Shadow Passion

Robin Gideon

ZEBRA BOOKS
KENSINGTON PUBLISHING CORP.

For Fred, Rita, Fug, Cliff, and Jim
For Brad Thompson
And for JS . . . who loves love more than anyone I've ever known.

rg

ZEBRA BOOKS

are published by

Kensington Publishing Corp.
475 Park Avenue South
New York, NY 10016

First printing: March, 1988

Printed in the United States of America

Chapter One

Sorren McKenna looked down at the pinpricks of light that shone through windows of the town below. He felt that familiar clutching sensation in his stomach and shifted his weight in the saddle. Something inside him was warning him not to go into God's Grace. The package from the War Department couldn't carry good news. It never had.

He thought once again of simply turning his horse around and returning to his ranch with the warm fireplace and hot brandy. He had worked hard to create a new future for himself, and he was loathe to see it dismantled by his former superiors in Washington.

"Damn me," he muttered softly, angry at his indecision.

It occurred to him that he shouldn't be afraid. Sorren McKenna had survived Quantrill assassination squads, countless fights with guns and knives, and many other skirmishes that cause blood to be spilled and men to die. Sorren's exploits during the great Civil War had taught him to survive, no matter the cost.

The war had been ugly, and it was something Sorren preferred to forget. The blind hatred the war had spawned shocked Sorren. Most shocking of all was that he had become such a critical part of it. As a spy behind the Rebel lines, he had been part of the very worst deception and treachery. He had learned that he couldn't prevent the fighting, but he told himself his work could speed its end. He did not realize until it was too late that his past—and the nightmares—would follow him, leading him, circuitously, to where he was now, looking down at the small valley town of God's Grace.

Lightly tapping the mare's ribs with his heels, Sorren headed for Angie's Saloon. At this time of the night, the package would be waiting at Angie's instead of at the stage station.

Minutes later, Sorren slipped off his mare and dropped the reins to the ground. He didn't need to tie her to the hitching post; Sorren had trained her to remain in place if her reins hung to the ground. Training horses was one of four things Sorren was extremely good at.

Pushing through the batwing doors, Sorren entered the familiar confines of Angie's Saloon. Four customers were seated in the back around a table playing cards. The rest of the tables were empty. Frankie, the bartender, was cleaning glasses behind the bar. He looked worried, too.

"Well, hello there, Mr. McKenna."

TENDER EMBRACE

"Don't cry," Sorren whispered. He stroked the satiny length of her hair, his hand gliding down Shadow's back to send tingles across her flesh. "Please, precious, it's killing me to see your tears."

Shadow's cheek was pressed into the arch of his neck. The warmth of his body, the suppressed strength, was more apparent to her now than ever. With a will of their own, her hands slipped around his trim waist.

When she tilted her face up to his, Sorren could not resist the temptation of her lips. Softly at first, his lips just brushing against hers, he kissed her. When he kissed her again, her wide, full-lipped mouth molded passionately to his.

Shadow held loosely onto Sorren, her fingertips uncertain along the small of his back. His kisses left her breathless, confused—wanting. She pulled away and looked into his eyes. Everything in the world was forgotten except this man who touched her so tenderly. She felt stronger, happier, but light-headed, for the air seemed charged with a strange, vital force that existed only within the circle of Sorren McKenna's arms. . . .

"Frankie." Sorren nodded a greeting to the bald-headed, red-nosed man, then turned his attention to the cardplayers in the back. Judging from the size of the pot, they were playing stud poker for small change. A waste of time, Sorren concluded.

The men were also drunk. They were fresh off the range, rank from it, with too much dust in their throats, too little money in their pockets for their labor, and too much steam to let off in too little time. They were trouble looking for a place to happen.

"Frankie, there's supposed to be a package here for me."

"Yes, sir, Mr. McKenna. Got it right here." Frankie reached under the bar and produced a large leather envelope. It was thick and heavy, bound with leather straps, and sealed shut with wax. "I ain't never seen a package quite like this one before. What kind of thing is that?" he asked, pointing to the red wax with the seal of the War Department in it.

"It's nothing very interesting, Frankie."

"Sure thing, Mr. McKenna," Frankie said quickly. Years of watching humanity from behind a bar had taught him when to talk and when to listen. "Whatever you say."

Sorren took the envelope and squeezed it. Curiosity made him want to break the seal to inspect the contents, but he felt it best to open it with Catherine and Carl Weatherly. He didn't trust them like he trusted their father, and Sorren knew they didn't trust him.

Sorren reached into the front pocket of his slacks and took out a gold coin. He snapped it on the bar in front of Frankie and said, "Buy yourself a drink on me. Thanks for your time."

"Hey! Thank you, Mr. McKenna. Don't you want a drink or somethin'? It's on the house. Aw, hell! It's on me!" Sorren had tipped him the equivalent of one week's salary. "Not the cheap stuff, neither! I'll give you some of Miss Angie's private stock!"

"Thanks anyway, Frankie, but I've really got to get back."

Behind him, Sorren heard the scrape of a chair and the lusty cackle of four men in unison. He looked up from his package, into the mirror that ran the length of the bar. The woman he saw was the most breathtakingly beautiful, self-possessed creature he'd ever seen in his life. He turned, unwilling to study her through the reflection of the mirror. She stood just inside the batwing doors, her head turning slowly as she took in everyone in the bar. Her eyes met with Sorren's, held his briefly, then moved on.

She dressed like a squaw, but she was of mixed blood. Tall for a woman, she had rather broad shoulders, a full bosom, and legs that were full, firm, and tapered. Her doeskin dress, Sorren noticed, had been slit up both sides so she could straddle a horse's back.

"Damn!" Sorren whispered. To Frankie he said, very quietly, "I think I'll have a whiskey. Scotch, if you've got it."

Around her waist was a plain leather belt, hand made, and fixed to it was a sheath carrying a bone-handled knife. The squaw's waist-length hair was held away from her face with a single leather thong tied around her forehead.

"Looky what we got here, boys! A pretty little

8

squaw! Hey, honey, you ain't working at Beth Ann's now, are you? Come over here and let ol' Joey show you what life's all about!"

Sorren's desire to keep his distance from Joey and the other three was in conflict with his concern for the young woman. He tried to guess the half-breed's age. Eighteen? Maybe a year older? It was hard to tell. As she walked toward the bar, Sorren saw how her breasts rose and fell, moving inside the soft tan doeskin dress.

"Hey, damn it, I'm talking to you!" Joey said in a voice just below a shout. "Squaw, don't you walk away from me!"

The woman kept walking, moving away from Joey and toward Frankie. Her right hand rested lightly on the hilt of the knife at her hip.

"What in hell is this? What's this, boys? Does this squaw think she's too good for me? Huh? Is that what you think, squaw?" Joey started for the woman. His eyes were red-rimmed from alcohol and lack of sleep. He smelled of a month on the prairie. "Hey! Damn it, I'm talkin' to you!"

The normally slow fuse of Sorren's anger had been lit by Joey's rage. Surprisingly, since he really hadn't planned on making the woman's fight his own, the moment the squaw was past Sorren, he stepped away from the bar, moving between her and the oncoming Joey.

"I don't think she's interested," Sorren said, his voice low, even. It was the voice of a man accustomed to giving orders that did not have to be shouted to carry authority. A man whose orders were followed. He smiled at Joey, but the smile was cold, without humor. "But I wouldn't worry too much about it. There are a lot of . . . the kind of women you're looking for in God's Grace. Maybe you should try your luck at Beth Ann's."

Joey had been drinking, but he wasn't drunk enough to let another man get between him and a woman. At least not without a fight. He looked at Sorren and squinted. Through the fog of lust and whiskey and contempt for the world around him, something shone through. He smiled crookedly and a thin trickle of spittle tainted with chewing tobacco juice ran from the corner of his mouth to his chin.

"Well, I'll be! If it ain't the high and mighty Sorren McKenna!" Joey pushed his sweat-stained, wide-brimmed hat back on his head with the tip of one finger. The Indian woman with the tantalizingly short dress and beckoning thighs was forgotten for the moment. "What are you doin' in Angie's at this time of the night, McKenna?"

Sorren said nothing. He tried to see in his mind's eye what Joey would look like without the whiskers. The voice was familiar, but not the face. Sorren had hired so many drifters and cowpunchers in the past several years. Most of the cowboys Sorren hired on a seasonal basis were all pretty much the same: hard-working, hard-drinking men trying to get a grubstake together as they made their way west to the Promised Land.

Sorren had been as far west as San Francisco. He no longer believed in a Promised Land. At least not on this earth.

Joey's jaw worked a moment, then he spat a perfect stream of tobacco juice between Sorren's black, highly polished boots. When he looked up, hatred showed plainly in his eyes. He had his left thumb hooked into the gunbelt around his waist. His right hand hung forebodingly close to the revolver's handle.

"You don't even remember me, do you, you son of a bitch?"

"No." Sorren didn't particularly care for lying. He'd done a great deal of it in his life already. He wouldn't do more of it for a man like Joey.

Sorren was a few feet from the bar, his dark eyes sharp and intent. It was utterly absurd for him to even consider the possibility of Joey being faster at the draw than he was, but he knew that looks weren't everything. Sorren hadn't lived as long as he had by being careless, by underestimating another man's ability. More than one grave had been filled by a seemingly drunk, sloppily dressed cowpuncher who knew how to handle a Colt.

"You son of a bitch," Joey repeated, shaking his head slowly. He sent another stream of tobacco juice flying, though it was aimed to the side this time. He'd gambled once already and lived to tell about it. "You mess with a man's life and you don't even remember his face? Somebody oughtta teach you to respect a guy like me."

From Joey's viewpoint, Sorren seemed perfectly unconcerned. He stood with his feet apart, his hands hanging limply at his sides. The flat-crowned, flat-brimmed black hat was pulled low over his eyes. He seemed, with the exception of his eyes, quite calm. But to look into Sorren's eyes was to catch a glimpse into the soul of a man who knew what combat was

11

about, who understood the permutations and possibilities of war, who accepted as unalterable the necessity for violence without cherishing or shirking away from that violence.

Sorren was less concerned about the cowpuncher in front of him than he was about the three others who were fanning out behind Joey. They slowly moved away from each other, making it impossible for Sorren to attack all of them simultaneously. One would not be hit by a stray bullet intended for another. They had done this before, Sorren decided. Pack wolves accustomed to fighting together against a single enemy. He knew what would have happened to the Indian girl had Joey gotten hold of her. They probably would have taken her right on the sawdust-strewn floor.

Where was she? Sorren realized with equal helpings of bitterness and admiration that after she had started this mess, she had disappeared, seemingly melting into the air. *Smart girl*, thought Sorren. Somehow Sorren had always known that when he died, it would be because of a woman, probably one he didn't even know.

"If you hadn't fired me, I'd be at Beth Ann's right now," Joey began, sizing up Sorren and wondering what chance he had in a fair draw, and how far his friends would back him up. "But you up and fired me, *Mister* McKenna!" He drawled the word out slowly, contemptuously. "Now I ain't got no job and no money. Can't even buy myself a woman! An' that's all 'cause of you, McKenna!"

Now, vaguely, the memory of Joey was coming back. Sorren hadn't even bothered firing Joey himself, delegating that particular responsibility to his ranch foreman. He remembered something about a man who drank too much, especially during the daylight hours, and who complained all the time. Sorren understood now why Joey was dangerous. He was poison, and he'd poison everyone around him.

"An' now, when I find myself a little Indian filly, you start steppin' on my toes again." Joey took a step backward. He needed the extra distance to make Sorren a better target. Also, when his friends opened fire, as he hoped they would, he didn't want to get hit in the back by a seemingly stray bullet. "McKenna, don't you know when you're not welcome? You always got to stick your nose into my business?"

Sorren shook his head slowly. The situation was getting worse. Joey felt bold with his friends backing him up. The potential for violence was so thick he could feel the air getting heavier. He momentarily recalled another night, another battle that was far away. "No, I don't have to stick my nose in your business, Joey. It's just that you need someone to tell you what you shouldn't do. I figure that's my job, Joey. I'm the guy that's going to teach you your manners and chase you back into your rat hole." Sorren moved closer to Joey. His dark predator's eyes were vital, alive. "Now why don't you just walk away from this, Joey? You and your friends have had enough to drink tonight."

"You messed up my life once too often, McKenna." Joey wiped his mouth with the back of a hand, smearing off the tobacco juice. "I think it's time I showed you a lesson."

Over Joey's shoulder, Sorren saw the men fanning out a little more. He was caught now in a cross fire. And Frankie was busy wiping out glasses. Frankie wasn't going to get killed fighting another man's war.

"Don't be a fool, Joey," Sorren said, his voice cool and even. "You'll get me. There's no reason for any of us to think any different than that."

"That's right, McKenna. I'll shoot you right in the guts and watch you squirm before you die."

Sorren shook his head slowly. His dark eyes never once left Joey's. "No," he said, correcting Joey as a teacher would correct a schoolboy. "You won't be the one to shoot me. One of the others will, but it won't be you. You'll be bleeding on the floor long before I ever get there. Want to know something, Joey? No matter what, I'm going to make sure you die. You know how fast I am. You know I can back up what I say. When the bullets hit and I start falling, you'll be dead before I touch the floor."

Joey tried to keep up his hard-edged facade. Something in that bastard McKenna's voice was entirely unnerving. Joey knew that McKenna wasn't lying. He glanced nervously at his friends for support. They were waiting for him to make a move.

For a second Joey wondered if it were possible to back away from this without looking like a coward, or a fool, or both.

Looking in Sorren's cold eyes was a sobering experience. Joey's better judgement now whispered inside his head to walk away from Sorren McKenna.

"You talk like a big man, McKenna," Joey said. He wiped his mouth with the back of his left hand. He blinked his bloodshot eyes several times. His mouth kept talking against his will. "Maybe me and the boys should shut your mouth for you."

The man to Sorren's left said, in a shaky voice, "Wait a minute, guys. Don't do nothin'. Please, Joey, for God's sake, don't do nothin'!"

"Pete? What in tarnation are you—" Joey stopped in mid-sentence when he saw the squaw's lethal-looking, razor-sharp knife touching his friend's throat just beneath the nervously bobbing Adam's apple. After a moment, anger replaced concern for Pete. "You dumb bastard! How did you let her get the jump on you?"

"I didn't hear nothin'! Damn it, Joey! You're here, too! Did you hear her?"

Pete's eyes were bulging, wide as saucers, wild with fear. He looked imploringly at Joey, then to his other friends. He tried to keep his head as still as possible.

Relief and respect were the two uppermost emotions Sorren felt when he looked at the young Indian maiden. She was behind Pete, keeping his body between herself and Joey. The knife at Pete's throat was held steady. There was enough pressure put behind it to indent the skin without drawing blood. Sorren had no idea where she'd disappeared to or how she'd gotten behind Pete. Like the others in Angie's, he hadn't heard a thing.

"Sweetheart, I owe you one," Sorren said to the squaw. When she glanced at him, he stopped breathing for a moment. She was wild, radiant with her energy . . . and so erotically enticing she could have been a fantasy. Sorren had to force his eyes away from the woman. To Joey he said, "Let's all walk away from this one. Makes no sense for any of us to

15

get hurt."

Joey looked at Sorren, then over at Pete. "Sure thing, McKenna. Just tell your squaw to take that bowie knife away from Pete's throat." He spit again, sending tobacco juice close to the tips of Sorren's highly polished, hand-sewn boots. "I always figgered you for a squawman."

Sorren could have killed Joey then, but he did not. He had done too much killing in his life already. If allowed, he would turn his back on violence. Looking over at the Indian, he noticed she did not seemed offended. She probably couldn't speak English.

"Let him go," Sorren said quietly to the woman. "They won't bother you anymore."

The woman looked at Sorren. She said nothing. The knife at Pete's throat was held in a steady hand. For that moment, she was in control.

"Hey, McKenna, tell that squaw to let Petey go," Joey demanded.

Sorren turned to the woman and said, in a reassuring tone, "It's okay now. Just let him go. These men won't try to hurt you."

So fascinated was he by the bold Indian woman that Sorren did not see Joey make his move.

Instinct took over as Sorren leaped to his left and reached for his gun, cursing himself for violating his personal rule of never turning his back on a coward. It came back to Sorren instinctively. All the moves, the reactions, the reflexes that had kept him alive behind enemy lines during the war. The same lightning, lethal instincts that had so impressed the War Department and repulsed President Abraham Lincoln.

Joey's bullet ripped through the hardwood bar and shattered bottles on the opposite side. Frankie dropped out of sight as the debris fell. Joey was thumbing back the hammer a second time, trying to get Sorren in his sights, when McKenna finished the head-over-heels roll and came up with his own Colt in hand. Sorren squeezed the trigger. A heavy, soft lead slug hit Joey in the chest, mushrooming on impact. Joey catapulted backward. He died before he hit the floor.

Sorren was moving and shooting. Turning to his left, he sized up Pete, now free of the Indian. Sorren shot as Pete ducked. The bullet struck the boulder fireplace behind Pete, ricocheting with a whine. Sorren thumbed back the Colt's hammer. The gun roared and bucked, spitting fire. Pete screamed, then died.

The other two were thinking the same thought when they died, guns smoking in their hands: How in hell could they keep shooting at Sorren McKenna and still miss him?

The entire gunfight had lasted only a few seconds. In that time, Sorren fired five shots, four men were dead . . . and one woman was injured.

"Damn! Frankie! Get over here!" Sorren rushed to the fallen woman. She was on her side, not far from the fireplace. Sorren dropped to his knees beside her. He rolled her over gently, turning her into the cradle of his arm. Blood oozed from a head wound that ran horizontal to her hairline, just above the left temple. "Frankie, damn it, get over here!"

She was breathing but unconscious. Sorren sat on the floor, holding the young woman's head in his lap.

"Get me a towel! And something to use as a bandage. She's been hit."

Frankie had been a bartender for a long time. Getting involved in other people's problems was something he avoided.

"Mr. McKenna, she's just a—"

"Damn it, Frankie! Do as I tell you!"

The flash of deadly, black rage that shot from Sorren's eyes changed Frankie's desire to stay out of the situation. He moved quickly around the counter, a clean bar towel in his hand.

"It's going to be okay, sweetheart," Sorren murmured, pressing the towel to the wound, talking in the same reassuring tone he used with wild horses. He looked up briefly. "Frankie, get Doc Madison over here."

"Mr. McKenna—"

"Frankie!"

"—he's over at the Boulter's place, Mr. McKenna! Been there two days already waitin' for Zachery's missus to have her little one! Everybody knows how bad a time she has dropping children! Had nine already and every one's like it's her first."

Sorren spat foul words. He checked the woman's head wound. She was still bleeding. The blood, however, was beginning to clot. In his mind's eye he saw himself shooting at Pete and missing. He again heard the whine of the ricocheting bullet. Had it been his own bullet that struck down this woman? Had he shot the woman who saved his life?

"I'm bringing her to my ranch, Frankie," Sorren said as he carefully pulled his legs out from beneath the woman. He squatted by her side and placed his arms under her knees and behind her back. "Make sure Doc Madison comes to my ranch as soon as possible. Hear me?"

"Yes, sir, Mr. McKenna. But you know ol' Doc Madison always goes on a bender after—"

Sorren was already headed for the front doors of the saloon. "If you get him to my ranch tomorrow, and he's sober, I'll give you fifty dollars."

"Yes, sir, Mr. McKenna!"

Sorren's mare did not like the additional weight of the Indian woman on her. She neighed and pranced a bit to show Sorren her feelings. A few soothing words from her master settled the mare down. Sorren held the women in front of him, her body sideways to his.

"What the devil are you doing in God's Grace?" Sorren whispered to the unconscious woman he held in his arms. He turned her head so that her cheek rested on his shoulder. There was something reassuring about being able to hear her breathe. "Come on, honey. I'm going to take care of you now. Everything is going to be just fine. Sorren's here and he's not going to let anything else happen to you."

But as Sorren's mare headed for home, her master's heart was chilled with agonizing questions. Was it his bullet that had struck this beautiful young woman down? Had he sidestepped Death again and caused the disappointed Fates to snatch this beautiful creature instead?

Chapter Two

Sorren ascended the stairs rapidly, his booted steps echoing through the empty house. In his arms, the young woman, her head on his shoulder, remained motionless. Only an occasional unconscious moan and the warmth of her shallow breathing against his cheek let Sorren know she was still alive.

He kicked open the bedroom door, crossed the room with several long strides, then placed her gingerly on his bed, resting her head on one of the three goose down pillows near the walnut headboard. He placed her arms at her sides and straightened her legs, then stood erect. Under other circumstances, her beauty would have affected Sorren powerfully. The motions he had just gone through—carrying a beautiful woman up the long, wide, winding stairway, kicking open his bedroom door, placing her on his bed—he'd done dozens of times with a dozen different women. But this time the woman was unconscious, blood matting her thick ebony hair, the possible result of his own richocheting bullet. It was this that prevented Sorren from finding any excitement in his action or in the beauty of the young stranger who now occupied his bed.

His mind worked fitfully, dashing off in different directions. Somehow the training and experience he'd gleaned during his War Department days had left him in the utter insanity of the senseless gunfight at Angie's.

"Think, damn it!" Sorren hissed aloud to himself.

The sound of his own voice was reassuring and helped him clear his mind, at least momentarily, of the sensation of guilt that kept pounding inside his skull like breaking waves against a battered shoreline. It was, he would later think, odd that the smell of blood—sweet, sticky against his cheek and shoulder—pushed him into what he did next.

He rushed to the kitchen and, within minutes, had a large copper kettle of warm water ready. He splashed alcohol liberally into the water, then washed his hands in the water. Then, for good measure, he added more alcohol. Returning to his bedroom, he began washing clean the young squaw's wound, just like he'd done before with wounded soldiers.

The stinging, alcohol-laced water caused her to moan and turn her head away from the cloth Sorren held. He took her head in his free hand and turned it to continue with his task.

"I know it burns," he said, not caring that she probably couldn't hear him or understand his words. "But the alcohol will keep away infections." When she raised a weak hand and tried to push the cloth from her scalp, he allowed himself a half smile. "You're a fighter, aren't you? You don't have to fight me. Just

21

let me do what must be done. It hurts now, but it has to be done. Trust me. I know what must be done. I'll take care of you. Sorren's here and he's going to take good care of you."

The wound was not as bad as Sorren had first feared. The bullet had followed the skull, leaving a two-inch jagged cut in the scalp. Sorren softly pressed the warm, damp cloth against her scalp until the wound was clean, then set about cleaning the dried blood from her waist-length hair.

When he was at last satisfied with his work, he emptied a kettle of rust-colored water. Sorren set the kettle near the door. The smell of blood still brought the memories of his war days back. He'd rather they remained buried in his past, locked away where they couldn't haunt him.

The shoulder of his shirt and jacket were stained with the squaw's blood. Sorren discarded the garments, casting them across the room as he stepped up to his closet. He withdrew a black silk shirt—one of ten identical hand-sewn shirts he owned—and put it on, leaving the buttons unfastened.

With the smell of blood no longer violating his senses, Sorren returned to his bed. He had three more things to do before his doctoring was finished. It only took Sorren an instant to decide he'd better save the most difficult for last.

He folded one bandage into a square and placed it directly over the woman's wound. Jostling her as little as possible, Sorren wrapped a second bandage around her head. Then, after a brief examination of her swollen right hand—Sorren concluded she had landed on it after being shot—he wrapped it with another bandage. The moan of pain that escaped her lips — those lips! — warned Sorren that she was not as deeply into unconsciousness as she appeared.

Sorren could not avoid the final step in his medical treatment any longer. Intuitively, he knew that this young woman, even in this state of vulnerability, held a power over him he could never deny. However pleasant the spell, a man like Sorren did not like being bewitched.

From the bureau near his bed, in the bottom drawer beneath several white dress shirts, he found the three nightgowns, left behind by previous bedmates. He glanced at the three gowns, trying to recall the forms that filled them, trying to remember which gown was the least revealing. It wasn't easy. The wearers had shed them quickly. Vaguely unsettled, he withdrew the top gown, deciding it was the most modest.

The squaw's blood-stained doeskin dress had to come off. Sorren's hands paused above her. Her full breasts rose and fell with her shallow breathing. Her legs, exposed to mid thigh, were quite firm. Sorren judged them to be the legs of a woman who'd spent many hours on horseback, and this puzzled him. The braves of the tribe did the hunting. The squaws gathered food, did the other teepee-bound chores, and usually did not ride much — if they rode at all.

He took a deep breath, forcing himself to be calm, fully aware of how ridiculous his reticence was yet unable to shake himself of the feeling that he was doing something wrong. He despised himself for his hungry thought, for imagining his pleasure even when confronted with her pain.

Sorren sat on the bed. He cupped the woman's head in one hand, slipping his other hand behind her back. She moaned softly, fighting him with what little strength she had left, as Sorren eased her up into a sitting position. He pulled her closer, his hands sliding around her trim waist. He caught her dress near the waist and pulled it up. She struggled a little more intently, but that did not stop Sorren from easing the unadorned dress above the curve of her hips, past her full bosom, then over her head and arms. Sorren felt the warmth of the young woman's smooth flesh as he held her for an extra moment in the sitting position. With his arm around her shoulders, a heavy, firm breast was pressed against his chest. He tried to look only at her face. His eyes could not help but stray downward to linger self-consciously on the crested peaks of her breasts, then lower still, to the juncture of her muscular thighs.

She was getting cold. He saw her shiver, her nipples growing hard, and she tried to turn to her side in a vain attempt to shield herself.

"Damn me," Sorren muttered angrily. "Let's get this over with."

Clumsily, he slid the nightgown over her head and worked her arms into the sleeves. After placing the squaw prone on the bed, he raised her hips and tugged the smooth material down to the middle of her calves. He stopped once again to look at her. She was much less disconcerting with the nightgown covering her, though Sorren mentally noted how much better she looked in the gown than the original owner.

Sorren placed a blanket over her and breathed a

small sigh of relief. He had done all he could for the woman who had saved his life. Now she needed rest.

"Who are you?" Sorren whispered, pain and confusion in his voice. "Why did you do it?" Sorren asked, knowing the woman would not—could not—answer him.

He stood in the dark, looking down at the unconscious woman in his bed. Her hair was a black spray over the fresh white linen pillowcase. Her lips were slightly parted as she breathed slowly, shallowly.

Feeling a powerful need for a brandy, Sorren stepped out of his bedroom, walking dazedly down the stairs to his study. He needed time to think, time to clear his head of the thousands of different thoughts that were bouncing around inside.

Shadow reached consciousness slowly, in stages, one painful step at a time. When she finally found the strength to open her eyes, the light was so intense she had to close them quickly. War drums beat angrily in her head. When she tried to put her right hand over her closed eyes to shield them, pain exploded in her wrist, causing her to wince.

Disconnected thoughts floated forward out of her foggy confusion. *I am in danger,* Shadow thought in the deceptively lucid manner of a strong-willed woman half out of her mind with pain and hunger. *I have been hurt. . . . Where am I? . . . what happened? . . . what happened? . . .*

Shadow had never felt so miserable, so beaten and defeated, in her entire life. Every muscle in her body ached. Her right hand was wrapped heavily with a white cotton bandage. She moved the fingers slowly, touching the tips to her thumb. The slight movement of the fingers caused excruciating pain. *What happened? What happened?*

There was another bandage around her head. Shadow touched the bandage tentatively with her left hand. High on the left side of her forehead, at the hairline, was a thick spot in the bandage. When she applied a little pressure to the area, pain that seemed to emanate from directly behind her eyes shot through her system. She only had the strength to gasp softly.

Minutes passed before she could open her eyes again. The smell of disinfectant assaulted her nostrils. It was a scent from the past. A scent she had not known since her days with Father Bradford.

She lay in a large bed. Her legs felt heavy under the blankets. When she pulled her knees up, they moved stiffly, as if they were not her own. *How long have I been here? And whose bed is this?*

She refused to give in to the pain. Through hazy, burning eyes, she looked around the bedroom. The room was extraordinarily large, perhaps as large as the Great Lodge teepee where the tribal council had decided that Shadow's banishment was best for the tribe. To her left was an ornately hand-carved chest of drawers. The cedar wood glistened from hand polishing. It was, Shadow noted in the still erratic wanderings of her mind, not unlike the bureau she had shared with six orphans at Father Bradford's years ago. Except, of course, the bureau she used at Father Bradford's was someone's castoff, having the carved-in initials of three boys who had used it before Shadow.

Beside the chest of drawers was a mirror mounted on a wooden swivel.

Next to the mirror was a smaller table. Upon it was a pitcher and washbasin, a razor, a soap cup, and three towels.

This is a man's room.

Using her left arm, Shadow pushed herself higher in the bed, her head and shoulders no longer propped against the goose down pillow. Though she had only raised her head a few inches, excruciating pain ricocheted in her skull. She felt like she was being stabbed behind her ebony eyes and squeezed them tightly shut. After several seconds the pain became bearable. Shadow waited a moment, then challenged the Fates again.

The blankets fell away from Shadow's ample bosom. Across the upper swells of her breasts ran a white line of lace that hemmed the smooth silk nightgown. Shadow ran a fingertip along the lace. The nightgown was beautiful.

New anxiety clutched her heart. *Whose nightgown do I have on? Who undressed me? Have I been violated?*

If I have been violated, how am I to feel? Shadow wondered, fighting against the merciless pounding in her skull that followed even the slightest movement. *Is this how a woman feels after she's been raped? Is that what has happened?*

She had to escape. Closing her eyes, Shadow listened carefully. Nothing. He, whoever he was, had apparently left her alone.

She pushed her feet out from beneath the blankets, over the edge of the mattress. She slowly tried to force her protesting body into a sitting position, but the sensation at the backs of her eyes came back with a vengeance. She leaned forward again, her narrow chin nearly touching her knees, her bosom against her thighs.

Shadow wanted to see her throbbing right hand. She pulled at the cotton bows that held the bandage in place, but her fingers were too weak to manage the tight knots. Angry with herself and despising her own weakness, Shadow bit at the cotton bandage until she tore free a thin strip, then began unwinding the wrapping. She let the cloth dangle from her wrist and drop to the floor, the white linen slipping between her bare feet.

"My God," Shadow whispered under her breath when she looked at her hand. "What have they done to me? What's happened to me?"

It didn't even look like her own. Instead of the graceful, delicate lines, the long, slender fingers, the hand that Shadow saw was angry purple, thick, and swollen. She moved her fingers and winced.

I must escape now.

Shadow blinked her eyes several times. Her vision was clearing. She pushed herself slowly until she was sitting upright at the edge of the big bed. The pain returned, but Shadow discovered that in time it lessened. It was still agony, but endurable agony.

But who did she need to escape from? And where would she escape to? The bedroom seemed safe enough, at least while she was alone. Did she fear the masculinity of the room? She struggled with herself, fighting against irrational fear, cursing her weakness and willing herself to be as strong and rational as possible.

Vague memories came to Shadow. She couldn't tell if they were memories or the reality that is left behind when dreams have come and gone. A soft, warm, soothing voice. The gentle, rocking movement of a horse beneath her. Strong arms around her.

"I'm here now," the voice had promised. *"There is no need for you to be afraid anymore. I'm here."*

Shadow slipped off the bed inch by inch. First her toes touched the hard wooden floor, then her heels. Her jaw was clamped shut, a muscle flickering in her cheek as she grimaced against the headache that all but blinded her. She had to leave now. She had some place important to go. There were so many things that she had to do.

As soon as Shadow tried to stand, she knew she had made a mistake. Her legs shook violently. Nausea and dizziness overcame her. With a cry of pain and frustration, Shadow tumbled to the hard floor, crashing into the nightstand as she fell. She heard more than felt herself hit the floor. A moment later the washbasin smashed into a thousand pieces beside her. She felt water against her skin and the nightgown.

As she lay limp and defenseless on the floor beside a stranger's bed, her mind screamed in silent rage. She fought against the overwhelming sense of defeat and waited for her captor to come, as she felt certain he would.

Shadow could not tell how long she had been on the floor when she heard the pounding of boots against wood. A second? A minute? She pushed herself up, struggling to get an elbow beneath her so that she could strike out with her uninjured left hand. The bone-handled knife, which had been her constant companion since her early teen years, was not with her. Shadow's dark eyes narrowed fiercely. No matter what happened next, she would at least fight.

He burst through the door, tall and lean, dressed ominously in black from head to toe. His eyes, Shadow noted, were as dark as her own, as dark as his hair and clothes. There was a scar on his left cheekbone, the mark left by the butt of a pistol or perhaps a man's swinging fist. His aura of danger took her breath away.

"What the hell are you doing, you little fool?" he demanded, rushing to the fallen Shadow.

Weakly, Shadow tried to hit him with her left hand. He caught her by the wrist. His fingers felt like steel. He released her hand.

"Don't fight me, damn it!" he hissed, slipping one arm under Shadow's knees. She hit him in the face with the side of her hand but he appeared not to notice as he picked her up and returned her to the bed. When Shadow tried to strike him again he caught her by the wrist once more, this time trapping it against the bed. The move brought him above her. He looked down into her dark, angry frightened eyes. "Stop fighting me, damn you! I'm not going to hurt you!"

Shadow half screamed, half moaned, and started to strike at him with her injured right hand. He moved so swiftly it was like he had read her thoughts. Pinning both wrists to the bed, he glanced from Shadow's eyes down to her heaving breasts pressed against the bodice of the white silk nightgown, then back up to her face.

"You really are a wildcat, aren't you?" He loosened his grip on Shadow's wrists but did not remove his hands entirely. "I'm Sorren McKenna, and I would really appreciate it if you'd stop fighting me."

He smiled and lights danced darkly in his eyes. Shadow said nothing. She just stared into his eyes, hating this man who had so much power over her. She found it little solace that the man who would ravage her was handsome.

"Damn," Sorren muttered, searching Shadow's eyes with his own. "You don't understand a word I'm saying, do you?" When Shadow allowed no sign of recognition to enter her eyes or expression, Sorren chuckled softly, shaking his head. "I don't believe it. The woman who saves my life doesn't even speak English. I can't even thank you properly. Damn." Sorren's eyes narrowed as he looked at the bandage surrounding Shadow's head. There was a hint of blood showing through the white cloth. "Sweetheart, you may be about the luckiest card I've ever been dealt, but I'm just not lucky for you at all. How's the head feel?"

The initial fear Shadow felt had subsided, but in its wake the headache, infinitely sharper than before, returned. She wanted to close her eyes but dared not. At least not with Sorren hovering above her, his hands lightly over her wrists.

"You're a pretty one," Sorren said, his voice soft and low. "Yes, you're pretty and you're scared right out of your wits. Sure you are. You just relax now. Let Sorren take care of everything."

Shadow got the distinct feeling that Sorren was talking to her in exactly the same way he would talk to a skittish colt. When he freed her wrists, she did not attempt to strike him. Sorren moved off the bed, pausing a moment to look at the young mixed-blood woman, his dark, piercing gaze savoring the length of her body.

"You definitely do that nightgown justice," he said in a husky voice that made a shiver ripple through Shadow.

I will give you nothing! thought Shadow as she felt Sorren's eyes on her body. She remained motionless, her hands on the mattress near her shoulders. She could not fight Sorren. She was too weak. Shadow swallowed dryly and turned her face away from him. She did not have to look at her defiler.

Sorren took Shadow's right hand in his own, turning it gently until the palm was upward. "You really landed on that thing wrong," he said, half to himself. "Why did you unwrap it?" He looked into Shadow's face again, nodding his head and giving her a smile. A dimple showed in his left cheek. "You like it when I talk like this, don't you? Sure you do. It calms you. Don't you worry about a thing now, I'm going to take care of everything."

Sorren's took the bandage from the floor and started rewrapping Shadow's right hand. As he wound the cloth around her bruised hand, she watched the way Sorren moved. His hands, she noticed, moved gently, efficiently, firmly. They had some calluses, but they weren't the hands of a working man. She wondered if he were a gunfighter. He looked like he could be. And all the while he bandaged her hand, Sorren McKenna kept up the silken, soothing words, telling Shadow in a dozen different ways how beautiful she was, repeating over and over that she was safe and that he wouldn't hurt her.

Shadow listened, occasionally grimacing as pain from her head or hand stabbed through her, wondering if Sorren McKenna were the type of man who would lie to her if he thought she didn't speak his language. Even though she didn't want it to happen, Shadow felt herself drifting off into a shallow, troubled sleep. The last thing she felt and heard was Sorren's fingertips gently smoothing an ebony lock of hair from her cheek and whispering, "Don't fight it, sweetheart. Sleep now. Everything is going to be fine. I promise you that. Sorren's here now, and he's going to take care of everything."

Chapter Three

It was nighttime when Shadow woke again. She was thankful for the darkness. The fierce pounding in her head, and the stabbing sensation behind her eyes were lessened considerably without glaring light. She blinked her eyes several times to focus them. The silhouetted objects in the room were less threatening now.

For Shadow, the darkness was not something to fear. All her life she had embraced the night. When other children at Father Bradford's orphanage were frightened of the dark, it was Shadow who had comforted them. The night was her ally.

Near the door, very faintly, Shadow heard the sound of slow, shallow breathing. Instinctively, she tensed. He was there. Had he been there the entire time she slept? Had he done anything to her? He had placed his chair near the bedroom door. Why? To prevent her escape? Shadow felt her body waking and she stirred. Even the slightest move brought back the pounding war drums of racking pain that rever

34

berated in her head. She could not leave now. It was best to lie still, recover her energy, then make her escape.

In the pale moonlight that filtered through the bedroom bay windows, Shadow had her turn to study Sorren. He was a handsome man, she noted. Probably in his early thirties. Maybe his middle thirties. The scar on his cheekbone was dramatized by a shadow, and Shadow wondered how he'd gotten it.

Who is this man, so powerful, so gentle? she wondered. The overall impression she received from him was that of suppressed power. Even in sleep, Sorren McKenna, his head now back against the wall with his arms folded across his chest, exuded an aura of power. It was as though he were not really sleeping, as though he were conscious of what happened around him at all times. She wondered whether he were ever completely relaxed.

Shadow stayed very still, afraid that any movement would cause the bed to creak. She intuitively knew that any noise, no matter how soft, would surely arouse a white warrior like Sorren McKenna. He had a warrior's instincts. The same instincts that Shadow herself took pride in possessing.

Sorren's eyebrows were pushed together in a frown, and his features showed the strain of the events of the past hours. Shadow thought it odd that Sorren should do so much for her. He had to want something in return for his kindness. There had to be an ulterior motive. No man, history had taught Shadow, helps a woman without demanding something in return, without exacting a price that seldom if ever measures up to the deed done.

As long as he is sleeping he will not harm me, Shadow reassured herself. *For this moment I am safe.*

She closed her eyes. Shadow's body felt unnaturally heavy, pressing deep into the plush softness of the downy mattress. The cool linen sheets and the nightgown caressed her flesh. She had not slept between sheets since her days at Father Bradford's orphanage.

The memory of Father Bradford struck an alarming chord in Shadow's consciousness. Father Bradford. She had seen him recently. When? When? *Oh, yes,* Shadow mentally reminded herself, reassured her mind was not so addled by the wound and with the pain that she could not think. *It was two days ago. He came to my camp. The will. The will* . . . The young woman drifted back two days in time to the exact moment her unhappy but understandable world was shattered into a thousand confusing pieces that she did not recognize . . .

Shadow saw him in the distance and a weary smile crossed her lips. It could only be Father Bradford dressed like that, riding his gray mule, wearing that silly wide-brimmed felt hat, the one that Shadow had teased him about when she lived at his school. It had to be him.

What could he want with her? It was at least thirty miles to the old school. Shadow knew that Father Bradford could move with relative impunity among the various tribes in the area, his legend as a peacemaker preceeding him wherever he went. But that still didn't explain what he was doing here now.

Shadow headed toward the grassy bluff where her buffalo hide shelter was. Father Bradford continued on his mule with no apparent alarm, not urging the animal to a greater speed than its slow, lazy amble. Shadow took this as a sign that nothing could be too terribly wrong.

In the thirty-one years that he had been a priest, since he took his vow of celibacy, Father Bradford had never seen anyone who had such an aura of impending trouble as Shadow. During Shadow's stay at his school, Father Bradford watched her transform from a tall, lanky, slender girl into a young woman of exquisite but undeniably dangerous physical charms. He had watched her, in effect, grow into her own woman's body. And, dear God, she was all woman . . and all trouble. Trouble whether she tried to be troublesome or not. Shadow could drive a man crazy even if she didn't try, and that's why Father Bradford knew he had to do whatever was necessary to save her soul. If she could draw his attention — a man who had given his life to God and vowed celibacy — then she could certainly enflame the senses of a man whose moral code was less stringent.

As he approached Shadow's camp, he observed that her status among the tribe members had not improved. Then he shook his head in dismay. Shadow looked so different from the young half-breed he had taught to read and write. In his school, Shadow had worn the prim hand-me-down dresses the congregation from St. Louis had provided for his students. Now she wore a soft doeskin dress she'd obviously made for herself with infinite care. The dress had been cut up both sides from the knee to

37

high on the thighs. When Shadow walked, it revealed a bronzed flash of her strong, tapering thighs. On her feet were soft-soled moccasins that came up above her ankles. Around her forehead, holding back her jet hair, was a slender leather thong. Father Bradford knew that she had been forbidden by the tribal council to wear any ornamentation because of her mixed blood. Otherwise, her dress, moccasins and headband would be adorned with beads. As it was, her simple clothing, as much as her complexion and smooth features, spoke of her social rank and genealogy.

"Hello," Shadow said quietly when Father Bradford pulled alongside her as she walked. The single English word felt good on her tongue. She much preferred speaking English to Kiowan. "It's been a long time."

"Yes, it has."

Father Bradford couldn't resist smiling. Shadow refused to call him *father*. Long ago she had vehemently explained that she had no father and would call no man such. He wondered how much or how little she had changed since leaving his school and returning to her tribe.

Shadow nodded her head toward the bluff. "Come to my camp. I'll make us some coffee."

It wasn't until the fire was burning nicely and the much-tarnished pot was hanging from the iron tripod above the flames that Shadow knelt on the soft woven hair rug. Father Bradford groaned a little as he shifted his weight, trying to get comfortable sitting on wood reserved for the evening's fire.

"The coffee is most civilized, but you look like

savage," Father Bradford said quietly, again shaking his head.

"I am a savage, remember?" Shadow remained kneeling, sitting on the backs of her heels. Only braves were allowed to sit cross-legged, which was more comfortable though sometimes immodest. She dropped several more coffee beans into a mason bowl and crushed them carefully with a smooth hand-sized rock.

"You don't talk like a savage," Father Bradford said. "Why look like one? That dress is terribly immodest."

Shadow shrugged her shoulders. "It makes it easier for me when I'm riding," she replied. "The squaws walk. I have to ride a horse to hunt. I'm only being practical."

"It's indecent."

"So is going hungry. If I don't ride, I'll be without meat. Tell me something . . . when was the last time *you* were hungry?" Shadow's gaze locked challengingly with the priest's. It could be uncomfortable to talk to Father Bradford. During the first couple of minutes, she could always tell whether they would argue or not. It looked like this would be a difficult meeting. Shadow's intense ebony gaze softened when she looked at Father Bradford's paunch. "I can see you've been eating well," she said teasingly. "Let's not argue now. Besides, I can't see how it makes much difference. The men wouldn't dare be near me." Shadow felt it best to lie about men to Father Bradford. Neither of them could change the past. Shadow leaned closer to the flames, toward Father Bradford. She cupped a hand beside her mouth, whispering as

39

though she were revealing some dark secret. "You know I'm tainted, don't you?"

Shadow realized her humor was not appreciated. He had always meant well, even if he often made her angry. Her tone softened, as did her black onyx eyes, and she asked, "Why have you come?"

Before Father Bradford began his story, he accepted Shadow's offering of a steaming cup of coffee. He sipped from the blue enameled tin cup, thinking of Shadow, thinking of her troubled past and uncertain future. She had so little control over her life. The illegitimate half-white child of a Kiowa squaw, she had been named Shadow by the tribal council because they judged her unclean. She would forever be only a shadow, never a part of the tribe. She was tolerated, never befriended. When she was very young, Shadow was given food by the successful hunters, though only after everyone else had eaten their fill. She was on this earth, but not of this tribe. Her dishonor and shame were hers to bear.

Father Bradford cleared his throat and began speaking, though he was consciously aware that he was avoiding a difficult subject.

"You always did make great coffee," Father Bradford said quietly. "When you moved away from the orphanage, I thought of you every morning when I had to drink my own coffee."

Father Bradford cleared his throat again, then began the story that left Shadow, for the first time in her life, speechless.

"I've known since you were an infant who your father was," Father Bradford said as Shadow battled with the confused buzzing in her brain to hear the man's every word. "He gave the school a lot of money over the years. It was under his specific instruction that you learn to read and write. Oh, dear me! You can't possibly imagine how proud he was of you. I had to write him regular reports on how you were doing in school."

"He—he knew about me?" Shadow asked in a trembling voice.

"Oh, yes! He knew all about you. Remember how I sought you out and practically begged your mother to send you to my school? And later, when she died—God rest her soul—how I kept on until you finally agreed to come and stay at the school? Well, that was all your father's doing. At least it was at first. Later, when I could see how you were progressing with your studies, I was really pleased with what I'd done. I guess there isn't a teacher in the world who doesn't take a personal pride in having a really astute student."

"Who is he?" Shadow's hands were folded together in her lap. Her knuckles were white with tension. "Please, I've got to know."

Father Bradford gave Shadow a sad smile. "First, I want you to know a little something about the man. Please, child, I know it is difficult for you, but please put your faith in me." He cleared his throat, unable to make his eyes meet the beautiful young woman's searching gaze. "He always felt guilty about what he put you and your mother through. You've got to understand that he had . . . pressures. He was a powerful man. A part of the landed gentry, as we like to call them around these parts."

Suddenly the reality of what Father Bradford was

41

saying hit her. Shadow couldn't understand why it hadn't come to her earlier.

"He's dead, isn't he?"

Shadow felt hot tears burning her eyes. She cursed the tears and cursed her own weakness. How could she cry for a man she'd never met? He was the man who had destroyed her mother's pride with his love! The man whose seed had caused her illegitimate birth! The man who helped to bring Shadow into a world he knew would never accept her. She kept thinking she shouldn't feel any pity or sorrow, but her will was not as strong as the pain in her heart and soul.

"I'm so—"

"That's why you're here. To tell me that he's dead."

"Yes, Shadow. I'm sorry."

When Father Bradford turned his eyes up to Shadow's misty gaze, she could not remember a time when he looked more sad. He swallowed and tried to keep eye contact with Shadow but couldn't.

"Why didn't you tell me earlier who he was?" Shadow asked, feeling anger rising inside her. "All my life I've been trying to find out who and what I am. You knew and wouldn't tell me!"

Father Bradford shook his head in denial. "It's not as easy as that, Shadow. There are powers in this world—in the white man's world—that you know nothing about. Powers that control things, people, everything. You see, he made me promise to never let you know that he was your father. In exchange—because I promised to keep his identity a secret from you—he was very generous to the school. He did a great deal of good for many children who otherwise would never have had an education. It's because of his generosity that you were able to stay at my school and learn the things you did." Father Bradford paused, then added, "It isn't like I sold your happiness for my own gains, Shadow. It was very difficult for everyone. For your mother. And for Matthew Weatherly, your natural father. Oh, Shadow, if only you knew the hours I'd spent praying for God to give me the wisdom to know exactly the right thing to do."

The tightness in Shadow's chest was unbearable. She pressed a fist between her breasts, finding it difficult to breathe.

Matthew Weatherly. She knew the name, nothing more. He had been important enough to get his name in the newspaper Shadow had practiced reading. Socially prominent. Shadow recalled him being something of a do-gooder, though she couldn't remember any specific incident that made her recall him as one.

How many nights had she lain awake on her mat, wondering who her father was? How many times had her mother skirted the questions Shadow had asked? She had been searching for her identity all her life without satisfaction. That's why Shadow had returned to the Kiowa camp, even when she was not entirely welcome. Even if she was scorned by her tribe, they were a part of her. And something, she unconsciously reasoned, must surely be better than nothing.

"Why? How? When did he die?" Shadow asked. Her tongue felt thick. Her lips refused to formulate words clearly.

"Three weeks ago. He couldn't come out and say you were his daughter. In some circles it wouldn't

43

look good to have—"

"An illegitimate squaw-child?" Shadow asked, finishing the sentence for him.

"Yes. Exactly. I know that isn't fair and I know it isn't right, Shadow. But that's the way it is." Father Bradford cleared his throat. He couldn't quite meet her eyes. "You see, he didn't know about you right away. Your mother got pregnant and she kept that secret from Matthew. He didn't know about you until you were almost a year old."

"But why didn't he do anything?" Shadow implored. "If he loved my mother, as you imply he did, why didn't he come to claim us?"

"When you were very young you got sick. Your mother, God rest her soul, was a very wise woman. She decided it was best not to stir up the water unnecessarily." Father Bradford cleared his throat once again. "It didn't look like you would live. Matthew wanted to help, but he couldn't. There really wasn't anything he could do but wait. I'll tell you this . . . he prayed with me a lot during those terrible days when we didn't know if you were going to live or die.

"He loved you as he did his other children, but he knew that bringing you into his world would turn everything upside down. He couldn't take the chance of destroying the happiness of Karl and Catherine . . . when it looked like you wouldn't live through the summer."

Father Bradford put a fist to his lips and cleared his throat. The words were coming from him slowly, painfully, being torn from his soul by Shadow's need and guileless sincerity.

44

"He carried that guilt to his grave, Shadow. It was, I believe, the only thing in his entire life he'd ever done that he was ashamed of."

Shadow could not explain how she felt. The initial shock was wearing off. Now all she felt was confusion. Weatherly? Matthew Weatherly. A masculine name. A name of the outdoors, of the skies and forests, the sun and moon. A name oddly fitting for the type of man that Shadow had always pictured him in her teenage dreams to be. She decided she liked it. Shadow Weatherly? No, that couldn't be. She had no white man's name. Only white man's blood. It pleased her, though, to know that her father had been successful. Shadow, in her fantasy image of her father, had always pictured him as a strong, powerful, wealthy man. Powerful and wealthy . . . but lacking the courage to admit to the world that he had fathered a child by a Kiowa squaw.

She struggled with herself, trying to think of how she *should* feel, trying to understand what she was actually feeling.

"Was he a good man?" Shadow asked quietly, staring into the flickering flames of her campfire. "Was he kind to people?"

The soft chuckle that came from Father Bradford's throat warmed Shadow's heart. "Yes, my child, he was a very good man. Very kind and very loving. You wouldn't believe the arguments he and I had over the years about you." The priest cleared his throat, speaking in a softer tone. "Sometimes he'd come over at night with a good bottle of his chokecherry wine. Mother Mary! That was potent brew! Anyway, we'd have a glass or two of that foul stuff,

45

then a glass or two too many. Pretty soon he and I would be at it. I'd be trying to tell him to do the honorable thing by bringing you in and he'd be screaming back that the best thing for you was to stay right where you were. His theory was that if you moved in with him, you'd be shown nothing but contempt. But if you stayed at my school, he could offer you the kind of education you otherwise couldn't get. And it wasn't so bad at the school, was it? You weren't treated too badly there, were you?"

Shadow's heart felt heavy. Had her father loved her? It was hard to say. He had definitely thought about her often and had gone to considerable lengths to insure that her life would have at least some advantages. But he had never once shown the courage to own up to what he'd done.

It was almost as if Father Bradford could read Shadow's mind when he said, "He wasn't a cowardly man, Shadow. He just did what he thought was best, considering everyone's position in this thing. You've got a half-brother and sister he had to think about, too."

Shadow's head snapped up. Her eyes glittered with vitality. "Family?" She looked into the priest's eyes, searching for more information there than he was willing to give her with words. "I've got family?"

When Father Bradford turned his eyes away from Shadow, she could tell that something was terribly wrong.

"Yes, I suppose you could say you have."

"But my brother and sister aren't going to consider me one of them, are they?" Shadow stood quickly and began pacing. Despite her rapid movements,

46

Shadow's footsteps were as silent as those of a cougar on the hunt. "So I've got family then. People who come from the same flesh as me." She considered this for a moment and added, "Well, we share the same father, anyway. That's something."

Father Bradford watched Shadow moving. The fluidity of her stride was like that of a huntress. Her strong, brazenly exposed thighs scissored smoothly. As Shadow paced, Father Bradford studied her, watching her ebony hair flowing like a satiny mane over her shoulders and down her back. He could not help being affected by the extraordinary combination of strength and femininity that Shadow possessed. Her beauty would get her in trouble if she ever entered into the white man's world.

She moves like a cat, the priest thought. *Will she ever fit in with polite society? Shadow may be able to converse fluently in the white man's tongue but she'll never fit in the white man's world. She's too much the savage. Or will she? I've always underestimated her in the past.*

"Take it easy, Shadow! Take it easy." His words fell on deaf ears, as Father Bradford knew they would. He wondered once again if he were doing the right thing by letting her know about her father. But what could he do? It was Matthew's decision to withhold information before his death; it was the family lawyer's decision to dispense information now. Shadow had always been restless, possessing a volatile, excitable spirit. He could not tell how she would react to the shocking news he felt obligated to give her. "You'll meet your brother and sister soon enough."

Shadow wheeled quickly, her full breasts rolling tautly inside the soft doeskin dress. She glared down at the priest, her jet eyes flaming, and whispered with deathly calm, "No, I'll meet my *half* brother and *half* sister! There's a difference."

"We'll just have to see how big a difference that is, won't we?"

"You already know that answer," Shadow snapped back. "I'm not a child. You don't need to coddle me."

Father Bradford sighed, choosing to ignore her stormy mood. "There's a reading of the will. I've been trying to find out where you were since I found out. The reading is scheduled for the end of next week. You've got to get to the Weatherly ranch by then. You're listed as a beneficiary."

"What?"

"A beneficiary. He's included you in his will."

Shadow knew what the word meant. It just didn't make any sense to her that a man who would refuse to accept her in life would leave anything for her after his death. Besides, she wasn't entirely certain what the laws governing Indians were in such matters.

"Can he do that? Is it legal?"

Father Bradford shrugged his shoulders, pushing his felt hat back on his head. "I don't know if he can or can't, legally speaking. And I haven't got any idea at all what he's left for you. But Matthew built himself a heck of a spread. I know you don't want to hear this, but I'll be there if you need me, child. You can handle this like you always do—all by yourself and on your own—but you can count on me."

Father Bradford looked at Shadow. She stared straight into his eyes for a moment. "But you won't ask anything of me, will you?" the priest said sadly.

"No, of course not. Not Shadow. The strong, independent Shadow. You're not alone in this world, whether you want to think you are or not."

"That," Shadow said in a voice so soft it was difficult for the priest to hear, "is a matter of opinion. One I doubt you're in a position to fully understand. You are accepted by the white man and by the Kiowas. I am rejected by everyone. We—" Shadow began, then cut herself short, "the Kiowas are afraid to harm you. It is said that evil will follow anyone who hurts the white man who speaks with God." Shadow laughed and there was condescension in her tone. She slipped unconsciously out of her Kiowan speech pattern just as quickly as she had gone back to it. "They are afraid of you because they don't understand you. The Kiowas are afraid of everything they don't understand. Fear and hate are their responses to ignorance . . . not entirely unlike your so-called civilized society."

"Or you, my child," he countered. "What are you afraid of? That you actually end up loving someone?"

Shadow sat at her place near the fire once again. "You're a good man, but don't tell me what I should or shouldn't feel. You'll never know those things."

They were silent.

"I'm afraid that I won't have the chance to love. And if I do, will I ruin someone's life, too?"

Father Bradford swirled the coffee around in his enameled tin cup. "You know, that's the first time I can ever recall you saying you were afraid of something." He shook his head, not looking at the young woman. "I haven't any answers for you, Shadow. Just love. And faith—my kind, of course," he smiled when

49

she looked up. She smiled back. "You've got to be careful when you go into the white man's world, Shadow. This isn't going to be like being at my school. There might not be anyone on your side, anyone to protect you."

"Thank you. May Akana bless you, too."

"Just be careful. That's all I'm going to tell you."

Father Bradford wished Shadow well and excused himself, saying he had to check on Red Feather's small band of Apaches that had made camp near the foot of the Rockies some twenty miles to the west. It was rumored there was sickness among the children, and Father Bradford was hoping there was something he might be able to do that the medicine men hadn't. What he didn't tell Shadow was his suspicion that another smallpox breakout had occurred.

"Say your good-byes to these people," Father Bradford said, his hands on Shadow's shoulders. "Say your good-byes and do the best you can. Maybe you'll find happiness in your new world; maybe you won't. If you really want my opinion, you won't be happy where you're going. But it's got to be better than—" As Father Bradford's words trailed off, he nodded his head toward the teepees in the distance, with the squaws and braves working hard, carrying firewood and setting up the remainder of the teepees.

Shadow gently eased the priest's hand off her shoulders. "I have nobody to say good-bye to." She turned away from him. "You'd better get moving if you're going to make distance before sundown. In the dark, you're just a man. You could be on your way to your god before your killer realized you were a priest."

Shadow's head wound kept her on the edge of consciousness for another twenty-four hours. The gnawing hunger in her stomach was her only solid reminder of time passing.

Judging from the sunlight coming through the bedroom's bay windows, it was nearly high noon when she finally awoke with a clear head. It was a beautiful, sunny day, the kind of day that Shadow loved. The large, soft bed began to feel like a trap.

Carefully, waiting for the pain to come, Shadow pushed an elbow beneath herself and raised her head. Inch by inch she raised her head and shoulders, waiting for the war drums to pound in her skull. But the drums were silent today. Soon she could leave, before the magnet that was the man McKenna bid her stay. *My weakness will not trap me,* she resolved. She issued a soft, grateful sigh. Very soon she would be able to leave Sorren's bed, freeing herself from the invisible bonds that kept her captive. Best of all, Shadow would soon be rid of that horrendous feeling of being totally dependant upon someone else. That, as much as anything else, cut Shadow to the marrow. She had worked hard not to need other people, to be self-contained and complete in herself; she had struggled long and even gone without food at times rather than concede defeat and accept cast-off food from her tribe. To need a man such as Sorren McKenna seemed a compromise of all that she had accomplished, taking away some of the emotional coup feathers that she had tucked into her own war bonnet like a proud chieftan.

51

She almost wished he had defiled her; it would make him easier to hate.

She started at the sound of boot heels clicking against wooden stairs. He was cooing to her again. She thought briefly of pretending to be asleep, then dismissed the idea. Sorren McKenna had in the past sat in the overstuffed leather chair and watched her sleep. Perhaps this time would be no different. Shadow didn't like the idea of having to pretend to be asleep just to keep Sorren away.

The footsteps stopped at the door. After a moment Shadow heard the muttered expletive "Damn!" issued through clenched teeth. The sound of metal rattling against metal preceded Sorren as he entered the bedroom, balancing a large silver tray on the palm of his right hand.

"Good afternoon, precious," Sorren said, giving Shadow the same smile as she'd seen before. He smiled with his mouth, but his eyes studied her intently. "I brought some food for you. I'm not the best cook in the world, but it should be edible." He kicked the bedroom door closed and returned the tray to both hands. The look of concentration on his face told her he was not accustomed to walking with a food tray and it was amusing to see all his efforts focused on such a domestic task.

The aroma of freshly cooked beefsteak doubled her hunger in an instant. Shadow couldn't remember the last time she'd eaten beefsteak. It was juicier and more tender and flavorful than buffalo, venison, or even rabbit, which had been her food staple while living on the outskirts of her tribe.

"How's the head?" Sorren asked, turning his attention away from the tray. He sat on the edge of the bed and Shadow tensed. Her heart accelerated. "Easy, precious. I just want to check the bandage. You know I'm not going to hurt you. I'd never do anything to hurt you, precious. You've got to believe that by now."

Shadow looked straight into Sorren's eyes. Still not trusting, she allowed him to inspect the bandage. His touch was gentle and kind. He seemed to have had some experience in such matters, leading Shadow to wonder once again about Sorren McKenna and where he came from.

"We're making progress," Sorren said, his eyes shining with delight as he stood. "At least you're not cutting me dead with a look anymore." He took a silver cover from the plate on the tray. The steak was fresh from the grill, its aroma more enticing than ever. Shadow salivated. She hadn't eaten a morsel of food in two and a half days. Aside from the few sips of water Sorren had forced down her throat while she was semiconscious, she hadn't had anything at all.

Sorren tested his willpower again, knowing he could not resist looking at Shadow's breasts. The blankets were only up to her waist. The lace-trimmed bodice, pulled snugly across Shadow's ample bosom, did nothing to hide its magnificence. The nightgown had not been tailored for a woman as voluptuous as Shadow. Sorren's eyes strayed downward. A single glance was intoxicating.

"Can you sit up a little for me?" Sorren asked.

Shadow started to move, then stopped herself. Sorren did not know she understood English, and that's the way she wanted to keep it. The less he knew about her, the more likely he was to underestimate her. Knowledge, Shadow had learned, is a commodity, fundamentally no different than the number of horses a warrior owned or the amount of money a cattleman had in his bank. The more she knew about Sorren McKenna, the better equipped she was to defend herself should that become necessary.

Shadow looked at Sorren, feigning ignorance at his request. He sat on the edge of the bed again, his weight on the mattress causing her to roll slightly toward him. With her right hand still heavily wrapped and extremely tender, it was difficult for Shadow to push herself away from Sorren.

"It's going to be okay, precious. Easy now . . . just let me help you."

Sorren examined Shadow's face as he slipped his hands beneath her prone body. He expected her to strike out at him as she had before. When she did not, he lifted her shoulders and Shadow helped him push her toward the headboard.

Sorren made his mistake when he leaned over Shadow to get another pillow to put under her shoulders. The move, done in innocence, caused his chest to press down momentarily against Shadow's bosom. In that instant, he felt the warmth and firmness of her breasts. Shadow's sudden intake of breath warned Sorren that his temporary ward had taken the contact between them as intentional.

"Sorry, precious." Sorren slipped the second pillow under Shadow's shoulders, easing her into a braced sitting position. "I didn't mean anything by it."

Finally satisfied with Shadow's position, Sorren

picked the silver tray off the nightstand and set it carefully upon Shadow's thighs. With a flourish, he pulled the brightly polished silver covers off plates of buttered fresh bread and a bowl of buttered green beans. Beside the steak was fried potatoes.

"Beyond steak and potatoes my culinary ability gets pretty limited," Sorren said. "But as long as I stick to the basics I can stave off starvation."

A knife, fork, and spoon were wrapped in a white linen napkin. Shadow reached for the utensils with her right hand, then grimaced as pain shot up her arm.

"Easy, precious. I know you're hungry. There's more where this came from." Sorren touched her bandaged hand. Their eyes met briefly and he swallowed, cursing himself for his thoughts. It was so easy to think of her beauty, so difficult to remind himself of her vulnerability and his role in that.

Shadow looked at the steak, then at Sorren. Without exchanging a word, she asked him how he expected her to eat the steak, which covered most of the ornately engraved silver plate.

"I'm not a very good host, am I?" Sorren took the knife and fork and soon had the steak cut into small pieces. He returned the utensils to the tray. "Try to be patient with me, precious. This isn't the kind of thing I do very often."

How often do you have women in your bed? wondered Shadow.

Shadow took the fork, jabbed a piece of beefsteak, then all but stabbed it into her mouth. She closed her eyes and chewed the steak slowly, savoring the flavor of corn-fed beef, seasoned lightly with salt and pepper and made even more delicious with mesquite wood smoke. The relief she felt made her eyes moist. She skewered a second piece of steak, holding the fork clumsily in her left hand. Before she could get it to her mouth, the meat slipped off the tines of the fork, landed on her chest, then rolled into the deep valley of her breasts just beneath the gown's lace-trimmed bodice. Shadow, too hungry to care, dropped the fork with a *clang* onto the tray and picked up another piece of steak with her fingers. She devoured the steak quickly, no longer savoring the flavor, now intent on sating the hunger that gripped her.

Sorren laughed softly as he watched the young mixed-blood woman attacking the her food. "Slow down, precious," he said, delight showing in his voice. "Here, let me help you. I should have known you've never eaten with silverware before."

Shadow looked up from her food, a cheek puffed out with potatoes, oblivious to the guilelessly enticing picture she presented Sorren. She wanted to tell Sorren that he was wrong, that Father Bradford had insisted on nothing less than impeccable table manners.

The notion of Father Bradford seeing her not only wolfing her food but eating with her fingers as well brought the tickle of a smile to the corners of Shadow's full lips, putting a pleasing gleam in her dark eyes.

"Precious, you really are amazing." The smile, however faint, gladdened Sorren's heart. He hoped it was a forgiving smile. "Let me help you so you don't make a mess of yourself."

The meat that had slipped off Shadow's fork drew Sorren's eyes. Famished as she was, she had ignored it until now. Seeing the direction of Sorren's gaze caused a shiver to ripple through Shadow. When he reached for the errant piece of steak she touched his hand with her own, stopping its progress.

"Easy, easy. I'm not going to do anything. I'm only trying to help."

Sorren considered it a victory, a show of faith, when Shadow took her hand away from his. With the fingertips of his first two fingers he removed the steak from its resting place between Shadow's breasts, just beneath the trim of the nightgown.

"Damn," Sorren hissed, dropping the steak onto the tray beside the plate. He shook his head slowly, looking into Shadow's eyes. "Precious, I've been trying to keep from looking at you, but you're not making it the least bit easy. No you're not. Not even a little bit." Sorren took the napkin and Shadow didn't stop him as he dabbed the juice of the steak from her golden skin. "Good God, woman, you are absolutely intoxicating. Do you know that?" It was Sorren this time whose eyes were filled with questions. "Do you have any idea how beautiful you are? Could you?"

Sorren picked up a piece of fried potato with the fork and brought it to Shadow's mouth, cupping his left hand under the food to prevent a second accident. His willpower had been completely spent on his hand's previous voyage to those tantalizing breasts. There was no telling what would happen if he were faced with such a challenge of honor again. "Open up, precious. Let me help you."

Not even the great hunger that chewed at Shadow's insides could lessen the impact of Sorren's words. Shadow had been told before that she was beautiful, but the words had come from an Indian brave, Bold Walker. Shadow knew exactly why he had given her honeyed words of praise. He wanted to be her lover, to be the man who would either accept what she could only give once or simply take her charms by force. Shadow had not been swayed by Bold Walker's flattery. She had seen through the gossamer veil he presented her, saw the calculating man lurking behind the mask of love words.

But could she accuse Sorren McKenna of the same deceit? Was he being honest or mendacious? He did not know that she understood every word he spoke. In light of that, what purpose would it serve to lie to her?

It was Shadow who was the first to turn her eyes away. She could not look at Sorren without questioning herself and her past. To look into Sorren's eyes made Shadow wonder about her future.

She could not include a man in her future, no matter how much she wanted to. She had to get to Matthew Weatherly's ranch—her father's ranch. She needed to know where she came from, to put the final piece of her incomplete past in her hands so that she could shape her own future. She could not allow herself to get sidetracked now, when the answers to the questions that had haunted her for so long were so close at hand.

"Come on, you need to eat." Shadow accepted the proffered forkful of green beans. The sweet, fresh butter was another taste from her days with Father

Bradford. "Do you realized you're a first for me?" Sorren grinned sheepishly as he fed Shadow another piece of steak. "You're the first woman ever to stay here two nights in a row. That's against the unwritten Laws of McKenna, but I'm making an exception in your case." His voice became very soft when he added, "I seem to be making all sorts of exceptions when it comes to you."

Now that the initial pangs of her hunger had been satisfied, Shadow again savored her food, eating slowly, taking the forkfuls from Sorren without embarrassment. It was the most delicious food she'd ever tasted in her life.

It was during the quiet moment, when Sorren had stopped speaking the words Shadow had waited so long to hear, that she had the chance to really look at the man. His hands were fascinating to watch. Long-fingered and dexterous, his fingernails clean and filed smooth. Sorren took care of his hands. It made Shadow wonder why.

At the corners of his eyes were crow's feet, leading Shadow to guess his age closer to middle than early thirties. His nose—a Roman nose with pronounced aquiline lines—had been broke at some time. There was a slight bump at the bridge. He was whipcord thin but well muscled, like the mountain lion Shadow had run into once while she stalked a mule deer.

"Feeling better now?" Sorren asked, slipping the fork from Shadow's mouth. The pleasure he felt showed in the lightness of his tone, in the timbre of his voice. "Do you have any idea what would happen to my reputation if it ever got around that I cooked a meal for a woman and then fed her? No one who knows me would ever believe that. Especially not for a woman I haven't slept with."

Shadow had to keep the recognition from showing on her face. How many women had this Sorren McKenna seduced? How many women had been in his bed, right where she was now? Apparently his reputation as a womanizer was common knowledge. At least Sorren talked as though it were.

"Precious, you really can throw a man right out of the saddle." Sorren sighed and shook his head. "If you could only look at your mouth. When you eat, your mouth is like a little animal. A shimmering, sexy little animal that ought to be kissed." Sorren took the napkin and dabbed at the corners of Shadow's mouth. "Last night while you were sleeping I watched you. It was the craziest thing. I just sat right where I'm sitting now and watched you. I've got so many things that need to be done, but last night all I wanted to do was watch you sleep."

Shadow could not raise her eyes to Sorren's face. She wanted to silence him, but any such action on her part would warn Sorren that she understood his words.

"Isn't that the craziest thing you've ever heard? I touched your hair." Sorren gently eased a thick strand of ebony hair from Shadow's cheek. "I touched your hair like this. It was beautiful to finally touch you without you hitting me or giving me those dagger eyes."

Where else, Shadow wondered, *did you touch me?*

As though he could read her mind, Sorren said, "You were on your back. I watched your breasts move as you breathed. It—" he cleared his throat, the memory still vivid, "it was too much for me. I pulled the blankets up to your chin and sat in the chair. I knew I couldn't control myself if I stayed that close, but I couldn't force myself completely from the room."

Shadow's heart was pounding. Her palms felt moist. She wanted to be away from Sorren and his confession. The tender, precious, loving words that she had waited so long to hear were now frightening, confusing, disturbing in ways Shadow had not expected.

"So I watched you from across the room. Not at an entirely safe distance though. In the darkness you were just as dangerously appealing as you are right now. I had to stop myself a hundred times from rushing to the bed and taking you into my arms."

Shadow squeezed her eyes tightly shut. *I won't cry! I'm not going to cry!* It didn't matter that she was hearing words that her soul had pleaded to hear. It shouldn't matter, she told herself, that Sorren had no reason to be anything but honest with her. She simply mustn't cry. But that couldn't stop the single crystal tear from trickling down her cheek.

"What's wrong?" Sorren asked quickly. He picked up the silver platter from Shadow's lap and returned it to the nightstand, getting it out of the way. "Precious, is it your head? Does it hurt?"

Shadow turned her face away from Sorren. Quickly she wiped the tear away with the back of her left hand. When was the last time she'd cried? Years ago. And even then, as a young girl when she could no longer take the taunting of the other children in the tribe, she did not let anyone see her tears. She would not give the other children the pleasure of knowing how deeply their insults cut her.

Sorren took Shadow's face lightly between his palms, forcing her to look up. He gave her that half smile that did not reach his eyes, the one that he used when he wanted to calm her while at the same time critically judge the extent of her recovery.

"Will you let me check the bandage?" Sorren asked in a husky whisper. His thumb slid with a feather's touch against Shadow's cheek. "It's going to be okay. Just let me look under the bandage."

Shadow wanted to stop him. He was sitting too close to her, his proximity and presence too powerful for her to be unaffected. She was becoming dizzy, disoriented again. Shadow wished she could completely ignore this enigma called Sorren McKenna. She knew that he was quite likely just a white man's version of Bold Walker—warrior and womanizer, a man known only for his conquests in battle and bed.

Shadow would not allow her eyes to meet Sorren's as he slowly and carefully untied the bows holding the bandage around her head. As he unwrapped the bandage, he rerolled it, his long, slender fingers twisting the cloth into a tight cylinder.

"Oh, yes. That's what I like to see," Sorren said. He moved several satiny strands of jet hair away from the cut. "It's mending nicely, precious. You won't have much of a scar at all, and what you will have will be hidden by your hair."

Sorren passed his thumb over Shadow's eyebrow, her face lightly cupped between his palms. He tilted her face up again, needing to see into her eyes.

"Look at me," he whispered. "Does it hurt bad?"

Shadow's eyes were closed, but that couldn't stop the tears from squeezing between her long, thick, curved lashes. The sight of her tears cut into Sorren and once again the weight of guilt pressed upon him, cutting jagged, torturous holes in his soul. "Damn it, precious, not in a thousand years would I ever do anything to hurt you again. I promise you that."

Shadow put her hand on Sorren's chest, intending to push him away. But her arm would not do the bidding of her mind. Instead of pushing him away, her hand slid slowly up his muscled chest, along his neck, then up to his face. She touched her fingertips to his lips, silencing the words that she could not bear to hear. She raised her eyes to his. Silently she pleaded with him. Didn't he realize how his love words tore into her heart? Couldn't he see that his beautiful words only emphasized the loneliness that Shadow had lived with her entire life?

When Sorren wiped the tears away, more came from Shadow's eyes.

Precious. He calls me precious.

Sorren took Shadow's hand in his, holding her fingertips against his lips. He kissed the ends of her fingers, first all at once, then each delicate fingertip individually. When Shadow tried to pull her hand away, Sorren gently but insistently held onto it, turning it to place the palm against his cheek.

"I'm sorry things turned out this way," Sorren continued, seeing the fresh trickle of tears coming from the onyx-eyed young woman. "I never meant for you to get hurt." He smiled wanly and explained, "Life seems to explode around me. It's always been that way with me." Sorren wiped a tear from

Shadow's cheek with a curved finger, then sipped the salty drip from his finger. "Tears again. I cause them too often. I never meant to make you cry. I promise you that." He chuckled mirthlessly. "Promises? Promises from Sorren McKenna? That's another first. Aside from the fact that no woman in her right mind would believe one that came from me, I've made it a point to never make promises . . . especially not to women. But . . . By God, sweet precious, I never thought I'd run into someone like you. Not in a thousand years."

Shadow could hardly breathe. Why did he have to keep talking to her like that? Couldn't he just leave her alone? She thought of talking to him. Since he did not understand her silence, perhaps words would make him leave the room. but that would mean giving up the one small advantage Shadow had over Sorren. She resolved to speak only as an absolute last resort.

A sob caught in Shadow's chest. She pulled her hand from his. Sorren's arms went to her shoulders, and before he was fully aware of what he was doing, he pulled Shadow in close, hugging her body with gentle force.

"Don't cry," Sorren whispered. He stroked the satiny length of her hair, his hand gliding down Shadow's back to send tingles through her. "Please, precious, don't cry. It's killing me to see your tears."

Shadow's cheek was pressed into the arch of his neck. The warmth of his body, the suppressed strength, was more apparent to her now than ever. She smelled the fragrance of his body, the manly scent of raw power. With a will of their own,

Shadow's hands slipped around Sorren's trim waist. The smoothness of his silk shirt was in stark, enticing contrast to the steelish muscles beneath.

Sorren never intended to kiss Shadow, but when she tilted her face up to his, he could not resist the temptation of her lips. Softly at first, his lips just brushing against hers, he kissed her. When he kissed her again, with more passion, her wide, full-lipped mouth molded to his. He could tell, without displeasure, that the young woman in his arms, in his bed, had not been kissed very often. Her lips were tentative against his own, mimicking his movements without copying them exactly. It was different for Sorren to be with untutored women. He was breaking another of the Laws of McKenna and he didn't give a damn.

Shadow held loosely onto Sorren, her fingertips uncertain along the small of his back, up his spine. His kisses left her breathless, confused, frightened— but wanting. She pulled her face away from Sorren and looked into his eyes.

"You are so beautiful," he whispered, each word coming out slowly, as though the mere act of pronouncing them was suddenly difficult for him.

It was Shadow who initiated the next kiss by simply closing her eyes. She wanted his kisses but lacked the boldness and confidence to be assertive. Sorren's warm, moist lips pressed tightly against her own. When his tongue passed lightly over her lips, Shadow opened her mouth to accept him. The deep, searching kiss was bewildering to Shadow. His tongue played with hers, darting, moving in a dance that Shadow did not yet understand. She responded instinctively, without reservation despite the fear and confusion she felt.

"So beautiful," Sorren murmured when the kiss finally ended. His lips nuzzled Shadow's as he spoke. "So damn beautiful."

For the next few moments, Shadow let Sorren's feelings surround her and touch her deep inside. She could not resist, did not want to resist. His kisses forced responses from her, burning with such intensity that everything in the world was forgotten — everything except this man who touched her tenderly, who spoke the loving words that Shadow only dreamed she would hear. He was making her body stir in a flush, wonderful way, bringing a rush of new feelings to the surface of her skin. She felt stronger, happier, but light-headed, for the air seemed charged with a strange, vital force that existed only within the circle of Sorren McKenna's arms.

Shadow opened her mouth wider, silently seeking the newly discovered pleasure of Sorren's tongue. She felt the pillow against her head and was vaguely aware that she was no longer sitting. Sorren now loomed above her, one hand beneath her, the other touching her naked shoulder. His weight bore down on her, pressing her breasts against his chest, pressing her deeper into the mattress. The pressure against her breasts charged like lightning through Shadow, unifying all her chaotic feelings. Sorren's weight felt good against her, his body a knot of corded muscle, a security against the outside world that Shadow — for a few moments — felt she could trust. With soft moans of pleasure, Shadow kissed Sorren, returning his kisses now rather than simply

66

eceiving them. She caught his lower lip between her
eeth and bit softly.

Sorren slipped his hand between them. He cupped
he fullness of one taut breast, catching the nipple
etween his finger and thumb. Even through the
ightgown, his contact with her nipple made Shadow
nhale deeply, gasping from the current of desire
orren's hands drew from her flesh.

She opened her eyes, defensive again. She looked
nto his face, her eyes filled with fear. This had gone
oo far. Sorren's sweet kisses, his tantalizing caresses,
ad made her forget who she was and what she was—
nd, more importantly, what she had to do. It was
is hand on her breast, stoking the fires of a need
hat threatened to consume her at any moment, that
orced Shadow back to the real world.

Instantly regretting his transgression, Sorren took
is hand from her breast and whispered, "No?"

"No."

Sorren shook his head, extricating himself from the
oman's arms slowly. He caught the satin-trimmed
em of a blanket and pulled it up to her chin,
overing Shadow, leaving just her head and arms
xposed.

"That's the one word I think we both understand,"
orren said in a husky whisper. "Precious, you're
ore beautiful than any woman has any right to be."
Ie started to touch Shadow's face but stopped when
he tensed. "I went too far, didn't I? A habit of
ine—in an out of bed, I'm afraid. I've got a streak
f greediness in me. And, precious, you could make
 man feel real greedy."

Sorren stood. For a long moment he looked down

67

at the woman in his bed, memorizing all the subtl features that made her so damnly, dangerously ap pealing. The blankets could not hide her opuler curves. He burned with the desire to take her onc again into his arms, to kiss away her fears, to feel th length of her body pressing warmly against his.

Her denial of him, whether she understood th single English word or not, was spoken from he heart and laced with fear and uncertainty. Sorre had heard affected protests before and knew tha some women felt obligated to put up resistance be fore accepting physical pleasure for its own sake.

"Easy," he whispered. "It's just me. You know I'r not going to hurt you." A punishing thought insinu ated itself into his brain. He swallowed and addec "It was a ricochet. An accident. I promise I'll neve hurt you again."

She rolled onto her side, turning her back to him Sorren felt that another moment in her arms, or more kiss from those soft lips and he, too, woul have been lost in the swirling emotions of the mo ment. He did not trust his own sense of honor whe she was involved.

Sorren was distinctly aware of feeling fortuna that she had stopped him. He had never felt this wa after tasting a woman's kisses and feeling her boc against his own. It was as though Shadow were dangerous narcotic, a drug of some kind that was to good, too pleasureable to be anything but pure da ger.

"I'm going to have to keep you at an arm's distanc from now on, precious," he said in a level voice. Sh did not respond to his words, keeping her back im. "I'm going to leave you for a while, but I will be ack soon. There's some work I've postponed too ong already." There was a weighty pause before he oncluded, "If I don't leave now, I may never leave."

He did not understand Shadow's soft sob as the ears returned. She hugged the pillow, squeezing it gainst her breasts, already trying to recapture the rief, blissful moments she'd spent in Sorren McKena's arms.

Shadow was soon alone in the room with her oughts and memories. She pressed her head into e softness of the goose down pillow. Shadow knew e would not force himself upon her, though in her eakened condition she would be helpless to stop im. It was the nagging doubt, the wondering about orren McKenna's true nature, combined with a ersonal past that Shadow could neither forget nor scape, that kept her wary, that fueled her suspicion.

The bone-tired fatigue started in Shadow's feet and rept swiftly upward. The adrenaline-induced mental cuity passed. Shadow closed her eyes and reminded erself that Sorren would return, then drifted into nother shallow, restless sleep.

Chapter Four

The view was always breathtaking to Sorren when
ever he rode over the crest of Two Arrows Valley an
saw the MW Circle Ranch. Matthew Weatherly ha
spent many years and much of his finances buildin
the palatial home below. His simple good taste — an
wealth — were evident, even from the distance of
half mile.

"Come on, girl," Sorren said to his mare, tappin
her sides lightly with his heels. "Let's find out wha
kind of deal the War Department is willing to mak
with this ol' soldier."

To the east of Matthew's home were the eigh
bunkhouses, built in rows in military fashion. The
reminded Sorren of his days spent in barracks lik
these half a continent away. Enough housing fo
eighty ranch hands. In the peak seasons, durin
branding and just before cattle drives to the stoc
yards, over a hundred men would be housed ther

Two familiar sensations came to Sorren as he roc
slowly into Two Arrows Valley, allowing his mare

set her own pace. Each time Sorren saw the MW Circle Ranch, he was reminded that he really wasn't — as he'd been accused of on more than one occasion — the richest son of a bitch in the valley. Seeing the bunkhouses and all the men brought back the only thing he missed from his soldiering days: There is a certain camaraderie that only men who have faced death together can share. The bunkhouses brought Sorren back to a time when he still believed in things being absolutely right and absolutely wrong. But those were his early days, in '62 and maybe '63, when he believed he saw the world around him clearly. Sorren no longer believed in absolutes. Dig deep enough and there is probably a skeleton in a locked closet somewhere, a little white lie hidden here and a dirty black lie hidden there. Life was easier for Sorren when he didn't see it quite so clearly.

As he drew closer, several of the Weatherly men shouted greetings to Sorren. He returned each wave. The men seemed nervous, he noted. They were as concerned as he was about the coming changes at the MW Circle Ranch now that Matthew Weatherly was gone and his son was taking the reins of the operation.

Matthew had ruled his men as a dictator, but with wisdom. He set very few rules of conduct for his men, but if those rules were violated, the punishment was receiving a final paycheck. Nobody *had* to work for Matthew Weatherly. He paid good wages for an honest day's work. He set down inviolate laws that didn't change like the winds, and everyone understood them. There was a line of men waiting to get on the MW Circle payroll.

Emma met Sorren at the door. Her wide black face broke into a beautiful smile at the sight of Sorren. The elderly nanny and maid took Sorren's hand and tugged him into the house.

"Land's sakes, child, you're skinnier than ever!" Emma admonished, looking up at Sorren with maternalistic intolerance. "You ain't been eatin' right, an' I knows it, so don't you try tellin' me no different!"

"Emma, I—"

"Don't you back talk me now," Emma cut in, taking Sorren's flat-crowned wide-brimmed black Stetson hat and placing it on the coat tree. "I don't take no back talk from my boys and I ain't gonna take none from you." Emma waggled a thick, short finger at Sorren, her face still cross but her eyes twinkling with pure pleasure. "I'll be over later and fix you some of my good stew. A big kettle so's you can eat proper for a couple days."

"Emma, you don't have to—"

"Mr. McKenna, do you think I got me a beautiful body like mine by not knowin' my way aroun' the kitchen?" Emma ran her hands down her sides. She was about five feet tall and nearly as wide. "I raised me five good boys, Christians every one. They don't back talk me and ain't a one of 'em is puny." Emma shook her head, her lips pursed tight with the kind of displeasure only an errant son can cause. She heaped on the guilt as thick as she could by muttering under her breath as she left, "Ain't right a boy your age not havin' hisself a good wife. Makes a man skinny."

Sorren adored Emma.

72

"Good evening, Sorren," Catherine said, crossing the foyer with a rustle of imported, hand-sewn petticoats. She took Sorren's hand and squeezed it, pleasure sparkling in her sapphire blue eyes. "I knew you wouldn't let us down tonight. Mr. Phillips is here for the opening."

"Couldn't miss this," Sorren said. He slipped his hand out of Catherine's, giving her a quick smile.

Jonas Phillips was one of the few men Matthew Weatherly trusted implicitly. As the attorney for the MW Circle Ranch, Phillips was the man who made sure all the *i*'s were dotted and all the *t*'s got crossed. And if anybody crossed Matthew Weatherly, they found themselves facing Jonas Phillips in the territorial courtroom in Denver City. He was rotund and bald, with a swatch of hair circling his head. When he was peaceful, he looked like a benevolent friar; in a courtroom, he was the wrath of God, Patrick Henry, and Joshua all rolled into one. Sorren had always gotten along with Phillips and would have hired him as his own attorney had there not been a problem with a conflict of interest.

"Evening, Sorren," Phillips said, extending a hand. "Glad you could make it."

Sorren gave the attorney a quick nod and firm shake. "Had to be here to find out what the War Department has to offer. And for what it's worth, I'm glad you're here. Nine times out of ten trying to read a contract gives me a headache. I cannot make heads nor tails out of that legalese."

Phillips emitted a chuckle. "That's why men like you and Matthew—God rest his soul—hire men like me. Come now, let's get down to business. The package is in Matthew's study."

An eerie feeling went through Sorren as he stepped into Matthew's private study. Sorren had spent hours in there with Matthew, sipping whiskey or drinking endless pots of coffee, depending upon the seriousness of their discussion, planning and plotting all manner of business ventures and private adventures. Matthew wasn't behind the desk now, but his son, Carl, was.

Sorren took one look at Carl and saw a virulent confidence that had never shone in the young man's face before. Whether Carl was or wasn't in charge of the MW Circle Ranch, he *felt* like he was, and it showed.

"So you finally found time to visit us, eh?" Carl was sitting in a high-backed leather chair behind an enormous walnut desk. It was where Matthew had done all his paperwork. Carl's blue eyes cut into Sorren, the contempt undisguised. "Not very bright of you to leave the package at Angie's." Carl leaned back in his chair, lifting a polished boot up on the desk. "I heard you had some trouble, but that's no excuse."

"A man has his priorities."

It tore at Sorren's heart to see Carl sitting in Matthew's chair, behind Matthew's desk, drinking Matthew's Scotch.

"I heard she's a squaw. Losing your touch, Sorren? I always thought you had better taste in women than that."

Sorren bit back the words that threatened to spill out. He couldn't let Carl work up his anger. Angry men make mistakes.

"Where's the package?" Sorren asked, his tone level and emotionless.

Carl pulled open a drawer and withdrew the leather-bound package Sorren had seen at Angie's. He dropped it on his desk and tapped it with his finger.

Sorren leaned over the desk and took the package, turning it in his hands. The sealing wax with the War Department seal pressed into it had been broken. Anger boiled inside Sorren.

"You opened it."

"I couldn't help myself. Catherine was making such a commotion after Emma said you were riding in that I just—"

"Carl! You promised you would wait until Sorren got here!" Catherine's cheeks had turned pink. She glanced at Sorren apologetically. "I'm sorry, Sorren. He had to have just opened it. Not ten minutes ago Mr. Phillips, Carl, and I were in this very room waiting for you. And the package wasn't open then. Then our man said you were coming, and Mr. Phillips and I left the room to greet you."

Carl, a glass of Scotch in hand, made a clucking sound with his teeth. "Now don't go apologizing for me, Catherine. If you don't want me telling Sorren about how you flit around here like a chicken in a coop when a fox breaks in, every time you know he's coming by, I won't tell him that. But don't cut me off just to apologize for me, okay?" Then, looking Sorren straight in the eyes, he said, "Business is business, right, Sorren? I waited as long as I could. If you put a squaw before business, that's your prerogative. But don't expect me to sit on a potential fortune

75

while you play nursemaid."

Sorren could picture it. Being left alone in the study with the package was too great a temptation for a man of Carl's character. He had to get the first look inside, even though the orders from the War Department made it very clear that Sorren and Matthew must be together when it was opened.

Sorren walked to the long leather sofa and sat on the padded armrest, near the window where the waning sun was peaking through the drapes. He thumbed through the documents quickly, skimming them for now. He would read every word with Phillips.

"Want to tell me what the deal is, or do I read all of this now?"

Carl, relishing the only time he knew more about a business deal than Sorren, took a long pull on his Scotch. He made Sorren wait several long seconds before answering.

"Well, I haven't studied the papers yet either, but in a nutshell, the deal works like this." He paused to sip his Scotch. All attention was on Carl and he was loving every second. "The MW Circle Ranch and you get sole distributorship for cattle and horses to the Army for the Colorado, Wyoming, and Dakota Territories. In return for this, we've got to promise full delivery of beef on specific dates to specific locations. There shouldn't be any problem in that."

Sorren exchanged an approving glance with Catherine. This would make all of them a lot of money. Carl sipped his drink, nearly finished with it.

"There's more. We've also got a standing order for horses. The Army wants them in groups of fifty.

They've got to be broken and trained to Army regulations. There's something in there about training."

Sorren paged through the documents until he found the contract for the horses. "I know some good men I can call on," Sorren said, continuing his perusal of the documents. "Great horsemen. They're expensive, but they're worth it."

"Calling in more men—expensive men at that— would increase our costs." Carl crossed the room to where the ornately carved crystal decanter of Scotch rested among the other bottles of Matthew's private stock. "Not a good business move. We'll work with the men we've got."

"Most of our men are cattlemen. We'll need at least a few specialists with us. I can't be everywhere at once."

"I said we'll use the men we've got. End of discussion. What else does it say?" Carl returned to the chair, avoiding Sorren's gaze, hoping McKenna would not challenge him. He kicked his feet up, crossing his boots on the desk.

"Daddy never put his feet up like that," Catherine said sternly. "Can't you show him some respect?"

"I loved him, too. But you've got to put the past behind you, Catherine. The old man's gone now and that's a fact. This is my desk now."

Catherine cast her eyes down to her pale hands folded in her lap. She blinked several times rapidly. Though Carl said he missed his father, he never showed any remorse over his death. Catherine also sensed that her brother relished the fact that he now held control of a million dollar cattle empire and

77

controlled the destiny of more than eighty men. Since Matthew's death, Carl had been a tyrant to the ranch hands.

"We also, by the way, get five thousand dollars apiece as upfront money. Operating expenses. Not a bad deal at all, I'd say."

While the prattle between Carl and Catherine continued, Sorren read several of the contracts. He trusted Phillips, but Sorren would have his own lawyer scrutinize every word before signing the contracts. On the face of it, everything appeared quite standard. By the time the contracts were completed, Sorren McKenna would be an exceedingly rich man by anyone's standards.

It wasn't until Sorren saw the smaller envelope, tucked into the training specification manual for the army horses, that he felt the first signs of danger. He picked out the small brown paper envelope. His name — only his name — was written on it in a familiar handwriting. The envelope was secured with plain sealing wax. No insignia had been pressed into the wax.

Sorren ripped open the envelope and pulled out the single sheet of paper inside. It read:

My dear friend,

I promised you that your service to your country was completed and that you, of all men, were entitled to retire in peace. You have served me and your country with pride and honor. So it is knowing how much you have already done, how much you have already sacrificed, that I now regret to inform you that there is one more vital task I must ask you to fulfill.

You remember, I believe, General Jean-Jacques La Roux.

During the war, he was known for his cunning and utter ruthlessness in his determination for a separate South. The war has never ended for LaRoux. This Rebel has kept together his ragtag band of renegades of the Stars and Bars. I've known for years about LaRoux's thievery, the raping and destruction he and his men leave in their path. I should have done something about it before this time, I suppose, but I honestly believed his men would naturally drift away from him. They haven't; he's as strong as ever. Now LaRoux has moved his men out of Mexico, and they appear to be making their way northward. These Rebels are once again taking American lives, preaching anarchy and violating the laws of these United States. For God's sake, this was why we fought the war — to bring the country together. LaRoux seeks to divide us again.

Intelligence reports are pathetically incomplete on LaRoux (aren't they always?). We do know that his men are fanatically loyal to him. They are even wearing the grey uniforms of their defunct regiment.

Please understand that I did not want to put this burden upon your shoulders, but I know of no other man capable of carrying the weight of such responsibility. A man was sent months ago to infiltrate LaRoux's cadre. He sent several intelligence reports, but he has not been heard from since just prior to LaRoux's northward push. Perhaps my first attempt is what prompted LaRoux to make his return to our Country. I do not know. The worst must be assumed.

LaRoux must be dealt with swiftly. Should the Powers that Be take an active involvement in this, LaRoux will become a martyr. Even in Hell, he can destroy us. His followers and sympathizers in the South are numerous. All that is needed is a martyr to galvanize their desire to again form their clusters of disunion.

79

We must realize this country cannot be divided against itself again. We are, as a Nation, in our infancy. Another childhood disease such as the one the People just suffered through would surely destroy the Republic.

I am sorry that this burden is placed upon your mantle and that it must come to you this way. But LaRoux must be dealt with, with swift finality, and in such a manner as to neutralize his power completely and for all time. Your Nation, though it will never know it, is counting on you. And so am I.

These contracts are my way, on behalf of this Nation, of rewarding you for your heroism in the past, and for future unheralded acts of Patriotism.

Good luck.

The letter was unsigned, but Sorren recognized the handwriting as surely as he recognized his own. It was from a man he had worked for during the war. An old drinking buddy. A man possessing one of the most brilliant tactical minds Sorren had ever come across. And, quite obviously, a man not averse to using a combination of bribery and blackmail to get what he wanted.

The letter was from Sorren's former superior officer, who had traded in the title of "general" for that of "president." The letter was from Ulysses S. Grant, President of the United States.

"Sorren . . . Sorren, what's wrong?"

He turned to Catherine, flashing a quick, feigned smile. "Nothing's wrong. Why do you say that?"

"You had the strangest look on your face just now. I've never seen it before." Sorren shrugged his shoulders. Catherine, concerned about Sorren and curious about the letter, pressed on. "It wasn't a cold look, or

80

even an angry one. It was—I don't know how to describe it—an empty look. Hollow."

I'm losing my edge, thought Sorren. On more than one occasion, his poker face had saved his life in enemy territory. A few years away from the action and Sorren was losing the fine cutting edge that had kept him a step ahead of those who would wish him dead.

"The squaw come to mind, Sorren?" Carl asked.

Sorren ignored Carl. To Catherine he said, "I was just thinking, that's all." He rose and walked briskly to the fireplace. "It's always a complicated business working with the government. You never can tell what the government really wants." Sorren tossed Grant's letter into the fireplace. Red and orange flames came to life.

Carl, seeing the envelope burning, bolted from his chair.

"What the hell are you doing?" He took two strides toward the fireplace, then stopped. The envelope and its contents were already engulfed in flames, just seconds away from being ashes. Violent eyes turned to Sorren. "What was that? Goddamn it! Sorren, you had no right! We're in this together!"

Catherine gasped. Her brother was capable of anything.

"Relax. It was nothing." Sorren returned to his spot on the arm of the sofa. Carl, livid, was close at his heels. "It was just some notes from the government lawyer. They got placed in the package by accident. Interdepartmental notes, that's all. Nothing of importance."

"What did they say?"

Sorren picked up the contracts and set them in his lap. He looked up at Carl, his face displaying confusion at Carl's anger. "Nothing much. Just some doodles from one lawyer to the next." He smiled coolly. "They don't trust us, you know. The lawyers think this order might be too much for just Matthew and me."

Carl sneered, "Don't you mean you and me?" Carl tapped his chest. "I'm in this now, not Papa. I'm running the show."

Phillips, who had characteristically remained out of the conversation, waiting patiently to be called upon, cleared his throat. When Carl looked at him, Phillips said, "It's true you're running the MW Circle now, Carl. But what has yet to be determined is whether the contract is with Matthew specifically, or with Matthew's ranch."

"What's the difference?"

"The difference is that if the contracts, which were drawn up some time ago, are with Matthew, they're now invalidated. If the contracts are with the MW Circle, they're still legally binding with your signature." Phillips placed his hands out, palms up. "I won't know until I see the contracts."

Carl, near panic, wheeled on Sorren and reached for the contracts. Sorren caught Carl's wrist. Sorren's fingers were like steel bands around his flesh.

"Don't." Sorren, seated, looked straight into Carl's eyes. "Don't ever do that." Carl cocked his fist. Sorren twisted Carl's wrist until the palm was up. He put a thumb to the back of Carl's hand and pushed. It took very little pressure to force Carl to his knees. "Make a fist on me again, and if you're lucky you'll need a doctor. But if you're not so lucky," Sorren said, pausing to let the truth of his words sink in past the pain, "you'll need a mortician." Agony was etched in Carl's face. "I asked you a question." He added more pressure with his thumb. Carl squealed. "Do you understand me?"

Catherine, horrified by violence of any sort, screamed out. "Stop it! Sorren, stop it this minute!"

Sorren stood slowly, his eyes never leaving Carl's face. He looked down on Carl. The contracts fell unheeded from his lap to the floor.

"You can have Mr. Phillips look at these contracts until he's blue in the face and it won't matter. I'm not signing anything. We'll all be happier without this business. Besides, I never did like working with the government." He paused. "And I'm sure not entering any partnership with you. If Matthew was still alive, maybe I'd go through with the deal." Sorren added a touch more pressure against Carl's wrist. He could see Carl's mind whirling, asking the question: Can I hit him hard enough to free myself, or will he break my wrist?

"Please, Sorren, let him go."

Sorren released Carl. "Matthew's not here." Sorren headed for the door. "He's not here now and he won't be coming back . . . and neither will I."

Sorren was on his mare and headed through the brick archway when he heard Catherine calling out to him. He kept going, his mare speeding to an easy canter.

Rage boiled in Sorren. "Bastards!" he hissed. The sound of his voice was reassuring. "Lousy, lying bastards!"

When Sorren and Matthew had first learned of the War Department's contracts, it had seemed too god to be true. And it *was* too good. General Grant, Sorren's old friend (he still couldn't think of him as *President* Grant), had manipulated the entire setup, making it difficult — if not nearly impossible — for Sorren to refuse the assignment to kill Jean-Jacques LaRoux.

Sorren could picture Grant in his office, pondering his options. How well did he know Captain McKenna? he would ask himself. What were McKenna's weaknesses? How could he use those weaknesses to force McKenna into accepting the assignment to solve the problem of LaRoux? How could McKenna be manipulated into coming out of retirement one last time without holding a grudge?

The hoofbeats of the horse beneath him chipped away at his anger with his friend, Ulysses Grant. Soon viewing the situation with an emotionless, critical eye, Sorren had to respect the foresight shown by the old soldier, by the brilliant military tactician turned politician. Grant had dealt the hand from the bottom of the deck, but he did it with style. He made sure there would be other people present when the contracts were opened. Matthew Weatherly, the cattleman, would concentrate on the contracts for the beef. Sorren, the horseman, would first check those contracts. That's why Grant's unsigned letter was in the training manual. Grant also made the stakes high enough to make them difficult to walk away from. And, as a coup de grace, he made sure that it was impossible for Matthew to fulfill the contracts alone. Matthew Weatherly would need Sorren's herd of iding stock if he were to sell his own cattle. Matthew would pressure Sorren into signing the contracts, Grant had schemed. Since the letter was unsigned and never mentioned Sorren's name, if it had fallen into the wrong hands, there was no way of tracing it to either its owner or to its destination.

There was just one thing Grant hadn't foreseen, and it was that uncontrollable variable that allowed Sorren to escape the trap. Grant hadn't counted on Matthew Weatherly dying. Matthew's death made it possible for Sorren to ride away from the ugly, bloody, manipulating scheme concocted by the President of the United States.

Sorren chuckled to himself. Grant was going to be furious when he found out the net he had cast had missed ensnaring Sorren.

"Serves him right for blackmailing a drinking buddy," Sorren murmured, patting his mare's neck. But in the back of Sorren's mind, he knew with a sad sense of certainty that if their roles were reversed, he'd have dealt a stacked hand, just like Grant.

Why was Carl so feverish to sign the contracts immediately? The contracts would make Carl a fortune, but he was already a wealthy man. Wealthy by all accounts. There was a definite edge of raw fear in Carl when Phillips pointed out the contracts might be invalidated with Matthew's death. It wasn't just anger from a business deal going sideways; it was more than just that. But what? What could Carl need or want that he couldn't already afford?

With the setting sun at his back, Sorren had to pull back on the reins to keep the mare from breaking into a trot. She was in a hurry, anticipating the ground oats she always got upon her return to the stables. She had been a good, trusty mount for Sorren for the past four years. He didn't need her tripping and breaking a leg in the dark.

He, too, had something special waiting for him upon his return.

When he returned to his ranch, Sorren had one of his men take care of bedding his mare. He usually handled such tasks himself, but tonight he had the woman upstairs to deal with.

At the doorway, Sorren pulled loose the knotted leather thong around his thigh. He took his gunbelt off and hooked it on the coat tree, along with his hat. He had to force himself to keep from running up the stairs to his bedroom.

What was her mood like now? he wondered. He made a point of clicking his heels against the wooden stairs. That would give her some advance notice of his arrival. He didn't want to startle her.

She was gone.

The inner turmoil that had started with Grant's letter was nothing compared to what Sorren felt when he saw his bed empty. He rushed through his house, searching. He couldn't even call out to her. He didn't know her name. He checked the bunk houses, but none of the men had seen her leave. Though several men halfheartedly volunteered to help him look for her, Sorren rejected the offer. They all knew that it would be folly to search for an Indian in the dark who didn't want to be found. The fact that any woman had left his home without so much as a good-bye was humorous enough to his men. He didn't need to make a complete fool of himself in front of them.

In the bedroom he found the nightgown he'd put on her. The doeskin dress he'd taken off was missing, as were her moccasins. He checked his bureau and found that nothing was missing—not the roll of cash he kept in the drawer with his silk shirts, not the heavy gold watch he'd received as a gift some fifteen years ago from a wealthy and grateful weekend companion.

"So much for the theory of thieving Indians," Sorren muttered angrily.

Sorren was getting the distinct impression that he was in a great deal of trouble. Not danger, just trouble. He had to force himself to keep from thinking about the raven-haired vixen who had kissed him with such fire, then left him pawing at the bedroom door.

He stripped off his clothes, tossing them onto the chair, and crawled between the sheets. Did the pillowcase still smell of her hair? Could he still feel the warmth of her long-gone body between the sheets?

Sorren closed his eyes, wishing for sleep to come quickly, knowing it wouldn't. His thoughts were wild and disconnected, one moving to the next without any central point other than the woman who had stayed in his bed, the bed he was now in. The bed he wished *she* was now in.

Jonas Phillips leaned back in a leather chair in the late Matthew Weatherly's study. He was enjoying the delay. Matthew, who had tried unsuccessfully to teach his children patience and respect for money while at the same time buying them everything they could ever want or need, would have enjoyed it, too.

Carl was particularly agitated. He had already helped himself to one whiskey. With his glass nearly empty, he was casting nervous glances toward the decanter. Carl was also giving Sorren McKenna red-eyed glares of such unqualified contempt Phillips made a mental note to tell Sorren to be on his guard.

"What in hell are we waiting for?" Carl's voice shattered the silence of the study. All eyes turned to him. "Phillips, can't we get this over with?"

"The reading of your father's will requires that certain legal formalities be followed. Besides, he wanted it done this way." Phillips was unbothered by Carl's outburst. It did seem quite likely that Carl would dismiss him and find a new lawyer after the reading of the will. Not working for Carl Weatherly would crimp Phillips's spending habits, but that was a fair trade-off for not having to see the self-centered, self-important would-be despot.

Carl tossed the last of his whiskey down his throat. "I shouldn't have to remind you that I'm running the show around here now."

Sorren smiled benignly. "Obviously not yet. If you were, the will would be open." Sorren glanced at Catherine, who sat on the sofa beside him. He gave her a quick, honest smile, not wanting her to be offended. "You see, Carl, whether you like it or not, Matthew is, as you so aptly put it, running the show. He may be dead, but you're a fool if you don't think he's in charge."

"You've got nothing to say about this!" Carl spat. "You backed out on a deal you made with Dad! What do you think he'd say about that? Huh? What would he think of you now?"

Sorren calmly rolled a cigarette. He scratched a match with his thumbnail and savored the sweet Virginia tobacco before turning his attention back to Carl.

"One thing your father never did was go back on his word. He never changed the rules after the game had started, either. You're right, I did back out on a deal; but only because the arrangement had been made with Matthew. And, as you've made it so apparent these past few days, you are not Matthew by any stretch of the imagination."

Carl was about to lash back when Catherine stopped his words with a huff and a wave of her hand. "Please, do we have to fight now? At a time like this? What would Daddy say?"

Under his breath, yet loud enough so everyone could hear, Carl said, "I'm so tired of hearing about Dad."

The study door opened and Emma stepped in, then moved to the side. Shadow walked in behind Emma.

"Here she is," Phillips said, his voice light but his mind speeding. He looked at Sorren and noticed the cigarette fall from his fingers to the Persian rug; Catherine seemed bewildered about the squaw's presence at her father's will reading; Carl showed instant libidinous interest.

It was Sorren's reaction that most pleased Phillips. *There she is!* Sorren thought. *My God, she's more lovely than ever.* The feelings in his heart were immediately enraged, exploding in his chest, tightening his throat. Barely a ripple of emotion crossed his face.

Emma spotted Sorren's smouldering cigarette and she waddled quickly over to it, the rustle of her petticoats breaking the spell of the moment. She bent over with a groan of exertion and picked up the cigarette. "Dirty, filthy habit, Mr. McKenna. You ain't never gonna find one of my good boys smoking these things. No, sir! That you ain't."

"That will be all, Emma," Phillips said. "I'm sure it was an accident. Thank you very much." He waved a hand to the single open chair in the room. "Please be seated and we can begin."

"Who's she? What's she doing here?" Carl's voice was icy, laced with suspicion. He wasn't thinking lusty thoughts about the half-breed now.

"That's a good place to start. Introductions are in order. Carl, Catherine . . . I'd like you to meet your half sister, Shadow."

Catherine sat open mouthed. She looked to Sorren, as though somehow he could explain something. Sorren's expression had changed from confusion to concern. Shadow had neither the head bandage nor the wrap around her wrist. Several fingers were still swollen. The bullet scar at her hairline was hidden by the way she had parted her hair and held it back with a leather thong headband. Her aura was that of something wild and proud and innocent, yet bold and eager. She reminded Phillips of a young doe approaching water — graceful and tentative, thirsty but cautious.

"What kind of joke is this, Phillips?"

"No joke, Carl . . . though I can see certain elements of humor in all this."

Shadow sat in the overstuffed leather chair. She crossed her legs at the knee, then tugged the doeskin dress down a little in a modest gesture. Her legs were exposed to mid thigh. She placed her hands lightly on the arms of the chair, never taking her eyes away from Phillips.

"Would you like to explain this?" Sorren was looking at Shadow but speaking to Phillips. "Apparently you're the only one who knows what is going on."

Shadow turned her head and looked directly into Sorren's eyes. "I can explain, Sorren, if you'd like?"

Phillips would have given a week's wages to be able to preserve the expression on Sorren McKenna's face. The old lawyer, who had seen so much in his life, thought he would never see a man like Sorren—which led him to wonder if McKenna was a type or a prototype—so thoroughly awestruck. Apparently men like Sorren could still be surprised, a thought that gave Phillips comfort somehow.

Then, as though he were shaking off the cold from a blustery night wind, Sorren looked away from Shadow for just a moment. His shoulders hunched inward and stayed there for a second. Then he squared his shoulders and when Sorren turned his eyes back to Shadow, they were dark and fathomless. It was an expression Phillips had seen before. An expression that was neither hot nor cold, an expression Phillips suspected was filled with emotion yet displayed none. McKenna's mind was moving fast, and he was blocking his thought out of his features.

He hoped that when Matthew's will had been read

and all was said and done, Sorren would still consider him a friend. Jonas Phillips always thought himself a man not afraid of anything. Still, the idea of having a man like Sorren McKenna as a personal enemy was horrific.

"Perhaps I could have a minute with you outside?" Sorren said to Shadow. Outwardly, he appeared perfectly calm.

"Of course," Shadow replied. She rose and headed for the study's oak double doors without looking back, without waiting for Sorren, her small feet, sheathed in moccasins, silent against the wooden floor.

"Will somebody tell me what in hell is going on around here?" Carl asked no one in particular.

Shadow's heart was pounding. Her palms felt sweaty. She had escaped Sorren's when she could, returning to Father Bradford's orphanage. Only the mentor from her youth wasn't there. He had left a note instructing Shadow to find a lawyer named Jonas Phillips as quickly as possible, and to explain who she was. The note promised that everything would be taken care of by Jonas, and that she shouldn't fear him.

Shadow had prepared herself for almost anything. She feared that Catherine and Carl would take the news of her being their half sister badly. That much was to be expected. What she hadn't counted on, what she hadn't steeled her resolve to cope with, was seeing Sorren McKenna in the same room.

Standing in the foyer, Shadow heard the door close behind her. She took a deep breath and turned. Sorren looked her up and down slowly, deliberately, taking her in with calculating eyes that were black and cold like marble.

"You speak English."

"Yes. Very well, I think." She tried to sound casual and friendly. The smile she tried didn't quite form.

"It might have been nice if you'd let me in on your little secret."

"I didn't—" Shadow's voice faltered. She looked away from Sorren. "I didn't know if I could trust you."

She heard the contemptuous exhale of Sorren's breath. There was a pause before he said, "You're hardly in any position to challenge another person's trust, now are you?"

"I know what you must think but—"

"Be quiet. I'm not finished."

Shadow felt a flush of anger. She'd never allowed anyone to shush her, not even Father Bradford. "Look, I'm sorry if—"

"Quiet!" Sorren's eyes met Shadow's. Now they were fiery. He'd stripped off his cold, impersonal exterior like a knight taking off his protective armor. Exposed now, he seemed more vulnerable and dangerous. "You let me do all the talking when you were in my bed, so let me do it now." Sorren took a step closer. Barely a foot separated him from Shadow. Refusing to bow to his intimidation, Shadow tilted her chin a bit higher, her shoulders square, her countenance defiant. "Why did you let me go on with that"—he searched for the right word—"that drivel? Why the tears? Was it really the pain, or were you crying to keep from laughing at me? My God, when I think of the things I said to you . . ."

"Then they weren't true?"

Shadow studied Sorren's handsome face. Where was the concern and tenderness she'd seen before? His words were not true? They had to be true! Why would he lie, thinking that she couldn't understand him?

"What do you think?" Sorren spit the words out as though only a child or a fool would have taken them at face value. "You were hurt. I thought you were in pain. Or was that all just a part of your act, too?" he took Shadow by the arms and for a moment she thought he was going to kiss her. Instead, his eyes went to her doeskin decolletage, then down to her exposed legs, and finally to her moccasins. He shook his head angrily. "Why did you leave?" Without waiting for an answer, he let his words keep tumbling out. "Can you write, too? Why didn't you leave a note? That would have been civil. . . ." He broke off, regaining some control. "Damn! And to think that I've been accused of wearing different hats. I'm nothing compared to you. You walk like a lady, talk like a lady, you glide into the study with more grace than Catherine could ever hope to have, and sit in a chair like a lady. But you're wearing that savage's dress."

"Stop looking at me like that." Shadow pushed against Sorren's forearm, knocking one hand from her. "I don't like it when you look at me that way."

"Then wear different clothes. Only a whore shows that much leg."

"You're one to talk! Whose nightgown did I have on? Was she some sophisticated *lady*?" Her voice dripped with sarcasm as she pronounced the word.

"Or was she just a savage squaw, like me?" Without warning, a sob caught in Shadow's throat. She cursed herself for it. She said, "You called me *precious*." And then her eyes glazed over with tears that she blinked back.

"I thought you were."

There. He'd said it. Shadow really didn't mean anything to him. She didn't need to hear any more. Words now couldn't change it. He was like all the rest. The damage had been done, the seed of mistrust planted and taken root. It hurt too much to hear his words.

"I'm going back inside," Shadow said. She slapped Sorren's other hand from her arm. "Mr. Phillips has to read my father's will, remember?"

"I can't believe you're Matthew's daughter." Sorren looked at Shadow now like a stranger, as though he'd never seen her before, as if he were seeing her for the first time and did not really understand what he saw. "He never said a word to me about you, and we talked about everything. At least I thought we had talked about everything."

"Obviously not."

Shadow couldn't stand looking at Sorren. Whenever she looked into his eyes, she searched for the concern she hoped he felt for her, the heartfelt concern that had been there when she was in his bed. But there was no concern in Sorren's ebony eyes now. Just anger and suspicion and emotions that Shadow didn't want to know about. She turned and headed for the study doors.

"I'm not finished yet."

Shadow held the doorknob in her hand when

Sorren's arm went over her shoulder. His palm smacked against the wood, keeping the door shut. Shadow could almost feel the heat of him.

"Why go on with this?" Shadow closed her eyes. Sorren had been the only man in the world to show her real tenderness. She wanted to be in his arms again. Instead, she kept her back to him. "You're angry. You feel betrayed. Nothing I can say or do now is going to change that. Why go on, Sorren?"

A soft chuckle came from behind Shadow. There was no warmth or friendliness in the sound. "It feels strange to hear you say my name."

"You still haven't said my name, Sorren. It's Shadow."

"Shadow Weatherly?"

"No," she said, her voice firmer, stronger. "Just Shadow."

"I doubt you're *just* anything."

"Can't you say my name, Sorren?" She turned, moving under Sorren's arm, their bodies nearly touching. "It's Shadow, not Precious."

"That's right. You're not precious." That one cut deep. The pain showed. Sorren shook his head to negate the words that could not be taken pack. "I didn't mean it that way. You've got to understand; this has all been so confusing." A stray lock of jet hair had fallen free from Shadow's headband. Sorren smoothed it back, his fingers touching her hair without ever touching Shadow directly. "When I saw you in Angie's . . . on the floor . . . I'm not a religious man, but I was remembering a lot of childhood prayers then." He touched Shadow's wound, now hidden with her hair. "How's the head?"

"I still get dizzy sometimes."

"Damn, you really had me scared."

"I remember some things about that night. Not much. Just some things." Shadow looked up into Sorren's face. Her heart felt full, heavy. Sorren was disconcertingly close to her. The feelings she'd only recently discovered she was capable of were coming back, warming her. "I remember being on your horse. You were holding me close. My head was on your shoulder. You kept promising me that you weren't going to let anything bad happen to me. You kept saying that you were there and that you would protect me." Shadow reached up and touched Sorren's face. "Say my name. Please." Her voice was softer than a whisper.

Sorren took Shadow's hand and turned it. He kissed her palm, as he had kissed it when she was in his bed. "Is it that important to you?"

"You've never said it." She ran her fingertips over his lips. "Please, Sorren. I want to hear you say my name."

"You shouldn't have deceived me."

"I didn't deceive you. I mean, I didn't want to. I was scared, Sorren. Scared like I've never been in my life. I didn't know where I was or how I'd gotten there." She gave him a faltering smile. "And I didn't know you. At least not right away. But I think in a way I began to understand you, to know you."

"Only because I thought you didn't speak English."

"Would you have said those things if you'd known? Would you have called me *precious*?" Shadow looked at his mouth. His kisses had sent fire through her, had taught her that not all men are evil. She wanted desperately to hear him say her name, or at least to call her *precious* once more. Just once more and then she would let him be. "Say it for me, Sorren."

Sorren gently pushed Shadow's hand from his face. "I've already said more to you than I should have. It seems to me you're the one who has some talking to do."

"Sorren?"

"Explaining is probably a better word for it. How long did you intend to keep me in the dark?" Sorren took a step back. "It's clear that you didn't expect to see me here. Did you just plan to leave while I was gone and never see me again?"

"Sorren, it's not like that." Shadow moved closer. She had to make him understand. "I've never had a—had a name. I didn't know who my father was until just a couple of days ago. You can't imagine what it's like not knowing who your father is."

"Oh? Did I reveal some dark secret of my personal past while you were in my bed? Hmm?" Sorren stepped backward again. "How would you know what I can't imagine? You know nothing about me. Nothing at all. You got shot and I took pity on you."

"I don't need your pity. I don't want it. I can take care of myself," Shadow replied, suddenly feeling defensive.

"Sure you can. And how would you have taken care of those men at Angie's?" He gave a short, angry laugh. "Did you think you could manipulate them as easily as you did me? I don't think that ploy would have worked with them."

"It wasn't a ploy, Sorren. You've got to believe me."

"I've believed too much of what you've said—and

haven't said—already."

Shadow moved closer, looking up into Sorren's handsome face. She touched his chest with her right hand and grimaced.

"The injury is real," he said coolly, looking first at Shadow's swollen hand on his chest, then into her ebony eyes. "What about your kisses? Were they real, or was that just part of the grand plan to keep me in line?"

"Stop it, Sorren. I don't like it when you talk to me that way." Shadow searched his face for the compassion she knew it could show. "Can't I hear the love words now? Can you only say them if you think I can't understand you?"

Before Sorren could speak, from inside the study, they heard the bellowing voice of Carl. "Hey! Let's get this over with today! Move it, McKenna!"

Sorren grimaced. "Be careful of Carl. He's dangerous."

"So are you." Shadow smiled. "In more ways than one."

"We'd better get inside. Carl's right . . . for the first time in his life." Then, quietly, he added, "I'm serious. You stay clear of Carl. He's as dangerous as a rattler, and more unpredictable."

Shadow resisted the urge to get up on her tiptoes to kiss Sorren. She wanted to taste his kisses, but she still saw too much distrust in his eyes. The thought that maybe she had destroyed her one chance at love by being suspicious pushed itself into her mind and she closed her eyes briefly, praying to Akana that it wasn't true.

They returned to their places in the study. Phillips,

holding the unopened will in his hands, looked around to see that everyone was ready. He opened the will, cleared his throat, and began speaking in his professional tone.

"This is the Last Will and Testament of Matthew Carl Weatherly, sole owner of the MW Circle Ranch . . ." The words washed over Shadow. These were her father's words, and hearing them brought him to life. It was difficult for her to concentrate. ". . . be it hereby understood that Shadow is my daughter, the half sister of Carl Weatherly and Catherine Weatherly. My entire estate is to be divided in thirds, with Carl, Catherine, and Shadow each to receive an equal share. Furthermore, let it be understood that if this will is contested, that portion of my estate shall be forfeited to those who are not contesting the will. In short, Carl, if you try to say this isn't legal, you'll lose everything." Shadow saw Phillips smile into the will. He didn't look up and appeared to be struggling to contain his amusement. "Also, Shadow may, if she wishes, live at the MW Circle. As her mother, whom I loved fully if wrongly, and the Lord knows, I have denied her a birthright long enough. If either Carl or Catherine try to prevent this from happening, their portion of my estate is forfeited."

Carl huffed violently. "That can't be legal!"

"Quite the contrary, Carl. I wrote it for Matthew. Everything in this will is legal."

"You're fired!"

"Very well. That doesn't change the legality of your father's will. There's more here. Can I continue now, or do you have more spleening to do?"

"He was out of his mind. Daddy couldn't have

known what he was doing." Catherine, ashen-faced, turned to her brother and said, "Is it really true?"

"Yes, Catherine, it is," Phillips answered. "Your father loved Shadow very much. He never came forward because he thought she would have a better life with her tribe. She also stayed with Father Bradford."

"That's why Daddy was always sending money to the orphanage," Catherine said in a faraway voice. "I was jealous that he seemed to care so much for those children."

"What is she, anyway?" Carl asked contemptuously. "Why don't you ask her?"

Without waiting, Shadow spoke. "I am a Kiowa," she said coolly.

Phillips cleared his throat and the room became silent. "So my children are all wealthy now. All of them, including Shadow. I'm sorry, my darling daughter, that I couldn't come forward before now. I hope that someday you will understand and forgive me. I have always loved you, as I have loved all my children, and I will love the three of you through eternity. I love you all. Matthew Weatherly."

Carl leaned back in his chair, looking at Sorren with fire in his eyes. "Did you know about this?" Sorren shook his head. There was amusement in his dark eyes, a pleasing glint that made Shadow's heart feel light. "Catherine, my God, Daddy gave her an equal share. Can he do that?"

Phillips answered, "He can. He did."

"Don't lie to me, you bastard!" Carl snapped. "I know the law! An Indian can't own land!"

"You should know it as well as I do before you

start mouthing off, Carl. While it is true that an Indian cannot own land, the definition of an Indian is important. You see, if Shadow's mother had been white and her father a Kiowan, she would be an Indian. However, with her father being Caucasian, she is, in fact, white. Or at least more Caucasian than Indian, in the eyes of the law."

Shadow met eyes with Carl. She saw the contempt he felt for her. "Your slut mother may have seduced Dad, but you're not my sister. Not by a long shot. No little half-breed bastard is going to take the MW Circle away from me!"

Shadow had faced such scorn before. She had no worries concerning Carl. She hadn't expected him to welcome her into the family anyway. She glanced at Sorren, but she had no idea what thoughts were going through his mind.

Had his love words been false? she asked herself once again. Had she, by remaining silent, protected herself too well from Sorren and pushed his love for her away forever?

Chapter Five

"Oh," Shadow whispered as she entered her bedroom. Emma smiled understandingly at the young woman beside her. "It's beautiful. It's huge. Do I really have this all to myself?"

"Yes, you do, missy," Emma replied. Her round black face beamed with pleasure. "Don't you worry about a thing now. Ol' Emma will set you up proper in here. You just trust me now, darlin'. Listen to me and I'll shows you how to get along with the Weatherlys."

The first thing that went through Shadow's mind was that her bedroom was larger than the room at Father Bradford's orphanage. But instead of a dozen or more children living in one room, Shadow had this one all to herself. To Shadow, who had lived her entire life — even by Kiowan standards — in abject poverty, this was an embarrassment of riches.

Along one wall was a marble hearth and enormous fireplace. Along another was a glistening polished oak bookcase that ran from the floor to the high ceiling. Another wall was dominated with windows that looked out over the rear of the Weatherly estate.

"Your closet's over here," Emma explained, opening the door to her left that Shadow hadn't noticed earlier. Shadow looked into the walk-in closet and again lost her breath. Along both walls, hanging from twin racks, were dresses. The hand-sewn dresses were Catherine Weatherly's history; were they Shadow's future? She fingered the seam on her doeskin garment self-consciously, suddenly uneasy and exposed.

"I can't believe one woman could own so many beautiful dresses." Shadow ran a fingertip along the intricate lace embroidery at the cuff of a blue velvet gown. "How can she ever wear them all?"

"She only wears them once," Emma explained. "Sometimes she don't even wear them that many times. Sometimes Miss Catherine just has 'em made, then sticks 'em straight away in here." Emma's voice took on a tone of quiet disapproval. "She's like that sometimes."

Shadow stepped away from the closet. She was smiling broadly, finding humor where Emma could not. "Emma, why on earth would I need a closet of any size, let alone one that big? This is the only dress I have!" she exclaimed, pointing to her doeskin dress.

Emma gave Shadow a stern maternal look. "That's another something I've been wanting to talk to you about. We'll get you some proper clothes tomorrow. You can't walk around my house dressed like that, missy. It just ain't ladylike."

"But, Emma—"

"Now, child, you do like Emma tells you." Emma crossed the room, moving purposefully to the large four-poster bed. She grabbed the goose down comforter and tugged it off, her short, heavy arms swiftly folding the blanket into a square with practiced ease. "I'll get you fresh linen." Emma avoided meeting eyes with Shadow.

"What's wrong with what's on there?" Shadow started to help Emma remove the next blanket on the bed. She stopped when Emma waggled a finger negatively. Understanding flooded Shadow's senses. She grit her teeth in rage, then forced herself to relax. "Oh, I see . . . Was it Catherine or Carl who told you to take off the good bedding?"

The breath went out of Emma in a huff of indignation and sorrow. She looked up and her dark round eyes were filled with helplessness. "I'm real sorry, missy. I gotta do what Miss Catherine tells me. She ain't a bad girl. She really ain't. But she's got her ways, and them ways just ain't gonna change."

"It's okay, Emma. It's not your fault. I understand." Enmity blazed anew inside Shadow. She bit back the insults that tingled on her tongue, insults toward Carl and Catherine and Akana and the entire Caucasian and Kiowan world. "I take it Catherine can't stand the thought of a bastard squaw sleeping on her good sheets."

"Don't talk about yourself that way, honey. It ain't right that you use those words about yourself."

"Why not? It's the truth, Emma. It's what I am." Shadow went to the bay windows and looked out. Her bedroom overlooked the bunkhouses of the ranch hands. Clearly, hers was not the choice room in the house. "Do I get any linen, or am I supposed to sleep on a bare mattress? It's all right one way or the other. I'm used to sleeping on a buffalo mat."

"Don't worry about a thing, missy," Emma replied. The anger she felt showed in her tone. "If Miss Catherine don't want you to have none of her linen, I'll give you some of mine. Couple years back, Mr. Weatherly gave my husband and me a bed this size. Gave us sheets and blankets and ever'thing, too. I'll make sure this room is done up proper for you."

"My father—he was a good man, wasn't he?"

Emma smiled softly, her full lips curling up in a mixture of pleasant memories and the sorrow of loss. "Yes, he was. The best man I've ever known. Not countin' my mister an' boys."

It pleased Shadow that her father had been kind and generous to Emma. But if Matthew could be that way with a black woman, why couldn't he openly accept his own daughter?

Stop asking yourself questions you'll never have the answer to! Stop it! Stop it now!

Shadow had her back to the door when she heard the sound of footsteps. She did not turn around. This was her room now. Her father had given it to her, and whoever was at the door should knock and ask to enter.

"You needn't worry, Emma. She can have the old cotton bedding. The ones in the storage room." Catherine's words and tone were icy with malice. "You know the ones I'm talking about, don't you?"

"Yes, Miss Catherine."

"The ones we usually rip up to make bandages for the men when they cut themselves."

She said that for my benefit, thought Shadow. *She wants me to know I'll only get from her what she no longer wants.*

And what about Sorren? Shadow hadn't missed the looks that Catherine had cast his way during the reading of Matthew's will. Catherine had kept looking to Sorren for support. It had given Shadow no small amount of pleasure to see that Catherine received little of it from the quiet, stony-faced man dressed in black who sat on the sofa beside her.

After Shadow heard Catherine walk away, she closed her eyes and breathed in deeply. Is anything worth this aggression? she wondered. Now that she knew who her father was and had been named in his will, could she face the open hatred that would be directed toward her? Could anything be worth the price she would have to pay? After all, all she had really longed for was the knowledge of who her father was.

Yes! Shadow mentally answered herself. *I have lived with open hostility all my life. And now — now more than ever — I have a reason to fight. I will not allow anyone to take from me what my father gave me.*

Shadow suspected Matthew would have wanted it that way.

So lost in thought was Shadow that she did not a first notice the three ranch hands standing below. They were leaning against the bunkhouse, looking up at her as she stood at the bedroom window in her doeskin dress. The wantonness in their hearts was etched like something foul on their faces. One of the men said something out of the corner of his mouth. The other two laughed softly and nodded in agreement. Shadow stepped back, moving out of eyesight.

"I'll be back," Emma said to Shadow's back. "Don't

you worry about nothin', missy. Emma knows how to take proper care of young ladies like you. You're family now, chil', an' don't you forget it or let anyone tell you no otherwise."

Shadow turned and gave the black woman a faltering but sincere smile. "Emma, I think you and I are going to be good friends."

"I hope so, missy. I dearly do."

"I've never really had a friend before."

"What about Mr. McKenna?" Emma's eyes twinkled mischievously. "He seems like he'd like to be your friend."

Sorren? What was her relationship with Sorren now? Shadow wanted to keep Sorren pushed away from the forefront of her consciousness. She had too many things to think about.

"I don't know if Sorren is my friend or not, Emma."

"Missy, if you don't know that, then you just ain't half as smart as I thinks you is." Emma huffed again and picked up the blankets she'd removed from the bed. "That Mr. McKenna's got an eye for you, darlin'. He surely does."

"Sorren's got an eye for every woman, Emma. I'm hardly exclusive."

"No, missy, no. I knows men and I knows that Mr. McKenna. He has an eye for the ladies — ain't no gettin' around that! But he's got a special eye for you. I seen the way he was lookin' at you today. Emma don't miss much. She knows everythin' that happens in her house. Yes, she does. So you listen to her when she says that Mr. McKenna's got hisself a special eye for you."

Before Shadow could say more, Emma was out of the room, mumbling something about young ladies not being able to see what's plain as day.

Carl leaned back in the chair, studying the amber liquor in his glass. The study belonged to him now, not Matthew, and he had decided to make it the room he would do his important thinking in. Carl had plenty to think about. Lately it had seemed like his world was crashing in around him piece by piece. His father had died; then Sorren chickened out on the War Department contract; and if that wasn't enough, Carl's half-breed half sister was now living at the MW Circle.

"We can't let her live her," Catherine said. Her blue eyes were filled with concern. The strain was showing on her face. "Carl, how will I ever be able to hold my head up in God's Grace once they find out she's living here?"

"They? Who's they?"

"Everyone who counts!" Catherine snapped testily, nearly hysterical. "You know who I'm talking about! The real people!" Catherine started to rise, then stopped herself. Since the reading of her father's will, she had been pacing about the estate, snapping crisp, superfluous orders to Emma and the other domestic staff, asserting her command. But someone had told her once that there is something undignified in showing agitation by pacing, so Catherine had resolved to sit and at least give the outward appearance of being calm. "Oh, no! Oh, dear God! I just had a thought."

"What?" Carl's lack of concern was displayed in his tone.

"What are they going to say about us in Denver City?" Catherine looked at her brother as though her entire world had just come crashing around her pearl-

109

buttoned shoes. "I'll never be able to go there again. I'm ruined. She's taken everything from me."

Carl was rapidly growing weary of his sister's prattle. He personally didn't give a rat's behind about what anyone would say concerning his having an illegitimate squaw half sister. In fact, Carl found it rather amusing that his oh-so-proper father had had himself a fling with a squaw. Damn shame, though, that he hadn't followed through with his early resolve of simply ignoring the little bastard by-product.

"I've got to think," Carl said, hoping it would quiet his sister. He wished she'd leave the room.

The Debt. There was, of course, the Debt to think about. Carl loved playing poker, loved drinking, and loved the ladies at Beth Ann's parlor. He'd won and lost small fortunes many times. Carl had always made good on his markers in the past — even if it meant borrowing money and consequently getting another lesson in temperance from his father. But how could he have known the bank would freeze all Weatherly assets after Matthew's death? And then it seemed like the War Department — like Carl's own personal cavalry — had ridden to his rescue with a hefty advance for riding stock and beef. It was that squaw-lover McKenna who put the jinx on that sweet deal.

"Carl, are you listening to me?" Catherine's tone was peevish. When she had concerns, she wanted them to be *everyone's* concerns. Her eyes took on a wild, frightened quality that Carl hadn't seen before as she wailed, *"What are we going to do about her?"*

"Not a thing," Carl said with more confidence than he felt. "At least not right away. As long as she's here at the MW Circle, we can keep an eye on her. She's our enemy now, Catherine. Dad always said that I should know my enemies even better than I know my friends. Dad taught me how to run the MW Circle," Carl lied, "and I'm not going to let you down." Matthew had, in fact, tried to give his son the training necessary to run a cattle ranch the size of the MW Circle, but Carl was not interested. He seldom listened to his father. "We'll let her stay here for now and get ourselves a good lawyer from Denver City to break the will. Somebody a lot better than Jonas Phillips. Tell your snooty friends she's a charity case. Tell them whatever you want."

That was not the answer Catherine was looking for from her brother. "What am I going to do?" she whined. "I'm so ashamed."

Jean-Jacques LaRoux felt splendid and thought he looked splendid in his new corduroy suit. Denver City was a busy, bustling boom town, filled with good saloons, good booze, and pretty women who could be procured by the hour or by the day. It was a city that appreciated money, and LaRoux only went first class. He didn't trust his own men to be in Denver City, of course. They were wild animals, killers every one, and with such easy access to their favorite entertainments, they would surely get out of hand, shooting up saloons and civilians and probably each other. He was anxious to conclude his business and return to his men. He didn't dare leave them for long. LaRoux was fully aware that his personal magnetism — and threats of retribution — weren't strong enough to hold them together for more than ten days.

The madam, a thick-bodied woman who wore too much facial powder to hide her wrinkles, stepped forward. "Mr. LaRoux, the gentleman caller to see you is here."

"Shoo him in," LaRoux said. When the madam turned, he gave her a pat on the behind. She flashed him an appreciative smile over her shoulder.

He didn't look like what LaRoux had expected. Instead of a cardsharp in a black gabardine suit, white ruffled shirt, and a pearl-handled hideaway derringer in an inside coat pocket, he was dressed in the dusty clothes of a cowpuncher.

"Mr. LaRoux?"

LaRoux remained seated. His gray eyes drifted lazily up to the cowboy's face. "It's General LaRoux. Why did he send you?" LaRoux's guess that the cowboy wasn't the man who'd won so much money was correct, and the cowboy's stammering lack of response confirmed it. "I don't make deals with underlings. Leave now. A mistake has been made. There's no need to prolong our association."

"General, I was told to give you this." LaRoux took the envelope from a calloused extended hand. He opened the flap. Inside were five crisp ten dollar bills. "It's to pay for your time so we can talk."

A respectable sum, LaRoux thought. "Sit. Whiskey?" LaRoux poured into the glass he'd had waiting. "Fifty buys you five minutes. Make the most of it."

The cowboy had rehearsed his speech. He didn't look up as he spoke, staring instead blankly into a space on the table between himself and LaRoux.

"My boss ain't nearly as rich as Carl Weatherly," the cowboy began. "The Weatherlys have got more money than they could ever spend. But this Carl, he ain't making good on his marker. He lost five thousand, give or take. If my boss tries to make Carl pay, it could get messy, business wise, I guess. Carl can make trouble, an' my boss don't want no trouble."

"So you want me to buy the marker, and if I collect the money from Carl Weatherly, the money's mine, correct?"

"Yes, sir. My boss says that if you buy the marker for twenty-five hundred, you can keep all five thousand for yourself. That's what he says."

"Your boss is a coward." LaRoux spoke slowly, his tone carrying the indignation of a well-bred, European-educated man faced with confronting a weak, plebeian man. He held the cowboy's boss in contempt but felt a certain professional appreciation for the dusty man seated before him. "He is less than half a man." The cowboy didn't bat an eye at LaRoux's insult. La-Roux wondered how much it would take to hire the cowboy. He always needed men who did not frighten easily. "I'll pay one thousand and not a penny more. Take it or leave it."

"I can't do that, sir. My boss said—"

"Your boss said you were to make the best out of a bad deal. Now either you accept my gracious offer or you don't. It matters little to me. Take it or leave it."

LaRoux had him cornered and he knew it.

The arrangements were made. The cowboy's boss was afraid of Carl Weatherly, but LaRoux wasn't. He'd read about the MW Circle in the newspapers. Carl Weatherly was just the kind of man General Jean-Jacques LaRoux loved to destroy. It was men like the Weatherlys who had plundered and raped his beloved South.

Jean-Jacques LaRoux might even have paid a thousand dollars just to see Carl Weatherly squirm under the blade of his knife.

"Can't you handle this without me?" Sorren asked anxiously. He wanted to leave, but his new bookkeeper kept asking him questions.

"Yes, Mr. McKenna, I can," the bespectacled man said. He pushed his wire-framed eyeglasses higher on his nose, but they immediately slipped down to the narrow tip again. "But you said you wanted to see all the figures yourself. You told me that last week."

Sorren smiled broadly. It was a false smile, the one he used with employees when he didn't want to argue with them. "That was last week. I trust you. Just make sure you tell Peter that the prime riding stock should stay separated from the nags. Okay?"

"Yes, sir, Mr. McKenna."

"Listen, I've got to get to the bank. I'm seeing Jonas Phillips."

"The bank?"

"That's where his office is."

"But I thought he was—"

"He was," Sorren said, cutting the man off and giving him another smile so he wouldn't be offended. This time when Sorren smiled, it was the genuine article. "Carl fired Jonas yesterday. I want Jonas on a retainer before Carl wises up and hires him back." Sorren put his hand on the bookkeeper's shoulder and bent down to whisper conspiratorially, though they were alone in the room. "Personally, I think hell will freeze over before Carl wises up, but let's not give him the chance." Sorren tapped the thick ledger on the desk. "I'm sure you're keeping everything straight. If necessary, I'll check it later. Just let me know if you're unsure of anything."

The bookkeeper, thrilled at being told he had Sorren's confidence, made a mental promise to himself to double-check all the calculations on cost of feed per head before he showed his boss the books. He wouldn't let Sorren's faith in him tarnish. Every penny would be accounted for.

In the thirteen years that Angelo Fantello had owned the Bank of God's Grace, no blacks or Indians had ever set foot on the brightly polished Italian teak floor. Angelo had imported the wood from Italy, and he even had a journeyman carpenter come to put it in place. So when Angelo saw a short, fat Negress flounce into his bank escorting a tall, tentative squaw in a revealing doeskin dress, he was stunned.

"Marcus! Throw them out *now!*" Angelo hissed under his breath to his bank manager.

Marcus's jaw dropped as he looked through his boss's glass-walled office and saw Shadow and Emma step into the bank. "Yes, sir! Yes, sir!" he responded in rapid fire, bolting out of his chair. Marcus had made the decision to fire Andy, the bank guard, even before he was out of Mr. Fantello's office.

Marcus almost trotted across the bank. He had no intention of letting the squaw and Negress get anywhere near the tellers. Good, honest help was difficult enough to find without having them deal with coloreds and Indians.

"You'll have to leave," he said as he approached the two women. "Please go quietly." He took another step and the squaw turned toward him, her dark eyes brilliant, wary. She put the heel of her right hand on the haft of the bone-handled knife strapped around her hips in a leather sheath. "Andy!" Marc shouted.

Andy, who years ago had been a deputy in God's Grace until he was found drunk in the streets too many times, tottered over to Shadow and Emma. He was only a little drunk at ten in the morning. It wasn't until after lunch that he got really drunk, though even then he maintained a certain decorum during banking hours.

"Yes, sir?"

"Throw these" — Marcus didn't want to use the word *ladies* in conjunction with a squaw and a Negress — *"people* out of this bank."

Andy had not lived as long as he had be challenging people who looked like they would resort to violence. He looked at the squaw and decided negotiating was safer than force.

"You ain't got no call to be in here now," Andy said. He half turned to Marcus and said, "I'll take care of this, sir. No need to concern yourself."

The squaw said to Marcus, "I'm here for my money. It's mine and I want it now." Shadow, smelling whiskey on his breath, had already dismissed Andy as nothing but a nuisance to her.

The look on Marcus's face went beyond contempt. "You haven't got any money here. The Bank of God's Grace does not allow your . . . breed to do business here."

Emma's jaws were clamped shut, her lips pursed severly. A muscle twitched in her heavy jowls. Her small hands were clenched into fleshy fists.

Shadow's voice was low, cool, emotionless. "I've never

116

had pretty clothes in my life. I'm going to buy some today. Now you've got my money and I want it." Shadow withdrew her knife slowly. Marcus's face turned pasty. "Now give me my money . . . just like you would for a white woman."

Sorren took one step inside the bank and stopped dead in his tracks. Shadow had her knife out and was pointing the lethal silver blade at the bank manager's stomach.

"Precious, you're the only person I've ever met who can find trouble faster than I do," he mumbled to himself. He took several long-legged strides, his boot heels clicking against the floor and echoing through the bank, which was now silent as a tomb. "Easy, precious," Sorren said, announcing his approach. He didn't want to spook Shadow. "Even in God's Grace there are laws against skewering bank managers."

Shadow's eyes flashed toward Sorren for an instant, then went back to the man she held at bay. She wasn't going to let her guard down.

"Do you know this woman?" Marcus asked in a derisive sneer tinged with fear.

"A little," Sorren said truthfully. "Not really very well." He touched Shadow's forearm lightly. "Put it away. You'll only get yourself in trouble." To Emma, Sorren asked, "What's wrong? What happened?"

Sorren had never seen Emma so enraged. She sputtered with anger when she spoke. "Miss Shadow needs some civilized dresses, Mr. McKenna. I said I'd help her pick out some nice, pretty ones. That's why I'm here. But this man here says Shadow ain't got no money here. Now you knows she has, Mr. McKenna. You were there when Mr. Matthew's will was read."

117

"Yes, Emma, I was there. But, quite obviously, this man has not heard yet. I'm sure it's nothing more complicated than having some papers signed. Jonas can handle that for us, then the money can be withdrawn."

The amusement Sorren saw in the scene vanished the moment Marcus opened his mouth. "Mr. McKenna, you're a good customer here. You always have been. But we don't do business with squaws and coloreds. What wo—"

Marcus's head snapped back on his shoulders when Sorren backhanded him across the face. He turned dazed, uncomprehending eyes on Sorren. A trickle of blood dribbled from one nostril into his pencil-thin moustache.

"Shadow and Emma are ladies and they'll be treated as such." Sorren cut Marcus dead with eyes black an cold as marble. The hand that had struck Marcus—seemingly coming from nowhere with the speed of a cougar's attack—now hung loosely at his side, ominously near the walnut-handled Colt strapped tightly to his thigh. "Unless they receive an apology from you now, Marcus, I'll close my account here . . . then I'll close *your* account."

Marcus's face turned pasty and colorless. Sorren McKenna had the second largest account at the bank—second only to Matthew Weatherly. He looked at Shadow. She still had the knife in her hand and was pointing it at his midsection. Andy, ever the coward, had slipped quietly away after Sorren McKenna's entrance.

"I'm very sorry," Marcus whispered.

"Louder. I don't think I heard you."

"I can fight my own battles," Shadow said to Sorren without ever once taking here eyes from Marcus. In a quieter voice she asked, "What are you doing here, anyway?"

"At present, I'm keeping you from getting charged with murder. I'm also looking for Jonas Phillips. Carl isn't smart enough to keep him on retainer."

Marcus, unable to look at anything but the razor-sharp blade pointing straight at his navel, licked his dry lips and said, "He's not here, Mr. McKenna. He left a note on the doors this morning that said he was going fishing for a couple of days."

Sorren chuckled. "That didn't take him long."

Sorren studied Shadow's profile and emotion surged inside him. In a flash he recalled the first time he'd seen Shadow. She stood now in an abbreviated knife-fighter's stance, legs spread to shoulders width, knife held at hip level, elbow cocked and ready to strike. Whenever she inhaled, her breasts swelled out, causing them to press a little more firmly against her dress. The tawny cleavage was tight, enticing. Sorren pulled his gaze reluctantly from the young woman's bosom.

And then, as he so often did when he thought of Shadow, he remembered how she'd been struck down by a bullet on their first meeting—possibly his bullet. He grimaced visibly at the recollection.

"There's no need for bloodshed," Sorren said, determined now to put an end to the conflict quickly. He looked at Marcus and saw the blood oozing slowly from his nose. A smile played with Sorren's lips as he said, "More bloodshed, that is."

"I only want what's mine," Shadow whispered. "That's all I want."

Sorren chose his words with economy in mind. It did not take him long to convince Marcus that the bank had much to lose and very little to gain by being stubborn. All eyes were upon them as Shadow, Sorren, and Emma followed Marcus into his private office.

"I'm sure you can find a way to advance Shadow some of her money until Jonas returns and all the appropriate papers can be written up, notarized, and signed." Sorren was giving Marcus the full benefit of his boardroom charm. The effect was enhanced by the fact that the bank manager's nose was still trickling blood, which he dabbed at with a white hanky.

"Well, sir . . . perhaps with your signature the bank could see it acceptable to advance some money."

"I knew we could find a suitable arrangement."

Shadow had never been in a bank before and did not have the slightest notion of how one operated. Nevertheless, she could see that she wasn't going to get a single cent without Sorren's signature.

"I don't want his money," she hissed. The palm of her right hand rested on the haft of her knife. "I've got money of my own. I've told you before. All I want is what's mine."

Emma, seated next to Shadow, placed her hand on the young woman's shoulder. "Easy, missy. It ain't like that at all. Mr. McKenna here is just puttin' his name down 'cause they know him here, that's all. It's still your money, not his."

Shadow turned hot eyes on Sorren. "I don't need your charity."

It was Emma again who spoke, her halcyon influence effective even on Shadow. "It ain't even charity. It's just legal things, missy. We gotta do this legal and proper, that's all. Trust me now. Emma won't steer you wrong."

Sorren issued a silent prayer of thanks to the heavens for having a woman like Emma in his life.

As Marcus pulled several sheets of printed paper from a desk drawer, Shadow swallowed the contempt she felt. She was a rich woman, but to the Bank of God's Grace, she was just another squaw. Men were still in control of her life. Did she really care about white man's money to fight for it? She decided that she did.

"Just put your mark here," Marcus said, pointing to the line he had placed an *x* by. His words were muffled slightly by the hanky he pressed to his nose.

"I can write," Shadow bitterly declared. She signed her name with a steady hand despite the untapped rage that boiled inside her.

Sorren added his signature on the lines beneath Shadow's. He saw how smooth and flowing her handwriting was — a clear sign of a formal education. He also saw that she used only one name — Shadow. Didn't she have a Kiowan last name? he wondered. He wished he knew more about the customs of her tribe. He wished he knew more about her. He wished he could figure out some way of being alone with her again.

Chapter Six

Sorren hated waiting. Patience, he futilely reminded himself, is a virtue. Though he had shown patience with Emma and Shadow — relenting under the portly black woman's insistence that he go along with them to give what Emma insisted was a necessary "man's" opinion on the dresses that Shadow was about to purchase — he did not feel patient . . . or very virtuous. He grew angry when he thought of the words he's whispered to Shadow when she was in his bed, believing she couldn't understand him. His anger was always dissipated with an innocent sidelong glance from the young woman with the deep brown eyes. Shadow's deception, he reminded himself, was unforgivable; what was equally true, and more pressing upon his immediate senses, was that her allure was undeniable.

He felt the desire to explain to Emma why he'd spoken the love words to Shadow. It was only because she was hurt, he would explain to Emma. He hadn't said anything to her that he wouldn't speak to a good horse that needed calming while he provided medical attention. But to do that would admit the words to another, and Sorren wasn't prepared to do that.

Had Shadow told Emma what he'd said to her when she was in his bed? It was a cloying thought. It was clear that Emma had taken an interest in the welfare of the young woman. How much had Shadow said?

Sorren had known more inner security and peace of mind when he was a double agent during the war. At least then people who were a threat to him could not wheedle into his heart with an innocent look or a graceful walk.

God's Grace had only a limited number of stores to buy fine clothes. Mrs. Anderson, Sorren and Emma mutually decided, probably had the finest collection of lady's apparel. Sorren had made a point of steering Shadow clear of the store where Beth Ann's girls bought their clothes. Emma would throw a fit if he even suggested buying a dress suitable for one of the town's working girls.

Though he had not told Emma as much, Sorren was enormously grateful to her for taking Shadow under her protective wing. Perhaps Sorren and Shadow could not mend their differences, but those boundaries would not bother Emma. She would guard Shadow from the traps and evils of the white man's world. And no matter how angry Sorren got with Shadow for her deception, he did not want to see her innocence and vulnerability trampled under the calloused, avaricious insensitivity of a man like

123

Carl Weatherly.

Sorren reached inside his jacket pocket for the makings of a cigarette. He glanced around for an ashtray. Instead, he caught a stern look from Emma. He sighed and pulled his hand—empty—out of his pocket.

"You're a good boy, Mr. McKenna," Emma said smilingly. She loved her victories, both large and small.

Inside the large dressing room, behind the heavy blue velvet pull curtain, Shadow was confused but enjoying herself immensely. Emma and Mrs. Anderson were being as gracious and helpful as they possibly could. And though Mrs. Anderson did at first show some hesitancy at helping a squaw purchase dresses in her store, that early squeamishness quickly vanished. Shadow hoped that Mrs. Anderson's helpfulness wasn't just the result of money changing hands from Sorren to the dressmaker.

"Here you go, missy," Emma said, placing a second armload of undergarments on the plushly padded settee beside Shadow, on top of the three dresses she absolutely insisted the young girl try on. "This should do you fine for starters. We'll get you everything you need."

"Emma, how can I ever thank you? You've been so—"

Shadow was silenced with a short, thick finger pressed against her lips. Emma gave her young ward a loving but stern look. "Now didn't I say we wasn't going to talk about things like that no more? You listen to Emma now. I don't talk unless I gots something to say. We'll make you a fine, proper lady, we will."

Shadow's lips curled into a smile under Emma's finger. "Okay, I won't say it any more." Emma turned to go out of the dressing room, peering around the thick curtain to make sure Sorren wouldn't catch a glimpse inside as she left. Emma was almost through the curtain when Shadow whispered just loud enough for her to hear, "But, thank you just the same."

Emma huffed, shaking her head and muttering, leaving Shadow alone in the dressing room.

Shadow had worn fabric dresses when she lived at Father Bradford's, but those dresses were hand-me-downs from the parish in St. Louis. They were usually loose-fitting and threadbare. Dresses that once belonged to portly middled-aged, middle-class women who took a bit too much self-satisfaction in their generosity. Those dresses were nothing at all like the beautiful, intricately hand-sewn dresses Mrs. Anderson made.

And the undergarments? She'd never had any before. The old women of St. Louis hadn't thought of sending such things to the orphanage, and even if they had, Father Bradford would have assumed that Shadow knew how they were to be worn. It was not the dresses that caused Shadow's confusion; it was all the other things that she, apparently, was supposed to wear *under* them.

Shadow picked up the corset. It looked violent, like an instrument of torture. The midsection was reinforced with whalebone and along the back ran a twin series of laces. Shadow studied the garment for a moment, then dropped it aside. She was voluptuous, not petite. She wanted to look civilized, but not at that price.

After a moment, Shadow picked up the corset. She stuck an arm through the curtain and called out, "Emma, do I really have to wear this?"

The corset was instantly snatched away. "No, missy," Shadow heard Mrs. Anderson say, "I didn't think she needed that. Not with her figure."

Shadow picked up a similar garment, a corselet, identical to the corset except lacking the restrictive, stiff whalebone supports. The corselet looked more helpful than hurtful and would not pinch her middle.

"Hmmm," Shadow murmured, twisting the pearl-colored silk and lace undergarment in her hands, inspecting it from all angles. It would do for starters. But why must "civilized" women wear so much *under* their dresses?

She pulled her doeskin dress over her head and dropped it to the floor, standing naked but for her angle-high moccasins. She worked her small feet through the legholes of underpants, drew the draw string tight, and knotted it. Underpants she'd had before, though never any as soft against her skin as these. That accomplished, her experience in such matters of feminine attire having reached its end, Shadow stepped into the corselet and tugged it up her legs, past the curve of her hips. The ties were in front, not in back like the corset. Instead of tightly woven string made for accepting great tension, the ties on the corselet were cloth, crisscrossing the full length of the front to a point between the half-cups of the bodice. The half-cups lifted her full, heavy breasts. Shadow snugged up the ties, knotted them into a bow at her bosom, then turned to inspect herself in the full-length mirror. She suspected the color was intended to be flesh-toned, but against her tawny skin it seemed bright white. The corselet had a way of putting her breasts on display, making them look fuller and more round. The nipples were partially exposed above the half-cups that were trimmed with lace. Shadow's confidence was diminishing rapidly. Perhaps it wasn't such a good idea after all to attempt the transformation from looking like a poor half-Indian to a half-white lady of wealth.

The next garment Shadow inspected was pleasing, both to the eye and to the touch. The camisole was smooth and pale. She pulled it over her head and it whispered down her body with a rustle of silk. She smoothed the hem along the tops of her thighs and adjusted the slender silk straps on her shoulders.

What next? There were petticoats and pantalets in layers and layers. Shadow suspected civilized women were dreadfully hot during the summer.

She turned and look at herself in the mirror again. Dangling from the end of the corselet, she noticed, were four straps, one at the front of each thigh and one at the back. At the end of each strap was a clasp. What in Akana's name were they for? Why had Emma left her alone to figure these things out?

The clasps were obviously there to hold something. But what? Shadow attached the garter clasps to her camisole. That accomplished nothing worthwhile. She hooked the clasps together. That didn't make any sense, either.

Shadow looked at herself in the mirror again. The undergarments covered as much of her as her doeskin dress, though the gossamer-thin camisole allowed her nipples to show.

Holding the front two garter straps cautiously between her forefingers and thumbs, as though they might strike her like a snake if she weren't careful, Shadow stepped through the velvet curtain and asked, "Emma, what are these for?"

In the next instant, Sorren's heart leaped in his chest, Emma's heart very nearly stopped, and Mrs. Anderson came frightfully close to dropping in a dead faint.

"Lord A'mighty! Missy, you get your body behind that curtain this instant!" Emma bellowed, pushing her bulk out of the chair as quickly as she possibly could, which wasn't very quick, but still too fast for Sorren's taste. She moved to block Sorren's view of Shadow with her own body.

In short order Emma explained to Shadow that proper young ladies did not show themselves to men—definitely not a man like Mr. McKenna—when they were in their underthings; she explained to Mrs. Anderson that Miss Shadow didn't understand some things and such matters would soon be made clear to her, because if Emma knew how to do anything, it was to raise proper youngin's; and Emma explained to Sorren, in no uncertain terms, that not only would his lips never speak a word of what had just transpired, but if he did not forget what he had seen—immediately and completely—he would suffer the wrath of God, or worse, the wrath of Emma. God, Emma explained, was a good and forgiving man; she, on the other hand, had an extremely long memory and an extremely unforgiving temperament. She was suspicious of Sorren's solemn vow to erase his vision of Shadow, a fantasy come to life.

Shadow accepted, but did not fully understand why, that she was never to show herself to a man when she was in her undergarments. Her doeskin dress covered no more of her than the clothes that Emma had selected. But after her etiquette *faux pas*, Emma stayed in the dressing room and helped Shadow with every detail of her attire.

When Shadow stepped hesitantly out of the dressing room the next time, she again made Sorren's heart leap in his chest. The floor-length blue gown was suitable for dress functions, though not formal affairs. Shadow did not like the way the petticoats clung to her legs as she walked and the bodice was uncomfortable on her breasts, its undersupports stiff and unyielding. She did, however, like to see the appreciative look in Sorren's eyes as he gazed at her. Maybe she could fit into this white man's society after all. But why did she have to wear the boots with the heels that hurt her feet and made her feel unsteady, as though she were walking on rocks?

"You'll get used to it, missy," Emma assured her, refusing to listen to the young woman's pleas that it was not necessary for her to wear so many layers of clothes just to be a "proper lady."

Shadow was in her third dress when Emma's son, Elijah, arrived.

"Mama, Miss Weatherly says you gotta come home now," Elijah said, holding his battered hat in his hands because well-brought-up young men did not wear their hats indoors. "She says I gotta bring you back."

Emma frowned at her son. It would do no good to argue with him. He was only doing as he'd been instructed. She turned to Shadow. "I'm sorry, Miss Shadow, but we gots to leave now. Miss Catherine don't want me spendin' my day with you when I can be fussin' after her."

Sorren saw the look of disappointment on Shadow's face. Still seated, he suggested, "If it is acceptable to you, Emma, I'll chaperone Shadow."

Emma moved closer to Sorren, standing so near her head was tilted far back on her shoulders so that she could look him in the eyes. "You ain't my idea of chaperone material, Mr. McKenna. Who's gonna chaperone the chaperone?"

When Emma gave him a fierce look, Sorren replied with just the right amount of soulful dignity, "I shall escort her directly to her home, careful to keep her away from strangers and whatever riffraff the streets of God's Grace have produced. She will be back in your protective custody as soon as we finish here."

"Mr. McKenna, I'm gonna trust you this time, though it seems to me like I got me a fox watchin my chicken coop," Emma said. She took a half step closer, looking Sorren straight in the eyes. With the soft-spoken authority of a woman who has raised many strapping boys and never once been rebuffed by them, Emma said quietly, "But ifin that chil' tells me you weren't a proper gentleman, not even God hisself is gonna save your hide."

Sorren promised Emma that he would be on his best behavior. Emma still was skeptical, muttering that Sorren McKenna's "best" behavior still had a long way to go before it would be "proper" behavior. She let Sorren know that he was not too tall or too old for her to take over her knee. Behind Sorren's smirk, Shadow saw the genuine affection the two had for each other.

After Emma left, Sorren excused himself and shortly reappeared with a carriage, his mare tied to the back.

"Hungry?" Sorren asked as he helped Shadow into the carriage.

"A little." Shadow sat in the carriage on her rumpled petticoats. She stood to smooth them under her legs, then sat again. She wasn't used to having such fine, multi-layered clothes on. "Not very much though. Emma makes a breakfast that lasts the entire day."

Shadow tried to ignore the questioning looks she received from the townsfolk as Sorren got into the carriage beside her and headed the old gelding away from Mrs. Anderson's store. She felt a certain uneasiness in being with him in public, not sure if the unreadable looks she received from people were the result of her Indian heritage or if she were being inspected as the latest sexual conquest of Sorren McKenna. Either way, Shadow did not like it.

In the trunk of the carriage were a dozen packages of varying sizes and shapes, containing the sartorial accoutrements of a young woman of means. One box, however, contained Shadow's doeskin dress, moccasins, and the sheath and bone-handled knife, all of which she had refused to throw away. Despite all the clothes she was wearing, Shadow felt strangely naked without her knife. She had carried it with her wherever she went. It was her one great defense against a world that seemed so hostile toward her.

"I don't have access to Emma's culinary excesses," Sorren said, turning down the main street. "And you've already eaten every dish I know how to make." He glanced at Shadow, trying to ignore the peach-colored summer dress with off-the-shoulder sleeves, doing his level best to keep his eyes from straying to her decolletage. She smiled. God, what a smile! "If you don't mind, I'd like to stop for a bite; I'm ravenous." *If she doesn't want to stop*, he thought, *I'll intentionally break a wheel on the carriage so I can spend more time with her*. But Sorren didn't like that idea much. He'd have to think of something more clever to keep Shadow near him.

Shadow nodded in agreement. It was nice being with Sorren again, especially now without the intimidation of being in his bedroom. So many new things were happening to her that she couldn't sort out what she felt to be true from what she just wanted to be true. When an attractive woman of about thirty, with blazing auburn hair curled and pinned in a flawless coiffure, gazed with wide-eyed astonishment as the carriage passed, Shadow wondered if she, too, were one of Sorren's lovers. Past or present? Sorren could, she knew, be a dangerously persuasive man. Shadow had seen how he charmed Mrs. Anderson. And even Emma, who alone appeared strong enough to openly stand up to Sorren, was not immune to his charm.

"Why did you give me the money?"

Sorren cast a sideways glance at Shadow. "Why do

your questions always come straight out of the blue?"

"Why did you do it?" Shadow persisted. She studied the profile of the man sitting beside her. Once again, he was dressed all in black. It was not difficult for her to see why he had a reputation as a seducer of women. "Please, I want to know. It's important."

"I didn't really give you any money. I just put my name on a piece of paper. The bank knows me, that's all. Don't make more out of it than is really there."

"But you didn't have to do it."

Sorren sighed, his shoulders dropping for only a moment. "Sometimes it's important to do the right thing. Can we change the subject?"

"And slapping that man? Marcus?"

Sorren's jaw tightened in response to the name and a dangerous brightness came into his dark eyes. His face softened after a moment, and he said, "To tell you the truth, I've been wanting to do that for a long time. He finally gave me a good enough reason to, that's all."

Shadow studied his profile. Just looking at him made her feel warm inside. She even liked the scar on his cheek and the bump on the bridge of his nose, remnants of fights long ago. His dark hair, combed straight back, curled near his earlobes at the sides, just licking over the collar of his black jacket in back.

"What about me?" Sorren glanced again at Shadow, this time checking her expression because her tone was low and serious. "If I gave you reason enough, would you slap me, too?"

Sorren chuckled. "You've already given me reason enough, but I haven't slapped you, have I?"

"That's not an answer."

"It's all the answer you're going to get."

"Look, you can't still be angry with me for not letting you know I speak English." In spite of herself and her desire to put her emotions concerning Sorren on an even keel, Shadow felt her anger rising. She wanted to turn the page on her past and start fresh with Sorren, but he wasn't letting her. "I was hurt and scared. I didn't know who you were or how I'd gotten into your bed. You can hardly blame me for being cautious." The memory of Sorren's powerful arms winding around her came back, causing a flush of excitement to go through Shadow. As though he were kissing her now, she could taste his lips softly touching her own, teaching her to kiss, showing her first how to receive pleasure, then how to give pleasure, and finally how to share. She could almost feel the weight of him pressing her deeper into the mattress, the masculine force of his broad chest pushing against her breasts, the heat of his body hardening her nipples, making them more sensitive to the touch than she'd thought possible. The memory of her own response made her cheeks warm. She turned her face away from Sorren, not seeing the buildings and people as she passed slowly by.

Shadow cleared her throat and whispered without malice, "You proved I had a right to be cautious with you."

Sorren's lips pressed into a tight line. He slapped the gelding's back with the reins. The old nag responded to his silent urging grudgingly, picking up the pace just slightly.

"I made a mistake and I'm sorry for it." Sorren did not look at Shadow as he spoke. "This isn't getting us anywhere," he said crisply. "We're just going around and around. The last word on all of this is that you don't trust me and I don't trust you." The words, spoken with such cold precision and finality, knifed through Shadow's heart. "I'll take you home."

"No." Shadow felt a tightening in her throat. She was finally talking with Sorren, even if it was in an argument. She wasn't ready to leave him yet. There was still so much that had to be answered. "Please, Sorren, don't take me home just yet." Shadow reached over and placed one hand lightly over the hand he used to hold the reins. "Please, not just yet. I've never had a pretty dress before. Can't you let me show it off a little?"

The chiseled granite features of Sorren McKenna cracked into a broad grin. He shook his head slowly and said, "I guess it doesn't matter where a woman is born or how she's brought up. All women like to do certain things."

"What kind of *certain things*?"

"Showing off!"

They shared a smile for a moment, not noticing that Miss Catherine Weatherly, standing in the doorway of the Bank of God's Grace, was cutting Shadow to shreds with blue eyes that were filled with utter, unqualified contempt.

The Golden Palace was the finest restaurant in God's Grace. Shadow remembered seeing it years earlier when Father Bradford had taken his orphans into God's Grace, paraded the pathetic-looking children around, hoping to receive donations from the townsfolk. She had heard stories of the grand, elaborate dances that took place in the enormous, oval-shaped ballroom. But, of course, she had never stepped foot through the ornamental archway leading into the hotel. The idea of dining at The Golden Palace was so absurd that she'd never even longed for it. If the cost weren't prohibitive, the unspoken whites-only policy was.

Sorren pulled the carriage to the side of the dusty street, tugging on the reins to stop the old gelding's progress.

"Will they let me in here?" Shadow asked quietly.

Sorren jumped out of the carriage and walked around it until he was standing in front of Shadow. "Of course they will. You've got to start thinking like a rich woman. That's what you are, you know." He reached for Shadow, but she hesitated in mid step in the carriage. Shadow's eyes caught Sorren's, holding his gaze.

"You're sure?" she whispered.

"Positive. Trust me. I won't let—" he said, then stopped himself before he finished the sentence.

Shadow reached for his hand, but Sorren did not take it. Instead, he caught her by the waist, his strong hands warming her through her dress. She leaned toward him, and for a moment he held her weight while Shadow was suspended between the carriage and the ground. He held her for a fraction longer than necessary. In that instant, attired in a soft, flowing peach dress, Shadow felt something she'd never really felt before—small and feminine, protected by Sorren. Her hands were at his biceps. The muscles beneath his jacket and shirt were rigid, flexed without straining. When her feet touched the ground, Shadow put a hand to her waist, her palm small and soft against the back of Sorren's hand.

"Thank you," she murmured. She looked into his eyes, searching there for some inner sign of what was going on in Sorren's mind, in his heart. Sorren broke the eye contact, taking his hands away from Shadow. The young woman whispered, "It doesn't seem to matter to you that I'm part Kiowan, but it does to other people."

"You're rich," Sorren replied, as though that alone answered everything. "Don't worry so much what other people think." Sorren took Shadow's arm, his hand at her elbow. It wasn't quite like being arm in arm, but almost. "It's what you think that really matters."

The head waiter, who passed himself off as a maitre d', recognized Sorren at a glance. He took several quick strides toward the tall, lean man dressed in black with the young dark-haired woman at his side. It wasn't until he got a closer look at Shadow's face — seeing her distinctly Indian features — that his rapid footsteps began to falter. God's Grace was on the edge of civilized society. The waiter didn't want Shadow's presence diminishing a reputation that was difficult to create and even harder to maintain.

"Uh-oh," Shadow whispered sotto voce. "Here it comes."

"Good afternoon," Sorren whispered. He gave Shadow's arm a small, reassuring squeeze. "We'd like a table."

The maitre d's eyes danced back and forth from

Shadow's face to Sorren's. He, like Marcus at the bank, was stuck between unwritten rules and a desire to please a man whose good graces were cherished and whose ill will was scrupulously avoided. He had already heard the whispered version of the incident at the bank. The waiter opted to break the rules. It seemed the safer choice.

"Yes, sir, Mr. McKenna," he said, giving a partial bow, his hand waving toward an undefined table in the dining room.

As they walked between tables, passing other guests, Shadow heard a man whisper to his male companion, "McKenna's bringing a squaw in here? What's he thinking, anyway?" Shadow resisted the urge to turn on the man and confront him. She was in her first new dress and she was going to act ladylike . . . even if it killed her.

They were nearly to their table when Shadow heard a woman whisper to her husband, "Darling, isn't that the dress you were going to buy for me from Mrs. Anderson? It doesn't look right on a filthy savage."

Shadow had bathed that morning. Her hair was neatly brushed and held back with small ribbons that Emma had put in. She might be a savage, but she definitely wasn't filthy, and she was going to explain as much. But she turned too fast. When she wheeled to confront the woman, she stepped on the hem of her dress. Shadow had never before worn a long dress, and the unfamiliar boots with two-inch heels betrayed her. She stumbled. She would have fallen to the floor if Sorren hadn't caught her. He pulled Shadow in close against his chest.

"Careful," he whispered, his eyes unsmiling. He, too, had heard what the woman had said.

The veiled snickers of the patrons washed over Shadow in a wave of condescension and mockery. The shame she felt was completed when the woman who had caused Shadow to turn whispered to her husband, "She looks like a little girl playing dress-up in mommy's clothes." A man said in a too-loud voice, "Another drunken squaw. McKenna must be losing his touch."

If she could have — if she weren't with Sorren and she weren't wearing the new stiff, heeled boots — Shadow would have run from The Golden Palace and never looked back. She didn't belong there. The people around her told her so, if not with words then at least with their condescending looks. The maitre d', who looked only at Sorren and completely ignored Shadow, pretended not to have noticed her near fall.

Shadow was hardly aware of Sorren helping her with her chair. This lovely afternoon at a fine restaurant was turning into a nightmare that she couldn't wake up from. She stared at her hands folded in her lap, willing herself to keep the tears from spilling out.

"Relax," Sorren said as he took his chair, looping his leg over the back to sit down. "The food here is wonderful. They buy their beef from Matthew, and it's absolutely the best. You can cut it with a fork."

Shadow forced her chin up, her face pale with shame, her large, dark eyes glistening with brimming tears. "They're laughing at me," she whispered in a trembling voice, her lips quivering.

Sorren pushed his chair away from the table. "Stay

here. I'll be right back."

"Don't leave," Shadow said, but Sorren was already gone.

It was a decade that lasted barely more than a minute. Shadow, staring at the folded hands in her lap, noticed the people around her were more vocal and loud with their insults now that Sorren was gone. Taking their direct insults was easier than their laughter. Nothing could be worse than being laughed at. She wanted her knife, but she knew that wasn't the answer. Even if she had her knife, Shadow wouldn't have drawn it, like she had with Marcus. If she weren't with Sorren, she would just leave The Golden Palace. Shame had taken away her will to fight.

When Shadow heard the woman inquire of her husband, "What in God's holy name is he doing now?" she raised her eyes. Sorren, with shoulders square, was walking slowly between the tables toward her. He was carrying something toward her, almost reverently: her handmade moccasins!

"I think you'll be more comfortable in these," he said as he approached her, his voice loud enough to carry to several surrounding tables. The right corner of his mouth curled up in a partial grin. He got down on one knee beside Shadow. "Turn your chair. I'll put them on for you."

Shadow was embarrassed and thrilled when Sorren turned her chair and took her tenderly by the ankle, raising her foot so that the pointed toe of her boot was on his thigh. He unhooked the eyelets of her boot, his fingers working slowly and precisely, just as they had when he'd put her bandages on. He took off her boot, then slipped on her ankle-high moccasin and tugged the leather drawstring tight. When he was finished with the other moccasin, he put Shadow's boots together, placing them near the leg of his chair.

"Better?" Sorren asked calmly, taking his chair. He was acting as though nothing strange had happened, ignoring the fragments of comments he heard.

Shadow wiggled her toes inside the soft leather moccasins. An odd sort of pleasure started in her chest, and by the time it worked its way up to reach her face, her eyes were bright with unabashed delight, mixed with embarrassment and adoration. "Yes," she said softly. "I feel much better. How can I ever thank you?"

The look in Sorren's eyes, which lasted only a second let Shadown know that he could think of many ways she could show her gratitude. The thought of it made her shiver.

Shadow ordered the things that she had never had as a child: a thick beef steak, baked potato, fresh lettuce, and cow's milk. Though Father Bradford had instructed that ladies are light eaters, it pleased Sorren immediately to see the young woman's hearty appetite.

They ate, for the most part, in silence. Occasionally a glance was exchanged. Sometimes their eyes held each other's, but never for very long. The early discomfort Shadow had felt in Sorren's presence had eased, and now it was acceptable for there to be pauses in their conversation. Neither felt the need for small talk.

"What would you like to do now?" Sorren asked

after the waiter had removed their plates. He pushed his chair away from the table, kicking his black-booted ankle up on the opposite knee. He had a steaming cup of coffee in front of him and a neatly rolled cigarette between his fingers. The contentment he felt showed on his face. The fierce intensity that was so much a part of him was missing, which delighted Shadow.

"I don't know," Shadow replied. A warm, soft pleasure seeped through her body. She wished that Sorren would look away so she could study his face without being seen. Suddenly she smiled brightly. "Yes, I do."

"What?"

"I want to see your ranch."

Sorren's eyebrows pushed together. "You've already seen it, haven't you?"

"Not really. I was in—" Shadow stopped herself. *I was in your bed most of the time*, she thought. *And when I ran away, it was too dark for me to see what it's really like.* Then it occurred to her that Sorren did not want his men seeing him with an Indian. A twinge of pain showed in the corners of Shadow's eyes.

Sorren read Shadow's thoughts and fears accurately. He was beginning to understand the way her mind worked. The more he knew and understood about her, the more tantalizing she was to him. "I'd be honored to show you the ranch," he said. "Now that we're neighbors and all."

"What do you call it?"

"Nothing."

"Why?"

Sorren looked away. He couldn't tell Shadow tha

he had never really felt certain how long he could keep the place, so he'd never named it. Just like his mare. He loved his mare, but he had never named her. You don't name something that may not be permanent. Sorren never knew when his past would reappear, and like the spy he had been years before, he would have to leave in the night without taking anything with him but his guns and his secrets and his deadly, deadly skills.

Quietly, Shadow said, "It should have a name, Sorren. It's not right for your ranch not to have a name."

And you know what it's like not to have a name, don't you? Sorren thought. He said nothing. Maybe Shadow was right.

"Someday I'll name it. For now it's just The Ranch."

When Shadow walked out of The Golden Palace, she felt more confident. She might still be an Indian squaw, but she was worth the attention of Sorren McKenna. There were no parting comments from the other patrons. They were afraid of him. It seemed like a lot of people were afraid of Sorren McKenna.

Shadow didn't know if it were good or bad that she felt attracted to Sorren, in part, because he was the inspiration of such fear. She'd been afraid all her life. Why would she be attracted to a man who inspired what she dreaded most?

Chapter Seven

Sorren's ranch seemed different to Shadow now. With the war drums beating in her skull each time she moved, his beautiful home had been a prison, with Sorren her jailmaster. Now, free to come and go as she chose and able to think clearly, she could see his home for its beauty, without the imaginary bars that had imprisoned her.

"It's not as large as the MW Circle," Sorren explained, "but it's been roomy enough for me these past couple of years."

"Do I get a guided tour, or are you just going to let me roam wherever whimsey takes me?"

"It's up to you."

Shadow felt a tickle in the pit of her stomach. The

light conversation she'd shared with Sorren for the past several hours had put her at ease. Now that she did not feel the urge to run whenever he came close, now that she did not flinch if his hand should touch hers or if he took her elbow when they walked together, she was anxious to get their conversation on a more substantive level. What did he like and dislike? He was a hearty eater and seemed to enjoy good food, but he was not a particularly skillful cook and apparently did not have a cook, though it was obvious he could afford one. Why not? Did he worry about a maidservant spreading licentious gossip? Was it to keep the identity of his overnight female guests anonymous?

He made a point of explaining how a man must do the right thing, yet he had not hesitated to use violence with Marcus in the bank. And it was clear that his wealth made it impossible for the maitre d' at The Golden Palace not to serve Shadow, even though she was not welcome.

"Since you refuse to answer, I'll make the decision," Sorren said, snapping Shadow out of her confused state of mind. "This is my house, and should you get lost, I would feel eternally responsible." Sorren gave Shadow a look of soulful, sarcastic sincerity. The humor in it pleased her enormously. "But before the tour begins, I believe that reinforcements are in order."

"Reinforcements?" Shadow did not want to share Sorren's company with anyone else. "Who?"

"In this case, the reinforcements are a *what*, not a *who*." He waved a hand to an interior door. "This way."

Shadow slipped her hand inside Sorren's arm, her fingers curling around the sinewy muscle on the lower part of his biceps. It was the first time she had initiated a touch between them. It seemed like such a simple thing, perfectly harmless, yet Shadow felt bold and adventurous just the same. When Sorren squeezed her hand briefly to his side with his elbow, Shadow felt the warmth of his flesh, the solidity of his body.

"I hadn't planned on company this evening," Sorren said as he pulled open the icebox door. "However, luck is with us." Sorren withdrew a bottle of wine. His eyes glowed with pleasure. "It's a very pleasant brut champagne."

"Brut? That's an odd name for a champagne."

Sorren chuckled warmly, easing his arm from Shadow's soft grasp. "You've got so much to learn. You own land, cattle. Hell, you own one third of the MW Circle. That means that you'll need to develop a certain sense of sophistication." Sorren withdrew a corkscrew from a drawer and pressed the pointed tip into the cork. "Whether you like it or not, people will expect certain things from you." He nodded to the cupboard door as he twisted the screw into the cork. "The flutes are up there."

"Flutes?"

"The long, skinny glasses."

Shadow found the slender glasses. They were odd-shaped and inefficient. The bases were heavy, the glass solid fully halfway up the flutes. Shadow thought the glass would tip easily and not hold very much champagne, and for the life of her, she couldn't see how it looked anything at all like a flute.

"These are champagne flutes." Sorren held the black bottle by the trunk and poured the golden liquid into the glass. "Have you ever had champagne before?"

Shadow thought of lying. Quite suddenly she was

feeling naive, almost like a little girl. She felt clumsy and awkward again. Did it bother Sorren that she understood so little of his world? That the things he took for granted, the things he took such pleasure in, were all a mystery to her?

"No," Shadow said in a voice just above a whisper. She studied the champagne fizzing to the rim of the glass.

"Then here's to firsts," Sorren said, his eyes holding Shadow's for a breathless moment. "Now the first thing to remember is that you must never—never ever—giggle and then say the bubbles tickle your nose. Even if the bubbles *do* tickle, *don't* tell me." Sorren transferred the bottle to his left hand, taking a flute from Shadow with his right. "And champagne has a way of sneaking up on you. Always be careful of how much you have."

Sorren positively glowed as he walked through the main floor of his home, showing Shadow this room and that. The den. The library. His personal study. The gun room with the walls lined with the mounted heads of trophy-size elk, mule deer, moose, prong-horn antelope, and mountain lion.

"You're a hunter."

"I used to be." Sorren's voice had lost the lightness it held earlier. "I've given that up."

"The Kiowas never could figure out why the yellow-eyes kill for sport. We only kill to eat."

"My eyes are as dark as yours. And with the exception of the cat, I ate everything I shot."

"Why'd you shoot the puma?"

"I was hired to. He was preying on cattle. Matthew put up a bounty on him and I went after him."

Shadow looked at the mountain lion. The taxidermist had done an excellent job. In death as in life, and now for all eternity, the big cat was snarling defiantly at the world. Shadow wondered if it meant anything.

"Why didn't Carl do it?"

Sorren gave a short, incredulous laugh and started to leave the room. "Two reasons," he said over his shoulder as Shadow quickened her pace to catch up. "The first is that it was too much like work for Carl. The second is that hunting a cougar—a rogue cougar at that—is dangerous business. Carl is many things I despise, not the least of which is being a coward."

"Let's change the subject." When Shadow's stride matched Sorren's, he slipped her hand inside his arm again. It surprised her to realize how much pleasure she took in touching him. She felt positively sinful reaching for him as often as she did. "I don't want to talk about Carl."

They went slowly up the long stairway as Sorren explained tidbits of information about his home. He took pleasure in explaining that the polished wood stairway and ornately carved hand railing came from the Northwest Territories. As he spoke, he allowed the back of one hand to glide against the smooth wood. Shadow sensed that Sorren was enormously proud of his home but perhaps a bit embarrassed by the riches it represented.

There were sixteen rooms in all. Sorren's bedroom was upstairs, and as Shadow approached the closed door of his private room, she felt her heart quicken. His bedroom represented good and bad memories. It was there that she had first known the rapture of a man's kiss, had felt the dormant passion in her soul come to life like a butterfly breaking free of its restrictive

148

chrysalis. But it was also in Sorren's bedroom that Shadow knew pain and terror. Her first awakening after the bullet had grazed her skull was still a vivid and painful memory that haunted her. The blinding pain and confusion . . . not knowing what had happened to her hand . . . and most of all, not knowing if she had been raped.

Shadow was inexperienced in the ways of the flesh. She accepted her virginity as a physical reality, as she did the fullness of her breasts or her height. All of these, for a maiden her age, had set her apart from the other maidens of her tribe. But Shadow had seen the transformation of other maidens after they had been taken to a warrior's buffalo mat. She would have been blind not to notice the glow and sparkle that surrounded a happy young woman who had been blessed with a powerful and tender lover. Still, she had guarded her virginity, instinctively sensing that it was something precious.

"What's this room?" Shadow asked quickly, indicating a closed door that Sorren had passed without comment. She wanted to avoid passing Sorren's bedroom for as long as possible.

"It's nothing."

Sorren continued, but Shadow stopped him by tugging lightly on his arm. "Please, I want to see."

Sorren smiled indulgently. "I'm telling you the truth. It really is nothing." He pulled his arm away from Shadow and opened the door. "See for yourself," he said. There was a chill in the timbre of his voice now.

Shadow regretted forcing the issue. But now that she had gone this far, she saw no reason not to look inside. When she did, a prickly sensation at the back of her neck gave her a warning she did not understand.

The room was empty. Empty of everything. Not one single piece of furniture spared it from its absolute barrenness. There was a faintly musty scent of stale air. Shadow wrinkled her nose at the smell.

"Like I said, it's nothing." Sorren closed the door while Shadow was still looking inside. He started down the hall without Shadow. He finished off the wine in his glass and then refilled it from the bottle. "Nothing . . . nothing . . . nothing," he said, walking past the closed doors.

Shadow walked fifteen feet behind Sorren. She quickly opened the door to each room and glanced inside to confirm her suspicions. Each room was empty. Sorren's enormous mansion, Shadow discovered, was a monumentally expensive wasteland, built with skill and care. Much of Sorren's home was hollow.

Questions danced like demons on Shadow's tongue. She kept the demons to herself, but they asked their questions just the same. *Why spend so much on a house where so little is used?* Sorren's big home suddenly felt like a ghost town unto itself. Shadow shivered and the air seemed to get cold around her.

"You've already seen this room," Sorren said, nodding to his bedroom door.

"Yes," Shadow replied softly. She slipped her hand into Sorren's muscled arm again, but he did not squeeze her hand against his ribs to show her he was aware of it.

At the end of the hallway, thankfully, was the guest bedroom. It was lavishly appointed, almost gaudily so. They turned together, and Shadow did not want to walk past the empty and unused rooms again but she had no choice.

"So that's the grand tour," Sorren said softly.

Shadow studied the side of his face. *He looked transformed,* she thought, *changed, suddenly tired and disillusioned beyond his years.* Shadow wondered if she had done something to cause this change in him. She longed to hear Sorren's slightly self-mocking laughter and see the gleam in his dark eyes when he found the world around him a beautiful and amusing place.

"All this walking has made me thirsty," she said, breaking the silence as they descended the stairs. She realized too late, only after Sorren had brought the bottle up, that her glass was still full. Shadow was not a skillful liar.

"It's gotten warm," Sorren said. He took Shadow's flute and set it on the stairway, then handed her his own glass. "Never drink warm champagne. It goes straight to your head."

Shadow sipped the wine. It was cold and bubbly and made her feel good as it went down. She took a second sip, then handed the glass back to Sorren when he reached for it.

"Let's get you a fresh glass."

"No, let's share," Shadow replied without thinking through what she was saying. She received a questioning look from Sorren, which contained a hint of amusement with life in general and her in particular, that played with Shadow's senses even more than the wine.

On Shadow's insistence, they returned to the hunting room to finish the wine. She had seen how pleased Sorren was to be in the room. It was a room he felt comfortable in, one of the few rooms he had gone to painful lengths to decorate to his own tastes.

"It's a beautiful house," Shadow said. Sorren did not acknowledge the compliment.

Shadow started for the sofa, then noticed the bear-skin rug on the floor beside the fireplace. On impulse, she went over to it. She spread her skirts in a halo of smooth pale cloth around her as she sat. Looking around the room, pretending not to notice Sorren's heavy gaze upon her, she could feel the masculinity of the room pressing in upon her in a way she found pleasurable.

"Sometimes when I look at you, it's like I'm looking at so many different women." Sorren tucked his left hand into his slacks, his head cocked slightly to one side as he peered down at Shadow through dark, lidded eyes. His eyes followed Shadow's glass to her moist, red mouth as she took a sip. "Different women all the time." He leaned down and took the glass from Shadow's hand, then set the bottle on the floor beside her.

"I don't understand," Shadow replied, her words soft, directed to the black-clad figure's broad back.

"I know you don't. That's what makes you so"— Sorren turned halfway around, looking briefly at Shadow—"beguiling."

Sorren took Shadow in with his eyes, his gaze moving over her approvingly. She sat on the bearskin rug, her legs tucked partially beneath her but to the side. The soft leather moccasins, peeking out beneath a snowy layer of lacy petticoats, were a reminder to Sorren that she was not the white debutante she tried to dress like. The moccasins were a reminder of the fiercely independent woman she was, a woman both capable and willing to draw a knife for her own defense—or his.

"Is that bad?" her tone was softly cautious.

Sorren's eyes continued roaming over Shadow, now moving slowly upward, pausing at the low bodice of the gown, pausing where they had drifted and dallied so many times since she'd first put the dress on, then up to her face. "No," Sorren replied slowly, the timbre of his voice deep, husky. "It isn't bad at all."

Shadow sipped her wine, taking a moment to pretend to study the glass. She could feel Sorren's gaze upon her. He seemed to loom not merely above her but all around her, surrounding her somehow. She could not find the inner strength to return his gaze, though she longed to caress his face, the breadth of his shoulders, and the narrowness of his waist with her own eyes, just as he was doing to her now.

"Why—" she began, her eyes cast down. She glanced up briefly at Sorren and began again. "Why do you always stand so far away from me?"

"Do I really?" Sorren seemed generally curious, as though Shadow had just articulated some character flaw in him that he was shocked to discover.

"Not all the time." With her courage building slowly upon itself, Shadow looked up, her dark eyes meeting and holding Sorren's. "But in this room you've stayed as far away from me as you politely could. Why? I wanted to be in this room because I thought you liked it here." Shadow ran her palm across the bear's head absently. "Is it because this is your room?"

"Every room here is my room." His tone held a casualness that he did not feel. "I own this house, remember?" Sorren moved closer and knelt beside Shadow. She handed him the flute.

153

"No, that's not it. This is your own room. It's private to you." Shadow felt an inner warmth color her cheeks as she pondered the next sentence. But the warmth did not stop at her face. She felt her nipples harden and, as the unwanted emotion passed downward through her, felt a tremor in her stomach and a moistening between her thighs. "Your bedroom isn't your private room. You take too many women there for it to be private. But the women . . . the women you share your bedroom with . . . you don't bring them here, do you?"

Sorren moved down, sitting beside Shadow, his warm body close without touching her. "No. I don't take anyone here." Sorren stroked a strand of ebony hair away from Shadow's eyebrow. His hand returned to her face, touching her lightly, brushing her cheek with the backs of his fingers. "Like I told you before, I'm making all kinds of exceptions where you're concerned."

"Does that bother you?"

"Yes," he said, then quickly amended, "it's different anyway. It takes some getting used to." Sorren twisted his broad shoulders to face Shadow. "Why am I telling you these things?"

Shadow had no answer for Sorren. His hand came up to lightly touch his palm against her cheek. Shadow's full, trembling lips parted as Sorren's fingers pushed into the dark, satiny fullness of her hair.

"Kiss me," he whispered. His lips were touching Shadow's as he repeated, "Kiss me, precious."

The heat of his kiss, however soft his lips touched hers, burned through Shadow. She leaned into him, pressing her mouth more firmly against his. When she felt his lips move, she opened her mouth, wanted to

154

know again the pleasure of his tongue exploring deeper.

It was not the first time Shadow had taken Sorren's tongue into her mouth, but she reacted as though it were. She darted her tongue against his, circling inside his mouth, shivering with the building passion that made her head swim with want and confusion. Her hand drifted upward, touching nothing but air, wanting to feel him yet not knowing exactly where to go or what to do. And as Sorren's mouth continued nibbling hers, as his tongue probed and tasted her sweetness, Shadow knew that she could not resist the carnal temptation that he elicited. She had denied herself before, had once pushed Sorren away when he wanted her. She had realized then that she wanted him, but fear and the years of denying herself had forced her to push Sorren away. But this time would be different. She was no longer an injured woman who could not defend herself. She was young and strong, and except for when Sorren kissed her, she was quite sane and capable of making her own decisions. She wanted Sorren to show her the mysteries of the flesh, to make her feel the way she knew the other maidens of her tribe must have felt when they were loved.

"Oh, Sorren," Shadow purred when the kisses paused, "you don't know how I feel when you kiss me."

Shadow's hand, still hovering in midair as though it were uncertain whether it should push Sorren away or pull him nearer, drew his attention. He took her hand in his and, just as he had done when she was in his bed, kissed her palm and then the fingertips, making the decision her hand could not. She watched, fascinated beyond words, as his tongue curled around one fingertip. He sipped lightly at the tip, then placed her palm against his chest.

"My heart —" he said, the words getting choked off in his constricted throat.

Shadow felt the wild beating of his heart. It was the life force within him, pounding madly with the want of her. Shadow spread her fingers out, and when her thumb grazed against his nipple, she felt his body stiffen at the touch. *He's sensitive there, just like I am,* she thought. She scratched his nipple through the shirt, experimentally, and Sorren's breath came out in a wavering hiss.

"Kiss me," she whispered, leaning forward again, hungry for the taste of his mouth, the touch of his lips. "I need —"

Sorren's arms wound around Shadow, pulling her in tight. His kiss, primal and hungry, bruised her lips this time, his reason and tender ways shattered by the innate urges that boiled in his veins.

Sorren pushed Shadow backward and their legs tumbled together as he rolled atop her. She felt his knee push between her own, forcing her dress up her legs. The heated moisture of her being pulsed with a need that was at once hungry and yet timid, frightened of the unknown but needing the knowledge that had been denied her.

"Sorren . . . Sorren," Shadow breathed as he kissed the silken, perfumed arch of her throat. She pushed her fingers into the thick sheen of his hair, pulling him tighter against her. He raised his head and his chest pressed against her breasts. Her nipples had been hardened by passion and now, with the weight of Sorren upon them and the pressure of her garments holding them, the rosy crests were sensitive to the

156

touch. He looked at her and Shadow kissed Sorren, one hand stroking the small of his back lightly.

Sorren slipped his arm beneath Shadow's neck, holding her head in the crook of his elbow. He kissed her lips softly and propped himself up to look down at her, his dark eyes barely open, the fire in them unmistakable in its intent. A hand roamed upward from Shadow's hip, running slowly over the cloth dress until it slid over the firm, sloping rise of one passion-hungry breast. Shadow inhaled deeply, her eyes widening as he caressed her nipple. She arched into his hand, pushing herself into his fingers.

Sorren watched his own hand manipulating Shadow's breast, touching her, kneading the ripe bosom. He stared at the hand, mesmerized by it, curious in a way. It was as though the hand somehow did not belong to him. Was he really touching her at last? And were her responses to his caresses real, or was this all some strangely vivid dream that he would wake up from? With his fingertip he traced imaginary circles in the fabric holding back her breast, and even through the chemise and corselet and dress, Sorren could see the distinct rise of her nipple. He knew exactly what it meant. The responsiveness of her body surprised and aroused him further. *She is a virgin,* the coldly rational and logical part of Sorren's mind whispered. That much Sorren was certain of. He could tell it in the way she had first kissed him. Her naivete was no charade to heighten his want of her. Her desire was no charade, either.

A sudden sense of duty went though Sorren, making his body tighten. Virgins were hardly his style, and given his past record with women, neither was fidelity.

His bullet had almost taken her life; was he to take her virginity, too? Was he taking it, or was she offering it? Sorren knew he was a master of self-justification. He could find an acceptable reason for having Shadow, without conscience or guilt. But could he accept her with a clear conscience, knowing from experience that he would not stay with her? Hadn't he done enough bad things to her already?

Shadow's shimmering lips, moist from Sorren's kisses, opened and closed. The fire that burned through her made words difficult but not impossible. She had needs, emotional needs that had nothing to do with the ravenous, mindless hunger of her body. Those needs had to be sated, too.

"Sorren, please say my name," Shadow said softly, her tone almost pleading. "You still haven't . . . oh, it's so beautiful when you touch me there . . ." — she shifted beneath his hand, twisting her shoulders to push her breast into the palm that seared her — "said my name."

Sorren's hand moved from one breast to the other. His fingers deftly worked the other nipple into aroused hardness. The dark pools of his eyes drifted slowly from his hand to the young woman's face. "Shadow," he whispered. The single word tasted sweet on his tongue. "Shadow . . . beautiful, precious Shadow."

Conscience be damned! thought Sorren. He felt weak against the desires this woman forced him to feel. Sorren had taken many women, accepting the charms they offered. He had also refused their offers if he felt there were strings attached. He could talk his way out of this one, he knew. Shadow would feel spurned briefly, but she would get over it eventually. Then some other man — a man who wanted her for his wife and for all time — could have her.

The notion of Shadow responding to another man's touch flared like wildfire in Sorren's heart. He clenched his teeth in sudden anger, as though Shadow were already looking for someone to take his place. With difficulty he pushed the distracting, uncharacteristically jealous thoughts from his mind.

"Say it again. I love the way my name sounds when you say it."

"Shadow." Then, with quiet authority, possessively, he whispered, "*My* Shadow."

Her eyes glistened with tears. At last he had said it. For reasons she did not understand, it had been terribly important that Sorren say her name. She blinked and a tear trickled down her temple, seeping into her ebony hair.

"Don't cry," Sorren purred. His hand slipped beneath Shadow. He kissed her lips briefly. She tried to kiss him again, but he lifted his face from hers. "Please don't cry. It kills me to see your tears."

One by one the small cloth buttons were unfastened down her back. Sorren's hand ran down one arm, and just as easily as before, he undid the buttons at Shadow's wrist. He kissed her again, and as he did, Sorren pulled the bodice of Shadow's dress beneath the taut mounds of her breasts.

Shadow blossomed in Sorren's arms, grew in the pleasure of his touch, swirled in the mindless ecstasy of his kisses. She felt him take her arm from around his shoulders, and Shadow wondered what she should do. Was she to touch him as he touched her? She wanted to please Sorren, to pleasure him, but how?

With a firm tug, Sorren brought the lacy cup of the

chemise and corselet beneath one breast. He touched the nipple, catching it between a forefinger and thumb. Shadow's mouth opened and she inhaled, her breathing suspended, her senses rioting. She put a hand on his shoulder, keeping her arm out of the way should it inhibit his straying hand.

"You have such beautiful breasts," Sorren sighed in a deep, rasping voice. He showered Shadow's face with kisses, kissing her lips and nose, her eyelids and cheeks. Then, kissing her jaw and neck, he kissed a naked shoulder, his lips moving downward with unmistakable intention. "Dark and sweet, like chocolate," he continued, his breath warm against Shadow's nipple. "See how they rise up for me?"

He circled the crest with his tongue. Shadow squirmed beneath him, wanting desperately for this teasing to end. She pulled her arm out of the sleeve of her dress. Sorren blew his warm breath against the moist nipple and it grew fractionally.

"Stop it, Sorren," she breathed.

He lifted his face, his dark eyes suddenly fierce, misreading the young woman's words. Shadow, feeling helpless and yet emboldened by the desires that coursed through her, looped her hand around Sorren's neck. She hugged his face to her breast, gasping, "Kiss me!"

He took the dark, round areole into his mouth. His tongue grazed against the aroused nub, then he bit lightly at the nipple with his teeth. His teeth felt sharp, and the touch of them was soon replaced by his rasping tongue. Shadow cried out softly, arching her back to press her breast into his mouth. *Nothing has ever, ever felt like this,* she thought. She whispered Kiowan words that Sorren could not translate, though he understood their meaning.

Shadow felt her dress rising, a hand sliding along the inside of one knee and then up to the silk-sheathed thigh. She gasped again, squirming on the bearskin rug, writhing as the warmth and moisture of Sorren's mouth caressing her breast matched the heated depths in the center of her need. When the hand moved above the stocking top, the fingers began a tight, slowly widening circle against her naked thigh, in the brief expanse of flesh between stocking and her lace drawers.

Touch me! Touch me! Touch me! Shadow's mind screamed, chanted the words that echoed in her brain but could not be forced from her throat.

The solid rap of knuckles against the front door of Sorren's palatial home startled Shadow. She clung onto him, unconsciously hiding her partial nudity with his body, holding tightly onto the security that was Sorren McKenna.

"Damn!" Sorren hissed in a flash of white-hot anger. "Easy, easy," he said, stroking Shadow's silky hair, his lips close to her ear as he spoke. "It's just someone at the door. Relax, precious. Let me get rid of whoever it is."

Clarity of thought had returned to Shadow, but she did not welcome it. She refused to release him. What was outside the room frightened her.

"They'll go away." Shadow tightened her grip on Sorren, her small hands bunched into fists at his back. "Don't leave me."

"I'd better go." Sorren tried to slip out of Shadow's arms, but she refused his silent request. There was a second knock at the door, louder than the first. "See? Whoever it is won't go away until I send him away. I'll be right back."

161

When Sorren pushed himself out of Shadow's frightened embrace, she crossed her arms over her chest, covering herself, suddenly feeling shy and embarrassed. Sorren rose to his feet and Shadow saw, for the first time, his arousal, fierce and solid, tenting the front of his denim slacks. She was awed and frightened by the size of him. The desire that had welled inside her had been destroyed by the intruder at the door. She pulled her eyes away from Sorren's body and thought, *I caused that. It shouldn't frighten me.* But it did. It frightened her to the core of her being.

Sorren closed the door when he left the room. Shadow felt abandoned, alone again like so many times before. Without fully thinking of what she was doing, she pulled up the strap of her camisole, then slipped her arm back into her dress.

Shadow curled her knees beneath her, sitting on the backs of her moccasin-shoed heels, her mind and soul and senses reeling under the impact of the thought that Sorren would return, soon, and he would want from her what she had promised without words.

Chapter Eight

Sorren paused outside the door to the hunting room. He breathed in deeply several times to compose his rioting senses, collecting himself and his thoughts. It was an easy thing to do now that Shadow was no longer in his arms and he wasn't intoxicated by the softness of her kisses and the firmness of her supple body.

He tilted his head back until it was against the oak door and closed his eyes for a moment. How many women had he made love to in his life? He couldn't remember. In his youth he had been arrogant enough to keep count, mentally marking each sexual conquest as a carnal victory. But Sorren McKenna had stopped counting his lovers long ago. So many of them were just diversions. Sorren always knew in advance how they would end. When the end came, in a day or a week or perhaps as long as a month, he was never saddened or surprised by it. It was nature. His nature, anyway, and a man just can't change nature. He accepted this phenomenon as simply the way things were, just as he had accepted his own peculiar and sometimes violent role in the war. Sorren took satisfaction in knowing that he was good at what he did, but that was all. Like his role in the war or his seduction of women, he was seldom truly happy about what he had done, but he did rest confident in the assurance of his own competence.

After a quick check to see if there were any telltale bulges in his tight-fitting denim slacks, Sorren walked unhurriedly to the front door. He opened the door wide, as the master of his own manor would at an intrusion, and faced Elijah, the third of Emma's sons. Elijah stood head and shoulders above Sorren, his broad, black body sturdy as the trunk of an oak tree, hardened by years of physical labor, nourished by three hearty meals a day from his mother.

"Evenin', Mr. McKenna," Elijah said, taking off his sweat-stained felt hat. "Mama sent me here to escort Miss Shadow back home. Mama says it ain't right that—"

"Yes, of course." Sorren gave Elijah a smile that he did not feel inside. Emma, in her own inimitable way, had been throwing Sorren and Shadow together every chance she had—like insisting that Sorren come along to provide a man's opinion of Shadow's new dresses. But now that Shadow and Sorren were together *alone*, Emma was pulling in the reins.

Sorren stepped aside and motioned for Elijah to enter.

"I'm real sorry, Mr. McKenna," Elijah said, his baritone voice soft, carrying the camaraderie that single men share. "Mama says I gotta come here for her."

"I understand." Sorren patted Elijah on the shoulder. It was like patting the side of a young bull. Sorren hoped he would never get into a fist fight with Elijah. Fighting the entire Confederate army would be easier. "I'll go tell Shadow you're here." Sorren led Elijah into the library. "The rye is on the shelf over there. Help yourself to a drink."

"Mama says drinkin' makes a man a fool."

Sorren knew that for years Elijah's father had been supplementing the family income with what was rumored to be the finest moonshine still in the territory. Elijah had been sipping strong liquor his entire life.

"Suit yourself," Sorren replied. "But if you do have some whiskey, I suggest you also have a chocolate mint. They're in the crystal near my reading chair. That way your mother won't smell the liquor."

Elijah's beefy face made an expression as he said, "Mama will know anyhow. She knows ever'thin 'bout ever'body."

"I suspect that's true, Elijah. I suspect that's true."

Sorren closed the library door. Thank God Emma had sent Elijah instead of coming herself. Emma would have stormed through the house until she found Shadow. And if she found Shadow languorously stretched out on the bearskin in partial dishabille, there would have been, in the truest sense of the phrase, hell to pay.

He went back to the hunting room and, though he wasn't sure why, knocked softly before entering.

"Elijah's here," Sorren said, stepping inside. "Emma sent him to chaperone you home." Sorren's face did not reveal his disappointment at seeing that Shadow had not only readjusted her dress, but had rebuttoned it, too. Sorren's conversation with Elijah had not been lengthy enough nor loud enough to warn Shadow. She had, immediately after Sorren had left her, put an end to the romantic interlude.

"Send him away," Shadow said after a pause. When Sorren's eyes lightened with amorous thoughts, she added quickly, "I don't need a chaperone. I can make it to the MW on my own. You'll let me borrow a horse, won't you? I lost my pinto after I got shot. Somebody stole him."

"Whatever you want you can have." Sorren felt a chill inside him. Shadow's lovely face, which moments earlier had so clearly displayed the passion she felt for him, was passive, emotionless. And the wide, dark eyes, which could touch Sorren so intimately from completely across the room, were now unreadable. Not scared, really; not cautious or wary; perhaps just a little sad.

Sorren looked at Shadow's new dress. "You can take the carriage if you want. I haven't any sidesaddles for you."

"I don't know how to ride sidesaddle." Shadow was on her feet, walking to the door with swift, determined steps, her moccasins silent against the floor. She waited for Sorren to move out of the doorway. "Excuse me," she said. "I'll tell Elijah myself."

"What's wrong?" Sorren's eyes narrowed, and when he reached for Shadow, she took a step backward, moving out of reach. "Shadow, I didn't send him here. Don't be angry with me."

"I just want to be alone, that's all." It was a lie.

166

Shadow didn't want to be alone, she wanted to be with Sorren. But she wanted being with him to mean as much to him as it meant to her . . . and obviously, that just wasn't the case with him.

Shadow studied Sorren's face, not sure of who she was looking at or what kind of man he really was. When Sorren was confused, the creases in his gaunt face that ran from the corners of his nose to the outsides of his mouth became more pronounced. He took another step toward Shadow, and once again she stepped back.

"What on earth is wrong? I'm not any happier about this than you are."

It means nothing to you, thought Shadow. *I was ready to give myself to you, and now you're only mildly disturbed. Elijah is an annoyance. You can't have what you want this time, so you're peeved. You won't have me tonight, and that displeases you. But you've had so many women before it doesn't really bother you.*

How could a man like Sorren McKenna ever understand the magnitude of the decision that Shadow had made? He had, by the hellish skill of his hands and lips and that sensual force that emanated from him, forced his will upon her, forced her to do as he commanded. To Shadow, it was even more than making love. She had been at the threshold of giving away her virginity to the dark-eyed man who dressed in black. But to Sorren McKenna, she was just another casual exercise of his lust.

Why couldn't he see how much it hurt her to dismiss so lightly what had almost happened? Was he so sure that he would have her later? Was he so sure that he could, at will, drive her senses insane with the hunger to taste his kisses and feel him against her?

"What's wrong?"

"Nothing is wrong." The words came from Shadow's lips flat and cold. "Why should anything be wrong?" She started to move around Sorren. When he touched her arm, Shadow paused just a moment to throw him an icy look.

"He's in the library." Their eyes held and Shadow saw that Sorren's nonchalant attitude had changed to mild anger. "I'm not the one you should be mad at."

"Like hell," Shadow whispered venomously, then walked out of the room before Sorren could respond.

It was not easy for Shadow to convince the towering, obedient giant Elijah to return without her. She would be along shortly, Shadow insisted. And Elijah mustn't worry about her because Shadow had been travelling alone most of her life, and despite the finery and femininity of her dress, she could be a very dangerous young woman if threatened. Elijah was stuck between the wishes of two extremely strong-willed women, but he relented to Shadow's wishes, trained by a thousand lectures from Emma that a gentleman *never* forces his company or companionship upon a lady.

Sorren was waiting for them at the door. Elijah put his hat on and turned to Shadow one last time. "Maybe I could jus' ride behin' you, Miss Shadow. You won't see nor hear me. No, ma'am. Wouldn't even know I was there. I'm quiet as a shadow, jus' like your name."

"That's very considerate of you, but it isn't necessary." Shadow's eyes involuntarily danced to Sorren's face, then went back to Elijah. "I would like to be alone tonight, Elijah. There are many things for me to think about, and a ride this evening will help me." Shadow was speaking to Sorren, though she directed her words to Elijah. "I'm well aware of the dangers of this part of the country. I can protect myself."

Elijah excused himself and left, and when the door was closed behind him, the silence between Sorren and Shadow was thick and heavy with words and emotions that wouldn't be shared.

"I'll take the carriage, if that's all right with you." Shadow did not look at Sorren as she spoke. The pain in her heart was sharp, like a knife wound. Sorren's indifference to not making love hurt Shadow as grievously as if he had taken her, then cast her aside. Where was his passion? She wanted it to be as important to him as it was to her. Shadow sadly realized that she was not as immune to pain as she wanted to be.

"Will you let me take you home?"

"Home?" Shadow turned to Sorren, her jaw set in a grim line, one eyebrow arched high. "You're smarter than that. The MW Circle isn't my home, it's where I happen to sleep right now, that's all. It's no more my home than this place. I slept here, remember?"

It was the wrong thing to say. Bitter words spilling from an angry heart. But Shadow wanted to hurt him. Why shouldn't he hurt, too?

Once again there was silence between them, a silence that neither knew how to break. Each wanted to cross the chasm that kept them separate, the chasm that had been leapt in the hunting room when

169

they clung desperately together, as though each were the other's lifeline. But it was too great an effort to cross that great divide twice in one evening, perhaps even twice in one lifetime, so neither even tried.

"Good night, Sorren." Shadow opened the door. A cool evening breeze played with her long hair. She wondered what time it was, how long ago the sun had gone down.

"Don't go like this." Sorren moved until he stood behind Shadow, close enough to smell the alluring aroma of her body. "Don't leave angry. I don't know what has happened, but—"

"Just say good-bye, Sorren!" Shadow snapped, cutting him off, fighting against the tears that wanted to spill forth. "Say good-bye or good night or whatever it is you say to the women who leave your house in the night." A sob caught in Shadow's chest, cutting off her words but making no sound of its own. She refused to let Sorren see the anguish he had caused. Her tone was flip and sarcastic when she continued, looking out at the starlit sky. "What is the etiquette for this sort of thing, anyway? You must know. You've said a lot of good-byes in your life, haven't you? Or course you have. The great Sorren McKenna, seducer of women, hunter extraordinaire, businessman par excellence."

"Why are you doing this to me? To us?" Sorren put his hands on Shadow's shoulders. Every instinct in him said to pull her close. He had no idea in the world why Shadow had turned on him so suddenly, and with such cold vengeance.

"Just leave me alone, will you?" Tears burned in Shadow's eyes, but she refused to let them run down her cheeks.

"Why? Damn it, Shadow, you owe me some explanation." Sorren's fingers tightened into the deeply tanned, tawny flesh of Shadow's shoulders. In the peach dress, Shadow's sun-burnished skin literally glowed. "You owe me that much."

Sorren was just about to kiss the slender, inviting arch of Shadow's throat when she whispered, "Can't you see what's happening to me? Since you came into my life . . . oh, God, everything is getting all messed up."

It was a justifiable explanation, one that Sorren could accept. He didn't *like* the reason she'd given, but he certainly understood. He had been trying to get away from himself in a dozen different ways, not the least of which was through his collection of lovers. He knew, with the savage clarity of a man who had no delusions about himself, that he'd "messed up" enough lives in his time. He couldn't blame Shadow for her decision, especially not now, when the Fates were dealing her a winning hand.

It occurred to Sorren that Carl might have said something to Shadow. It was entirely in keeping with Carl's nature to bad-mouth others. Especially since Sorren had refused the War Department contract. Carl knew enough about Sorren to frighten off any woman. And Sorren was absolutely certain that Carl wouldn't hesitate to throw in a bold-faced lie, just to add more spice and venom to his story.

"Leave," Sorren whispered. There was no malice in his tone, only sadness. He really could understand Shadow wanting to distance herself from him. Perhaps it was meant to be this way, perhaps it was

171

better for both of them. "I won't try to stop you again."

Sorren felt a shudder go through Shadow, and he knew she was crying. He felt a new sense of respect for her. She was agonized by leaving him but determined to do the right thing anyway. He wished like hell she'd be foolish enough to stay with him.

"Good night, Sorren," Shadow said.

She opened the door, stepped through it, then closed it behind her without ever looking back.

Sorren's house had never felt so large and empty as the precise moment the door closed behind Shadow.

"This is ridiculous," he whispered aloud. In a raised voice, hoarse with turmoil, he spat, "She's just a goddamn girl!"

But he didn't really believe it. Sorren McKenna had been with enough women to know that there damn sure was a difference in what he felt. With the others, a sense of relief had always come over him whenever they were gone. Once his passion had been spent, their company was something he felt obligated to tolerate. It was the price he paid for seducing them — or accepting their seduction. It was Sorren's turn to feel empty and alone.

"I can't stay here." The words, even softly spoken as they were, echoed hauntingly through the enormous, barren house.

He would saddle up his mare and take a ride alone, head out to the west range. A night sleeping under the stars, then a hard day checking the stock, would surely keep his mind off a finicky half-breed woman he really had no business being with in the first place.

It would work, wouldn't it?

Shadow had never heard a more lonely sound than the heavy front door to Sorren's house closing behind her. Hearing the latch click into place released the tears that she'd held back so long. They flooded from her eyes and ran in streams down her cheeks. As she had done since her early childhood days when the Kiowan children, then the words of the orphanage, had taunted her, Shadow had held her tears back just enough to conceal them from her tormentor.

The tears came unchecked, blurring her vision. The horse and carriage Sorren had rented in God's Grace was tied to the rail, just off the porch. She headed for it, stumbling when the tears prevented her from seeing the two steps leading down to the hard-baked ground, and untied the reins.

Shadow got in the carriage and agony washed over her. It was as though all the humiliation she had suffered in her life had only been in preparation for this single moment. She dropped the reins and buried her face in her hands, her shoulders heaving as great sobs roiled out from her heart.

She did not hear the door open. It was Sorren's boot heels on the porch that drew her attention. Shadow bolted upright, wiping away tears guiltily with the backs of her hands.

Sorren's face was taut, pale. He walked over to the carriage, looking up at Shadow. Very softly he said, "Don't leave me."

Shadow was still crying, though softly now as she moved into Sorren's hands, allowing him to help her out of the carriage. When her feet were on the ground, she leaned into him, pressing her cheek against his chest, sliding her hands around his body to squeeze him tightly.

"Love me, Sorren," she whispered. "I'm so scared. All I want is for you to love me."

Shadow never moved her face from Sorren's shoulder as he lifted her, carrying her into the vast house, empty but for two fragile souls.

Chapter Nine

Sorren set her gently to her feet in his bedroom. She leaned into him, her arms looped softly around his neck. The warmth and strength of his body felt reassuring against the supple softness of her breasts.

"I'm scared," Shadow whispered. She tilted her head back, kissing Sorren's neck, then accepting a deep, probing kiss from him. "I don't know what to do. I don't know how to please you."

"Everything you do pleases me," Sorren replied. He slipped his arms around Shadow's waist, pulling her in tighter. When he did this, Shadow became distinctly aware of his aroused maleness. She inhaled deeply, simultaneously frightened and yet inquisitive. His hands moved upward, pushing brusquely over her breasts to cup her face in his palms. He smoothed away residual tears with his thumbs, looking deep into Shadow's dark, glistening eyes. "Precious," he whispered. "My precious, don't worry. I'm going to make everything all right."

"Love me, Sorren."

His hands were at her shoulders, and when Sorren turned Shadow around so that her back was to him, she offered no resistance. She was on the edge of the unknown. Her youthful fantasies hadn't been like this. They were always vague, a faceless man and caresses that never quite really touched her silken flesh, let alone touched her heart. She felt his lips, warm and soft, against her neck. Shadow tilted her head to the side, inviting more kisses. The buttons running down her back came free under his experienced touch. The gown was slipped from her shoulders and arms in a rustle of new fabric. A moment later, Sorren's fingers curled into the thin shoulder straps of her corselet and that, too, was brought down. The garment caught at the fullness of her upsweeping breasts.

"Precious . . . Shadow . . . precious," Sorren whispered in the luxurious mane of ebony hair flowing over the young woman's naked shoulders. His breath was warm against the cool places on Shadow's neck where his lips had moistened her flesh. "You really are dangerously beautiful. So damn beautiful."

The corselet and gown were tugged down. Her full breasts, taut with desire, burst free. She stood, swaying slightly with the intoxication of passion, until she felt the garments pushed lower still. She raised her feet and the soft leather moccasins were removed one at a time.

"Sit," Sorren said. There was an underlying command in his tone now. Desire burned through him, eating at his judgment, tearing away at his sense of control. Feral need boiled like a volcano, pressure building against pressure. He wanted to take Shadow fiercely, devouring her with his aching, pulsing need, but he knew, too, that he could not. Not this time, not the first time.

Shadow sat at the edge of the bed and her stockings were tugged down her long, slender legs. Naked now, unsure of herself, a flicker of self-consciousness awoke in her dazed brain. She crossed an arm over her breasts and placed one hand between her thighs to cover herself. Her body, newly heightened to the possibilities of pleasure, tingled softly. Even the touch of her own fingers, softly pressed against the moist center of her need, caused a warm rush of sensations to flow through her. Shadow sighed, eliciting a half smile from Sorren.

"Don't be shy." Sorren took Shadow's hand, removing it from her breasts. "I like looking at you."

Shadow put her head down, unable to look up. Her hair tumbled in a wave down her shoulders, hiding her breasts, running down to tickle her trembling thighs. She shivered softly when Sorren smoothed her hair over her shoulders, allowing it to cascade down her back. He touched her chin with his fingertips and gently forced her head up.

Shadow had seen half-naked men all her life. The men of her tribe often wore little other than a loincloth. But somehow her past experience at viewing the male body meant nothing to her now. Nothing in her past had prepared her rioting senses in the least as she watched Sorren's long, tanned fingers working free the buttons of his black silk shirt. He stripped the shirt off, dropping it to the floor at his feet. Each muscle in his

177

sinewy chest rippled beneath the surface of his skin, moving like the muscles of some stalking mountain lion in his physical prime.

She could not take her eyes away from Sorren, though something inside Shadow whispered that she should not enjoy the sight of him as much as she did. When he bent over, balancing on one foot to remove a boot, she studied the muscles in his arms. The veins were pushed close to the surface of his skin by the sleek, steelish muscles. Even bent over, his stomach was flat, the line of each rib delineated. When his boots had been removed, Sorren stood upright again, his fingers hovering near the snap of his slacks.

The telltale swell down the left leg of his slacks made Shadow's mouth open in shock. She inhaled tremulously. Unconsciously she held her breath. *Now* she was frightened. She glanced up and saw Sorren's eyes bright with want and slightly mocking.

This man knows the power he has, thought Shadow in an oddly petulant way. She wanted, for a reason she wasn't sure of, to be less affected by Sorren's physical charm. Sorren's confidence, that if she looked at him she would want him, bothered her. Why couldn't he be as unsure of his sexuality as she was? Shadow's fragile confidence demanded.

Sorren flicked open the buttons of his fly. The slacks opened and, very slowly, he pulled them down his legs. He stepped out of his clothes and the long, pulsing length of his arousal was too close to eye level for Shadow not to look at it.

Confusion welled in Shadow. He was too big. This was all wrong. Father Bradford had told her stories, stories that were as vague and faceless as Shadow's sexual fantasies. But this wasn't a teenage dream, it was happening right now. This had to stop this instant! This had to stop right now! This must stop right—

He stretched her out on the bed and slipped beside her. Shadow's head was on Sorren's forearm. The fingertips of his right hand trailed softly along her body in desultory caresses. The heat of his hardness burned Shadow's hip.

"I could look at you forever," Sorren whispered hoarsely. He circled the crest of one breast with the tip of his finger, causing Shadow to tremble. The nipple became visibly harder.

"Sorren . . . I . . ." Words failed her when the hand moved downward, trailing over her stomach. She quivered. She wanted to tell Sorren that she was frightened, that she didn't know what to do or what was expected of her. Something in her demanded that she participate rather than simply, passively accept. But Shadow could not be so bold. Though she felt the frightening length of his arousal pressing against her thigh, branding her as his in some unknown way with its red-hot heat, she could not reach for him. With eyes closed, she listened to his words and felt his touch, accepting the exquisite sensations he so easily drew from her.

Sorren kissed her and Shadow rolled toward him, pressing more of her tingling, ready body against him. The heated depths of her passion ached to be caressed, yet Shadow twisted toward Sorren, turning in such a fashion as to prevent his straying hand from moving between their bodies.

"Don't be frightened, precious," Sorren purred, kissing Shadow's throat, forcing her onto her back as he slipped lower on the bed. "I won't hurt you." His tongue

179

left a thin trail of moisture between Shadow's mounding breasts. "I won't ever hurt you."

Shadow stretched her arms out, giving up the last vestige of her fear and uncertainty. What would happen would happen. It was futile to try to think coherently. All she wanted was to *feel*. Her chaotic thoughts were her enemies, inhibiting her senses, demanding that there be a *reason* for the way she felt, for the incredible abandonment of all that she had previously held dear.

"So soft . . . so soft and sweet and precious." Sorren circling Shadow's naval with his tongue. His tone was casual; his tongue and his caresses weren't.

He pushed her legs further apart, and again Shadow did not resist. She was beyond thinking, beyond embarrassment and self-consciousness, above and beyond the demons of desire that Father Bradford had warned her about. His fingers, stoking the fires of her need, played softly over her skin. She felt his teeth, in sharp contrast to his feathery touches, nip at the taut flesh of an inner thigh. In a disembodied way, Shadow realized she had one leg up on Sorren's shoulder. A hand pushed over her sucked-in stomach, moving higher to roughly cup one breast, crushing it to her rib cage.

"Shadow . . . sweet Shadow," he whispered, then kissed her.

She flinched. Fire raced through her veins.

"Don't!" Shadow gasped, squirming. But he was much to strong, and passion had made her weak. Or, just perhaps, she really did not want him to stop. The point was rendered moot when Sorren kissed her a second time and his tongue darted inside and Shadow had never known anything could ever, ever, ever feel like that.

She could hear words. Disconnected words that meant nothing to her addled brain. "You must tell me what you want," he was saying, coaching her, insisting that she respond verbally to his oral caresses. Coherent words were impossible for her. Shadow didn't even try to speak. Her body, speaking the universal and irrefutable language of desire, told Sorren everything he needed to know.

He played her body with consummate skill, teasing, cooling, and heating, heightening Shadow's anticipation until she ached with want. And when the white fire of ultimate pleasure coursed through her in a shuddering release, Shadow was swept away into the unknown. She was catapulted high into the clouds as her voluptuous and absurdly responsive body trembled in a spasmodic and unprecedented outburst of physical emotion.

Later—how much later, Shadow wasn't sure—she felt his lips against her, kissing the juncture where hip and thigh meet. She felt lazy, deliriously sated.

"Come here," Shadow whispered. She needed to look into Sorren's eyes. Only then could she know that this was not just some beautiful dream. She pushed her fingers into Sorren's thick jet black hair, hugging his head briefly between her breasts. Holding him close, she could again feel the fierce pounding of his heart. She whispered, "You make me feel precious. You say that to me, but now I feel precious."

Sorren moved above her, his hips sliding between Shadow's parted thighs. She felt the conical end of his manhood pressed against her moist honey entrance. He seemed huge. Frighteningly, enormously huge.

This time fear did not insinuate itself into her mind, it exploded like dynamite.

"Sorren, I —"

"Shhhh!" Sorren kissed her, gently but insistently, stopping the words that Shadow really did not want to speak.

He moved slowly, with suppressed strength. The overwhelming need Sorren felt to take Shadow, to possess her body and soul, was tempered only by the continual whisper in his brain that warned him she was a virgin. *Gently, gently,* he kept reminding himself.

Shadow raised her knees, forming a velvety valley with her thighs for Sorren's lean hips. Sorren raised himself up, resting his weight on his elbows so that he could look down into Shadow's face.

"No," Shadow complained, her arms twisting around his body. She pulled at him, feeling the sinewy muscles in his back. "I want to feel you . . . all of you . . . against me . . . inside me . . . please . . . please, Sorren, please."

She opened for him, soft feminine resistance giving way to steelish masculine force. Shadow was kissing Sorren now, her mouth pressed hungrily against his, when she felt the pain inside, the tearing. She made a soft sound of pain, and when Sorren tried to stop, Shadow urged, with a searing kiss, that he continue. She had known little other than pain her entire life. This one brief moment of pain she would endure, would gladly accept, because the pain was so short-lived, and the pleasure that followed, the sheer ecstasy of feeling Sorren moving inside her, above her, seemingly all around her, was worth any possible price.

She did not reach that peak of ecstasy she had earlier.

But in place of that mindless, world-shattering ecstasy and release, Shadow felt loved, felt the power of Sorren's body and the need he had of her. She tasted the saltiness of his shoulder, felt him straining to push deeper and deeper. She gave herself to him, holding tightly onto his shoulders, clinging to him desperately, her body locked to his by more than what was physical.

And when at last the deep, rumbling groan of ecstasy went through Sorren and with a cry of pleasure he thrust deep into Shadow and released, she hugged him fiercely, stroking his satiny hair, feeling his heart pounding against hers as his body untensed above her.

"Don't move," Shadow whispered when Sorren started to roll away. "Not yet. Not just yet." He was still inside her. She didn't want to feel empty again. The old fears had come to the fore once again, and she was fighting them off as best she could. She kissed his neck, shoulder, cheek. He was salty. Shadow did not know yet that the blissful minutes she'd had Sorren pressing into her, moving inside her had, by his standards, been embarrassingly abbreviated. She could not know that his intense need of her had shattered the calm detachment that helped to make him such a masterful lover. And, hauntingly, she did not know if she had really pleased him. He was an experienced lover. Surely he would need — would demand — skill to match his own.

"My head is spinning," Shadow whispered, her cheek against Sorren's chest, his arm looped around her. She felt him tense protectively at her comment. "No, it's not the wound. That doesn't bother me anymore. It's you, us, all this that's making my head spin."

Sorren chuckled, and Shadow, with her ear against

his chest, heard the sound reverberate through his ribs, the rumbling sound of contentment seeming to emanate from deep within his soul.

"Say something," Shadow said.

"What?"

"I don't care. Anything. Just say something."

"Why?"

"Because I'm listening through your chest!"

Of course . . . Shadow had never lain in bed with a man. Everything she saw, touched, heard, felt, and tasted was new to her. Her guileless curiosity, her complete lack of affectation, brought a surge of joy to him. Sorren laughed heartily, drawing giggles of appreciation from her.

"Mmmmm!" Shadow murmured. "If I were a cat, I'd purr." She snuggled a little closer to Sorren, one leg over his, her left hand on his stomach. She shifted a little, not knowing where exactly to put her right arm. It didn't seem to fit beneath her, or between her body and Sorren's very well. "Sorren, can I ask you something?"

"Sure."

"Are you comfortable?"

"Extremely." His fingers played along the smooth, warm, soft flesh of a naked shoulder. Taking a lock of waist-length hair, he idly began twisting it around and around his finger. "You?"

"Yes. More comfortable and at peace than I ever thought possible. But I have one question."

"Let's hear it."

"Promise you won't laugh?"

"I promise," Sorren replied, affecting great solemnity.

"What am I supposed to do with my right arm?"

184

Sorren very nearly bit his tongue trying to keep from laughing. He struggled with it, holding back a great and powerful joy. Shadow was giggling, her head on his broad, heaving chest as he fought against the waves of laughter. When at last the pressure was too great, the pleasure too powerful to hold back, Sorren's loud, booming laughter filled the bedroom.

Shadow twisted her knees beneath her, her ebony hair flying around her shoulders and down her back and arms. She beat Sorren's naked chest with small fists and giggled, "You promised! You promised you wouldn't laugh!"

Sorren rolled away from Shadow, covering his head with his arms to shield himself against the playful on-slaught of tiny fists smacking against his back, biceps, and shoulders.

"Stop laughing at me!" Shadow put her palms against Sorren's back. The touch of him made her tingle. "Stop laughing or I'll push you out of bed!"

"Don't!"

Sorren spun to defend himself, and how exactly he ended up with Shadow beneath him he wasn't quite certain. One minute they were laughing and tussling like misbehaving children, and the next he was looking into her eyes so close to his and so filled with the fire of desire. He felt again the voluptuous, exquisite length of this extraordinary woman against him. And when he felt her small hand tentatively take his suddenly roused manhood, the laughter was replaced with a throaty purr of carnal hunger from Shadow.

"Again, Sorren," Shadow whispered between kisses. She guided him into her. "I want you again." She felt the long, powerful measured thrusts enter her, taking

185

her breath again. "Love me, Sorren. Love me."

Shadow felt for Sorren, but he wasn't in the bed. Before she could panic or feel abandoned, she heard the long, slow exhale of breath. She turned her head slightly. Sorren was standing near the open window. A crack of lightning illuminated his naked profile for moment.

My God, he's beautiful, Shadow thought sleepily.

"Come to bed. It's cold without you," Shadow whispered. Slow, rolling thunder echoed through the Colorado hills outside.

Sorren flicked his cigarette out the window. He walked around the bed slowly. Shadow raised the sheet for him as he slipped in beside her. She moved in close, placing her cheek against his chest as Sorren's arm slipped around her shoulders.

"This is better . . . much bet—"

Shadow was sleeping peacefully before she finished the sentence.

Sorren awoke first. He blinked his eyes. Sun was streaming through the window. He closed his eyes again, wishing he'd had the foresight to draw the curtains before going to sleep. He hugged Shadow a little tighter to him, savoring the warmth of the bed and the soft body against him. Shadow moaned sleepily, a hand drifting up his chest to his face. Her fingertips touched his lips. He kissed them and felt her smile against his naked chest.

"Good morning," Shadow whispered. Her shoulder moved a little. She kissed his chest. They were in exactly the same position they'd been in when sleep and exhaustion overtook the lovers in the late hours of the evening. "This is nice. I like waking up with you."

Sorren shifted a little beneath Shadow. He had a morning erection that had absolutely nothing to do with her. He felt—though he'd never felt this way with other women in similar situations—absurdly embarrassed by it.

"Excuse me," Sorren whispered, starting to slip out of bed.

"Don't leave me," Shadow insisted, her waist-length hair tossled all around her head and shoulders, spreading over the white linen and Sorren's naked chest. She held onto Sorren's chest, not entirely oblivious to the fact that this caused her breasts to rub against him.

"I'll be right back."

Shadow squirmed a little higher on the bed, pressing more of her body against Sorren. She kissed the point of his chin. "Don't leave yet. It's too nice and warm here." Shadow raised her knee, sliding her thigh against Sorren's and touching the hardened length of his manhood. "Oh, my!" she whispered in a breathy rush of words, entirely misreading the cause for Sorren's arousal.

"You don't understand. It's—"

Sorren went a little crazy inside when Shadow put a finger to his lips, stopping his explanation. He looked into her eyes and saw lightning that would have put the previous evening's thunderstorm to shame.

"I may not understand everything, but I'm learning." Shadow's body moved with sleepy, feline grace, as much of her touching as much of Sorren as possible as she straddled his hips. "Kiss me, Sorren. Kiss me and call me precious and . . . ohhh! I love how you feel moving inside me . . . love me awake."

Emma was not amused. She was not in the least littl bit amused.

"It was raining so hard," Shadow said, stepping be hind the dressing curtain in her room. "Sorren wa afraid I might get dizzy again. It wasn't all that lon ago that I couldn't even open my eyes without feelin faint."

"Yes, I know that," Emma muttered as she too Shadow's peach dress from the curtain and put it awa in the closet. When she returned, her lips were presse tightly together, arms crossed under an enormou bosom, jaw thrust forward with determination. "Missy me an' my man never had us no little girls of our own. guess the good Lord jus' didn't think it should be so. say this 'cause I got me a deep-down feeling you're special chil', Mr. Matthew's love chil.' An' you ain't go yourself no mama, neither."

Shadow looked over the lacquered Chinese dressing curtain. Emma appeared uncomfortable but deter mined, her stout body planted between Shadow and the door. Shadow wondered whether this was coincidenc or planned. Questions played in her mind. Did she loo loved? Could Emma tell that she was not the sam young woman who had gone shopping with her onl yesterday?

"I had a mother," Shadow said quietly.

"An' you got one now, missy." Emma nodded he head, approving of the words that were forming in he brain. "Now maybe I ain't really your mama, an maybe we both ain't quite the same shade of dark, but don't see as how that's got much truck in these kin' o things. Me? I'm a mama. Only thing I know how to do is be a mama. I mama'd my boys proper, an' I did justice to Mr. Carl an' Miss Catherine. Now I needs to be me a mama jus' like you need one. So you ever got yourself any questions, you jus' come to Emma. I got a pack full of answers."

This was the most glorious morning of Shadow's life. Waking up in Sorren's arms, making sweet love with him, and now Emma's beautiful sentiments.

"I will, Emma. I promise."

Emma flipped a white cotton casual dress over the curtain for Shadow to wear. "I'm real glad as how we got that all settled, missy, 'cause there's been somethin' been playin' on my mind. An' me bein' your mama, in a way, gives me the right to ask you somethin'."

Here it comes! thought Shadow playfully.

"Men got themselves a dark side to 'em," Emma continued. "Even good men got that dark side. It's jus' the way men is somehow." Emma shifted her feet, looking down at the floor then up again. She was uncomfortable with the subject. "This dark side, it can creep up on a man, surprise him real quick like, quick like the work of the devil himself. When this dark side takes a man, missy, it got the power to turn him mean, like an evil thing, like somethin' that ain't even hisself. I don't want to scare you none, missy. All men got this dark side in 'em. My man's a mighty good man, missy. He surely is. An' even my man gets the dark side in 'im. The devil comes a callin' an' the dark sides takes my man complete, jus' as sure as I'm standin' here now. Just like in the Good Book when that whale swallowed Jonah whole. But you see, missy, when the devil's dark side has got my man, he's such a good man that even

189

that dark side don't make him mean. No, missy, the devil's darkness gets upon my man real regular, and i ain't never made him mean." Emma blushed a little. She smiled for a moment, then pushed the smile away. It wasn't the time for memories like that. Emma nibbled thoughtfully on her lip for a moment. "I taught my boys proper, too. I says that the dark side don't have to make 'em mean. I says that ifin I get word they don't treat their ladyfolk like ladies or act like proper gentlemen, even God hisself won't switch 'em like I will."

Emma looked up, sincerity in her tone and countenance. "Now you was with Mr. McKenna last night, missy. I ain't accusin' you o' nothin'. I know you're a good girl. I see that in you. An' I love Mr. McKenna like one of my own. So tell me true now . . . was the dark side upon Mr. McKenna last night? Did he treat you like a lady?"

Shadow danced on the line between truth and lie. "Sorren has always been good to me, Emma. When I was hurt"—Shadow's fingers unconsciously drifted up to the mending bullet wound, hidden by her hair—"he treated me very . . . gently. And last night he was very gentle with me, too." Shadow spoke the truth, but she still felt guilty for artfully misleading Emma.

Emma's face broke into an enormous smile, brimming to the top and spilling over with pride and relief. "I know'd he was a good man! I know'd it all along! Last night my mister say to me, 'Emma, what you worryin your head for? You know that Mr. McKenna's a good man brought up proper.' That's what my mister says to me."

"You love your husband very much, don't you Emma?"

190

"Missy, I married my man when I was jus' fourteen. An' since that day, his face is the first I see in the mornin' and the last I see at night. That's just the way I likes it."

"I'm happy for you," Shadow said, her voice dipping lower as questions began playing with her mind. "Maybe some day I'll be lucky enough to find a man like that for myself."

"You will, missy," Emma said. She patted her enormous stomach. The conclusion to any conversation, especialy an important one, should always be followed by a solid meal. "Lord willin', you'll find yourself a good man. You'll find him, missy, 'cause I know me the Lord, an' he ain't gonna let a beautiful lady like you go lonely."

Chapter Ten

"There's something I want you to do," Carl said, almost spilling the glass in his hand. Catherine was beginning to worry about her brother's drinking.

"What's that?" Catherine asked cautiously.

"I want you to chum up to Shadow."

"What?" Catherine exclaimed, her voice brittle with indignation. "I will not! Why on earth should I do that?"

"Because it's important." Carl got up from his chair and began pacing the room. "You see, if you can get close to Shadow, then maybe we'll find out something."

"Like what?"

"I don't know yet. That's the point. I want to know how she thinks and what she thinks about. That's going to be important. I want you to gain her confidence. While you're doing that, I'll be able to figure out some way of getting Shadow out of our house. And, with a little luck, some way of keeping her away from our money."

"I'll never know why Daddy did what he did. I just can't understand it." Catherine sipped her tea. It had gotten cold in the cup. "Do you really think she'll ever trust me?"

Carl turned toward his sister, his eyes shining with evil thoughts. "Shadow? Of course she will. She's dying for friends and friendship. She's no more happy with us than we are with her, but you can change that." He sat in his father's chair and kicked his boots up on the desktop, oblivious to the scuff mark he put in the polished wood. "Talk with her, tell her things about yourself. You do that and she'll talk about herself. Women are that way."

"Just women?"

"No, not just women, but you've got to admit that women are more open about their lives than men are." Carl finished the whiskey with one big gulp. He grimaced as the liquor burned down his throat. "Men fall for the same thing, too, I suppose. It's like a poker game, sis. That's the way you've got to look at this. Dad made a big mistake. He let himself get seduced by an Indian slut. He thought he could make up for it later in life. He wasn't thinking straight. Maybe he was drunk. Something was wrong with him. Something inside."

"Yes, I suppose," Catherine said, her voice sounding far away. She didn't like thinking bad thoughts about her father, but there were facts that just couldn't be avoided. "That had to be it. He just wasn't well. That's why he did it. We can't blame him for it."

"Of course not. He must have gotten sick and it

muddied his thinking. He was a smart man. Hell, Dad was smart as a whip. But he had flaws, just like anybody else. And in the end it was those flaws that did him in." Carl shrugged his shoulders. He plopped into the chair and slouched deep down. "It's up to us to rectify those mistakes, sis. We've got to see that the legacy Dad leaves behind doesn't include some half-breed bastard squaw. The best way I can see, at least for now, of putting an end to the trouble Dad's caused is for you to get close to Shadow."

"I don't even like the sound of her name. What kind of name is Shadow, anyway?"

"Some crazy Indian name. You know how primitive they are." Carl looked straight into Catherine's eyes, stabbing his finger against the desk as he continued. "Get close to her. Find out what her weaknesses are. Once I find out, once I know where she's vulnerable, I'll know how to destroy her. Trust me on this one, sis. I'll get her out of this house and out of our lives completely. And she won't be taking a single copper penny from us, either. I promise you that. I give you my guarantee."

Catherine set her tea down and rose from the sofa. She didn't like the notion of having to pretend she was Shadow's friend. She also didn't like the way her brother used the word *destroy*. Catherine wanted Shadow out of her life, but she didn't want to see Shadow ruined.

Catherine wondered if she could make the charade work, even if she put her heart and soul into it. Playing coy with a man was second nature to Catherine. Befriending an Indian would require the acting job of her life.

"I'll try," Catherine said softly, looking out the window. It was going to be a warm day. The sun had burned the storm clouds from the sky. "I'll do my best, but I'm not going to promise anything." Catherine turned away from the window, looking at her brother with a self-protective gleam in her crystal blue eyes. "But only in this house! I'm *not* going to be seen in public with her! Not in God's Grace, and I most certainly am not going to be seen with her in Denver City. That's where I draw the line! Good Lord, Carl, what decent man would have anything to do with me if he knew I was friends with a half-breed? I mean, we can't be held too accountable for what Daddy did. We'll eventually be forgiven for that." Catherine shook her head, mentally seeing her suitors dwindling rapidly in number and quality. "I'll be as nice to her as I can in this house, but I'm *not* going anywhere with her."

There was a soft knock at the door. Emma stepped into the room. "There's a gentleman here to see you."

"Who is it?"

"Don't know. Nice dressed fella though."

"Did he say what he wanted?"

"No, Mr. Carl. He jus' tol' me he wanted to see you."

Carl shooed Emma away to fetch the man. Moments later, a tall, slender man with long, wavy blond hair, which touched his shoulders, and a neatly trimmed moustache and goatee stepped into the study. His knee-high boots were brightly polished and the corduroy suit was new and expertly tailored.

"Good afternoon, sir," the fellow said, approaching with long, confident strides and extending his hand.

195

"Allow me to introduce myself. I'm Jean-Jacques LaRoux."

Carl shook the proffered hand and sat back in his chair, sizing up the intruder. When Carl looked over at Catherine, he saw the interest she felt was written plainly all over her face. He wondered if she'd be able to fool Shadow into thinking she was a friend. If she couldn't hide her true feelings any better than that, Carl's scheme was in serious trouble from the outset.

"And good afternoon to you," LaRoux said. He took Catherine's hand softly in his own. His eyes were on hers as he bent forward, clicking his heels together smartly in military fashion while kissing the back of her hand. "I presume you are Miss Catherine Weatherly. This is a treat for me. So far from home and yet I find such beauty. I must write my friends to tell them not all beauty is in the South."

"Why, sir! You flatter me!" Catherine blushed prettily as she slipped her hand out of LaRoux's. "There are so few real gentlemen in these parts."

"You will find, good lady, that there is no gentleman quite like a southern gentleman." LaRoux gave Catherine one last smile and the final benefit of his undivided attention before turning away from her. "And though I find the company of your sister most delightful, perhaps it would be best if we could talk in private. I have business matters I wish to discuss with you."

"Of course," Catherine replied, obviously quite impressed.

Carl wondered what kind of business the southern gentleman could have in mind. He looked wealthy enough and cultivated enough to be an influential partner. Now that the business association with Sorren McKenna had gone up in flames, Carl could use a new partner. LaRoux knew their names, so he'd probably done some checking into the Weatherlys' background.

Carl settled comfortably into his chair, folding his hands on the desk, sitting the same way he'd seen his father sit when dealing with business matters.

"Please, take a seat," Carl said, nodding almost imperceptibly toward the straight-backed chair beside his desk. "Let's hear what you have to say."

LaRoux smoothed his trim moustache and sat. He crossed his legs at the knee, flicking at an imaginary piece of lint, pinching the crease in his slacks to keep it perfect.

"Mr. Weatherly, I have recently purchased a marker of yours," LaRoux began, his timbre smooth and polished, perhaps from a European education. "The marker is for five thousand dollars." Carl's face blanched visibly. "Now while it is true that I am a gentleman, it is also true that I am a businessman. And believe me, sir, I am not in the business of losing money. So, sir, when precisely tomorrow can I come to pick up my payment."

"Marker? I didn't sign any marker." Carl's tone was annoyed, but his face showed the fear that had crept into his soul. "There's obviously been some mistake. Mr. LaRoux, I've never seen you before in my life."

LaRoux pulled a neatly folded sheet of paper from his pocket. Carl recognized it and swallowed with some difficulty. "Remember this?" LaRoux asked, flipping open the paper. He remained seated. "Remember a midnight game of poker in Denver City? At Scott's Saloon?" Carl began to crumble.

LaRoux calmly stood. He placed his left hand on the desk in front of Carl. His right hand slipped into the pocket of his coat, and when it reappeared, he was holding a double-barreled derringer. He touched the twin muzzles to Carl's forehead and thumbed back the hammer. He was perfectly calm, a man at ease with himself and his surroundings, a man accustomed to handling business matters as quickly, efficiently, and effectively as possible. "Mr. Weatherly, I will either receive my payment or I will—and I promise you this—blow your brains all over this room. Now while it is true that killing you will not get me my money, it is also true that the next person I must deal with—namely, your sister—will have a fine example to go by." LaRoux sighed wearily, appearing bored with a speech he'd given before. "The choice is yours. Either you pay me and live, or you don't pay me and die, thereby becoming a valuable example for me in future debt collections."

LaRoux held the hammer with his thumb and let it down without taking the muzzle from Carl's forehead. When the hammers made a soft click when placed down, Carl flinched, squeezing his eyes shut.

"You have the reputation of being a man who likes having things his own way, Mr. Weatherly. It is not a reputation I dislike. In fact, I have something of the same reputation myself. Just imagine what people would think of me if I let you slide out from under a marker? It would grievously damage my ability to conduct business."

LaRoux pocketed the derringer and stood. "I'll

send a man here tomorrow. Please be sure to have the money ready by noon."

LaRoux was almost to the door by the time the small thing that constituted Carl's courage finally came to the fore. "You don't — you don't know who I am," he said in a faltering voice. "I own this valley! You can't threaten me!"

LaRoux chuckled, shaking his head wearily. "Mr. Weatherly, you may own this valley, but you don't own me. Please, I find this kind of talk so . . . superfluous. And it may damage our future business relationship. Do as you are told and you will only feel a minor financial pinch. You're a rich man, Mr. Weatherly. You can afford to pay off the marker." With deathly coldness, LaRoux concluded, "By noon tomorrow, Carl. I'll send my man. If I have to see you again, they'll bury you the next day."

LaRoux left the room. Carl heard him give a cordial good-bye to Catherine. A moment later she burst into the study, every movement and gesture animated with pleasure. "Wasn't he just the most handsome man you've ever seen in your life?"

Carl went to the liquor cabinet and poured himself four fingers worth of whiskey. His hands were shaking so badly he spilled nearly as much as he got in the glass.

"Carl, aren't you listening to me? Isn't he just so *gallant?*"

General Jean-Jacques LaRoux took the long, thin black cheroot from an inside pocket. Using a silver cutter, he snipped off one pointed tip. He rolled the cigar between his lips briefly, moistening the rich, flavorful tobacco wrapper. With slow, savoring puffs he started the cigar, then settled in for the final three-hundred-yard ride into his camp.

He did not need to give the secret signal to identify himself as he slipped past the first wave of sentries. Even at this distance, they would recognize him. He couldn't see the men, but he knew they were watching him carefully. LaRoux looked up when Smitty stood and moved to his right, positioning himself so he would be outlined against the sky. At fifty, Smitty was the oldest man the renegade general had in his outlaw army. With a long-barreled Winchester cradled in the crook of one elbow — the much-prized gift coming from LaRoux himself — he waved his hand. LaRoux touched his fingers to the wide brim of his gray hat and nodded in a slightly exaggerated manner, enhancing the gesture to accommodate the distance that separated them.

LaRoux liked Smitty. Smitty was an old-time soldier, a man who knew how to take orders. He was also an extraordinary marksman, never talked unless he had something to say, and he only occasionally drank to excess.

"Evenin', General!"

LaRoux turned to the voice as he entered camp. It was Johnny Stones. LaRoux again touched his hat and gave a curt nod, though this time his face was impassive. Johnny was more like the other soldiers he had now. He was rash, young, and violent. Headstrong and willful, Johnny could be a cold-blooded killer, and for that reason, LaRoux kept him around.

There were more greetings, the men showing the

respect due their leader. But they didn't stop their stride when they greeted him, like they used to. And they had a lightness in their tone that was more friendly than respectful. It was as though they were beginning to think he was really one of them.

LaRoux blew a stream of smoke and contemplated the thought of actually being part of the rank and file. It was an altogether disturbing thought. The men were filthy, unwashed, and unshaven. And all that drinking and whoring! LaRoux was smart enough to provide plenty of liquor for his men. They got restless without it. And there were the three women who he kept in camp for the men. A year ago the three had been beautiful, but the same slow, creeping dissoluteness that was affecting his men was affecting them. Hard lines were beginning to be permanently etched on the women's faces. They had stopped caring about keeping their gaudy, suggestive dresses in immaculate condition. Spreading their legs for too many men they really didn't know and certainly didn't love had taken its toll.

At least he had Francine. She'd been with LaRoux two months already. She showed the promise of staying as his personal, private paramour perhaps another month. Two on the outside. Then he would turn her out, giving her to his men as a prize. At first it would be just one man, with Francine being the reward for some particularly heroic or violently effective command being followed through. Francine would complain, but she'd follow through with what LaRoux demanded of her because everyone in the camp knew that LaRoux's word was the law, and violating that law meant death. Death quick and

201

painless or death slow and torturous. It didn't matter. The men would all see the execution, and LaRoux would tell them how order had to be maintained, that the only reason they stayed together to fight for the South—even though many of them were too young to actually remember the war firsthand—was because of his masterful command of their skills. The men really weren't soldiers, they were criminals, and LaRoux knew it. But they needed leadership, they needed someone to point them in a direction so their baser instincts could run wild, and LaRoux gave them that direction. And then he'd lead them on a raiding party, making his men believe that he really was one of them—only smarter, that's all.

In a week, the dead man who had been killed by LaRoux or on LaRoux's orders would be completely forgotten.

The men were drinking more than they used to. They were restless, spoiling for a fight. It had been weeks since they'd had a good raid. Nearly two months. No amount of liquor and women could fully satisfy the violent drives that pushed these men on.

And then, as he stopped his horse near the post and started out of the saddle, a thought struck LaRoux with such force he froze, his leg stopping in mid swing over the gelding's rump.

The men were losing their fear of him. It was only as long as they were afraid of his retribution that LaRoux knew he had control over his men.

All the signs were there. And why he hadn't really noticed this earlier, before it had reached what he considered to be an advanced state, he couldn't guess.

"My God!" LaRoux whispered, amazed at himself. "Can this really be?"

"Can what really be, darling?"

Francine, looking pretty as ever in a blue dress with the matching bonnet that LaRoux had picked up for her in Denver City, was waiting for him at the entrance flap of his tent.

"Nothing. I just had a thought, that's all. Nothing for you to worry about."

Even before he was in his tent, LaRoux was making plans to regain the full dictatorial control over his men. And, even more importantly, LaRoux was going to regain his mental acuity. He had allowed himself to get sloppy, he concluded. The men could think him to be "one of them" because the intellectual difference between himself and his men had lessened. It mattered little to him that his mind was still as sharp as the sword he had in his footlocker. All LaRoux could think about was the fact that he wasn't honed to a razor's sharpness intellectually.

A man like LaRoux lived by his wits . . . or died by the lack of them.

He'd get rid of Francine. He'd reward someone with her. Maybe being without a woman for a while would sharpen his mental skills. It was so easy to get by with an obtuse intellect when there really wasn't a war going on. And Francine was doing everything she possibly could to see his every whim and wish were satisfied. She was helping him get soft inside.

LaRoux had let his men get lazy. That was it. He'd let his leadership slip. What he really needed to hone his skills was a new challenge for the men, something really enticing. Something that would require all their most violent skills.

This thought was immediately followed by the mental image of Catherine Weatherly's beautiful, pristine face. Now, she would be a challenge that LaRoux would take joy in! With that white flesh and those high-blown ways of hers, she would be something special that he could parade in front of his men. Miss Catherine Weatherly would be his latest prized bauble. And when the time came to give Catherine to his men — the time for such things, however regrettable, always came — they would know that he had a woman even better, even more beautiful and ardent, waiting in the wings. He had a more beautiful woman waiting for him because he was *General* Jean-Jacques LaRoux, and that was his style.

"Leave me for a while," LaRoux said, moving to his desk. At one time he'd studied maps on the desk. That was during the war, when he was getting fresh intelligence reports by the hour on enemy troop movements. Now the desk held a fine bottle of Kentucky whiskey and a box of cigars. "There is something I need to do."

"But I haven't seen you in so long."

Francine trembled when LaRoux shot a look her way. She had already tasted his wrath when she defied him. LaRoux, without warning, could be utterly vicious. When she had once talked back to him in front of a soldier, he waited until they were in the tent together, then he beat her. He struck her with his fists, hitting her in the arms and stomach and legs, drawing as much pain as he possibly could without damaging the face he loved to look at. When the beating was over, Francine had learned her lesson.

Francine wasn't pleased with being forced to be outside where all those filthy soldiers could surreptitiously look at her—none dared openly gawk at the general's woman—but she didn't have any choice in the matter. As she stepped out of the tent, Francine opened her parasol to protect her skin from the sun.

LaRoux looked over his men in the starlit evening. The tension, the adrenaline pumping in his veins and in the veins of his men, was so thick and potent he could almost taste it in the air.

LaRoux could feel himself getting stronger with each passing second. He felt power growing inside him. He wouldn't again take his leadership for granted.

He gave the order to break camp and for his men to be battle dressed, which, given the impoverishment of the soldiers, only constituted carrying extra supplies of ammunition. Then, as the soldiers began preparing themselves for a night ride, LaRoux took Francine and Josie, the freckle-faced woman who more than a year earlier had been his favorite, into his tent. Francine was jealous when LaRoux brought Josie into the tent, and she was almost openly hostile when he insisted the women touch each other. But Francine's morality was malleable enough to accommodate LaRoux's latest quirks. He was in total command and control—of himself and the men and women around him. LaRoux felt masterful, and Francine could never remember him being so physically active or emotionally detached in bed before.

Francine did not guess that she had just lost her prized position in LaRoux's bed, or that on that night she would sleep with many men.

"All set, sir," Smitty's cheek was swelled out with an enormous wad of tobacco. He had twin Remington revolvers strapped around his hips and was carrying the Winchester rifle LaRoux had given him. A fully loaded bandoleer with ammunition for the Remingtons and Winchester cut a diagonal swath across his chest.

"How are the men?" LaRoux was checking his own weapons as soldiers took down and stored his tent in one of the three wagons.

"Loaded for bear and ready to run."

"Drunk?" In earlier days LaRoux would never have even thought of asking such a question. Now it was necessary.

"Some of the young ones have had a nip or two. Nothing too much."

"Excited?"

"Hell, sir, all of us have been itching for a ride. We've not done much funnin' lately."

"You're right about that, Smitty. But that's changing tonight." LaRoux withdrew his revolver from the crossdraw holster and slowly turned the cylinder, checking the rounds. "Tell me something, Smitty. Do you think Francine is a pretty woman?"

Smitty's eyes narrowed suspiciously. He was not sure of his general's motive for asking such a question. Being a soldier for most of his life had made Smitty cautious of officers, though LaRoux did seem to be more talented than the others he'd served with.

"Well?" LaRoux repeated.

"General?"

LaRoux gave Smitty a smile. It was always a rare thing for him to smile at a soldier, and the significance of it was not lost on Smitty. "After tonight," LaRoux said, his voice low, "I'm giving Francine to you." LaRoux paused and smiled dryly. He never gave anything away. "Provided you prove yourself worthy."

Smitty spit a long brown stream of tobacco juice into the dirt. "Why, that's right kindly of you, sir. Right kindly, indeed."

"You can have her first, but then you've got to share her with the rest of the men."

Smitty mulled that over for a moment. "Fair enough. Hell, I'm a soldier, sir. Ain't it true that a good soldier always shares what he's got with his fellow soldiers?"

"Make one last check on the men. I don't want anything to go wrong tonight. Come back to me when you're done."

"Yes, sir," Smitty said. He saluted smartly before leaving.

LaRoux could feel the power growing inside himself. An energy, like a life force all its own, distinctly separate from the rest of his physical being, was taking control of him. Within the hour he'd be on a night ride with his men, covering ground and hunting for something. His target wasn't important. The power LaRoux had over his men was an aphrodisiac to him, making him strong, whole, complete in himself. His men needed to fight something or they were going to start fighting among themselves. La-

Roux hoped they'd find women. The soldiers craved women in the same way LaRoux craved power.

"Men are all set, sir," Smitty said upon returning.

There was a gleam in Smitty's eyes, placed there by fantasies of himself with Francine.

"Tell the men to mount up."

As a unit, the ragtag band of mercenaries, murderers, criminals, and displaced soldiers slipped into their saddles. Even the horses seemed to smell death in the air.

LaRoux waved a leather-gloved hand and twenty-three men rode into the night.

"Spread the men out," LaRoux whispered to Smitty when they'd reached their destination. "Move in slow and quiet."

The old soldier disappeared into the night, and LaRoux was once again amazed at Smitty's stealth and agility for a man his age. During the war, LaRoux had a dozen men of Smitty's caliber under his command. Solid soldiers every one. All but Smitty had been killed by the Yankees. Smitty was the last of the true professionals LaRoux had in his command.

It was a small caravan, just four Conestoga wagons in all. Four families travelling westward in search of gold or fertile land or God knows what other dreams went through their heads and hearts.

The caravan would be good for LaRoux's army. There were two civilian sentries, each one probably no better trained for such duty than a farmer watching out for the fox who makes nightly sojourns into his chicken coop. Those two men would be the first to die; dying, if all went according to LaRoux's hastily made plans, by a knife. Only the gurgle of a man with his throat slit would be emitted to warn his family and the family of his friends. And that sound, LaRoux knew, wouldn't be enough. By the time the families realized an all-out attack was underway, it would be too late to mount a defensive stand.

Kneeling in the high grass, LaRoux looked overhead. The stars were out, and so was the moon. *Poor fools,* thought LaRoux, looking back to the wagons pulled into a tight circle. They were in the wrong place at the wrong time. For that simple, pathetic reason, they would die. All of them.

LaRoux knew the booty in such an attack would not be much. He had no illusions about the money he'd make. The travellers certainly had little or nothing of value that he would want. If they had money, they wouldn't be seeking out new lands. It was their poverty that they were running away from.

The men, women, and children in the caravan would never know the riches they dreamed of.

The prairie was quiet a moment longer. Then LaRoux sensed movement around him, and it began.

LaRoux stayed out of the foray, watching his plan turn into bloody reality. By the time the first futile shot was fired, the struggle was over. The men were dead or dying, the women fared much worse.

LaRoux watched the carnage from a distance, the scene illuminated by moonlight and a single burning Conestoga. He watched as Johnny scared a young woman from her hiding place beneath one of the wagons. She wore a cheap cotton homemade nightdress. Johnny was much faster and the chase didn't last long. He tackled her to the ground, and other men quickly surrounded the laughing soldier and the screaming girl.

LaRoux turned away. He felt no overriding remorse over what was happening thirty yards away, but he did not have much stomach for voyeurism of this violent nature. His solders were behaving in precisely the fashion he knew they would. Tomorrow, when the debauchery was complete, his men would be stronger, more deadly and powerful, than they were now. The men would sense it in themselves, and they would know that their leader was responsible for their change.

LaRoux pulled out a cheroot and lit it, his back turned to the woman on the ground.

She was screaming very loud. It was a hideous, high-pitched scream of primal horror. LaRoux got to his feet and began walking into the night. He'd wait until it was all over.

Chapter Eleven

A soft knock at the door pulled Shadow away from the book. "Come in, Emma," Shadow called out. She closed the book, leaving a slim finger between the pages to mark her place.

It was not Emma who entered her room. Miss Catherine Weatherly, with barely a trace of malice in her azure blue eyes, took a single, hesitant step into Shadow's bedroom.

"May I please come in?"

What's this about? Shadow silently mused.

"Sure," Shadow said after an uncomfortably long pause. "Why not?"

Catherine frowned at the last comment. She stepped into the room, leaving the door open. "Mind if I leave the door open? We can get a nice breeze going through here if we do."

Shadow was sitting in a chair by the window. She nodded her head. Her eyes, dark and unpenetrable, never left Catherine.

"Are you getting things set up around here the way you want them?" Catherine's tone was light and cheery, but her movements were quick and furtive, her eyes never staying in one place very long and never meeting Shadow's directly. "My, we simply must have Emma cut some fresh lilacs and bring them in here. It'll brighten this room just *so* much." Catherine sat on the edge of Shadow's bed, facing the chair. She leaned toward Shadow, her voice dropping discreetly. "Lilacs will chase out that musty smell. This room hasn't been used in so long. That smell of stale air will go real soon."

"Why are you doing this?"

Catherine reacted as though Shadow had slapped her. Shadow's tone wasn't brittle with suspicion or laced with venom. It was curious and nothing more.

"Doing what?"

"Catherine, you are not a stupid woman. Neither am I. Now, please, tell me what this is about. Why are you here?"

Catherine gave a small huff of resignation and looked away from Shadow. "I thought—I thought that since you're going to be living in this house, we might just as well be friends. I know we didn't start off on the right foot, but you've got to admit that I had an awful good reason to be shocked." She produced a small lace hanky and began to twist it between her fingers. "Maybe we won't become the best friends either of us have ever had in the world, but we don't have to claw each other's eyes out every time we're in a room together."

Shadow looked out the window. What a day! Wake up in Sorren's bed, in Sorren's arms, then make love to him; Emma's declaration she had appointed herself Shadow's mother; and now the grand dame of the MW Circle, Catherine Weatherly, was making the first steps toward calling a truce. Does one person deserve to get a lover, a mother, and a friend all in one day?

"As long as you own one third of the MW Circle, you should do some of the work, right?" Catherine continued. Golden eyebrows arched over playful blue eyes. "You're not going to believe the paperwork it takes to run a ranch this size. It's incredible! Carl's not very good with the books, so I did most of the paperwork when Daddy was—"

Catherine's voice faltered for a moment. Shadow felt unsure of her position and what she should do. Though Shadow and Catherine both had Matthew Weatherly's blood running in their veins, he was really only a father to one of them. Shadow felt it hypocritical to show open remorse—even though she felt it—for the loss of a man she'd never met.

"When Daddy was alive," Catherine continued after a moment. "I did all the stock inventory, handled all the paperwork for buying and selling, and I did the payroll."

"How do you know I can read and write?"

Catherine looked annoyed. She didn't like being on the defensive. She'd spent most of her life without having to justify her behavior. "You were at Father Bradford's. Everybody knows that nobody teaches the Good Book and the three R's like he does. Why, it's some little orphan from Father Bradford's that wins the Denver City spelling bee year after year. Everybody knows that."

213

At last the iron-hand wall of Shadow's defenses gave a slight tremor, which grew into a crack and finally showed itself on her lips as the smallest of smiles. If Catherine's motive was to unload some of her work off on her, Shadow was willing to accept it. She'd never gotten anything without paying a certain price. Why should her inheritance be any different?"

"What would you like me to do?"

"What about payroll? I know it's simply dreadfully boring, but it would be a good place to start. After you get the hang of that, we can move you into more interesting things."

"That sounds fine to me."

Shadow suspected Catherine's sudden good will was motivated more by the desire to avoid work than to get on speaking terms with her half sister, but she didn't mind. If the end result was satisfactory, Shadow was willing to put up with some sibling politics. However, Catherine had never struck Shadow as a lazy woman. Vainglorious? To a fault. But not lazy. It made Shadow wonder.

"When do you want to start? Are you busy now?"

"Not really." Shadow laid the book on the floor at her feet, open and face down. The action drew Catherine's attention.

"That's how Daddy did it, too. Never used a marker to keep his place." An affectionate softness spread across Catherine's face at the gentle memory. "Daddy and Emma used to go round and round over it. Daddy would have open books scattered all over this house. Emma would always pick them up, close them, and return them to the library. She doesn't know how to read or put books in alphabetical order, so she'd just put the books back any old place. Daddy would get so mad! He'd have to hunt and hunt to find the book, and then when he did find it, he'd have to hunt again to find his place."

It gave Shadow an odd feeling inside to be hearing stories about her father. For so many years she'd only imagined what he was like. Now she was learning personal details from a most unlikely source.

Shadow was absurdly pleased that she, like her father, didn't use markers in books. And what other similarities, she could not help but wonder, did she have to her father, Matthew Weatherly?

It was hours later that Shadow sighed, rubbing the back of her neck as she rolled her head on her shoulders. She seemed stiff all over, her muscles tensed and knotted. She also felt mentally exhausted. Going through the payroll records of the MW Circle had made her feel like she was back at Father Bradford's school. The ledgers seemed endless, columns and columns of figures and dates. Each man at the ranch got paid according to the value Matthew had placed on his labor and according to the seniority he'd gained at the MW Circle. Consequently, no two men got paid exactly the same amount.

It was, as Catherine had promised, time-consuming and brain twisting.

At least she told me the truth about something, Shadow thought with a twinge of humor.

Shadow stretched her arms above her head as she entered her bedroom. Her neck and shoulders were so stiff it seemed like she had over exerted herself physically, straining the muscles, though the opposite was the truth. She wasn't accustomed to sitting at a desk for hours on end. She felt like she used to feel as a little girl when she labored over her textbooks at the orphange.

Shadow glanced at her bed. Sleep would be a comfort to her . . . but she'd be sleeping alone tonight.

Soft, pleasing memories drifted across the surface of her mind. Sometimes the memories were embarrassing. She never thought she would be so unrestrained in bed. Under Sorren's exquisite touch, Shadow's body had come alive. The pleasure was of such blinding intensity all the other joys Shadow had known in her life became mere trifles. When she was in Soren's arms, her body trembled with the want of his touch.

Stripping off her dress and petticoat, Shadow hung the garments in her closet. She didn't have anywhere near the number of dresses that Catherine had, but at least she had *something* in the closet now. Seeing her doeskin dress on a wooden hanger brought a smile to Shadow's lips. It was an incongruous sight. A plain, simple, unadorned Kiowan leather dress on a hanger, mixed in with ornately embroidered, hand-trimmed dresses of lace, silk, and velvet.

So much has changed! thought Shadow reflectively. And of all the changes, it was the changes inside herself that most pleased Shadow. Now she *knew* what it was the other young Kiowan women knew. She now shared that secret knowledge. Did the change show on her, like it showed on the women of her tribe? Could people see that she was a woman now? But why, she pondered, hadn't her mother told her anything about it? Loving Sorren was so beautiful.

216

There couldn't possibly be anything wrong in loving him, in taking pleasure from his powerful, gentle body.

Shadow pulled the one nightgown she owned out of her closet and slipped it over her head. The soft silk drifted over her sensual curves. Tailored to her physique, it was more comfortable than the one she'd worn at Sorren's. This one was cut to accommodate the fullness of her breasts and her sweeping hips. Cream-colored lace danced just above her bare feet as she crossed the room to her big, empty bed.

Sweet thoughts of Sorren kept coming to mind. Shadow didn't want to think anymore, only rest. She was mentally exhausted. The enormous responsibilities of running a ranch as large as the MW Circle were staggering. If Sorren were waiting for her, she would not have minded going to bed. But he was four miles away, probably sleeping in his own bed right now.

He's alone, isn't he? Don't do that! Stop thinking that way!

Shadow pulled back the blankets and slipped between the cool white sheets. She hoped that she was tired enough to find sleep quickly. Thoughts of Sorren had kept her from fully concentrating on other matters all day, making mental exercises even more difficult. For now, all she wanted was mindless, thoughtless sleep.

The bed seemed an acre wide. It was big and lonely, and its softness offered Shadow little comfort. Tonight she would sleep with her head on a pillow. Last night she'd slept with her head on Sorren's chest, his arm curled gently and protectively around her shoulders.

Nothing is the same without Sorren, Shadow thought. *This morning I woke up in Sorren's arms. Tomorrow I'll wake up alone.*

She took one of the three pillows on her bed and hugged it tightly to her bosom. The goose down pillow was a poor, lifeless substitute for the virile man she ached to hold, but it would have to do.

Don't think, Shadow told herself. *Just sleep. Sleep and don't dream.*

Closing her eyes, Shadow willed herself to sleep. She pushed Sorren from her mind, but in his place came memories of other men. Memories that were just a year old. Memories still new enough to be hauntingly, agonizingly real in the netherworld of a dream . . .

It came back to her then. The vision. The agonizing memory of that first time when Shadow realized she was not a little girl anymore. Was it just the previous spring?

Graywolf and Little Feather were Shadow's age. When she had found them swimming in the spot she thought was her own secret place, she was at first annoyed, then pleased when they invited her to join them.

As she splashed in the stream with the teenage braves, Shadow did not realize how heady a sensation it was for the young men. Shadow's raw, unintended yet undeniable sensuality had gripped Graywolf's young soul. To see her running on the riverbank, breasts rolling beneath the doeskin dress, strong, naked thighs scissoring, her entire body moving in smooth unison with the universe pulled at Graywolf,

218

teasing him with feelings he did not fully comprehend, making his mind whirl devilishly . . . and violently.

Shadow dove into the water. When she surfaced, laughing, Graywolf stopped breathing. He watched the water running down the front of her body, following the valley of her beautiful breasts. She pushed a few heavy strands of wet hair away from her face. The movement of her hands caused her breasts to rise and strain slightly against her dress, tawny swells of satiny flesh raised and pressed together in what Graywolf saw as a tormenting, unavailable feast.

Shadow was unaware of the impact she had on Graywolf and Little Feather. They had been kind to her, treating her as a friend. But then, tussling with Graywolf, she looked into his eyes. What she saw there frightened her beyond words. She saw no warmth, no compassion. She did not see any emotion that she recognized.

Shadow felt a terror that had never before touched her soul.

She tried to run, but Graywolf caught her at the riverbank, wrestling her to the ground. Shadow struggled with all her might, screaming and kicking. Graywolf was chuckling, his face close to Shadow's, saliva glistening on his lips. She could feel the heat of his breath against her face. Rough, bruising hands pushed her dress up, grabbing at her.

At that moment, when Shadow thought she would die, when she knew that she could never live through a terror this consuming, in the one shining instant when the teenager recognized and understood her defilement would happen and there was nothing she could do to stop it, her thumb ripped into Graywolf's eye.

Graywolf screamed in pain, rolling off Shadow. She ran as fast as her legs could take her, fear propelling her on, wondering whether she had done something wrong and wondering why she had deserved such treatment by two young warriors who had regarded her first as a friend, then as an enemy.

From that point forward, Shadow was never without her knife. The nightmares that followed made each evening a litany of horror as she relived each vile touch against her body, the heat of Graywolf's breath against her face as he writhed above her. Eventually the nightmares stopped becoming a nightly occurrence, but then each time Shadow thought they had stopped altogether, they would return to torment her, to remind her of what had happened and what had almost happened. Shadow could never forget what Graywolf and Little Feather had done no matter how much she wanted to.

They had not taken Shadow's body, but they had taken the night away from her.

Alone in her bedroom, Shadow moaned, struggling to escape her nightmare. In her sleep, those wild eyes, harsh hands, and violating fingers were hurting her as much as they had when it had first happened. She fought the nightmare, struggling to get away from it just as she had struggled to get away from Graywolf.

Chapter Twelve

Shadow bolted upright in bed. *It's just a bad dream,* she thought. As though hearing the sound of her own voice would help, she whispered, "Stop thinking about them. Sorren's not like that."

The sound of her voice was hollow in the bedroom.

Sorren! Sorren! Sorren!

The name rang in her ears.

She had to see Sorren to prove to herself that he wasn't like Graywolf. Sorren McKenna would never force himself upon her.

Don't be silly! It's late! What will Emma say if you go to Sorren now?

When Shadow realized that she was trying to talk herself out of going to Sorren's, she knew she'd already made up her mind. She had to see him. Now. Tonight.

In a moment, the nightgown was pulled over her head and thrown to the floor. Shadow took her doeskin dress from the closet and drew it on. A moment more to slip into her moccasins, then she was flying out of her room and down the hallway.

Shadow stopped to put a bridle on the big roan gelding. She didn't bother with a blanket or saddle. She'd never required a saddle before.

"What in tarnation are you doin'?"

Shadow leaped headfirst onto the roan. When her stomach was against the horse's broad back, she spun sideways to get properly seated. She pinched the roan's ribs with her knees.

"Hey! I'ma askin' you a ques—"

Shadow shot a look at the sleepy old man in long johns who tended the Weatherlys' personal riding stock. She saw the recognition spread across his beard-stubbled face.

"Sorry. Didn't recognize ya at first," he mumbled.

"Hee-yaa!" Shadow shouted, her moccasined heels hitting the roan's flanks.

Horse and rider shot out of the stables at full gallop. Shadow leaned over the horse's neck, her hair, like the roan's mane, dancing in the wind as the pounding hooves thudded against the rich green pasture land, eating up the ground and shortening the distance between Shadow and Sorren with each great stride.

The gelding started to lather. Shadow had picked a good mount. He was big and strong and liked to run.

She eased the horse down to a canter. She kept wanting to push the roan on, but something inside her would not allow her to be cruel to the horse just to satisfy her own needs.

The last mile seemed to take forever.

What if Sorren wasn't alone? What if the woman—or women—who owned the nightgowns in Sorren's bureau was there? She would have heard by now that Shadow had stayed with Sorren during her recovery. Sorren had too many ranch hands who couldn't keep that kind of secret to themselves for the neighbors to not have heard. Sorren's lover who owned the nightgowns would have to see him to restake her claim on him. Shadow could expect no less from her.

Or what if Sorren didn't welcome her intrusion into his night? She could hardly blame him for that, either.

No! He'll want to see me! He'll be ecstatic to see me! a frightened, unsure heart prodded in hopes of gaining confidence.

She first saw the illumination of a lamp burning in a bunkhouse over a late night poker game, then she saw Sorren's massive, empty mansion. The roan sensed Shadow's impatience and picked up speed.

Hope welled up inside Shadow. Unashamed by her own raw need to see Sorren, to touch him and hold him close, she covered the last stretch of ground quickly.

Shadow jumped off the gelding and looped the reins quickly around the hitching post. She leaped onto the porch and tested the door. It was locked. Her palm felt sweaty against the smooth doorknob.

She looked over at the bunkhouses. She didn't want to arouse the ranch hands' curiosity or give them more reason to talk about her and Sorren. If Sorren was upstairs in his bedroom, where she was sure he would be at this time of night, she'd have to pound very hard on the door to get his attention. She certainly couldn't ring the triangle on the porch.

Neither option seemed feasible. Both would draw the attention of too many men, when all she had was one man in mind.

The first window she checked was open slightly. Shadow pushed against the window and it slid up easily. She crawled through, her heart pounding, fully aware that she was doing something wrong but not caring.

She had to see Sorren. She had to see him without waking up his men. This was the only way.

It was something that had never left Sorren, and he doubted it ever would. The ability to awaken instantly from a deep sleep, with the clear-thinking, lucid mind of someone who knows he is hunted.

He rolled out of bed in a smooth motion, landing soundlessly on all fours. He opened a drawer in the bedside table and withdrew a revolver. He thumbed back the hammer, listening for the three distinct clicks to indicate it was completely cocked. Just under one pound of pressure on the hair trigger would fire the Colt.

He walked on the balls of his feet to the side of his closed bedroom door. The assassins would need to come through the door if they were to get to him. It would not be impossible to get through his second-story bedroom window, but it would be difficult. Too chancy a proposition with so many of Sorren's ranch hands sleeping in the bunkhouses nearby.

Sorren wondered who was coming for him. He always knew in the back of his mind that it would happen sooner or later. Someone would recognize him, someone would remember that right after he'd left a Rebel camp it was attacked by the Union army. He had so many people who would want to kill him if they knew all that he had done. Many of his enemies would spend their last dollar to have him killed.

Sorren thought, *This peaceful life has made me weak*.

The intruder bumped into the small table at the stairway landing, the one Emma had placed a potted plant on.

Amateurs, Sorren thought. It was disconcerting to him. A professional insult. He would much rather the person who had found him out had hired an assassin. It would be less personal that way. A business transaction. A point of honor — revenge — would be met without any personal savoring of Sorren's spilled blood. During his years working for President Lincoln and then General Grant, Sorren had done many violent acts, but they were never personal. He was just a soldier, doing what he could to to end a terrible, costly war.

Spreading his feet, he pushed his shoulder against the wall, holding the revolver in both hands, raised to shoulder height. The first man through the door was a dead man. He just didn't know it yet. No matter what happened after that, Sorren told himself, at least the first man through the door was dead. If there was more than one assassin, he'd have to step over his fallen comrade to get to him.

Sorren waited. Logic told him that it had been little more than thirty seconds since he had heard the window slide open. Still, the waiting was unbearable.

He felt it in his knees, in the pit of his stomach. He wanted to action to begin. He wanted to see what would happen.

Now! Come through now! his restless mind demanded.

He was ready and waiting.

It was time for shooting first and asking questions later.

He felt intensely alive.

Sorren was ready.

Shadow waited outside Sorren's bedroom door. She knew she should have announced her presence before this, but she just couldn't find the courage to do it. What if he were angry with her for coming over? Though Shadow didn't know that much about Sorren's past, it was painfully clear to her that his female guests did not stay very long and apparently weren't welcome without an invitation. Shadow sensed that Sorren demanded he write the rules for things like that. It occurred to her then, somewhat ludicrously, that he had not invited her to come back to his home. Shadow didn't want to think of things like that now.

She put her hand on the knob to his bedroom door. Shadow inhaled deeply, summoning up courage she didn't feel.

The worst he can do is throw me out . . . throw me out of his house and his life and cast me back into the emotional cauldron of disappointment and despair. That's the most he can do to me tonight.

She turned the knob slowly, her heart pounding in

her chest, pounding with fear and anticipation.

Slowly, very slowly, she opened the door just a crack. First an inch, then two. She still couldn't see Sorren's bed. One more inch and she'd be able to see him.

What did he look like when he was sleeping? He'd looked at her when she slept, but Shadow had never watched Sorren sleep. Was his face passive and at peace, so dissimilar to what it was like when he was awake and his brilliant mind was moving just a little faster than anyone else's?

Now she saw the bed. The bed was empty. The blankets were mussed. He wasn't there.

The doorknob was jerked out of her hand and the ugly black hole of a pistol muzzle was shoved in her face.

I'm dead, Shadow thought in that split second.

It took a moment for her to see the face behind the pistol was Sorren's.

"Damn you! Goddamn you!" Sorren shouted, recoiling away from Shadow, jerking the gun away from her. He turned sharply, as though he were jolted by some powerful force, and Shadow noticed that he, like herself, was trembling visibly. "Goddamn you! Damn you! Damn you!"

"Sorren—"

He turned on Shadow, his eyes dark and wild and full of fear. "I could have killed you! Don't you realize that? I could have killed you!" Sorren's hands were shaking and he realized, as he set the hammer down softly, that he was losing his killer's instincts. He had held back on the trigger. In earlier days, he would have fired the moment his revolver had found its target. Shooting would have been the smart thing to do.

"I'm sorry," Shadow said, her voice small and pleading for understanding. "I had to see you. I had the most terrible—"

Shadow was shocked when Sorren wrapped his arms around her, hugging her fiercely close, molding her body to his. He hugged her, squeezing the breath from her, holding her with such strength it hurt.

"Promise me you'll never do that again."

Shadow's arms were trapped at her sides. She wanted to hug Sorren back, but she couldn't. He squeezed her a little tighter as he repeated, "You've got to promise me that you'll never do anything like that again."

"I promise."

"My God, Shadow, I could have killed you. Don't you realize that? Please, God, Shadow, don't ever, ever do anything like that again."

Sorren buried his face in Shadow's neck, inhaling the warm, feminine aroma of her. His naked body was still trembling. How close had he come to shooting her? It was a haunting, horrible question to ask himself. For a second time, he had nearly killed her. He felt cold inside. Had she forgiven him for wounding her before? What must she think of him now? It was worse than just feeling empty, he felt guilty. It was a hideous sensation to not know whether he'd shot the woman who'd saved his life. Did she have any concept of how close he had come to shooting her now?

Sorren held Shadow for long moments before he finally asked, into her downy jet-black hair, "What are you doing here?"

Shadow did not fully understand the intense fear she could feel in Sorren's sinewy body. She buried her face in his chest, wrapping her arms around his middle. His flesh felt warm, feverishly so, against her cheek. She kissed his muscled pectoral.

"I—I had a nightmare," she whispered, her voice quivering a little. Later, perhaps, she would tell him the details. Now, all she wanted was to hold him, to be shielded from the world and from her past in the warm, secure embrace of his arms. If she had that tonight, she could handle the problems of her world tomorrow.

"It's okay," Sorren said soothingly, his breathing becoming even again. "Everything is going to be fine. You're with me now and nothing bad is going to happen to you." He shuddered and his arms, like thick bands of steel, squeezed her tighter. "I just lived through a nightmare, too."

Shadow closed her eyes, fighting against tears that wanted to spill forth. She was in his arms now. She was holding Sorren and that was what had driven her through the night.

"Promise me you'll never hurt me," Shadow said as tears pooled in her brown eyes. "Please, Sorren, promise me that you'll never be mean to me."

"I promise. My God, precious, don't you know by now that I would never—"

"Promise me!"

"I promise you, Shadow. I promise that I'll never, never ever, do anything to hurt you."

It was all that Shadow wanted and needed to hear. He was not like Graywolf and Little Feather. He would not force himself upon her, no matter how great his desire for her. She was certain of that now. She heard the truth in his words and in his tone, and she felt the truth of it in his arms. Sorren McKenna was not capable of that kind of evil.

They stood for silent minutes at the doorway of Sorren's bedroom, clinging to each other. It was as though both were afraid to be the first to break the embrace. Shadow played her hands over Sorren's back, hugging him, feeling his leathery muscles. He was naked, but she did not think of him in a sexual way, though in the past such close proximity to him had fired her desires.

"Can I stay here tonight?" Shadow asked in a whisper.

"Of course you . . . what about what people will say?"

"Sorren, I don't care what people say. I want to be near you, with you. Can't you see that that's all that matters to me?" Shadow eased herself out of Sorren's arms. She held his strong, lightly calloused hands, looking up into his devastatingly handsome face. She saw the last traces of what had been fear still in the corners of Sorren's eyes. "Hold me while I sleep," Shadow whispered. She hated her need to feel him, to be comforted by him, but she was helpless against her want.

Sorren led her to his bed. Shadow stripped off her doeskin dress, dropping it to the floor as she kicked off her moccasins. She slid into the bed beside Sorren, sighing softly when his arm went around her shoulders.

"This is what I wanted," she whispered

into Sorren's chest.

Sorren had never slept with a woman before without making love to her first. He sensed that Shadow did not have loving on her mind when she rode through the night to him. She had needed something else entirely. It mystified him when he did not try to seduce Shadow, when he didn't try to make love to her before she drifted to sleep. That just wasn't like the man everyone knew Sorren McKenna to be.

He was experiencing so many different feelings when he was with Shadow. He didn't react to her like he had with all the women of his past. Sorren McKenna found it a curious phenomenon, and it comforted him in small put important ways.

He kissed the top of Shadow's head, pulled her a little tighter against his chest, and squeezed her leg for a moment between his own, then she went gently to sleep.

Emma's emotions were mixed, chaotic. She didn't know whether to feel happy, sad, disappointed, or betrayed.

The commotion started with the sound of a horse riding at full gallop away from the MW Circle. Emma, who just happened to be awake at the time, saw in the dim starlight the gleam of a strong, naked thigh and the swirl of endless ebony hair. It would be absurd to believe it was anyone other than Shadow.

Emma sent John, her husband, to the stables to find out what had happened. When he returned, his obvious good humor was infuriating Emma.

"She was ridin' like the wind, headin' straight as an

arrow to Mr. McKenna's," John said. He stepped up behind Emma, sliding his hands around her enormous middle. "Seems as though you ain't lost your touch none for matchmakin'."

Emma refused to turn away from the window. She was not unmindful of her husband's hands touching her softly through the voluminous cotton nightdress.

"Don't you be jokin' none about this, John." Emma shook her head sadly. "I thought I taught that Mr. McKenna better than that." Emma turned inside her husband's hands. Her round eyes were dark and accusing. "It ain't my Shadow who's to blame here, John. It's that Mr. Sorren! He's the one gots her all crazy inside. It's all you men that makes us good womenfolk crazy inside."

"Now don't go talkin' this personal." John squeezed Emma a little tighter. She wriggled in his arms, turning away from him and toward the window again. "You ain't responsible for what Mr. McKenna and Miss Shadow does. That Mr. Sorren was full grow'd before you started motherin' him."

"Don't make no difference," Emma replied sullenly, staring out into a warm, vast, beautiful evening sky. "I shoulda had my mark on the boy by now. I don't know nothin' if I don't know how to mother."

Emma could feel her husband chuckle, and despite herself, she sensed her anger dissipating slowly.

"They ain't doing this to spite you," John explained in a deep baritone voice that softly rumbled through the bedroom. " 'Sides, ain't you the one who's been throwin' 'em together every chance you could?"

"John, are you blamin' me 'cause them children got swallowed up by the dark side?" Emma's tone was hard-edged and accusatory. "You know I wouldn't do that!"

John was not accepting the seriousness of the situation. The more humor he found in it, the more angry Emma was getting, her ire turning away from Shadow and Sorren, getting redirected to her husband.

"Dang fool kids," Emma muttered miserably. "Turn your back on 'em for one second an' they can't help but find themself some mischief."

"Now there ain't nobody sayin' there's blame to go round." John moved fractionally closer to his wife of many years. "Ain't nobody sayin' that at all. You always a talkin' 'bout the devil's dark side, but I don't recall you bein' so dead set against it for yourself."

"Don't you go blamin' me for the dark side, John Elijah!" Emma snapped crisply. "I didn't know nothin' 'bout it 'til I met you!"

"Don't you remember when we was just kids? Come on now, Emma, it weren't *that* long ago." John's fingertips played lightly over Emma's stomach, straying slightly but never moving too high or low. "Now my memory o' those days says there weren't much fun at all. Seems like we was just livin' in the night, the dark side upon us so heavy we couldn't see nothin' in this ol' world but each other." John inched forward, his body nearly touching his wife's. She rocked back on her heels a little, ending the distance that separated them. "Ain't always the man whose got the dark side in 'im. Sometimes it's the ladies. Even fine, proper ladies like you and Miss Shadow. You can't go a blamin' Mr. McKenna. He's home jus' mindin' his own business."

"He's still to blame." Emma's tone was softer. She sounded distracted. Though she looked out at the stars, her mind was divided between the work-roughened, gentle hands touching her, the familiar voice flowing through her, and loving memories both old and new.

"Now maybe you're right an' maybe you're wrong. I'm only sayin' maybe and ain't saying so. But maybe that Miss Shadow is a fine, proper lady, the kind of lady we always wanted for a baby girl ourselves. Maybe she's jus' as right as rain, but she's got herself a powerful need to see her man." The pressure between them increased when Emma leaned more firmly into the broad, enormously powerful expanse of her husband's chest. She put a hand over John's, pressing his palm a bit more firmly against herself. "Now that Mr. McKenna's a tomcat. I won't lie to my missus 'bout that. But jus' maybe he's been tomcattin' so much 'cause he ain't never met Miss Shadow 'til now. Maybe this Miss Shadow—right proper young lady that she is—is jus' the medicine to cure that boy's fever. An' maybe that Mr. Sorren wouldn't even a know'd how right Miss Shadow was if you hadn't o' flung 'em together playing your matchmakin'."

Emma closed her eyes. She could feel John's chest moving as he breathed. The touch of him, even after all these years, was exhilarating.

"The dark side—" John continued after a brief pause, the motion of his hands now moving in slowly expanding circles, "the dark side ain't always gotta be somethin' bad. It's the dark side that brung us our boys. An' look at them." There was pure pride in

234

John's tone, pride laced smoothly with amorous feelings toward the mother of his sons. "Dark side can't be bad if somethin' so right comes of it."

Emma inhaled deeply when her husband's hands simultaneously moved higher and lower. "John," she whispered, her voice so soft he had to tilt his head and bend down to hear. "John . . . is the dark side upon you?" She felt him nod his head, his rough cheek against her smooth one. Emma slipped her hand inside her husband's and led him to the big, comfortable bed they'd gotten as a gift from Matthew Weatherby.

Shadow woke first. A rush of emotions went through her with the dawning of clear consciousness. It all came back to her. The hideous nightmare of her attack by Graywolf and Little Feather. The wild ride through the night. The single moment when she thought she would die from Sorren's own revolver. And then Sorren holding her close, whispering love words to her, stroking her back and shoulders. With the knowledge that she was safe inside Sorren's arms, sleep had come quickly, gently enveloping her, soothing her fears and giving her the comfort she so desperately needed.

She did not know that sleep did not come to Sorren for hours. He had felt the pressure of his finger against the hair trigger of his nightstand Colt. He knew, even if Shadow did not, how close he had come to squeezing the trigger.

They had separated during the night, Shadow moving more toward the middle of the bed. Sorren lay on his back, his right hand under his head, his left hand out, reaching for Shadow even in sleep. She twisted slowly onto her side, mindful not to wake the sleeping man beside her.

The dangerous edge to Sorren wasn't with him as he slept. At least Shadow couldn't see it in his face. He seemed at peace with himself and his world. Perhaps it was just because she couldn't look into his eyes. It was always Sorren's dark, piercing gaze that let Shadow know how intense he was. She recalled seeing him for the very first time in Angie's, during the standoff with those foul men so late at night. Though Sorren's posture gave the appearance of a man thoroughly at ease, it was his eyes, black as midnight and sharp as the edge of a razor, that had shown the inner, precise, rapid workings of his mind. And again when Shadow saw him in her father's study for the reading of the will, it was only Sorren's eyes that had given away his mental acuity.

The lines that ran from the corners of his nose to the edges of his mouth weren't so deep now. Shadow wondered if Sorren would ever be at ease enough with her while he was awake to look like this. Peaceful. That was it. If she had to think of a single word to describe Sorren McKenna at this very moment, she would use the word *peaceful*. It seemed an odd concept to her to think of Sorren that way. Until this moment, *peaceful* was about the last word she ever would have used in conjunction with the man.

During the night Sorren had sprouted a shadowy growth of beard. *I'll bet he has to shave every day,* thought Shadow. Shadow realized how little she really knew about this man. She reflected how Kiowan men

236

have little or no beard growth. In a strange way, this helped to define for her how far she had come recently. She was years away, or so it seemed, from her Kiowan tribe and from Father Bradford's orphanage and school. In her closet at the MW Circle were dresses that had cost her as much money as she usually made from her sale and trade of furs in a year, or more.

It was then that Shadow remembered that she'd left her knife behind in her haste to see Sorren. Her knife was her protection against a hostile world. But she'd left it without a thought, her fear unable to make a connection between Sorren and the need for defense. She liked that and smiled sleepily.

Is this the way I'm supposed to feel? Is this what love is? she wondered.

Shadow wasn't sure. Her brows pushed together in thought. Love. What she felt didn't seem like love. At least not like the concepts of love she had grown up with. Her mother had loved a man, and because of that love she was cast out from her tribe, hated because of her love. Her mother had made love to a man, and the product of that union was an illegitimate child that was held in scorn by the tribal council.

She wondered if Sorren knew what her name really meant. If he did, would it make any difference to him? How strong was his need for social acceptance? Shadow had never reconciled in her own mind the need to belong to something greater than herself. She could not say why she had stayed close to her tribe when she got nothing tangible from the relationship other than derision.

Stop questioning everything! a sleepy mind gently chided. *Didn't Sorren prove last night that you can trust him? Didn't he know — without you having to tell him — that you just wanted to be held? He's not like the others! He's not like anyone else!*

Shadow remembered their night of lovemaking. Even in her semiconscious, sleepy state of mind, it brought back a warmth of memories that made the surface of her skin tingle. Sorren had made love to her many times, each time more pleasing than the next. He'd brought her senses to the summit of ecstacy time after time, forcing Shadow up into the world where nothing existed but her body. Her body and Sorren's, joined together by something much greater than their own bodies.

It occurred to Shadow, in a half-humorous way, that she had a new teacher. She'd traded in Father Bradford, who had taught her how to read and write and think, for Soren, who had taught her how to make love like a woman. No, that wasn't quite true. She wasn't making love like a woman. She responded to Sorren making love to her. And though it appeared as though the emotions going through Sorren were as intense and powerful as those going through Shadow, she didn't really make love *with* Sorren. She responded to him and covetously accepted his lovemaking, but he was the one making love. She was the one who received his love. She accepted his skill as a child would a gift; passionately, but selfishly and passively.

*Will he tire of making love *to* me?*

Shadow had spent just one night of making love. It was clear that Sorren had spent many, many nights making love. Would the teacher become bored with

238

his pupil, however infatuated he was with her body now?

"Hmmm," Shadow murmured aloud. She was a bit more awake now, and the more she thought about making love with Sorren, the more she realized how she had taken glory in his desire to please her but had done nothing really in return.

What have I ever done to make him happy? she wondered. Words came back to her, whispered words in a darkened room that slithered erotically across the surface of a passion-fogged mind. *What do you want? Tell me what you like? Does this feel good? God, you're beautiful. So beautiful. Precious . . . my precious.*

In her mind, Shadow heard Sorren's whispered voice, deep with passion, heavy with desire for her.

Sorren's extended hand was very near Shadow's face, just above her head. She moved slightly and kissed his palm. His fingers curled a little. She kissed his wrist and again the fingers curled softly into the palm, as though he were caressing Shadow's silky hair.

She watched the rise and fall of Sorren's chest as he breathed softly. A tremor went through her as she remembered what it had felt like to have his chest pressed against her breasts, feeling the pounding of his great heart beating so close to her own.

Are his nipples excitable, like mine? It was a curious thought. Shadow realized she really knew very little about Sorren's body. *Does his body come alive when it is touched?* Shadow had certainly touched Sorren, but she hadn't really *caressed* him. Not in the same way that he caressed her. She touched him and held onto him as he made love to her, but she didn't really caress him. She was just now beginning to sense the difference. She felt selfish and a little insecure.

The white sheet was at Sorren's stomach, stopping Shadow's gaze. A thin peninsula of hair grew upward on Sorren's stomach from regions below, the hair growing to his navel like an arrowhead. Shadow, a sleepy smile curling that mouth that had received so many sweet kisses of late, came to the realization that she could now, for the first time, objectively study Sorren's body.

She curled her knees beneath her and sat upright slowly, careful not to jostle the bed or awaken Sorren. If this was to be done in a thoughtful manner, he had to leave her alone. She never could think straight when he started touching her and those damnable dark eyes of his began igniting the fires of desire within her.

No, this has to be done, done now, done while Sorren sleeps. It is the only possible way.

That, anyway, was Shadow's logic as she very carefully took the sheet between her first fingers and thumbs and gently peeled it back until she had exposed Sorren to the middle of his calves.

He tells me I'm beautiful all the time, but what do I ever say to him? Do I tell him how beautiful his body is to me?

It bothered Shadow that she had not, in fact, told Sorren how incredibly handsome he was. He complimented her continuously when they were making love, telling her she was precious, telling her how magnificent he thought her breasts were, her legs, her thighs, how he loved the touch of her waist-length hair against him. But she never said much in return, too afraid that she would say something wrong,

240

something that would destroy the loving golden mood that Sorren had created for them.

She caressed Sorren with her eyes, feeling a kind of illicit pleasure in what she was doing.

He really is a lion, she thought, looking at how the muscles in Sorren's powerful legs rippled the surface of his skin even though his body was completely relaxed. She decided that Sorren had spectacular legs. The thighs were thick with muscles that tapered in at the knees, then the calves swelled out again. They were the legs of a man who'd spent much of his life on a horse.

Her eyes travelled upward and a shiver went through Shadow. It was this body that had shown her a pleasure so all-consuming she now judged everything else by that pleasure. With a gentle, inquisitive hand, she reached for Sorren, taking him into her grasp. Sorren's phallus twitched, eliciting a soft, throaty purr from Shadow.

Shadow's fingers curled tentatively around him. She felt him grow in her hand, the warmth of him seeming to go through her palm to spread throughout her body.

"What the—?"

Shadow recoiled from Sorren, sitting back on her heels. A look of guilt spread spontaneously across her face. She was oblivious to how she appeared to Sorren, sitting on her knees, her naked body hidden only by all that long ebony hair that flowed over her shoulders and breasts down to her thighs.

"I didn't!" Shadow began, not sure if she had done anything to warrant an apology but feeling as though she should.

She received a sleepy smile from Sorren. He reached for her, and in that instant, she realized she had done nothing wrong. It was Shadow who caught Sorren's wrist this time, stopping his hand just short of her. Seeing the playfulness in Sorren's dark, lidded eyes was all the reassurance she needed to continue.

"Come on," Sorren coaxed, trying without much effort to pull his wrist out of Shadow's grasp. He reached for her with his right hand and she caught that, too.

"Don't," Shadow replied. She leaned forward, trapping Sorren's wrists to the mattress above his head. The move brought her forward, hovering above Sorren. Her hair tickled his stomach, the tips of her breasts brushing against his flesh to draw another purr of contentment from Shadow. "This is a very scientific experiment," Shadow said, her voice filled with false sincerity, carrying an undercurrent of amusement and amorous anticipation. Very sternly she added, "Just lay there and be quiet."

"Shadow, you may not have noticed this about me before, but not being in on the action isn't something I'm accustomed to." Shadow's heavy breasts hung inches above Sorren's face, tantalizingly close. He raised his head and caught one nipple between his lips, putting his tongue in motion against the tip. His beard stubble was rough but not unpleasant against her soft flesh.

"Ohhh! Now stop that," Shadow chided. She did not, however, pull away.

Continuing to hold onto Sorren's wrists, Shadow arched her back. She swayed, stretching her voluptuous body, moving as a cat does upon awakening. She rolled her head back on her shoulders, swilling in the erotic emotions and feelings going through her. Twisting her shoulders, she fed Sorren her other breast. She licked her lips to moisten them. She was rapidly losing control of her senses. "I'm serious now, Sorren. This is a very scientific experiment, done under the most . . . um . . . ideal situation." Sorren continued with what he was doing, paying only partial attention to what the young woman was saying. "You see, sir, it's simply not fair that you continue making love to me when I actually never make love to you."

Sorren's head dropped back to the bed. He looked into Shadow's eyes, not understanding what she was saying.

"There, at last I have your attention. Now as I was saying, it simply is not fair of me to continue receiving your considerable skill at lovemaking when I, in truth and in fact, do little more than simply receive your skill. The cold, hard facts—"

"Warm," Sorren quickly corrected.

"Whatever." Shadow was swaying from side to side, moving so that her breasts rubbed softly across the hard-muscled surface of Sorren's chest. "Anyway, what I'm trying to say is that if I am to learn how to make love, it is clear that you must leave me alone." Again Shadow received a quizzical look from Sorren. She was enjoying this game. "The problem is that every time you touch me, I . . . well . . . I lose control of my intellectual faculties. That is very . . . entertaining, but hardly conducive to learning."

Shadow released her grip on Sorren's wrists. Her fingertips trailed lightly down his forearms. Her ebony eyes were smouldering, locked onto Sorren's hungry gaze. "Please, Sorren, indulge me just once and do what I ask of you without arguing." Shadow's hands moved over Sorren's neck, down to his chest. She touched his nipples lightly with her thumbs. "Are yours sensitive, too? Sensitive like mine?" She kissed him there and felt the rumbling groan of pleasure come from his chest. "Oh, I see they are." Shadow moved lower. The hard length of Sorren's erection slipped between her breasts. Her heart skipped a beat. He was fiercely aroused. Her fingertips went across Sorren's stomach, touching him light as a feather. "Now surely a man of your intellectual ability can understand how important it is for"—Shadow inhaled deeply, grasping Sorren, struggling to maintain the steady, even tone in her voice—"the untutored to experiment. It's the only way I'll ever learn to please you."

Shadow studied Sorren for a moment, battling against her own rioting senses. He had bunched the blankets up in both hands. His legs were taut, the muscles in his powerful thighs knotted and flexed. His stomach was rippled with muscles like a washboard. She brought her hand up and down. She watched his throat work as he swallowed dryly. Shadow released her tender hold on him.

"Just relax, Sorren," Shadow whispered. "Just close your eyes and relax."

Shadow took one thigh between her hands and kneaded the taut muscles, pressing her fingers into the hard flesh. She did the same to his other thigh, then worked down to the calf. Satisfied with her work, she moved higher on the bed and massaged the muscles in Sorren's shoulders, biceps, and forearms. She pushed her thumb into his palm, working it in a circular motion.

"Just relax, just relax, close your eyes and let your mind wander," she purred.

Sorren closed his eyes. And though he was able to unknot the muscles in his arms and legs, he was most definitely not relaxed.

When Sorren gave the outward appearance of calm, Shadow again took him into her softly trembling hands. She was, as she was so often with Sorren, both frightened and curious. Leaning forward, her breasts straddling one heavily muscled thigh, she kissed Sorren softly.

"Tell me," she whispered, her breath warm against the moist spot on Sorren where her lips had been, "if this feels good."

She took him in deeply, and Sorren McKenna began to shiver.

Chapter Thirteen

Reason told Sorren that this type of feeling couldn't last forever. He'd been in lust with women before, and the lust never really lasted very long. But Shadow wasn't like any of the women he'd ever known. She was *nothing* like the women he'd known in his past.

He kissed her lustrous mane of ebony hair and slipped out of her grasp. "Much as I hate to say it," he said, kicking his feet over the edge of the bed, turning away from Shadow, "it's time we got out of bed."

Shadow watched Sorren walk to the closet. His buttocks drew her gaze and she blushed a little, feeling positively sinful in the pleasure she took in looking at her lover.

When Sorren was standing at the entrance to his closet, Shadow quickly jumped out of bed. There was no comfort in his big bed when he wasn't there with her.

Sorren took a summer-weight dressing robe from a

hook on an inside wall and slipped his arms into it. He pulled the rope sash tight, knotting it around his waist.

"Do you have something for me to put on?" Shadow asked as innocently as she could, standing naked in front of Sorren.

"I'm sure I've got something."

Together they spotted the mauve dressing gown. It was beautiful and feminine . . . and the possession of some woman Shadow resented with all her heart and soul. She would rather walk around Sorren's great mansion naked than wear another woman's robe.

Sorren looked at Shadow and gave a shrug of his wide shoulders. He couldn't hide his past and he couldn't change it. He could, however, do something about his future.

"I'll pick a robe up for you today," Sorren said quietly, but without apology.

"I'll find something." Shadow turned away from Sorren, not wanting him to see the disappointment on her face. "Do you like coffee?"

"Can't wake up without it," Sorren answered. Shadow glanced over her shoulder at him, her eyebrows raised in mock amazement. "Well, not usually." Sorren cleared his throat. "I'll make us a pot. Meet you downstairs in the kitchen."

When Sorren was gone, Shadow went through his closet, looking for something to wear. She would *not* wear The Other Woman's robe, and the only other robe Sorren had in the closet was a winter-weight robe for himself. It was much too warm for that one, even if it was Sorren's.

She went to the dresser and pulled open a drawer. Inside was a stack of fresh silk shirts. She touched the shirts. They were soft, expensive, immaculately tailored. She picked one up and pressed it on her face. The silk was gentle and smelled fresh and clean.

Shadow was just about to put on one of the shirts when she spied, on the overstuffed chair near the bedroom door, the clothes that Sorren had worn the day before. He'd tossed them on the chair before going to bed. Shadow abandoned the dresser and picked up the discarded black silk shirt. She pressed the garment to her face and inhaled again. She smelled the faint aroma of burnt tobacco . . . and Sorren.

Slipping her arms into the silk shirt, Shadow pulled it on, a smile of absolute pleasure crossing her face. The shirttails came down low in the front and back, to about mid thigh. At the sides, where the shirttails were not as long, it came to a point at the tops of her thighs. She buttoned the shirt quickly and rolled the sleeves up several times.

The shirt felt better than the nightgown that she'd worn before, even though both were made of silk. The shirt was much more like her doeskin dress; it didn't have anything slapping against her legs as she walked.

Shadow left Sorren's bedroom, pausing at the door to look at the rumpled bed, smiling inwardly at her own daring, her body tingling with the illicit satisfaction she'd taken in seeing Sorren's total abandonment to her.

* * *

Sorren got the fire burning in the stove and put the water on for the coffee. He felt superbly happy. It was quietly disconcerting to him that his happiness was only partially due to the amorous experimentation Shadow had relished upon him for more than an hour.

She's definitely different, thought Sorren as he measured out the coffee, using less grounds than usual. She might not like it as strong as he did, he decided. In a thoroughly uncharacteristic way, Sorren McKenna wanted desperately to please Shadow in every manner possible. Though pleasuring women was one of Sorren's avocations—his skill at such pursuits was whispered about in polite and not-so-polite company—his desire to please had previously ended with the consummation of lovemaking.

As he spooned the coffee into the water, which was nearly at a boil, Sorren made a mental note to get rid of the robe he'd purchased for Nancy. He'd also have to get rid of the nightgowns. Shadow's disapproval, her profound disappointment at seeing the evidence of other women in his life, had bitten deeply into Sorren's conscience.

What in hell am I doing with a virgin, anyway? a part of his mind inquired, the pre-Shadow part of his mind that knew a man like Sorren McKenna was monumentally unsuited, socially and emotionally, for settling down with a single woman. It was this part of his mind that cruelly amended the *virgin* part of the thought. Shadow's innocence had been lost, not entirely without reservation, to his years of experience and smooth, practiced charm. *She never had a chance,* a cruel mind taunted.

When he heard the soft rap of knuckles at his front door, Sorren welcomed the intrusion. He needed to stop thinking so much about the way his life had been and how different his world now seemed with Shadow so deeply involved in it.

He opened the door, unmindful of the light knee-length robe he wore. His foreman, Nelson, was standing there with a pained expression in the set of his mouth and in his eyes. It was more than just troubles with the men or with the cattle and horses. Sorren could tell that in a glance.

"What happened?" Sorren asked, cutting through whatever preamble Nelson might have put forward.

"It was a massacre," Nelson began. "Thought you'd want to know." He shifted his feet, taking his hat off and squeezing the curled brim in his hands. "About fifteen miles or so south of God's Grace. Four families. All of them dead." Nelson gave Sorren a soulful, sorrowful look. "You should have seen the bodies. They weren't just killed, they were massacred. Bodies with ten and twenty holes in them. The women, too."

"The women?" Sorren left the question unstated.

"Yeah. They all were—"

"Okay, you don't have to give me all the details about that." Nelson looked gratified that it wasn't requested of him. "Any posse go after them?"

"No. There wasn't much to go on." Nelson took a pouch of tobacco and some papers from a shirt pocket. He spilled much of the tobacco as he tried to roll a cigarette. Sorren took the makings from him and quickly rolled two cigarettes, lighting both of them with Nelson's offered match. "They were awful, Mr. McKenna. Downright awful. I was in town this morning picking up the new hitch for the busted chuckwagon when the bodies were brought in. I couldn't help myself, Mr. McKenna, I just had to look. Nothing like that's happened around these parts in years."

"Who found the bodies?"

"Stage coming from Denver City." Nelson inhaled deeply on his cigarette and grimaced. The taste had gone foul on him. "I'm not a weakling, Mr. McKenna. You know that. I've seen my share of death and such. But I've never seen anything like that before. 'Cept in the war. What kind of animals kill like that?"

"Why wasn't there a posse?"

"They followed the stage trail. There's no way to tell whose prints are whose. And nobody is real anxious to tangle with them."

"Were the horses shod?" This answer was vital.

"The horses were shod."

"That rules out an Indian attack."

"We haven't had trouble with the Kiowas or Apaches in some time." Nelson dragged on his cigarette again, then flicked it off the porch. "The redskins leave us alone and we do the same with them."

"Talk to me," Sorren persisted, trying to balance the line between commiserating with the good-hearted Nelson's feelings of sorrow and his own need to know exactly what happened. "What else can you tell me?"

"I wasn't thinking so clearly after I saw the bodies," Nelson continued hesitantly. "Good Lord, Mr. McKenna, one of the women looked like she was only a girl. A little girl." Nelson had had a daughter once, now dead. He looked like he was going to be sick. "What else did you hear?" Sorren's eyes darkened, his face set sternly now. "Think, damn it! I need to know everything!"

"They're not rightly sure of how many there was. They know they had two wagons with them. It was lots of men—all knives, no guns." He paused. "They cut letters into each body, Mr. McKenna, like they were branding cattle."

Sorren felt his insides tighten up. LaRoux. Only Jean-Jacques LaRoux killed that way. Only LaRoux would have his men attack a wagon train of poor families. The man Sorren McKenna had refused to hunt and kill. A whisper of guilt began to creep into his conscience. Because he had refused to do what it was he was so capable of doing, however, distasteful he found it personally, because he had refused to do what he had done before, four families were raped and murdered.

"Can you think of anything else that you saw or heard?" Nelson shook his head. "Thank you, Nelson. You've been very helpful. I'm sorry to have grilled you." Sorren smiled wanly in sympathy with his foreman. "Why don't you take the day off?"

"I can do my job, Mr. McKenna. I don't need—"

"Don't take it as an insult. You've just seen something that no man should ever have to see. Take the day off. Get drunk. Go to Beth Ann's. Do whatever it is you have to do to erase what you've just seen from your mind." Sorren put his hand on Nelson's shoulder. "Trust me, I know what I'm talking about. If you tried to work, your mind wouldn't be on the job. We both know that that's a good way of getting

252

stomped by one of the maverick horses. I've had to do the same myself on occasion. The only thing to do is erase it from your mind. Do it now before the memories are permanent. It's important to me because soon you'll be in charge. For a little while, I think. Maybe longer. I need you thinking clearly."

Sorren was lying a little. When he had seen massacres and human savagery during the war, he didn't have the option of getting howling drunk to forget the horrors of war. He was too much an integral part of those horrors, and his position within both the Rebel and Yankee armies was too tenuous for him to accept the solace of an alcohol-dulled mind.

He was paying for those memories now. Sometimes at night they came back to him, stark in their clarity, haunting and real to him. It was those memories, Sorren believed, that made it impossible for him to sleep more than four or five hours a night.

When Sorren returned to the kitchen, he found his coffee boiling over.

"Damn it to hell!" he hissed through clamped teeth. Sorren grabbed a towel and used it to move the pot from the burner.

"Such language so early in the morning!" Shadow said through a smile, stepping barefooted into the kitchen.

Sorren glanced over at Shadow. He was surprised to see her wearing one of his shirts. Under other circumstances, she would have been bewitching in the black silk. But Sorren couldn't think of things like that now. Not even if he wanted to. Shadow got up on tiptoes to kiss him and he turned his cheek to her.

The full knowledge that he, Sorren McKenna, a

man who prided himself above all else in doing the *right* thing, had turned his back on his President, ignored his own skills, pretended he had no responsibility to his neighbors, was burning like wildfire inside him.

Four families were horrifically murdered. All because Sorren McKenna was trying to pretend that he wasn't really the man the President thought him to be, the man he really was. Sorren could not, no matter how ardently he tried, turn his back on his past or ignore a future that now seemed preordained. He couldn't hide from his past in the arms of women he hardly knew. He couldn't even hide from his past in Shadow's arms. What was it the President had called him? "A criminal with a conscience" were Lincoln's words. Was the President right? Was he, as Lincoln had accused, a necessary evil in times of war. Wasn't there ever going to be a time when there were no wars to fight? Could Sorren ever be more than just a man with a gun?

"The cups are up there," Sorren said, nodding his head toward the cupboard. He took a towel and wiped at the coffee.

Shadow took two heavy glass cups and set them on the small breakfast table. She sensed a difference in Sorren's mood, and something warned her to be still and listen and watch. Shadow tucked the tail of the black silk shirt under her as she sat on one of the straight-backed, hard wooden chairs.

Sorren poured the coffee through a tight metal mesh screen, filtering out the grounds as the rich brown liquid flowed into the two cups.

He placed the coffee pot back on the stove, not

knowing what to say to Shadow. What could he say to her? He had to leave quickly, before the trail got cold. He had killing to do. He was Sorren McKenna, hunter of men.

What was he doing with an innocent woman— nearly a child—like Shadow, anyway?

There was an assignment for him, a ugly task that he'd turned his back on before, that was calling to him. The longer he waited, the worse his chances were of finding LaRoux and his soldiers. What he would do when he found LaRoux was another matter entirely.

An irrational thought shot through Sorren: Perhaps this was the last time. If he hurried—and lived—he could be back home within the week, hugging Shadow and watching her while she slept beside him in his huge bed. He stiffened, absently wiping the stove. He was a fool. There were hundreds of men like LaRouox. It would never end for Sorren.

"Sit down with me," Shadow said, her voice warm with affection, just above a whisper. She crossed her legs femininely at the knee, tugging Sorren's shirt down her thighs modestly. Sorren was continuing to wipe the stove, his back toward Shadow. "Honey, please sit down with me."

Sorren turned slowly. When his eyes met Shadow's, they were cold. The warmth that had been there while they were in bed together was gone now. He was in a dozen different ways an entirely different man. Sorren sat in the chair kitty-corner to Shdow's and picked up his cup. The coffee was weaker than he liked.

Shadow reached out and placed her hand over Sorren's. She smiled at him. "What's wrong? You seem . . . distant."

Sorren shook his head. What could he tell her? That his refusal to kill General LaRoux had caused the deaths of four families? That he was going to hunt LaRoux as soon as possible? That he was going to kill LaRoux just as he would a rabid dog? Whatever he told Shadow, if it were the truth, she could never understand. No one ever did. Sorren felt a profound sense of alienation, of self-imposed isolation. Then he felt guilty for feeling this way.

"Honey, you can talk to me," Shadow persisted. "Something is bothering you. Can't you tell me about it?"

"Nothing is bothering me." Sorren's words came out icy and he knew it. Lying to Shadow felt terrible. Especially when he was doing it this badly. And when did she start calling him *honey?* "I can't talk about it. It's just something from long ago, that's all."

"A woman? Sorren, I know something of your past." Shadow squeezed Sorren's hand lightly, wishing that the jealous twinges she felt tingling inside her would go away. She knew she couldn't change the fact that Sorren had slept with a great many women. She couldn't be the only woman in his past, so she was resolved to be the only woman in his future.

"It's not a woman." Sorren stared at the coffee swirling in his cup. He sipped the coffee without tasting it. "It's not that at all. You don't understand."

"I might understand if you'd talk to me."

"Drop it, will you?" Sorren snapped with brittle anger. "It's my business, not yours."

Shadow took her hand from Sorren's, stung by his words. "Then keep it all to yourself. I mean, it's not exactly like you and I have any reason to talk, is it? We've never shared anything, have we?"

Sorren stood, turning his back on Shadow. "Don't do this to me now," he said without looking at her, crossing the kitchen to where his tin of tobacco and papers were. "I've got a lot on my mind right now."

"Am I part of it?"

Sorren scratched a match with his thumbnail before answering. "Yes . . . you're a part of it."

"Is that good or bad?"

Sorren turned quickly to face Shadow. His eyes were hard. She sat upright in her chair, unconsciously defending herself. "Yes, damn it, you're a part of it! But you're just a part, that's all! Now please don't ask me any more questions!"

Shadow could not look at Sorren when his handsome face was so altered with anger. What had she done wrong? Hadn't she done everything she could think of to please him?

Was she no longer appealing? Did he think of her as just another conquest? The sensation of being used and then discarded overwhelmed Shadow with such force she did not even feel like crying. The shock of it just left her numb.

"Perhaps I should leave," she said to Sorren's back. She waited for him to respond. Even his telling her to leave would be preferable to his not saying anything at all. "I don't know why you're treating me this way. I don't know what I've done to make you so angry with me."

"I'm not angry with you."

257

"Then who are you angry with?"

"Myself."

"Why? Shadow's hands were balled tightly on the kitchen table. She was more confused by Sorren now than before. "You didn't . . . what happened between us wasn't your—" Shadow searched for the right words, struggling for the right tone to convey the feelings that were too precious for words to adequately express. "What happened between us was beautiful. It *is* beautiful. Please, Sorren, don't feel like you've done something wrong."

Sorren began to feel himself crumbling, weakening inside. Never before had he wanted to be completely honest with a woman. He wanted to now. And if he followed his impulses, he was certain Shadow would despise him.

"Sit down with me," Shadow said, but even as she spoke the words, she was rising from her chair. Moving up behind Sorren, she placed her hands lightly on his shoulders. "A little while ago I felt closer to you than I've ever felt with anyone." Shadow hurt inside, hurt in a way that was a reflection of the anguish she sensed in Sorren. She still did not know what had changed Sorren so dramatically. She did know that whatever it was, she could overcome the obstacle. She knew how to fight, and for Sorren she would fight the entire world.

Shadow watched the way Sorren inhaled his cigarette. He was drawing the smoke in deep and exhaling it with a sigh. He wasn't savoring it, as he sometimes did. Shadow slipped her hands along Sorren's shoulders until they were near his neck. The moment she began massaging the knotted muscles,

Sorren twisted his shoulders, knocking Shadow's hands from him.

"Don't. It isn't the time for that."

"But, Sorren—"

"Will you just leave me alone?"

"Okay. Have it your way." Shadow went back to the table. Her cup was half empty; the liquid had gone tepid. "Can I have more coffee, or am I only allowed one cup before you throw me out?"

"Help yourself."

"You go to hell!" Shadow spat, and the tears she had been able to hold back could no longer be stopped.

For long moment Shadow stared at Sorren's back, willing him to turn around and apologize for his behavior. All she wanted was to understand, to be included in Sorren's world so that she could help him battle whatever challenges life had thrust upon him. But she could not, no matter how hard she tried or how much she wanted it, be a part of Sorren's world, a part of his life, until he invited her.

In a soft voice laced with pain, Shadow, with crystal tears running down her cheeks, whispered, "You promised you wouldn't hurt me."

Chapter Fourteen

Sorren forced himself to sit at the table alone. He drank his coffee slowly and rolled another cigarette. All the old habits were coming back to him: the excessive use of tobacco; forcing himself to appear calm while his insides were turning; the slow, burning sensation in the pit of his stomach; the tingling at the back of his neck that let him know he was at his sharpest.

In a way, Sorren hated himself for the excitement that was slowly building inside him. He did not like the fact that he was reacting to the hunt for LaRoux with anticipation. Not just anticipation, but with pleasure. Now that his decision had been made — and, most preferably, made *for* him — he knew what he had to do, knew he possessed the skills to get the job done, and knew that in a secret corner of his heart he would enjoy the hunt. He wouldn't enjoy the outcome, that final bloody conclusion that signaled the end of the hunt. Though Sorren had killed many men, he never took any pleasure in it. He did, however, to the very core of his being, enjoy the hunt. It was the thrill of pitting himself and all his skill and wit against another man. And Jean-Jacques LaRoux was much more than just another criminal. He was the best of the worst. It would be a great, final encore performance for Sorren McKenna.

Sorren wondered if President Lincoln had seen this side of him. Perhaps that was why Lincoln had counted so heavily on him during the war but had never really liked Sorren. He held limitless respect for President Lincoln, as a man, as a politician, and as a war strategist. But he suspected the respect was one-sided: He respected President Lincoln, but the President viewed Sorren McKenna as something akin to an efficient and essential tool, a distasteful piece of equipment he didn't want to know too much about. Sorren, to Lincoln, was a some*thing* not a *some*one.

Sorren crushed out his cigarette. A cold curl had settled on his lips, in no way diminishing the facial features women found so dangerously appealing. He would have to control his tobacco use. Long ago Sorren had learned that self-denial led in a natural way to self-discipline. And the more self-discipline a man had, the more control he had over his own life.

And control is what it's all about, isn't it? *Of course it is*, thought Sorren.

But no matter how much control he had over his life — or how much he *thought* he had — Sorren couldn't change the fact that he had hurt Shadow, hurt her deeply. He had made promises to her — something he hadn't done with other women — and then he had willingly and consciously destroyed those promises.

It did not help his conscience much to know that

he had very little choice in his behavior toward Shadow. The simple, hard fact was that she had trusted him, and he had betrayed her.

Sorren sighed and closed his eyes. By the time he opened them again, he had transformed himself from businessman to manhunter. He rose from his chair. The manhunter's instincts, dormant for many, many months, sprang full force into his body and spirit. He touched his fingertips to his thumb. Even his sense of touch now seemed heightened. He ran his fingers through his hair, pushing it back off his forehead. His scalp tingled. Thoughts and images seemed to be coming into his head so fast he couldn't view them distinctly.

He was ready. Almost ready, anyway. Within the hour Sorren McKenna would be ready to do whatever was necessary to end the violent reign of a human parasite named Jean-Jacques LaRoux.

As he walked out of the kitchen and headed toward his bedroom, Sorren's mind was faraway, working in the crisply functional, military fashion he had learned so many years earlier. He was thinking about what he would take with him. A bedroll. Plenty of jerky for the hunt. The Remington Rolling Block with the scope and the Winchester carbine. Shotgun? It was always a difficult process trying to determine what he'd need when he really had no idea of what situations he'd face or what enemy he'd come up against.

When he reached the bedroom, he was surprised to see that Shadow wasn't there. Surprised and disappointed. He found his shirt on the chair, the one she'd put on to go down to the kitchen. The one he thought she looked so attractive in but hadn't said anything about. Her doeskin dress was gone.

"She moves even more quietly than I do," Sorren murmured, pleased with Shadow. He felt in that instant that she would have made a good spy for the Union army. But perhaps not. Her Indian blood would have made her stand out too much, would have caused too much attention to be drawn toward her. That was always a liability in being a double agent. Besides, he knew what female spies ended up having to do with their quarry to gain trust. He couldn't think of Shadow in anyone's arms but his own.

He selected his clothes slowly and carefully. Black denim slacks with a black silk shirt. The boots with the riding heel and the small holster sewn inside the right one to hold a derringer; inside the left boot he had sewn in the sheath for a thin stiletto-bladed throwing knife.

From his closet Sorren withdrew the bedroll. It was the same one he'd used during the war. He hadn't used it in years, and now the touch of the coarse wool fabric felt good against his hands. He withdrew a light black denim jacket and slipped his arms into it. Finally, he neatly folded a black silk scarf into a line, then knotted it around his neck. It was his signature. Colonel Jean-Jacques LaRoux of the Rebel army, now the self-appointed General La-Roux, knew that Sorren McKenna, Rebel soldier, always wore a black silk neckerchief.

As he walked slowly down the stairway, his boot heels clicking against the wood and echoing through the empty house, Sorren wondered if he would ever see this place again. It had never quite materialized into the home he wanted. It was a house. A grand, spectacular house. But it wasn't a home.

It might have been, the part of his mind that wanted peace and tranquillity taunted. And just as quickly the analytical part of him demanded, *Stop thinking about her! If you lose concentration, you die!*

It really was all quite logical. He had to be logical. Sorren McKenna just didn't have time for love right now.

Shadow ran her hand along the smooth surface of the wood and glass gun case. She could feel Sorren all around her. It was the feeling she had sought the other night when she was first in his arms and the fire of true passion had exploded in her soul.

Shadow's eyes were drawn to the bearskin rug. It was there that she had decided, either consciously or unconsciously, she wanted to make love with Sorren, to share her body with him. It was in this room, this room that was so *Sorren*, that she had ceased to think like a frightened girl and began thinking like a woman. It was in this room that Shadow had pushed her defenses away and allowed a man to touch her heart.

Somewhere in this room was the clue that would give Shadow the reason for Sorren's sudden change. She believed that if she looked hard enough and was in touch with her senses enough, she would be able to find the clue she sought. Something had made Sorren change drastically in a matter of just a few minutes. Though she had at first suspected he was angry with her, she didn't believe that now. And it wasn't sex. If he was angry with himself for taking her virginity, he sure had a strange way of showing it, she mused grimly. There was no guessing how many virgins Sorren McKenna had deflowered in his long and apparently successful life as a lover. She decided guilt was not something that played on his mind very often.

She heard the boot heels clicking against wood, then the opening of the door. Shadow's body tightened momentarily, then she forced herself to relax. She would not react guiltily. She had done nothing wrong. If there were any guilt to be levied, it should be directed toward Sorren. He was the one acting irrationally.

"Oh," Sorren mumbled, stopping at the door when he saw Shadow. "I didn't know you were still here."

"I wasn't quite ready to leave yet," Shadow replied, not looking at Sorren. She wondered if he could tell that she had been crying. Would he care if he knew? That was something Shadow didn't even want to think about. "I hope you don't mind."

"No. I don't mind." It was a parody of social convention, two people talking calmly and casually. Small talk from people who hours earlier were exploring the mysteries of each other's bodies. "I just came in here to find something."

"Me, too."

Sorren went to the gun case. He reached above the cabinet and found the small key he kept hidden there, then unlocked the case. He tucked the key into a back pocket. He noticed that Shadow had turned enough to watch him but was trying not to be seen doing it.

"Guns." It was a statement, not a question. Shadow walked over to Sorren. She watched the way his fingers curled around the forearm stock of a Winchester carbine. His action was almost a caress. "You don't need to put on war paint for me to know what you're doing."

"Something has happened," Sorren began, his speech coming out slowly, in a matter-of-fact fashion. "There was killing. Four wagons were ambushed. Everyone was killed."

"And you're going after whoever did it."

"Yes."

Shadow watched as Sorren pulled down on the lever of the Winchester, sliding open the action. She saw, too, the vitality in him. The excitement he felt was a palpable thing to her. She could taste it and feel it in much the same way she could when she knew that he desired her. Only this time it wasn't her he wanted. It was action.

"Heaven forbid there be a killing in the territory that you're not a part of."

"Don't start, Shadow. There are things I've got to do. You don't understand."

She refused to bow to Sorren's quiet dismissal. "You're going alone." Another statement; not a question. "How very much like you to do that, Sorren." A brittle, cold anger was creeping into Shadow's voice. "Of course, it probably doesn't matter to you that it's dangerous as hell to go against these men. I assume there is more than one man who did this killing, right? I mean, why would Sorren McKenna go after just one man?"

"Stop it, Shadow."

"Aren't there posses for this sort of thing?"

A derisive, short laugh came from Sorren at the comment. "Posse? And who would I ride with? Carl? I've got a couple of good men working for me, but they're not experienced trackers. Besides, I need them here to look after the ranch."

"Do you know the people who were killed?"

"Not really."

"That means you don't even know their names, right?"

Shadow received a cold black stare for that one. "That's right. I don't know them. I never met them. Satisfied?"

"No."

Shadow watched, fascinated and horrified, as Sorren thumbed cartridges into the Winchester, then set it carefully down, leaning the muzzle against the gun case. Next he withdrew a long-barreled weapon with an optical instrument fixed to the barrel. Shadow had seen such guns before in the hands of buffalo hunters, but never had she seen such an attachment.

"What's that?" She was less curious than she pretended. All she wanted Sorren to do was talk. The only way she could understand is if he talked with her.

"Telescopic sight. It's the latest thing. Makes a target at three hundred yards seem like he's right at your nose." There was something in Sorren's face as he studied the single-shot rifle in his hands. It was a quality that Shadow had never seen before and she wished she hadn't seen now. "This is a Remington Rolling Block in .45-.70. Probably the finest long-range weapon ever made." He sounded like he was talking about a prized horse or a beautiful woman. Shadow hated the warm timbre of pleasure she heard in his tone.

"Just the sort of thing you need for some long-range killing, I suppose."

Again Sorren glanced over at Shadow. It wasn't difficult for her to tell that he didn't appreciate her sarcasm. She wasn't pleased with herself for it, either. But somehow she just couldn't help herself. Anger and the sense of being forced out of a part of Sorren's life were making Shadow behave in ways she didn't like.

They both knew she had to ask.

"Can I come with you?"

"No," Sorren snapped quickly. In a softer tone, he added, "You don't want to do that." His eyebrows pushed together in confusion. "Why would you want to do that?"

"So that you wouldn't be alone. It's not safe being alone."

"It's not safe being with other people, either."

"I could help you. I've hunted most of my life." Shadow affected a lighthearted tone as she added, "Who knows? Maybe I could save your life again." Sorren saw no humor in the comment. The right side of his face curled up in a mirthless smile. Quietly, sadly, Shadow said, "Don't do this alone. If you don't want me with you, at least take one of your men. Don't go alone."

"Alone? I'm always alone."

"Damn you, Sorren!" Shadow suddenly burst. "Why are you doing this to me? I'm trying so damn hard to be reasonable with you, and all I get are one-word answers that say nothing at all!"

Sorren's eyes were cold, black, impassive. He turned his gaze upon Shadow. "Listen to me," he said, the words again coming out very slowly as he chose them with infinite care. "You can't go with me because hunting these killers isn't like hunting for something that you're going to skin and eat. It's not going to be anything like that at all. It's going to be dangerous, and that's why you're not going with me."

"Do you know where they are?" Shadow was, for the first time, afraid for Sorren's life.

"Not exactly. But I'll find them in a couple of days." And then, to himself, almost sadly, he added aloud, "I always do."

Shadow grabbed Sorren's arm. Her fingers dug into his solid biceps. "I'm going with you."

Sorren jerked his arm out of Shadow's grasp. "Don't be a fool!" he spat. "You're not going with me. You're going home. That's the last I'm going to say about it." Sorren shook his head, the anger he felt now directed toward himself. "I simply cannot believe I'm getting in this argument." He shed his jacket and slipped his arms into the figure-eight-shaped leather straps of a shoulder holster. "Damn, I really am getting weak inside. I've never allowed anything like this to happen before."

Shadow squared her shoulders. Her hands were tight fists at her sides. "Okay, Sorren . . . have it your way. Go alone and hunt them, if that's what you really think you have to do. But answer me just one thing."

"What?"

269

"Why you? I need to know why you have to do this. Why not someone else? And why do you have to do it alone?"

"That's hardly one question," Sorren said. His mouth curled again into a half smile that never came close to reaching his dark, glittering eyes. It wasn't really a smile at all. "I'm doing it because I have to. I have the ability to catch the people responsible for the murder. Therefore, I have a responsibility to do what I can."

"You're a liar!" Sorren's head snapped in Shadow's direction as though he had been slapped. "Don't give me some weak story about duty! I can see it in you, Sorren. You're doing this because you want to! This isn't some duty that I just don't understand. It's not that at all. You *want* to do it!"

"That's not true." Sorren *hoped* that what Shadow said wasn't completely true, though he knew there were elements of excitement in the hunt that was about to begin. "You don't know what you're talking about."

"If you believe that, you're not only lying to me, you're lying to yourself."

Sorren tucked a pistol into the shoulder holster under his left arm. He turned to Shadow with eyes that wanted understanding but gave little in return. "I don't blame you for feeling the way you do. I'll make it up to you later. Right now I must get started on this . . . hunt."

Sorren took a knife from inside the gun case and slipped it into the sheath in his boot, then smoothed his pant leg over the boot.

Shadow walked to the door and stopped. She

turned and watched Sorren with his guns. A shiver went up her spine and she hugged her arms around herself. Sorren exuded a coldness that seemed to invade every part of the room, including herself. He had frozen inside, and with the frigidity of ice, he was more alive than she'd ever seen him.

He's a hunter, thought Shadow. *I can't deny it. I knew it from the first time I saw him, but I ignored what I knew. Look at him. Sorren McKenna, the hunter in his gun room with his guns. He loves it. He loves the hunt even more than he loves making love.* She looked at the walls and saw the stuffed trophy heads that lined them. *The hunter surrounds himself with his kills. And the white world calls me a savage.*

"You're a fool," Shadow said quietly. There wasn't anger in her voice any more, just resignation. "You're willing to risk everything. And for what? Some twisted sense of duty? No, you can tell me that's the reason, Sorren, but I know you better than that. You like doing this. You'll risk yourself and me and us just to go on this hunt."

"That's not true." Sorren was thumbing cartridges into his Colt. "I wouldn't risk your life for anything. That's why you're not coming with me."

Without another word, Shadow left the room, leaving the door open.

She had no idea whether she would ever seen Sorren again . . . or even if he would live through the week.

"What made you come to your senses?" Carl asked, a cocky smile playing with his lips.

Sorren looked at Carl and wanted to slap the smile from his face. The more he talked with Carl, the more he despised everything about the man.

"I changed my mind, that's all."

Sorren was pretending to study the contract from the War Department one last time, but his eyes weren't really reading the words. What could he tell Carl? That he had decided Shadow might as well profit from his accepting the assignment to kill La-Roux? That he wanted to make sure she would be financially secure in case something happened to him? Sorren didn't want the money. It was blood money. Nothing good could come of it for him. But it wasn't tainted in Shadow's hands. The money wouldn't stain her soul as it had his own.

He signed his name. "There. Now it's legal."

Carl extended his hand without rising from his chair. Sorren looked at the hand, then into Carl's eyes. After a moment the hand was withdrawn.

"I'll have my bookkeeper going over the books day and night, Carl," Sorren said smoothly. "If you're thinking about dipping into the coffers, you can forget about it. I'll have you up on theft charges in the territorial court so fast your head will spin."

"Now that's hardly a way to talk to your new partner, partner." Carl forced himself to laugh softly. He was already a little tipsy. "You don't even shake my hand. Some businessman you are."

Catherine piped in, "Now, Carl Weatherly, I want you to quit being mean this instant! Do you hear me?" She gave Sorren a look of apology, her sapphire-blue eyes wide and filled with concern. "I'm terribly sorry for my brother's behavior, Sorren. I just don't know what's gotten into him lately."

"Booze, mostly, I think," Sorren replied with a shrug of his shoulders. He didn't care what Carl had to say one way or the other. "Don't worry about it."

Sorren headed for the door. He didn't want to be at the MW Circle longer than necessary.

"Catherine, didn't I tell you to stop apologizing for me?"

Sorren's steps hesitated a fraction of a second as he made his way to the door. He had his problems with Catherine. There was no getting away from that. But she was essentially a good woman. Spoiled lousy, self-centered, often childish and petty—there was no denying that. But there was also a good heart inside her, and it was that good heart that Carl took such joy in shredding. Sorren wondered if he would ever have the chance to teach Carl a lesson in respect. He'd enjoy giving Carl Weatherly just one lesson. That's all it would take.

Carl deserved it.

Sorren was almost at the front door when Catherine called out to him. "Sorren, can you wait just a moment? I want to talk with you."

He wasn't in the mood for small talk. Sorren seldom was inclined to put up with trivial banter, and he certainly wasn't in the mood for it now.

"Yes?"

When Catherine approached, her stride slowed as she got closer to Sorren. She stepped up slowly, like she was not sure whether he would strike out at her or not.

"Can I ask you something?" Sorren shrugged his broad shoulders. "Don't be angry with me now. I just need to know something."

"What?"

Catherine looked up into Sorren's eyes, then turned her gaze away. "Why—why did you decide to go through with the War Department contract? You seemed dead set against it before."

"I changed my mind, that's all."

"Does it have anything to do with Shadow?" Catherine smiled wanly. "I know what happened last night. I heard the men talking about it. And then when Shadow came back this afternoon, she was—"

"She was what?" Now Sorren was genuinely curious. He hoped the damage he'd done to Shadow's feelings wasn't unrepairable. If only she would leave him alone until he finished this one last assignment, then he could show her all the love, attention, and *honesty* that she needed and deserved.

"She was . . . I don't know the right word for it. It wasn't like she was hurt. Disappointed, maybe? No, that's not the word for it." Catherine looked up again, and Sorren couldn't read what the concern showing in her eyes was supposed to mean. "Shadow's different than the rest of us who have wanted to be with you, Sorren."

"I know that," he said, then left the house.

Chapter Fifteen

Shadow leaned over the thick ledger, trying hard to concentrate on the columns of numbers. It was a futile effort. She couldn't get Sorren out of her mind. She tried to think about the money she would get now that he had signed the War Department contract. But even in her fantasies of wearing beautiful new dresses, Shadow kept picturing Sorren's image as she showed him the clothing for his approval. She wanted to see that special look in his eyes that came when he was pleased with her.

A soft shuffle of feet drew Shadow's attention to the study door. Catherine was standing there with an expectant look on her face, holding a silver tray with a tea set on it. Shadow, still suspicious of her half sister's sudden change of attitude toward her, did not welcome the intrusion.

"Did you want to see me?" When Catherine nodded, Shadow felt a twinge in her stomach. Catherine was different. Not just in the expression on her face, but in her movement and gestures. "Come in." Shadow put down her pen. "I need a break from this anyway."

Catherine came in hesitantly. "You're sure you don't mind?"

"I'm positive. Come on, Catherine, you've got something on your mind. We'll both feel a lot better if you tell me what it is."

They went to the small two-cushion leather settee, and when the tea was poured and Catherine had added two lumps of sugar and a splash of lemon juice, she appeared ready to release what she was holding inside.

"I know it's none of my business—"

"—but you'll ask anyway," Shadow cut in.

Catherine blushed in embarrassment. It wasn't the pretty, false coquettish blush she saved for men; it was the real thing, and this made Shadow wonder even more what was happening.

"Yes, I'll ask anyway." Catherine sipped her tea and studied the swirling liquid for a moment. "Like I said, I know it's none of my business, so I'll understand if you don't answer. And that's just fine." Catherine's blue eyes met with Shadow's and held. "You were with Sorren the other night. You spent the night with him." Catherine turned her gaze away. She couldn't look at Shadow and say the things that had to be said. "But when you came home, you weren't happy. That's not like Sorren. I'll admit that there have been times when I've thought about what it would be like to be with Sorren. I've thought about that more than I care to. But I've never really followed the idea because he was Daddy's business

276

partner, and because he's . . . you know . . . with friends of mine."

"I'm still missing the point." Shadow felt strange inside. It was odd having someone like Catherine know that she had made love to Sorren. Shadow wasn't embarrassed by it. She wouldn't deny that she had made love to him. It just seemed terribly strange that something so private should become so public. "I know this is difficult for you, but I just don't know what you're getting at."

Catherine sipped her tea. She was stalling. Decisiveness wasn't her strongest trait. "I've had friends sleep with Sorren. And after they had . . . you know . . . were with him, they were happy. They didn't act like you did. They had this glow to them and they smiled all the time. The day you came home from Sorren's you hardly said a word to anyone. And I was watching you. You didn't smile. Mary Beth kept staring off into space with this smile on her face and this twinkle in her eye. You weren't like that at all."

Shadow swallowed dryly. She did not feel like confiding in Catherine. "Things didn't exactly . . . turn out like I had thought they would."

"Was it your first time?"

Shadow was taken aback. She hadn't expected Catherine to get that personal.

"I'm sorry. I know it's none of my business." Catherine put her hand lightly over Shadow's. "If you want to talk about it, I want you to know you can come to me. You can tell me anything, and I promise you, it'll go no further than my own ears."

"Catherine, I appreciate the offer but I really don't—"

"Please, don't shun me just because we didn't start off on the right foot." Catherine looked into Shadow's face again. "I'm serious. If you want to talk about it, you can come to me. Despite what my brother thinks, I'm a very good listener."

Shadow didn't know what to say. She wasn't sure she could trust Catherine. She was positive that she didn't want to give her half sister the intimate details of her argument or of her lovemaking with Sorren.

Finally, she said, "Thank you, Catherine. I'm not very good at thanking people, but I want you to know that I appreciate what you're doing. I know I haven't been very good company lately." Shadow shrugged her shoulders, trying to pretend the differences between herself and Sorren weren't that important. "It's just something that happened between Sorren and myself. That's all."

"He wasn't . . . I mean, he didn't force himself—"

Shadow smiled inwardly. What would Catherine think if she knew what had really happened? If there was any truth to it, it was Shadow who had forced herself upon Sorren, not the other way around.

"No. Sorren is very loving. He was loving and tender and everything I ever dreamed a man would be." Shadow saw the concerned expression change on Catherine's face. She could not tell if her half sister was jealous or not. "Don't worry, Catherine. Sorren was wonderful to me."

"Then why weren't you—?"

Awareness dawned on Shadow. She kept herself from smiling broadly and contemplated if she should say anything or not. Finally, returning the squeeze to Catherine's hand that she'd neglected so far, Shadow said, "Someday you'll find the right man, Catherine. And when you do, I hope it is as beautiful for you as it was for me." She squeezed Catherine's hand again. "The problem Sorren and I had came later. It was a misunderstanding."

Shadow smiled, and for the first time in her life she felt like she actually had a sister. Though, most oddly, she felt as though she were the older sister rather than the younger one. She sensed that Catherine was wanting details, wanting to know what it was really like to make love.

Catherine looked up, her blue eyes filled with doubt and confusion. "I'm sorry to be such a bother to you. It's just that you're the only one I know who would tell me the truth about . . . certain things. My girlfriends . . . oh, I think they exaggerate." Catherine rose and sighed, looking rapidly about the room as though she'd forgotten something. "Well, I thank you just the same. We all appreciate what you've done for us."

Shadow's eyebrows pushed together in confusion. "Appreciate what I've done?"

"Yes. I hadn't thought of it, but even if I had, I don't think I would have had the courage to go through with it."

"Catherine, what are you talking about?"

Blue eyes met brown ones and held. Catherine gave a small, humorless smile. "Sleeping with Sorren."

"What?"

"Sleeping with Sorren so he'd sign those War Department contracts. They'll make us all rich . . . including you."

Shadow felt the blood drain from her face. "Is that what you think?"

Catherine looked at the tea set on the silver platter. "I'll send Emma for that later." She turned toward the door. "I think it was very courageous of you, Shadow. I never would have thought of doing that."

Shadow wanted to scream at Catherine. She wanted to tell her half sister that it wasn't anything like that at all. She was too stunned for words though. Too stunned to do anything but think, *So that's what they think of me now? That I slept with Sorren for money?*

Carl finally felt like his power at the MW Circle was consolidated. It had been two days since Sorren had signed the contract with the War Department. Shortly after that, he disappeared. Carl had no idea where Sorren had gone, and frankly, he wasn't concerned. Carl was no slouch with the books. He could doctor them so that even if Sorren hired a team of bookkeepers, they wouldn't find any improprieties . . . no matter how much money Carl decided to skim from the top.

And then there was the slight problem with Jean-Jacques LaRoux. The *ex*-problem of Jean-Jacques LaRoux, that is. Though Carl now had access to his funds at the bank and would soon be getting the first advance from the government, it looked like he wouldn't need it to pay off his marker. LaRoux hadn't shown up for his money. Carl suspected that he had finally realized how much power the Weatherly name really had in God's Grace, and in the entire territory, and had decided to cut his losses and run.

It bothered Carl that he hadn't stood up to La-Roux. The man was all bluff with not a trump card to back his hand. Carl made a promise to himself to never back down to anyone again.

He was in charge now. He held the power. He would never again defer to anyone under any circumstances.

Carl's fingertips grazed lightly over the contracts on his desk. It had taken a couple of days to find a new family lawyer. Through a friend, he had heard of one who specialized in what he called the "gray area" of the law. That meant that with enough money under the table, he could do whatever he wanted and the lawyer would make sure it all looked legal. He was just the kind of lawyer Carl wanted and needed, much more suitable for the MW Circle than that old fool Jonas Phillips.

Jonas was Matthew's lawyer; with his firing, the last of the old guard was gone. Carl Weatherly now had complete, unchallenged control of the MW Circle.

The knock at the study door caught Carl's attention. He'd been daydreaming a lot that day, he suddenly realized. His dreams were all happy ones "Come in," he said after waiting a bit. Whoever was outside the door could wait to meet the king of the MW Circle.

Shadow took a step into the room. "Emma said you wanted to see me."

"Yes, Shadow," Carl replied, taking on the authoritarian tone he'd picked up from his father. "Thank you for coming here. There's something very important I would like you to do."

"Oh?" Shadow moved closer.

Carl saw the suspicion in Shadow's face. He thought, *She doesn't trust me. She will soon.*

"You know about the War Department deal we're working on with McKenna, correct?" Shadow nodded her head and fought back the tears that welled up at the memory of the last time she'd heard those contracts mentioned. "Good. Well, we need someone to take the contracts to our lawyer. I could send one of the men, but I don't trust them with something this valuable." Carl looked straight into Shadow's eyes as he said, "We're family, whether we like it or not. And as long as you're part of the family, I think I can trust you to deliver this contract to our new lawyer in Denver City. Will you do that for"—Carl caught himself before he said *me*—"us?" Carl saw the change in Shadow's face and thought, *I knew she'd fall for it.* "Will you do that for us?" Carl repeated.

"Of course I will. I want to be of help around here. I think you must know that by now."

Carl gave Shadow a smile that was pure gold. "If you bring the contracts to our lawyer, you'll be very, very helpful." He lowered his tone slightly and added, "I don't want to give this work to someone outside the family."

"I understand," Shadow said, and she really thought she did.

"There's a stage going to Denver City tomorrow morning," Carl continued, his confidence soaring with each second that passed. The enthusiasm he saw in Shadow's expression let him know she now was letting her guard down. Very soon he would be rid of her for good. "Make sure you bring plenty of money with you. Take it from the expense account, not from your own account. You'll stay at the best hotel in Denver City; eat at the best restaurants." Carl smiled winningly. "It's going to be a hot, dusty trip there, so don't be afraid to unwind a little once the business is concluded. Ask Catherine about what stores to go to. She's shopped in every one that's worth anything."

Shadow's joyous expression changed slightly at Catherine's name. Nevertheless, she said, "I'll do that."

It really wasn't difficult to pick up LaRoux's trail. It had taken less than half a day for Sorren to find where LaRoux and his band of renegades had cut off from the stage trail, moving back in the general direction of God's Grace, angling toward the foothills of the Rockies.

"Simple tricks," Sorren muttered under his breath. He wondered whether or not the original expedition had intentionally ignored the signs so that they wouldn't have to follow the murderers, or if they really had been tricked by LaRoux's gambit.

Sorren got an odd tingling in the pit of his stomach as he slowly followed the signs of LaRoux's movement. He was a mediocre tracker as far as game was concerned, but when it came to tracking a man, he doubted there was anyone better. It wasn't egotism that drove him to this conclusion; he simply had not seen any evidence to make him believe there was a better tracker of a criminal than himself.

283

For two days Sorren followed LaRoux's trail. He knew he was getting closer. The fires he found were warmer than earlier ones. Manure was fresher. What bothered Sorren most of all was the desultory path taken by LaRoux. It didn't seem to have any specific direction. He had moved his men toward the foothills of the Rockies. Then, after camping there for a day, he had headed back in almost a horseshoe move toward God's Grace.

"What the hell is he doing?" Sorren asked aloud one night, staring up at the stars. His hands were folded behind his head as he lay on his bedroll.

Sorren closed his eyes, wishing for sleep. He didn't feel tired. He felt more awake than he wanted to, and this was never good for him. He wasn't a man who could sleep for very long. Whenever he tried to get rest and couldn't sleep, his mind always wandered to subjects that were uncomfortable to him. Subjects like Shadow.

What was she doing now? What was she thinking? Was she in bed? Alone? Wearing what?

A smile played teasingly on Sorren's lips. Different feelings came back to him, each one more pleasing than the next. Like the feel and weight of Shadow's warm breasts against him as she slept with her head on his shoulder. Her thigh on top of his whenever she curled in close to him. And there was always that smoky look in her eyes, the one that appeared just as he entered her. That was the look he thought of most.

Sorren felt himself becoming aroused. He grit his teeth and cursed angrily, speaking words that he never used with anyone. It wasn't right of him to think of Shadow when he was trailing a man like Jean-Jacques LaRoux. It wasn't right . . . and it wasn't safe. LaRoux *had* to have all his attention. If Sorren allowed himself to relax, to be at ease, it could mean his own death.

He tried to force Shadow from his mind, and when he tried, she became more entrenched in his thoughts.

How angry was she with him? Sorren wondered if he could have handled their parting better. At the time, he couldn't think of a way to get separated from her without making her feel left out of his life. She now felt hurt, and probably betrayed and used. With hindsight working for him as he stared at the stars twinkling in the night sky, he could think of all sorts of things he could have said. Loving, honeyed lies that would have covered the real reason he was forced to leave.

Stop thinking about her!

How in hell could he escape a shadow? Not just *a* shadow, *his* Shadow?

It wasn't until Sorren remembered how close he was to LaRoux—by his estimation now less than eighteen hours—and that LaRoux was headed back in the direction of God's Grace, that he was able to shake Shadow from his consciousness.

That night Sorren did not sleep well. He had been without Shadow for two days, and if he understood how much this affected him, he would have been greatly disturbed.

Shadow snapped the valise shut and took a final

look around her bedroom to make sure she hadn't forgotten anything. She inhaled deeply and felt her breasts strain against the square-cut décolletage. After the initial thrill of wearing the expensive, sophisticated clothing that Emma said was absolutely necessary for a lady of Shadow's wealth, the voluptuous young woman now found the garments too clingy and constrictive.

She sighed. So many things were changing in her life. She was going to Denver City alone. Travelling alone did not bother her, but she would so much rather explore the bustling city with Sorren at her side. Already they were growing apart. This was something they should have shared. And she had no idea where he was, what he was up to, or even if he was alive.

Shadow sat on her bed, then leaned back on her elbows. Catherine's words had cut her deeply. As time had trickled by, she began to wonder more about Sorren's motives for signing the contract. Why change his mind? It infuriated Shadow that she could never convince Catherine she hadn't made love to Sorren so that he would sign the contract.

She's just bitter, Shadow thought. *She wanted Sorren and she's mad that he doesn't want her. He wants me and that makes her mean and jealous.*

A secret smiled played on Shadow's wide, sensual mouth. Though she was still unsure of her own sexuality, she felt more confident now than before. Her "experimentation" had done as much for her own confidence as it had done Sorren's pleasure. To see him so completely helpless against the pleasure she gave him, to see his total surrender to her, was something that she would never forget.

In a vindictive corner of her mind, Shadow suspected that Catherine could never keep a man like Sorren McKenna satisfied. Catherine was too selfish. She wouldn't concern herself with a man's pleasure. Was she still a virgin? Part of Shadow felt sorry for Catherine.

Thinking about her lovemaking with Sorren gave Shadow a warm, naughty feeling inside. She liked the feeling. Sorren wouldn't become bored with her as he had with his other conquests. Tired, perhaps, exhausted beyond words—but never bored.

Shadow couldn't be sure if Sorren could love her. She wasn't even sure if she loved him, or if he simply made her feel like she was in love. She wondered if it were possible to *feel* like you were in love without actually *being* in love.

Is it possible to make someone fall in love with you? How does one go about doing that?

Stop thinking like Catherine!

Shadow sat upright, then bolted to her feet. She wasn't wearing the heavy petticoats under her dress, though Emma had insisted that proper ladies wore such things. It didn't make any sense to Shadow, and since it was devilishly hot and the ride to Denver City would be a long one, she had opted to go without them.

Shadow was beginning to enjoy making her own decisions about her life and about the things that she would and would not do. She adored Emma, but she wasn't going to let the older woman dictate her life's plans; she wanted the respect of Carl and Catherine, but she wasn't going to fall apart if she didn't get it;

and she wanted Sorren's love above all things . . . but she didn't know what she would do if he never returned for her.

Shadow's moccasins made no sound as she crossed the bedroom with the valise in hand. Inside the valise were the War Department contracts. Outside, a waiting buckboard would take her to the station in God's Grace, where she would catch the morning stage to Denver City.

Chapter Sixteen

Carl wasn't lying when he said it would be a hot trip on he stage, Shadow thought miserably as she dabbed at he perspiration on her neck with a lace hanky.

She was already looking forward to getting to Denver City. First she would find a good hotel, then he'd get into the biggest, cleanest, coolest tub of water possible. When she was squeaky clean and efreshed, she would find the new Weatherly lawyer nd finish her work. Then she would go to a fine estaurant and order a thick steak, like the one orren had cooked for her when she had stayed with im.

Shadow rested her head against the back of the eat. There wasn't much cushioning on the stage seat nd none on the headrest. She felt like crabbing bout the conditions, but that only made it worse. Besides, she didn't want to strike up another conversation with the two men who shared the stage with er. One smelled as though he hadn't bathed in a month; the other was only slightly less offensive because of cheap cologne. He kept looking at her and smiling, as if they were sharing some intimate secret. Both men made Shadow feel ill at ease.

It had been ten hours since she left the station at God's Grace. Ten hours of bumps and jolts, of swirling clouds of dirt and dust that came through the open windows. Shadow could no longer smell the unwashed cretin who sat on the seat facing hers. Her sense of smell had grown dull over the hours, and for that she was thankful.

"How long will it be until we reach the way station?" Shadow asked the man who had such a difficult time keeping his eyes off her.

The man smiled and Shadow saw again that he was missing two teeth on the right side of his mouth. He pulled a thick watch out of his pocket. Pressing a button, the watch snapped open. " 'Bout another two hours, maybe three if we're on schedule."

"Thank you."

"No trouble. You need anything, you just come see ol' Billy Bob. He'll fix you right up."

Shadow looked out the window, feeling the eyes of the man called Billy Bob undressing her. "That's okay," she said after a long pause. "I'll manage nicely on my own."

"Suit yourself. "Cain't tell ya what yer missin'."

Shadow wanted to give him a final retort, but it would do no good. She had already discovered this man was immune to insults.

Tomorrow at this time she would be in her hotel room. Maybe she would order a bottle of wine to sip while she soaked in the tub. A smile played on her lips. She felt cooler just thinking about the bath and the wine.

The sun will be down soon, thought Shadow. *I'll be spending another night without Sorren.*

The first night after their argument was hell for Shadow. Even Catherine had noticed that she wasn't herself. The second night wasn't much better. What shocked Shadow was that what she missed most was not his wonderful lovemaking but the times when they were together, just touching each other, holding each other. That was the closeness Shadow missed the most. There were things that she had learned to love about him, like the way he ran his fingertips lightly over her naked shoulders while they talked in bed. The joy that she had seen in his eyes when she was threatening to push him out of bed was something Shadow would never forget. It was much more precious than gold, more rare than anything else in the world.

But then he had changed. The warmth in his eyes had turned to an icy, calm intensity. He wasn't simply a warrior. Bold Walker was a warrior, but Sorren wasn't like him. Not exactly, anyway. Thinking about Bold Walker made Shadow wonder about her Kiowa tribe. Did anyone there miss her? Did they even know she was gone? Though she had lived much of her life on the outskirts of the tribe, she did not miss them at all.

Shadow was looking out the coach window when she first shot rang out. A moment later, there was a second and third shot. At the same time that Shadow noticed the riders coming out of the woods on her left, the body of the stagemaster rolled off the side.

She watched his body hit the hard, sunbaked trail and rapidly drop from view behind the stage.

"What's happening?" Shadow asked.

The fellow named Billy Bob pulled a pistol from his holster. He looked out Shadow's window, then out the opposite side window. The other man did nothing. He sat and stared at the multitude of riders now surrounding the stage without saying a word.

"Slow it down!" someone shouted.

Shadow peered out the window. There were four or five riders leaning over to grab the reins of the stage horses. It seemed like there were men everywhere, and all of them had pistols and rifles trained on the stage.

"Come on out now!" the same voice boomed. "Out of the stage with your hands held high. If your hands aren't empty, consider yourself dead right now!"

The man across from Shadow dropped his pistol to the floor of the coach. "I ain't no hero," he mumbled. "Ain't got nothin' worth stealin' nohow."

Shadow couldn't move. She was a fighter. A fighter by spirit and by necessity. But every fighter knows when to fight, when to run, and when to stall for time. Decisions that are thrust upon people do not always have to be made immediately. If Shadow tried to run, she would be gunned down.

"Hey, we got ourselves a women in here!"

Shadow didn't bother looking at who had spoken. She would know soon enough. Already she was fighting with herself to ignore her fear. It was as though there were two of her, one frightened beyond conscious thought, the other assessing the situation and looking for a way to escape. She had to keep her vits about her. Fear was her greatest enemy now. Fear would keep her from thinking clearly.

They were pulled roughly out of the stage. Shadow and the two other passengers were lined up against the coach. Men had boarded the stage and were throwing boxes and packages out of the trunk attached to the back and those tied to the roof. A tall, rather handsome man dressed much more lavishly than the others stepped forward. He had blond hair that curled at the collar of his jacket, and he sported a moustache and goatee.

"Did either of you men ride with the Stars and Bars?" the tall man asked.

The two male passengers, their backs against the stage, shook their heads.

"Men, these men were never Rebel soldiers," the tall blond man said in a casual tone. "What do you think we should do about that?"

The volley of gunfire drowned out Shadow's scream. She stood motionless, holding her face in her hands, and screamed with a primal horror so real that she believed this had to be a nightmare. Perhaps fifteen of the twenty or so men who were facing the stage had opened up with their pistols and rifles. Each man fired two or three times. Shadow waited for the bullets to strike her, but they never came.

As gray clouds of gunsmoke hovered around her and the smell of gunpowder burned in her nostrils, Shadow summoned Akana to protect her.

"Bring whatever valuables they have to me when you're finished," the blond man said, then turned and walked through the crowd. Over his shoulder, he said, "You men can have the woman."

293

Shadow looked through her fingers at the men. *Please, Akana, take me now. Don't let me live through this.*

The men began to advance, their eyes burning and their mouths hung partially open in foul carnal craving.

"What a minute, boys!"

It was a grizzled voice belonging to an old man. Shadow took her hands from her face. A single man was advancing toward her. She did not see compassion in his eyes, though he had been the one to stop the others.

"Damn it, Smitty! You ain't stoppin' us now!"

"Shut up, Johnny." Smitty looked at Johnny impassively. The old man spit a long stream of tobacco juice into the ground, twisting his upper body just enough to make the Winchester, cradled in the crook of his arm, point directly at Johnny's naval. "Yeah, I am doin' jus' that." Smitty's flinty gaze left Johnny to travel to the other faces studying him. "We're on a run here now. Things is goin' good. The general coulda had this little filly for hisself, but he didn't do that. He left her fer us. Now I say we show the general we appreciate his smartness and ever'thin' else he does. I say we give this little filly to the general. Hell, we'll all have our chance eventually." Smitty smiled and turned, but each man there noticed the muzzle of his deadly Winchester pointing at himself in turn. "Whatcha say we all jus' hold our horses an' wait 'til the general gives her back, eh?"

Shadow did not know if she was being spared or not. For now, anyway, she would not be taken by all twenty men.

Sorren heard the gunshots and tapped his horse's ribs. When he was closer, he heard the hideous volley of gunfire.

He kept the horses moving at a smooth canter. The mare's nostrils were flared. The smell of blood was in the wind, frightening the animal. Sorren wanted to go faster, but he dared not. This was not the time to forget caution.

"Easy, girl," Sorren whispered soothingly to his mare, patting her neck as they rode closer to a group of men now less than thirty yards away. She instinctively feared the smell of blood.

Several men turned to face him. He saw longarms being raised and trained on him. Holding the reins in his left hand, Sorren raised his right hand until it was near his shoulder. Nobody in his right mind would ride into LaRoux's troop alone unless he had been summoned, and that was what Sorren was hoping the soldiers would understand.

"Stop right there, mister!" a baby-faced killer said. He was holding a pistol on Sorren, pointing it at his face.

"Relax," Sorren muttered. Baby-face moved to block Sorren's approach, but the mare moved quickly, darting away. "I haven't the patience to deal with snot-nosed little boys right now."

Sorren heard several men laugh at his comment. He hoped Baby-face wouldn't shoot him in the back. A soldier, perhaps Sorren's age, though he looked older from years of hard living and heavy drinking, caught his eye.

"Tell LaRoux that Sorren McKenna is here to see

him."

The man's eyes squinted in thought. "You mean *General* LaRoux, don't you?"

Sorren was going for effect. He had to have the soldiers wondering who he was and what his relationship with LaRoux was. It was only their confusion that had kept them from gunning him down immediately. He had to keep thinking so they wouldn't start shooting. "He's General LaRoux to you, not to me."

"Big talkin' guy, ain't ya?"

"Just tell LaRoux that Sorren McKenna is here."

Sorren pulled his mare to a stop. He kept his face calm and impassive, but his eyes kept searching for LaRoux. Questions flared in his mind, the answer to each one crucial to his continued existence in the next few minutes. How much did LaRoux know about him? LaRoux, at one time, believed him to be a mercenary working for the Rebel army. Did he still believe that? Had he heard anything about Sorren in the years since the war. Would LaRoux see him as a threat or as an asset to his private army?

Sorren was surrounded by at least ten men. Though he knew he was a better gunman than any of the ragged, dusty soldiers, he also knew he didn't have a chance against all of them.

He felt a trickle of sweat dribble down his spine. The sun was setting. It wasn't hot enough for him to be perspiring like he was. How does a man make himself *not* perspire?

Be calm, he told himself. *Be calm. Get in close. Pick your own time and place. That's the only way you'll get to LaRoux. From the inside and on your own terms.*

Sorren sat back in the saddle, affecting his most

bored posture. To his right he saw the stagecoach. One half of it was riddled with bullet holes and splattered with blood.

There was a commotion to his left and then the sharp, laughing voice of Jean-Jacques LaRoux bellowed, "Bring that traitor to me!"

Half the men reacted to the words literally; the other half heard the humor in their leader's voice and relaxed.

"You might say the general and I are old friends," Sorren said to nobody in particular. He swung a leg over his horse, dropping to the ground. "Somebody take care of my horse. Make sure she gets water. It's been a long ride."

Sorren walked slowly and he smiled inwardly when the men parted to make room for him. From behind he heard someone say, "Bossy kinda fella, ain't he?" and Sorren knew that at least for the time being, he was in control of the situation.

When Sorren got his first look at LaRoux, from a distance of twenty yards or so, his first thought was, *He's gotten so old.*

"McKenna! You rascal you!" LaRoux said, his face beaming with pleasure, walking with a hand already extended.

When Sorren looked into LaRoux's eyes, he felt a chill go through him. *The man has lost his mind. LaRoux has gone completely insane.*

They shook hands, clasping each other's biceps with their free hands. Sorren smiled and looked into LaRoux's eyes as a man would who had shared dangerous adventures with another. But all he could think about was how strange it was that LaRoux should be so happy to see him. It wasn't like they were ever truly close friends during the war. Sorren hadn't even *pretended* to be his friend.

"It's good to see you!" LaRoux said. He ushered Sorren to a path and they walked several yards to a small clearing. A tent had been set up. "Damn it, McKenna, what brings you here?"

"I was looking for you."

LaRoux turned, and though he tried not to look shocked, Sorren could see the wheels turning in his mind.

"Now why would you be doing that?"

Sorren shrugged his shoulders. "I've been riding for days. If you want me to talk, you're going to have to bribe me with a little whiskey first."

LaRoux laughed at that, but Sorren sensed that he hadn't relaxed at all. The general gestured to the trunk of a dead tree that had apparently been brought over to serve as a bench. Then he stepped into his tent, and when he returned, he held a bottle in one hand and two glasses in the other.

"To your health," LaRoux said after pouring shots into each glass.

Sorren swallowed the whiskey in a gulp and felt it burn down his throat. As he did this, he never once took his eyes from LaRoux's. The two men were studying each other, neither willing to give away too much. Sorren extended his glass and it was refilled.

"Now, why were you looking for me?"

Sorren sipped the whiskey before answering. "Heard some stories and they kind of sounded like your work," he began, his dark eyes still trained on LaRoux. "I've been here and there since the fighting stopped."

"The fighting hasn't stopped," LaRoux cut in.

"I've been here and there trying to figure out what I was any good at," Sorren continued, as though he had not heard. "I even tried being a sheriff once, if you can believe that." He took another sip and sighed, affecting the posture of a man relaxing. "Now I've got a spread for myself. Some horses I raise and break."

"Big?"

Sorren waggled a palm. "Too much like work. Then I started hearing stories about you in Mexico territory and I said to myself, 'Now that's something I'm good at!'"

"You were the best."

In a dead-serious voice, just above a whisper, Sorren said, "I still am."

This time it was LaRoux who pretended Sorren had said nothing. "You still haven't explained why you were looking for me."

"A while back I heard about an ambush in this area. Four wagons full of people got it. Seemed like your style."

"There was a time when it was your style."

Sorren could feel LaRoux's eyes on him, studying him, looking at him as a potential enemy. "I thought you might need a good man at your side. We worked together before and didn't do too bad for ourselves. Thought we might try it again."

"Why would I want to cut you in?"

"I've seen your men. Now I didn't get a real good look at them, but they don't strike me like the kind of men you had with you from '62 to '64. Sorren tilted his head back and smiled. "We're not fighting the war anymore, so whatever you're doing, it's got to be for a profit. I just want my share of it, that's all."

LaRoux leaned over and poured more whiskey into Sorren's glass, even though very little of it had been drank. "Maybe I could use a man of your skills," he said warily. "On the other hand, maybe you're too expensive."

Sorren gave LaRoux a sly smile. "It's not just the money I'm after. I can find a job anywhere." Sorren cleared his throat and chuckled softly under his breath. "There was this woman, you see, and she had a husband—"

"Jesus Christ, McKenna, don't you ever learn?" LaRoux exploded hysterically, a smile now spreading across his face.

"Now just be quiet and listen. We were going at it like crazy and he comes home early."

"Did you kill him?" There was a look of expectation on LaRoux's face. Sorren's didn't have to guess what answer he wanted.

"He went for a gun. He didn't leave me any choice." Sorren leaned closer to LaRoux. He was pleased with his own acting skills when he actually felt himself blushing with embarrassment. He talked in a confidential whisper. If the truth was known, she was happy as could be I dropped her husband. But when the law started snooping around, she went nuts and said I raped her." Sorren chuckled softly. "I should have known the law wouldn't let that one rest. She was the sheriff's wife!" LaRoux howled, then hugged his sides with laughter.

"So you're on the run again." LaRoux slapped his

knee with pleasure. "McKenna, you'll never change! Not in a thousand years will you ever learn your lesson." He took off his hat and shook his head, spreading his long, wavy blond hair around his shoulders. "You always did have a special something for married women."

"That's the only way you know they're any good. If nobody else wants to bed them, why should I waste my time?"

The sexual banter went on for a while longer. Sorren did not feel at ease, but LaRoux seemed to be buying his story. In time he also understood why the general had been so happy to see him. LaRoux had nobody to talk to. He considered his men grotesquely inferior.

They exchanged stories of the war, both the good ones and the bad ones, stories about women seduced and women rejected. A dozen different times Sorren thought about drawing his knife and putting it into LaRoux's chest, but each time he thought of it, he quickly discounted it. LaRoux, after years of being hunted, was not a man to let down his guard. He always had men around him. Sometimes it was just one or two, but they were always strategically located. At other times, there were more than six or seven men. If Sorren would try anything, he might succeed in killing LaRoux, but it would surely cost him his own life. At present, he just wasn't willing to make that sacrifice.

"Smitty, come here!" LaRoux called out. A moment later Smitty, his face flushed with alcohol, came forward. He eyed Sorren suspiciously. "Bring my present to me now." After the older man had left,

LaRoux turned to Sorren. "Best damned soldier in the world, Smitty. I gave him my woman the other day, and he turned around and gave me one in return. We just got her from the stage."

Sorren fought against the nausea that welled up inside him. LaRoux wasn't a soldier anymore. He was vicious during the war. Truly savage. But he had been savage, at least, for a purpose. Now he was savage because he liked it.

Through the trees Sorren heard a masculine gasp of pain and then a man say, "Don't hit her, goddamn it! She's the general's woman!" Sorren thought, *She's fighting them. Good girl. I just hope you don't get yourself killed for it.*

LaRoux turned to Sorren. "Smitty's a good man. He knows better than to bruise up my favorite woman."

A moment later Smitty and another man dragged a scratching, clawing, biting Shadow into the clearing.

Chapter Seventeen

Shadow was thrown to her knees. She kept her chin down, her eyes on the ground. Her hair, so lovingly pinned and swirled into a delicate coiffure by Emma, was now a mess, tumbling down her shoulders in a mass of tangles. A few barrettes and combs were still in her hair, just enough to show that it had been pinned up at one time, just enough to display the turmoil and trauma she'd gone through during the last hour.

Shadow did not feel like crying. Horror had turned to rage.

"Isn't she something?" It was the rich, cultured voice of the man she knew as General LaRoux. "A real fighter, that one. She'll be wild in bed." LaRoux spoke for the benefit of his audience. He found all nonwhites distasteful to one degree or another.

Very slowly, Shadow rose to her feet. Pride refused to allow her to remain on her knees in front of LaRoux. With a forearm, she swept her hair back from her face and looked up, her eyes dark, angry, and defiant.

And then she stopped breathing, because the man she thought she was beginning to know, the man she had shared her body with, the man she wanted so much to please, was sitting beside General LaRoux, sharing a drink with him.

"You bastard!" Shadow spat, using the epitaph so often used against her, the one she found most reprehensible. "So—"

Shadow's reflexes were fast, but not fast enough to block the stinging slap from Sorren that snapped her head around. The smack of a palm striking against a soft cheek seemed to echo in her ears. She slumped partially, her knees giving way beneath her. She heard her blood racing in her ears. Before her knees touched the ground, Smitty and the other soldier grabbed her arms and hoisted her up.

She felt fingers pushing into her hair. Her head was jerked back. Shadow gasped as she felt strands of hair being yanked from her scalp. When she opened her eyes, Sorren's face was frightfully close to hers, his eyes glittering with a kind of wildness Shadow had never seen in them before.

"Lesson One," Sorren said, and to emphasize his words, he jerked her head back another inch, "You don't talk unless you're spoken to. And when you do talk, you'll find your life here will be a lot easier if you keep a civil tongue in your mouth."

Different sensations were all slowly coming back to Shadow. Her cheek was burning now, turning crimson where Sorren had slapped her. She caught the nauseating, putrid smell of whiskey on his breath.

He loomed above her, the violent man dressed in black. Flashing in her mind's eye was the image of his face as he slept. It was calm then, truly peaceful. Now it was a twisted caricature of the handsome man she thought she was in love with.

"Do you hear me?" Sorren demanded, his fingers tight in Shadow's hair. He shook her head. "I want an answer!"

Shadow spit in his face, and for her defiance, she received another slap. This one, surprisingly, was not as hard as the first one. It hardly hurt at all, or perhaps she was just becoming numb to pain.

Closing her eyes, Shadow thought, *This isn't really happening to me. This isn't really Sorren. It's someone who looks like him, that's all. It's just a terrible nightmare. Open your eyes! Open your eyes and wake up and end this ugly nightmare!"*

When Shadow opened her eyes, she watched Sorren wipe her saliva from his face with the back of a hand.

"Get her away from me," Sorren hissed through clenched teeth. His face, always gaunt, was more defined now as he glared angrily down at Shadow. He untangled his fingers from her thick hair. "Put her in a safe place. And I don't want anyone touching her." He gave Shadow a look of malevolent lust. "At least not until I've had my fill of her." Sorren looked straight at Smitty. "I don't want anyone touching her. When I'm good and ready, I'll come for her."

For a moment, the camp stopped. Men did not simply take women away from LaRoux. Sorren knew he was forcing LaRoux to make a decision—and he could get himself killed in the process.

"When *you're* good and ready?" LaRoux said evenly. He paused, feeling the eyes of his men on him. He smiled. "Allow me to make a gift of that which you have already taken." Then he laughed, and everyone began to breathe again.

Smitty looked back and forth between Sorren and LaRoux. "Do what he told you to do," LaRoux ordered. To Sorren he said, "Consider this a professional courtesy." Sorren returned his thin smile, acknowledging the gesture with a slight nod of his head.

"And Smitty"—LaRoux paused and gave the old man a wicked smile—"when the time comes, you'll be the first."

Smitty nodded his head. He understood perfectly. Better to be third in line for the raven-haired, razor-tongued vixen than twentieth.

Shadow was dragged down the path through the trees again, but this time she wasn't fighting. Her will to fight, that spark of life inside her bosom that she thought could not be extinguished, had gone out.

There was no fight left in Shadow.

She was brought to a Conestoga wagon and practically thrown through the canvas flap at the rear. Shadow landed with a thump on her knees. She heard the tear of her dress giving way. The dress that morning had been new and cherished. Now it was dirty, torn, ruined.

Shadow looked around the interior of the wagon. It was packed with food, and jammed into the front part was a mattress. She didn't have to be told what that was for. This wagon was what constituted the bordello for the soldiers in LaRoux's command.

She crossed her legs beneath her and buried her face in her hands. How had her life taken such a turn? First the ambush of the stage, and then Sorren, sitting with that evil General LaRoux.

Shadow could still see Sorren's evil face leering at her. She remembered how his strong hand, which had once caressed her with a connoisseur's touch, had slapped her face. And that look in his dark eyes as he jerked her hair, his face so close to hers, his breath smelling of whiskey.

How had she been so gullible as to believe his love words? For the first time in her life she had let her defenses down, and the end result was that she was betrayed by the man she'd given her virginity to.

She knew then that Sorren had not left her to "hunt" for the killers of the wagon train; he'd gone to join them. There they were, LaRoux and Sorren, drinking whiskey and chatting happily. And to think that he had tried to convince Shadow it was duty that had made him leave her.

Shadow thought, *What am I going to do when he comes for me? I won't let him touch me. I won't! He'll have to rape me. I won't let him enjoy it. I'll scratch his eyes out. I'll kill him before I let him touch me.*

"Akana," Shadow whispered to herself, her voice softly pleading to the heavens, "why did you ever make me love a man like him?"

"Overstepping yourself a bit there, aren't you?" LaRoux's eyebrows were raised in question as Sorren sat on the tree trunk beside him. Though it annoyed him that McKenna had both given orders to soldiers not under his command and seemed to think he could usurp the squaw in white woman's clothes, LaRoux was pleased with Sorren's reactions. He was as quick as ever, and though he'd never seen Sorren lose his temper before, LaRoux wasn't dismayed. He only wondered if Sorren still knew how to accept orders. If he did, he'd be the lieutenant LaRoux had been looking for. Smitty was good, but he wasn't officer material.

"Name your price," Sorren said quietly, not looking at LaRoux. "You can have my percentage of the next take, or you can have cash up front. Just name it and it's yours. Just so long as I have that"—he gritted his teeth as though blood-thirsty rage boiled in his veins—"bitch to myself."

Women are his weakness, thought LaRoux, looking reflectively at the man beside him. *They always have been. If I can keep him in women, he'll be under my thumb for the rest of his life, and he'll be glad to be there.*

"You want her that much?"

Sorren reached for the whiskey bottle at LaRoux's feet before looking up. "Nobody spits in my face," he said quietly. "Nobody." He pulled the cork from the bottle and took a long swig of liquor. "I'll be done with her soon. Then you can have her, or let the others have her. But first I want to teach her a lesson."

It made perfect sense to LaRoux. Sorren would show the squaw a lesson in subservience. The squaw was attractive, LaRoux had observed, but he wasn't interested in her himself. He never slept with the coloreds or squaws. He knew that kind of thing made a man dirty deep down in his soul. If McKenna wanted to spend his soul on a squaw, that was his problem, not LaRoux's.

"Here's the deal," LaRoux began slowly, formulating his plan as he spoke. "You'll get your share of everything, and I don't want any money. Consider the squaw as a bonus for riding with me. But from this point forward, don't ever countermand one of my orders. When I talk, you listen; when I give you a command, you follow it. You don't ask why, you just do it."

Sorren tilted the whiskey bottle to his lips. He allowed air bubbles to rise toward the bottom, making it appear like he was drinking much more than he really was. When he replaced the cork and set the bottle down, he exhaled softly, pretending the whiskey had seared his throat as he gulped it.

"No problem there. You know me. I'm a good soldier."

"This isn't like during the war," LaRoux said, looking directly at Sorren. He couldn't allow the slightest misunderstanding. "You're not working alone behind enemy lines. You're riding with me and you'll take orders from me. You can't just accept assignments and then work on your own from there on."

"I know that. You won't have any problems from me." Sorren stood abruptly. "Is she some place where I'll have a little privacy?"

"She'll probably be in the hotel."

"Hotel?"

"Smitty'll show you." LaRoux watched thoughtfully

as Sorren turned away. A hundred stories he'd heard about the legendary Rebel soldier, Sorren McKenna, came to mind. He remembered a particularly impressive one. At the time, it seemed too improbable to be true, even for Sorren McKenna. "Sorren!" he shouted. The black-clad man stopped in mid stride. He turned slowly until he faced LaRoux. "Is it true that you were the one who assassinated General Becker in New York?"

Sorren registered no emotion whatsoever, but his mind was working rapidly. Sorren, President Lincoln, and General Grant had concocted so many schemes and planted so many stories in the newspapers during the war it was hard to remember them all.

"Why?" Sorren asked, stalling for time. His mind was racing.

"I just want to know, that's all. You're under my command now. I like to know what my men are capable of."

It came back to Sorren, all the little details that had made his reputation, his identity within the Rebel army, so unquestionable. General Becker had died at home, alone with his wife, of natural causes. A heart attack, the doctors believed. Lincoln had his agents make sure the newspapers carried the account of a grieving widow who told of a man, matching Sorren's description, slipping past the general's bodyguards and knifing Becker to death in his sleep. The assassin "escaped" past the guards without ever being seen. The rumor that the assassination had been done by Sorren McKenna was planted in the South by agents working for General Grant.

"Yeah. I did it," said Sorren after long moments, his tone carrying neither pleasure nor sadness.

"How did you get past the guards?"

"It was easy," Sorren replied, then turned and walked away.

The "hotel" was the Conestoga wagon with the large feather mattress in it. It was the storage wagon, carrying food, clean water, bandages, and other necessities of travel.

Sorren muttered his thanks to Smitty for leading him there. He stepped past the soldier standing guard at the rear of the wagon, wondering if he was there to keep Shadow in or the other soldiers out. He stepped into the wagon and put a finger to his lips. Shadow, sitting on the floor of the wagon near the mattress, turned dazed eyes toward him.

Sorren smoothed the canvas curtain over the rear of the wagon again. The heat inside was oppressive.

He got down on one knee near Shadow. He placed a fingertip to her lips to keep her quiet. Then, in a voice loud enough to carry through the canvas walls to the guard on duty and any soldiers with voyeuristic tendencies who happened to be lurking around, he said, "Now, let's find out if you can do more with that mouth than insult me!"

The stupor Shadow had been in vanished with his words. She snapped out of it fully conscious . . . and filled with hatred.

"You filth! I trusted—"

Sorren clamped his palm over Shadow's mouth. When she began to fight him, he pushed her back-

ward, knocking her onto the mattress. He intentionally kicked over a stack of pans nested together. The
effect was satisfactory.

"Shut up!" he hissed, his body pinning Shadow to
the bed. He had his hand pressed so tightly over her
mouth the skin near his fingers had gone from tawny
to white. "Don't say anything! Just let me explain!"
Sorren's face was almost touching Shadow's in the
stifling hot, closed wagon. "Don't say my name. For
God's sake, Shadow, *don't say my name!*"

Sorren felt her relax, and he released some of the
pressure of his hand over her mouth. The burning
contempt he saw in Shadow's eyes cut through him
like a knife. "Just let me explain," he whispered. "Just
give me a chance and I can explain everything."

But Shadow did not want an explanation. She was
not looking at the man who had made sweet love to
her, the man who had turned her life around with his
affection. She was looking at the devil incarnate, a
silver-tongued liar who smelled of liquor and drank
with murderers. The moment she felt the hand
loosen over her mouth, Shadow caught the middle of
one finger between her teeth and bit with all the
strength in her jaws.

"Owwww!" Sorren gasped in agony, feeling sharp
teeth sinking to the bone on the ring finger of his
right hand.

He jammed the fingers of his left hand into
Shadow's mouth and, with all his might, pried open
her jaws enough to free his bleeding finger.

"You damn fool!" he shouted, unafraid of what
ears outside the wagon would hear his words. "That's
my gun hand!"

The look in Shadow's eyes was of pure triumph. "Good!" she spat.

Sorren wanted to slap that smile from her face. Didn't she realize how important his hands were to their safety, especially now? Had she completely lost her mind?

The black silk shirt was sticking wetly to Sorren's body, defining his leonine strength. He rolled off Shadow, cradling his wounded hand in the other. "You damn fool," he whispered, his voice hollow in the wagon. Blood, warm and sticky, pooled in his left palm. "How does it feel to know you might just have killed me?"

"I wish I had." Shadow got off the mattress, sitting on the floor once again. She would not sit on a mattress used by the whores who rode with LaRoux's men.

Sorren tested the finger. It hurt like hell to bend it, but at least it wasn't broken. It was going to swell mightily. Would he even be able to hold a gun in the morning? He wanted to scream at Shadow for making an impossible situation even worse. She'd hurt his gun hand. Hadn't she learned *anything* about him? The stabbing pain went from his finger up to his elbow.

"You stupid little fool. You don't know what you've done."

"Yes, I do. I nearly bit your finger off! I wish I *had* bit it off."

The triumph Shadow felt in hurting Sorren was short-lived. As her anger subsided and the blind rage to lash out at Sorren—to hurt him as much as he had hurt her—lessened, she found herself sinking

313

into a low, pitiless sorrow.

Shadow watched as Sorren took off his neckerchief and wrapped it tightly around the damaged ring finger. She slid a little ways across the floor until her back was against the short wooden wall of the wagon. She wanted to put as much distance between herself and Sorren as possible. She hugged her knees to her bosom and tried to ignore the oppressive heat and the taste of stale air on her tongue.

"This is why you left me," she whispered. "So you could meet up with your old friends. Did you see their handiwork? They killed four men. They gunned them down without giving them a chance."

Sorren tested his finger again. The makeshift bandage would keep the swelling to a minimum. If he developed an infection in the finger, he'd have to have it amputated. If he did that, he'd lose the critical edge to his marksmanship. It would only be a matter of time before someone challenged him. In his mind's eye, Sorren could see the scenario of his own death being played out. He saw himself facedown on a dusty road with a crowd of people slowly gathering around his corpse, some of them saying how they never thought Sorren McKenna would ever get beat, others saying confidently that they had known all along it was only a matter of time before someone drew faster.

"Okay, I'm calm now," Shadow said quietly. She remembered not to use Sorren's name. She wondered if Sorren McKenna were really his name. Shadow wondered if she really knew anything at all about the man who called himself Sorren McKenna. "Tell me some lies. That's what you wanted, so go ahead and do it. You're so good at lying, aren't you?"

"I went looking for LaRoux," Sorren said. He sat on the mattress, moving closer to Shadow so that his voice wouldn't carry. "I knew he was the man behind the attack on the wagons last week. I didn't want to join up with him, I just wanted to find him." Shadow gave Sorren a look that asked if he really thought she was gullible enough to believe him. "I can only tell you the truth. If you don't believe me, I can't help that."

As Sorren spoke, he wondered how much of the truth he could give Shadow. She was in no mood to get the whole truth. He sensed that much. This was a touchy situation being in LaRoux's camp. And now with his gun hand burning like hell's fire, he might have to rely on Shadow; it was always dangerous to rely on amateurs.

"I met LaRoux a long time ago." That was at least partially honest, Sorren told himself. He still felt the guilt of deception. "I was lying to LaRoux when they brought you to him. I told him I was on the run from the law and that that's why I had been looking for him. He believed me. I said I wanted to ride with him."

"Why?" Shadow was looking at Sorren over her knees, her mouth and chin hidden by her legs.

"Because the only way LaRoux is going to be"— *think of the right words, McKenna!*—"brought to justice is from the inside. I couldn't just ride into camp and arrest him, could I?" Sorren waited a moment, then asked, "Well, could I?"

Shadow shrugged her shoulders. She wasn't going to give up her skepticism that easily. She'd trusted

Sorren too much already and that trust in him had cost her dearly, in ways that would never show up on one of the MW Circle's financial ledgers.

"I didn't want to slap you, but I couldn't let you say my name. If LaRoux realized that you and I know each other, he could use that against me." Sorren tested his finger again and grimaced. The pain was getting worse, not better. "I had to slap you, don't you see? I couldn't risk you saying something that would endanger both of us."

Shadow asked a question whose possible answer frightened her. "Is Sorren McKenna your real name?" *Say it is*, she thought, and at the same time cursed herself for wanting to believe in Sorren.

"Yes."

"What have you lied to me about?"

"I haven't —" Sorren stopped himself. He needed Shadow trusting him. Pouring fresh lies on top of old lies wasn't going to gain her confidence. "I haven't lied to you unnecessarily. I had to tell you some things that weren't true, but I didn't want to."

"I find little consolation in that." Her eyes were glassy with withheld tears. It was only then that she realized she was nearly crying once again. She peered over her knees, her eyes shining wetly in the pale light that filtered through the canvas. "What about the things you said to me? Were they lies?"

"What things?"

"You know what I'm talking about. For God's sake, don't think that I'm *that* stupid."

Sorren closed his eyes. The pain this time was not in his hand, it was in his heart. She was questioning everything about him now. Everything he had ever said to her was under suspicion. The grand irony of it was not lost on Sorren. The one time in his entire lecherous life he had actually been honest about his feelings with a woman, had told her the truth about how he really felt about her, even though he had actually said very little, he wasn't believed. All the lies he had told to all the other women were believed in their entirety. A joyless half smile, nothing at all like the one Shadow found so endearing, curled the lips that had kissed her so tenderly.

"When I said those things to you, I wasn't lying. I promise you that."

"You also promised you wouldn't hurt me." Shadow rubbed her cheek, though it no longer hurt. It was a cruel gesture, done as much to remind herself what Sorren had done as to remind him. "You've been doing a lot of that the last couple of days."

Sorren felt a trickle of perspiration from his temple to his jaw. He wanted to open the rear flaps of the wagon, but for security reasons he couldn't.

"Help me with my jacket, will you?" Sorren extended his hand toward Shadow, indicating he wanted her to grab the sleeve of it. She didn't move. He pulled the light jacket off himself, wincing when fresh pain stabbed through his hand up to his elbow.

He leaned back against the mattress again, his elbow on his knee, keeping his hand raised above his heart in the way an army doctor had once told him.

"What were you doing on the stage, anyway?" Sorren asked. He'd been so shocked to see Shadow, so involved in trying to protect her from LaRoux, that the cause of her being there hadn't touched his curiosity until now.

317

"I was delivering the contracts to our lawyer in Denver City." Shadow's speech paused briefly, then she added, with a touch of regret, "Then I was going to say in the best hotel around and soak in a tub until I felt human again."

Sorren shook his head wearily. He felt a thousand years old. It seemed like he had been fighting in wars for hundreds of years. "Carl," he muttered disgustedly. "That damn Carl. I suppose he's the one who sent you?" Shadow nodded and pushed thick hair away from her face. "Let me guess. . . . You were to see the lawyer first, then go to the hotel?" Again Shadow nodded. "He was lying to you. There isn't a hotel in Denver City that would allow an Indian woman to take a room. Certainly not an unescorted Indian woman."

"What?" Shadow exclaimed, her eyes widening.

"You would have been lucky to sleep in a livery stable." Sorren vowed that if he ever got away from LaRoux, he was going to make Carl pay for his mendacity. "I'll bet he bought the stage ticket for you, too?" Again Shadow nodded. "One way?" Nod. "You probably would have been stuck in Denver City until hell froze over. They don't sell stage passes to Indians. If they did, it would cost you three times as much as the going rate. When you finally made it back to the MW Circle, Carl would have been apologetic as hell and say he never knew that would happen."

"That lousy—" Shadow's voice trailed off.

"That's Carl. He's always been like that. At least as long as I've known him." Sorren sighed and rubbed his eyebrows together. It was something he did whenever he was physically and intellectually tired. "Come on, let's get some sleep. We're going to need our wits about us tomorrow if we're going to get out of here."

Shadow shook her head slowly. "I'm not going anywhere with you."

Sorren huffed and shook his head in disbelief. "Listen, the only thing that's keeping you from getting raped by every man in this camp right now is me. Now you can hate me if you want, but you'd better understand that the only thing separating those men out there from you," he said, jerking his thumb at the canvas behind Shadow, "is me. You've already hurt our chances of getting out of this alive by damn near biting off my finger."

Shadow didn't want to believe Sorren. It was inconceivable to her that this man could be trying to help her now. She wanted to believe him, but she didn't want to be hurt by him again, to be misled and lied to. In the face of her skepticism, she could not deny that Sorren was her only barrier from the soldiers. She had seen the way the men looked at her when she was hauled away. And when they wrestled her to the ground, their hands had been all over her body, cruelly grasping her breasts and forcing her dress up.

"Come on, let's get some sleep. We'll need our rest." Sorren grimaced as he moved over on the mattress, leaving enough room for Shadow to get on it. He placed his right hand on his chest.

"I'm not sleeping there, or with you," Shadow replied, hugging her knees tighter against herself.

"It's here or on the floor. If you take one step out of this wagon, I won't be able to stop the men from

319

doing whatever they damn well please."

Shadow made a disdainful expression. "That's where they do it," she said. "This is just a whorehouse with wheels on it."

"I know that."

"And you're going to sleep there anyway?"

"I haven't many options right now."

Sorren placed his left forearm over his eyes. He didn't want to argue any more with Shadow. He had too many problems on his mind right now — problems that could become fatal ones — for him to fight with her.

"You no doubt are unaccustomed to sleeping on dirty mattresses used by willing whores," Shadow whispered, her tone soft and filled with derision. "I'm not. I won't sleep in that bed and I won't sleep next to you." Her tone deepened slightly as she added, "You've already proven that you can't be trusted."

Shadow saw a muscle flicker high on Sorren's cheek as he grit his teeth in anger. "The only way we're ever going to get out of this mess alive is if you do what I tell you to do. If LaRoux finds out that you and I know each other, he'll kill us."

"You've lied so many times I don't know what I can believe anymore."

Sorren twisted onto his side, turning his back to Shadow. "I'm getting some sleep. You can sleep on the floor if you want. If you don't like that, you can share the bed. Don't worry, I won't try to touch your precious body."

Sorren could feel a marrow-deep anger, burning like a long, slow fuse toward dynamite, sizzling inside him. Someday he would make Carl pay for what he'd done to Shadow. Her opinion of Sorren may have changed, but his emotions toward her were just as strong as ever. All he had to do was convince her that he wasn't a liar, wasn't a cold-blooded murderer, and that the man who treated him like a friend wasn't really his friend.

It seemed impossible.

All he had to do was make Shadow believe in him again, make her trust him like she used to.

He rolled over and looked into Shadow's eyes.

It *was* impossible.

Chapter Eighteen

Sorren awoke first. The old instincts were still with him now that he was once again living a double life. He awoke without moving a muscle or even flinching. With eyes closed and his breathing continuing at its even, steady pace, he listened carefully. What did he hear? The sound of Shadow breathing as she slept on the floor beside him. The sound of a campfire coming to life outside. A few men talking quietly, either respectful of those who still slept or not awake enough to raise their voices any more than a whisper. What did he smell? Coffee, and beans that were laced with pieces of pork and beef for flavoring. Memories came back to him of the awful food he had endured during the war. Why was it neither the Union nor Rebel army could find decent cooks? Was it the difficulty in cooking for so many hungry men at one time that made the food so abominable?

When he was convinced that he was alone and unwatched, Sorren opened his eyes. He was fully awake by this time, his mind and body ready for action.

He sat upright and kicked his feet off the mattress. Shadow was sleeping on her side, her hands under her cheek, her knees curled up to keep her legs beneath the small blanket she had. She looked frightfully uncomfortable. Sorren wanted to take her into his arms and hold her gently, but he did not. Shadow had made it quite clear that Sorren's touch was no longer welcome.

He looked at his wounded finger. Sorren tried to bend it and stabbing pain lanced through him. The finger bent, but not easily.

He unwrapped the neckerchief from the finger. Almost instantly, the finger began to swell. He smiled at the finger and at the pain, though there was nothing funny in it. He'd never seen Shadow that angry before. Not even when she was in the bank and had drawn her knife on Marc.

He looked at Shadow again. God, she looked beautiful. Even with her hair all mussed up and fatigue showing on her face, she was astonishingly beautiful. And she loved him. Or Sorren was pretty sure that she did, anyway. He wondered if she *had* loved him, if his betrayal had caused a crevice in her affection that no amount of love words could close.

Sorren got up slowly and stepped over Shadow, careful not to disturb her. She would need more rest. If yesterday had been harrowing for Sorren, it had been doubly so for Shadow. And sleeping on the floor of the Conestoga hadn't helped matters any.

Sorren slipped through the partially open rear flap of the wagon and stepped outside. The air was fresh and clean, smelling of morning, of dew. In the distance, he saw the Rockies. Sorren inhaled deeply. The air in the wagon was stagnant. Outside, he could almost smell the snowcapped mountains.

Only one soldier noticed him. He gave Sorren a grin and Sorren smiled back. *Everyone must surely think that I raped her last night,* thought Sorren. I've got to play up to their game. Idly, Sorren wondered what time the last guard on him had gone off duty. Perhaps he'd had one all night, and only now, with the entire camp rising, were his movements unwatched.

"You got coffee there," Sorren asked, seeing the large enameled pot on an iron tripod above the flames. It helped, with soldier types, to ask the obvious.

"Yeah. You want some?"

Sorren accepted the cup and tasted it. The coffee was hot and weak. It was pure army coffee, just like the slop he used to drink. Some things never changed. The soldier gave him another grin, but Sorren didn't smile back this time.

"Suppose y'all didn't get much sleep last night," the soldier said, leering at Sorren.

"Not much," Sorren replied, then turned and walked away. He just couldn't make sexual jokes about Shadow with this man. Perhaps if she were someone else, he might have at least tried to make lighthearted banter about his sexual conquest. But with Shadow, he couldn't. Besides, who among these murders and rapists would believe him if he said he *hadn't* raped her? The truth, Sorren understood, was seldom his friend.

The camp was coming to life in segments. Old feelings came back to Sorren, along with the burning sensation in the pit of his stomach. It was the burn he always had when he was in a Rebel camp, pretending to be a Rebel soldier, pretending to fight side by side with men he was actually sending to their graves. Sorren wondered how many of the men in the camp he would kill and if one of them, or all of them, would kill him.

He thought, *No one here, including myself, will die a natural death. We'll all die violently.*

Sorren moved to the tongue of a wagon and sat down, sipping his coffee. He wanted a cigarette, but he wouldn't have one. Now was not the time to let his defenses down, to let his discipline slip even a fraction. His mind was sharpest when he denied himself his vices.

How many times have I seen this same scene? Sorren mused. Men rolling out of their blankets, stumbling around to the nearest tree to relieve themselves, then staggering toward the closest pot of coffee. Men stretching, yawning, scratching themselves and looking around as though they couldn't remember where they were and had no idea how they had gotten there.

He heard the canvas curtain rustle behind him, but Sorren didn't move. A soft, bare foot touched his back. He turned slowly to look up over his shoulder.

"Oh. Good morning," a sleepy-faced Francine said. "I didn't know it was you." She seemed oblivious of the fact that the strap of her petticoat had slipped off a smooth shoulder nearly to the point of exposing one breast. "I thought you were one of them other coots." She gave Sorren a smile and made an attempt to push her hair into place with her fingers. "I must look a mess. You'll have to forgive me."

"No need to be forgiven," Sorren said quietly. He did not miss the look of interest in Francine's eyes. Perhaps, under other circumstances and before having met Shadow, he would have been interested enough in her to pursue his carnal urges. As it was, he was mildly flattered by her obvious interest in him, and a little annoyed by it. He didn't need a woman clinging to him while he was with LaRoux. Having Shadow with him and having a painful gun hand was going to make his job difficult enough as it was.

"You're the new man." Francine moved so that she sat on the tongue of the wagon beside Sorren. Her hip was touching his. He noticed how low her petticoat had fallen on her bosom. She saw the direction of his gaze, but she did not readjust the garment. She introduced herself, then said, "You're that man Sorren McKenna. I guess you and the general go back a long ways. Fought in the war together and all that."

"And all that," Sorren said noncommittally. He wanted to get rid of Francine or leave himself, but he didn't want her offended.

Sorren heard a grumble from inside the wagon. Shuffled footsteps preceded the curtain being opened, then Smitty, in long johns that hadn't been washed in the recent past, stepped out.

"Francine, get me coffee," he said in a sleepy, gravelly voice.

Sorren was a little surprised. He knew that Smitty

was one of LaRoux's top men, but he hadn't figured the old soldier warranted one of the two wagons. The wagon he had slept in last night, Sorren concluded, was used only when the soldiers were allowed the private services of one of the women. On most nights the women just chose a tent, with a man in it, to sleep.

Shadow had been right all along. It was just a whorehouse on wheels.

Francine, not wanting to leave Sorren but afraid of what would happen if she openly refused Smitty's command, got to her feet grudgingly. She looked at Sorren, gave him another smile, then bent low to take his cup from his hand and, in doing so, exposed much more of her bosom to him. "Can I warm this up for you?"

"Please," Sorren replied.

Smitty took the place vacated by Francine, and Sorren breathed a sigh of relief. At least Smitty wasn't appearing angry with Francine's undisguised flirtation with him.

"Morning," Sorren said without looking at Smitty. He would like information from the old soldier if possible, but he wasn't going to push his luck.

"Ya gotta be careful fer that woman," Smitty growled, rubbing his eyes and scratching his beard stubble. "Damn woman'll talk yer ear if ya let her." Smitty and Sorren watched Francine return with three cups of steaming coffee. "I prefer 'em quiet like, but I ain't gonna get it that way with her."

Sorren grinned. "We've all got our crosses to bear." Smitty didn't understand Sorren's reference, and the look on his face showed it. "At least she's pretty. She could talk too much and also be ugly."

"Yeah," Smitty acknowledged. Francine returned and Smitty took the cup she offered. "Ya got a point there."

Francine squeezed herself between Sorren and Smitty. Though she did not actually reach out and grab Sorren, both men there knew she was thinking about it. Her eyes never strayed far from the younger man.

"Any idea where we're headed next?" Sorren asked, hunched over his coffee, appearing as though the answer to his question meant nothing more to him than small talk.

"The gen'ral didn't say. He ain't one for talkin' much 'les he's got somethin' special to say. We're one place and then we're ridin' someplace else. He lets us know we're there when we git there."

"Makes sense." Sorren thought, *I probably won't get much from Smitty. He's been a soldier too long to have a loose tongue.* "How long have you been riding with General LaRoux?"

Smitty's eyes twinkled with pleasure as he glanced over at Sorren. "Long enough to know that he's got somethin' big planned inside that head o' his." Smitty handed his cup to Francine and nodded toward the fire. She pouted but nevertheless rose to get him more coffee. "He's got somethin' goin'," Smitty said confidentially after Francine had left. "He ain't seen it fit to tell me ever'thin about it jus' yet, but I knows that man and I knows when he's got a ride planned inside his head."

Sorren sipped his coffee reflectively, nodding his head with mild interest. He thought, *Tell me what you now, you damned old fool! Quit stalling and just tell me what LaRoux has told you!*

When Sorren said nothing, Smitty couldn't let his insider's knowledge go to waste. He had to tell someone, and apparently Sorren was going to be the man. Sorren guessed he wanted to prove how close to the general he was.

Smitty sipped his coffee and pulled out a plug of tobacco from the breast pocket of his long johns. Francine grimaced when she watched Smitty bite off a cheek-stretching chew, and Sorren guessed she didn't like the taste of it in the old man's mouth.

"We're gonna be takin' on somebody strong," Smitty said after waiting long enough to make sure he had Sorren's attention. "The gen'ral tol' me las' night to make sure the boys got themselves sobered up. He always tells me that jus' before we go on a run."

"Hmmm," Sorren murmured. Trying to guess where LaRoux would go next, whether he was planning some carnage in particular or just looking for a victim, was about as easy as trying to guess when a rogue mountain lion would come out of the hills to make a meal of a rancher's sheep. That's what had made LaRoux so devastatingly destructive during the war: Nobody in the Union army had ever been able to guess what his next move would be. He kept his troops moving back then, and he kept them moving now. His tactics hadn't changed. The direction might appear meaningless, but Sorren doubted it was. LaRoux had not lived outside the law for as many years as he had without thinking his maneuvers through. He knew what he was going to do next, even if it was

no more than something that was unexpected. It wa
Sorren's job to figure out what that move would be

Stop thinking that way! Sorren suddenly demanded o
himself. It took a moment for him to realize h
wasn't in the war anymore; his job was not to stop
LaRoux's whole army, it was to kill LaRoux. Once
LaRoux was dead, his soldiers would separate
quickly. Without a leader, without the catalyst o
Jean-Jacques LaRoux, they would not be so danger
ous.

"If you hear anything else," Sorren said, risin,
slowly from the tongue of the wagon, "let me know i
you would. I haven't ridden with LaRoux in a lon,
time."

"You'll hear when the rest of us do, McKenna,
Smitty said, no longer casual.

"It takes a while getting used to not riding alone,
Sorren said. He looked away, as though confessin,
some dark secret. "There's safely in numbers."

Sorren glanced at Francine. She was not pleasee
that he was leaving.

"McKenna, is it true you was the one who blowe
up the *Indigo Doll?*" Smitty asked without warning

Sorren smiled, looking down at Smitty. There wa
hardly a Confederate soldier that hadn't heard abou
that one. Sorren remembered the story easily, be
cause he himself had been the one to plant the tale i
the newspapers.

In 1863 the *Indigo Doll,* a passenger paddleboa
that roamed the Mississippi River from St. Paul t
St. Louis, had exploded, killing most of the nearl
one hundred passengers, who had either died in th
explosion or drowned. The cause of the explosion, i

was believed, was a faulty boiler. The stories the newspapers carried, however, suggested that a Rebel spy, matching Sorren's description to a T, had planted explosives on the civilian-laden paddleboat. For months afterward, all civilian vessels were given security by the Union army. Citizens as far north as Minnesota were terrorized, afraid to use water transportation.

"Why would I kill civilians?" Sorren asked rhetorically, the smile in his eyes saying he had done it.

"Had a cousin on that boat."

Sorren's smile waned slightly. His wounded right hand strayed an inch closer to the smooth butt of his Colt. Smitty was unarmed.

"He was a Yankee scum, that man was. Born an' bred in Missouri. But instead o' fightin' with the Stars and Bars, he joined up with the bluecoats."

"His mistake," Sorren replied, his tone even.

"Sort of the way I looks at it, too."

Sorren nodded a good-bye to Francine and left Smitty. As he walked, he felt their eyes on the middle of his back. He wondered what LaRoux had in mind for his men. He knew that he shouldn't worry about it. His first priority was to get Shadow out of camp, to allow her to escape. Only when that was accomplished could he worry about finishing his assignment. In many ways Sorren was like Smitty: He was a professional soldier, he'd always been a professional soldier, and no matter how hard he tried or how much he wanted to change that basic fact about himself, he couldn't.

Shadow awoke, and instantly the old fear came back. All the events of the previous day came back to her in a rush of emotions, each one more frightening than the one before. The worst feeling was when she was being dragged down the deer trail through the trees to LaRoux. She remembered the sensation of abject helplessness as the two soldiers held her arms, their free hands touching her body, gouging their fingers deep into the soft, lush mounds of her breasts, trying to kiss her on the mouth.

Just thinking about what had *almost* happened caused nausea to well up inside Shadow. After she had been attacked by Graywolf and Little Feather, she had known fear, but the thing she feared then was an unknown. Now, after knowing Sorren and tasting the sweetness of temptation, desire, and fulfillment, she was fully aware of how beautiful physical and spiritual lovemaking could be. Intuitively, she knew how vile and defiling a forced experience must be. She knew now, in mental concrete images that horrified her, what she was most afraid of.

Shadow sat up slowly, groaning as she did so. She felt as tired now as she did last night. Sleeping sideways on the floor in the wagon had made it impossible for her to stretch out. Her back ached and so did her neck. On her hands and knees, she stretched, arching her back catlike. Then she got unsteadily to her feet, testing her muscles to see which ones would do as she commanded.

Her dress was clingy and soiled. It had been hideously hot and close in the wagon during the night. Shadow would have liked to open one of the many flaps in the canvas, but to do that would allow the soldiers outside to look in. The feel of their gaze on her body was something so physical and disgusting that she would suffer any inconvenience in air circulation to avoid it.

Sorren was not in the wagon. Shadow wondered where he had gone. To talk with General LaRoux? To discuss plans of what massacre they would perpetrate next?

Though she knew it was all in her mind, Shadow could still feel the stinging slap Sorren had given her. She could also smell his squalid whiskey breath as he spoke to her, his eyes bright with rage, dark as midnight. She remembered, too, how she had spit in his face and later sank her teeth into his finger. She wondered why he hadn't slapped her after that. Certainly biting his gun hand was a much greater offense than . . . what was the word she had used to describe him? . . . Filth? Yes, that was it. Filth. At the time, it seemed to fit him perfectly, fit him like a glove to a hand. Now she wasn't so sure.

Don't believe his lies! a wary mind cautioned. *You've done that before, and look where your faith in him has gotten you.*

A mirthless smile toyed with Shadow's sensual lips. The dark side. Those were the words that Emma had used when she was talking about sex. Sex wasn't the dark side of life. It was beautiful. The dark side of life was what Shadow was witnessing now. The dark side surrounded her; it was closing in on all sides and had the faces of soldiers, old and young, all of them ready for violence, ravenous with the want of her.

She was hungry, but she didn't feel like eating. She was dirty, and she desperately wanted to bathe. *How quickly I learned to enjoy the comfortable life!* thought Shadow, the joyless smile still taunting her wide, full-lipped mouth. The meals with many courses, the big, soft bed, feather pillows, the ready availability of a bath and plenty of fresh laundered clothes . . .

She thought, too, how quickly she had ignored her own vulnerability. She had not brought her knife with her on her trip to Denver City. The knife would have at least offered her some protection against the renegade army run by a lunatic general.

No, that wasn't true, she told herself logically. Had I fought back harder, they might have killed me . . . or worse. She had already witnessed the savagery of the men who held her hostage. They had gunned down the two people who'd shared her stage with her, gunning them down with a vengeance. It was not simply an act of murder, it was more than that. They had fired thirty or forty bullets into the corpses. It was mutilation, not just murder.

Could Sorren really be a part of such behavior? Even if he wasn't an active participant, could be tolerate such things?

A boot scraping against the rear step of the wagon was Shadow's first warning that Sorren had returned. She tensed instinctively. She stepped up onto the mattress, moving back until she was against the canvas wall of the Conestoga.

"Relax," Sorren said, stepping into the wagon. "It's just me."

"I know."

Sorren made an expression of disdain when he saw Shadow's posture and countenance. "Listen," he said, his voice soft, filled with thinly suppressed anger, "I don't know what else I can say to make you believe that I'm not going to hurt you. You can believe me or not. I can't make you do anything. But if you hinder what I'm trying to do here, you'll only end up getting both of us killed." He stopped, his eyes locked onto Shadow. "That's just a little something for you to think about." He shook his head with disdain, his eyes dark and penetrating with his anger. "Spend more time thinking about how you can escape this hellhole and less time thinking about how I've lied to you. It'll be time well spent."

Sorren took a step closer to Shadow, extending the coffee cup. "Consider this a peace offering. I know you like coffee." Shadow's eyes went from the cup back to Sorren's face. "Suit yourself. You can starve yourself to death, too, if you really want to."

Shadow felt herself crumbling inside, felt her will to fight Sorren and Carl and Catherine and everyone else in the whole miserable world slipping from her. What choice did she have? She had to trust Sorren. He was her only chance to escape from LaRoux. If she didn't trust him, she would have to trust someone else. Escaping from LaRoux and all his men was too difficult a task to handle alone. Besides, what did she have to lose by once again placing her faith in Sorren? Nothing. Her situation couldn't get worse.

Yes, it could. You could get passed around from one soldier to the next. Shadow closed her eyes against the thought.

Sorren sat down on a cracker barrel and looked at his right hand. He flexed it. The ringer finger was thick and swollen, but it bent. He would be able to hold a gun. How much pain he'd feel when the Colt was fired and the heavy-caliber pistol recoiled into his palm was quite another matter. He'd have to make his first shots good. The finger wouldn't take the pounding of repeat firing.

Shadow studied Sorren's profile as he worked his finger. The excitement she'd seen in him when he was preparing in his gun room to ride after LaRoux had been replaced with a quiet, deadly professional determination. She could see it in the set of his jaw and in the way he forced his finger to flex despite the pain. He was preparing himself for a gunfight. She couldn't help but wonder how many times he'd gone through exactly the same thing, how many times he'd gotten himself mentally and physically prepared to kill.

"I really hurt you, didn't I?" she said, not knowing what else to say.

"Yes. Satisfied?"

"No." Shadow moved and sat on the edge of the mattress beside Sorren. "I'd like some of that coffee, if the offer is still good." She picked up the cup and tasted it. The coffee was acidic and weak. Looking at Sorren's wounded finger, she saw the swelling and the cuts on either side of it in a half-moon shape where her teeth had buried into his flesh. It didn't look infected, at least. "Are we going to get out of here alive?" Shadow suddenly heard herself ask.

"Possibly." Sorren withdrew the Colt from its holster at his hip. He hefted the weapon thoughtfully, curling his fingers around the smooth walnut butt. Thumbing back the hammer made him grimace. A muscle flickered high on his cheek. "LaRoux doesn't trust me. He's got men watching us."

"Can we get past them?"

"I'm not sure yet. Once I see how he is operating now, I'll know a lot more." Sorren looked at Shadow, his eyes touching swiftly along her face and down her shoulders and arms. She looked a mess, but he still found her desirable. "We've got to make it through today. Maybe tonight we'll make our move."

"Good. I hate it here. I just want to—" Her voice trailed off, though Shadow was not conscious of it. What did she want? She wanted to bathe in Sorren's big tub and walk naked and unashamed from room to room, as she had before. She wanted to go to sleep in Sorren's arms and wake up in his arms. She wanted her life the way it was then. It seemed a lifetime ago, though it was really only a couple days.

Sorren read Shadow's mind but without great accuracy. "I want to stop running and stop fighting, too," he said, his voice a low rasp inside the Conestoga. "I want to go home and forget all about LaRoux and the others. But I can't do that, Shadow. Not just yet. I've got responsibilities that you know nothing about."

"Only because you won't tell me," Shadow countered.

"It's best that you don't know. Believe me, it's best for both of us. The less you know, the safer it is."

They'd been through this before. Shadow let it drop.

"I'd like to bathe," she said, her voice dropping a decibel to match Sorren's. "At least wash up a little. I feel grimy." Shadow pushed her hair back. A comb was entangled in the long tresses and she began separating it from the knotted strands. "I feel filthy

337

. . . inside and out."

Sorren slipped the Colt back into the holster. He glanced sideways at Shadow, watching her fingers moving as she removed the comb from her hair. "Don't give up on me yet," he whispered. "Not just yet. I can get you out of this. I know I can. Just believe in me one more time and I'll get you out of here. You'll be safe." He pushed the flat-crowned hat back on his head. He seemed to be forcing the words from his throat with great effort. "Just one more time. That's all I'm asking."

Shadow's lips quivered. The horror of this place, the head and fetid air of the Conestoga, Sorren sitting so close to her and yet being so distant, had all worn on her until her will had been reduced to a shell of what it once was. This was not the type of battle she understood. She knew contempt and derision. She knew how to fight against people who felt she was inferior, and she knew how to hate those who cursed her to her face and behind her back, saying her blood was tainted and cursed. She did not know how to fight a war with guns, where men shot and killed men they did not know.

"I'm — I'm sorry," Shadow said, her voice trembling. She didn't know why she was apologizing or why, suddenly, she felt like crying. "I'm sorry. I'm sorry. I'm sorry."

She was repeating that line over and over when Sorren put his arm around her shoulders and pulled her in close, molding her soft body against his hard one. Shadow pressed her face into Sorren's neck and the tears came. She cried softly, burying her face into the arch of his neck, her arms encircling his trim waist. She hugged him tightly as tears moistened the collar of his black silk shirt and his neckerchief.

"Shhh," Sorren said softly. He stroked her hair, his hands running down from her shoulders to her back. "It's going to be all right. Don't worry. I'll get you out of here. You'll be safe. I'll get you out. Everything is going to be all right. Trust me. Trust me one last time and I'll make everything all right."

After long moments, Shadow finally pushed herself gently away from Sorren's chest. She looked into his eyes, her face close to his.

"I'm so tired," she whispered. "I just want to rest. I don't want to fight any more." She moved closer and kissed the tip of his chin. Her cheeks were stained with tears. "I'm in love with you, you know. You do know that, don't you?" Shadow searched Sorren's eyes for understanding. She touched his cheeks softly with her fingertips. "Don't you? You've known all along, haven't you?"

Sorren nodded, unable to look at Shadow. He had not, as she had claimed, known that Shadow was in love with him. *She still loves me,* Sorren thought. Ecstasy swelled inside him but did not spill out. *I should say something. I should tell her I love her. I do love her, don't I? Of course I do! I've slept with enough women to know the difference between love and lust.*

Shadow waited, but she did not get the confirmation she so desperately needed. Her lips curled up at the corners, quivering slightly with resignation. *So that's it then,* she thought. *At least he was honest with me.*

"Last night you said you'd need my help to get us out of here," Shadow said, her voice faltering slightly. A dull, empty ache had started in her stomach.

Though she was hungry, the ache was not from lack of food. Shadow had gone without food so many times in her life that the pangs of hunger were no longer something that distressed her. What she needed was words from Sorren, to hear that he felt about her the way she felt about him. Not getting them, she was determined to push on, to plunge forward into a world that was uncertain and frightening. "Tell me what you want from me and I'll do it. I won't fight you any more."

"First, let's get you washed up. I'm sure there's some place you can get that accomplished in private. After that, I'm just not sure. We're going to have to play this minute by minute."

Sorren stood, cursing himself for his own cowardice, knowing full well that he was hurting Shadow by not being able to say the words that filled his heart, yet unable to open up the gates that kept his love mute. "We'll be on the move soon," Sorren continued. "LaRoux can't stay here long. When the stage doesn't show up in Denver City, they'll send a posse looking for it."

"Of course," Shadow replied, her mind and soul numb with the dreadful picture of a one-sided love.

Chapter Nineteen

Shadow never got the chance to wash before they were up and riding again. LaRoux allowed his men twenty minutes to eat, and then they were moving again. Shadow rode in a wagon with Francine and three other women — Betty Sue, Pauline, and Janey. She did not try to start any conversations with them, and they looked at her with suspicion. She saw in in their faces the hard life that they had led. The effects of their vocation showed plainly on their faces, in the way they held themselves, in all their movements and gestures. They were tired young women, aging rapidly and much before their time. Sometimes they would laugh, but it sounded brittle, hollow, and dishonest to Shadow. Pauline only laughed *at* someone. Her jokes always had a victim. They talked among themselves, and their bitterness toward the world was often undisguised. After two hours of eavesdropping on their conversations, Shadow was quite certain the women, with the possible exception of Francine, who had yet to be shared among the men, hated everyone and everything, including themselves.

In the middle of the pack, Sorren rode beside Smitty for an hour or more. Then he tapped the ribs of his mare and moved up until he was beside Jean-Jacques LaRoux.

"Morning," Sorren said, touching the brim of his hat in a gesture that might have been a salute. He wasn't certain yet of the proper military protocol in this army.

"Morning." LaRoux smoothed his moustache, curling it around his mouth in a downward arch. "I'd ask how your evening was, but by the looks of that finger, I can guess myself."

"She's a fighter, all right."

"Get the job done?"

"I don't mind a little fight," Sorren replied. "A spunky woman has never stopped me before. Just makes it more fun."

LaRoux nodded in understanding. "The men have been curious, though. They want to know how long you intend on keeping her all to yourself."

"A while. She's not ready for them yet. She's like a good mare. Unless she's broke just right, she won't be any good for riding."

"Like Pauline?"

"Hmmm?"

"Pauline. The skinny one with the bad attitude," LaRoux explained. "She figures that if she spreads her legs, that's good enough." He shook his head in disgust. "Worst excuse for a woman I've ever met." LaRoux shrugged his shoulders, dismissing the thought—and the woman who had caused it—as inconsequential to his life. "You going to be able to handle a gun with that hand?"

"If I have to," Sorren replied honestly.

Though he rode loose in the saddle, Sorren's eyes moved restlessly. He knew now that during the night he always had someone watching the wagon. It wasn't in LaRoux's nature to let his defenses down, even for a moment. When Sorren had moved up to ride beside LaRoux, Smitty had followed, keeping enough distance between himself and Sorren to be out of earshot, yet close enough to put a bullet between his shoulder blades.

LaRoux doesn't trust me, thought Sorren, his body passive, his mind ticking off all possible ways for Shadow to escape. *The moment she's gone, LaRoux's going to know I've had a hand in it. He's too wary to assume any different. He wants me with him because he knows I've killed before, but he doesn't trust me at all. How can I put an end to this lunatic without becoming a corpse myself?*

"What are you thinking about?" LaRoux asked.

Sorren looked over at him and smiled. "Nothing in particular."

"We'll get along a lot better if you just let me do the thinking."

"No problem," Sorren said. He thought, *This is a man who must die.*

"What?" Carl exclaimed, his eyes wide, the excitement he felt evident in his tone.

"I said the stage got held up," Catherine replied, a worried look on her face. "It got shot to pieces!" She looked away from her brother, dismayed at his obvious pleasure. "They didn't find her body. Only the men."

"So we don't know yet if she's dead or not," Carl said, speaking to himself.

Catherine was on the borderline of panic. "She's our sister!"

"She's Daddy's bastard child," Carl snapped. "And what the hell is wrong with you, anyway? If she's dead, we're her only relatives! We'll get her one third of the MW Circle. Can't you see that?"

Catherine knew her brother could be unpleasant, even ruthless, but she never thought he had a murderous heart. "Good Lord, Carl, are you that cold? It's been a shock to me, too, to find out I've got a sister. And I'm not any happier than you are that Daddy left her part of the MW Circle. But she's our *sister*, Carl! My God, doesn't life mean anything to you at all?"

"Of course it does," Carl replied, his tone soft and mildly offended. "What kind of man do you think I am?" He rose from his chair, crossing the room to stand near his sister. He put a hand over her shoulder and gave it a squeeze. With his left hand he touched Catherine's chin, forcing her head up. "Do you really think I want her to die? Can you really believe that I would want that?"

"Well, you said—" Catherine pulled her chin away from Carl's hand. She couldn't look into his eyes. "No. I don't suppose that—"

"I resent her taking what is rightfully ours, but that doesn't mean I would want to see her dead." Carl thought, *I can play my sister like a violin. She's weak inside. She hasn't the heart for business. She can't do what*

344

eeds to be done. He said, "If something bad has
appened to Shadow, that isn't our fault. You can't
blame me for trying to find a silver lining in every
loud. That's only trying to see the good side of
hings. There's nothing wrong with it. It's natural."

"Natural for you, maybe," Catherine said, but from
he tone of her voice, Carl could tell that her anger
nd disappointment in him was waning.

"I'll send a cable to St. Louis today. From there,
t'll go to Washington. In no time at all they'll send a
luplicate contract. Everything will be just the way it
vas . . ." he said, and concluded in his head, *but
Shadow's name won't be on the new contract!*

Emma stared at the candle, not knowing what to
ay or do. She hadn't felt this way since the first—
irst and *last*—time her oldest son had stayed out all
night without warning her. Worst of all, Emma knew
his wasn't just an overnight thing between Shadow
nd Sorren; it was something deadly and dangerous.
t was caused by people who didn't love Shadow like
Sorren did.

"Come now," John Elijah said, standing behind his
vife at the kitchen table. She had been staring, for
over an hour, into the flame of the single wax candle
hat burned. "The child will be all right. She's a
ough girl. Tough like you. She'll be all right."

John placed his hand on Emma's shoulder, and she
placed hers over his. "She really ain't tough, John,"
Emma said. "She ain't tough like she wants us to
believe. The girl's tender inside. I can see that, John
Elijah. I can see that just as plain as I see you right

now." Emma turned her eyes to the flickering flame "I'm scared for her."

"You're scared 'cause you've got so much love in your heart," the tall black man replied softly. "It's that love that's seeing her through right now."

"I want to pray."

John moved until he was beside Emma. He got down on one knee, taking both of her hands in his "I'll pray with you," he said in a low tone. "Me an you an' the good Lord will get Miss Shadow through this."

Emma closed her eyes and, together with her husband, began saying, "Our Father, who art in Heaven, hallowed be thy name . . . thy Kingdom come, thy will be done. . . ."

Shadow had lived through shame before, but never had she known anything like this. Not only did the soldiers all gawk lasciviously at her whenever they thought Sorren wasn't seeing them, but the other women were also cruel to her. And Francine, Shadow strongly suspected, wanted Sorren.

It wouldn't have been half so bad if Francine, Betty Sue, and Janey, apparently in some strange ritual that Shadow did not understand, stopped talking about things—sexual things—that they'd done to this soldier or that one. Sometimes they laughed, sometimes they just nodded in quiet understanding and sympathy. Shadow discovered that Johnny liked a woman on her hands and knees, and as he took her from behind, he would pull on her hair. It seemed utterly dehumanizing to Shadow, but the other

omen didn't seem to mind all that much. It was his
tish, they explained, and since he didn't really pull
eir hair that hard, they didn't particularly mind. As
ey recited the litany of fetishes and favors of the
en, Shadow felt herself become further withdrawn.
he tried to stop listening.

"Maybe you're just like Pauline," Betty Sue said,
rning her amber, accusing eyes to Shadow. "Maybe
ou think you're better than we are. Or maybe you
st don't know how to treat a man right. Huh? Do
ou know how to treat a man? Maybe you just lay
ere dead like. That's what Oscar tol' me Pauline's
ke. She don't do nothin'!"

"That's 'cause I ain't a whore like you!" Pauline
at.

"No . . . you're just a lazy slut," Janey chimed in.

Francine looked up momentarily from her sewing,
here she was mending a hem on the green satin
ress LaRoux had bought for her a month earlier. "Is
at true?" she asked Shadow. "Don't you know what
man needs, what a man likes? That Sorren fella
. . now that's a man!"

The other women, again with the exception of
auline, chimed in their agreement on the masculine
ualities of the newcomer, Sorren McKenna. Pauline
id nothing, and Shadow wondered why.

Shadow remained silent, but the women would not
t her be. What did he like? they inquired, three sets
f eyes locked onto Shadow, three faces turned her
ay, three women thinking they had a chance to
duce Sorren away from her. How did he kiss? Does
e like to kiss you, they asked with smiles, down
ere? The question brought giggles from all of them,

347

though Shadow had refused to answer.

"How long does it take him?" Francine asked, h[er] tone serious. When Shadow didn't reply, Francin[e] with apparent frustration and burning curiosit[y] asked, "Well, tell me this then—is he big? Bigg[er] than most? Longer? Thicker? He's hung like a sta[l]lion, isn't he?"

Shadow felt her cheeks coloring. How on ear[th] could she possibly know what he was? She had n[o] one to compare Sorren to. She wanted to believe th[at] Sorren was superior to any man in the world. Sh[e] believed, for emotional reasons, that he was. But d[id] she really know? It didn't matter to her. When h[e] touched her, when he caressed her and kissed h[er] and made love to her, he made Shadow feel like sh[e] was turning inside out, made her flesh burn wi[th] desire and her body ache for the release that h[e] always caused.

"Hey, how do the Indians do it?" It was Jane again. "I heard that these squaws know how to kee[p] their bucks hard for an hour or more."

"Who'd want these bums for that long?" said Pau[l]ine. They all laughed as they turned to Shadow, wh[o] looked away, embarrassed.

"Well, honey," Francine said, her voice drippin[g] with sarcasm, "if you can't say it, you sure as he[ll] can't do it!"

And as if on cue, Sorren pulled his horse alongsi[de] the wagon and gave Shadow a smile. "Hello," he sa[id] in that resonant voice of his. His eyes held Shadow for long, portentous moments before he appeared [to] notice the other women in the slowly moving wago[n.] "Ladies," he murmured, touching the brim of h[is]

348

black hat. "Shadow, will you ride with me a bit?"

"Of course," Shadow said above the sound of three women laughing to themselves.

After Shadow had leaped off the tail of the wagon onto the back of Sorren's arm, Francine said, "Mr. McKenna, I can't jump on a horse like that, but I know other things. Whenever you want it done right, you come see me, okay? I'll do things for you that Miss Prissy here's never even thought of."

Sorren never lost his half smile. "That's an interesting proposition," he replied. "Give me some time to think about it."

When they had ridden a little ways from the rolling bordello, Shadow hissed in Sorren's ear, "I suppose you think that's funny!"

Sorren put his left hand on Shadow's knee. He raised her skirt until he touched her bare skin, and she tightened her hands threateningly around his middle.

"Don't you dare!" Shadow whispered, her eyes hot with anger, boring into the back of Sorren's head.

"Don't fight me on this," Sorren replied, the smile never leaving his lips. "Now you and I both know that I haven't touched that precious body of yours since we've been here, but nobody else knows that. And the moment LaRoux suspects that you're anything other than my latest whore, he'll pass you to the other guys. He might even kill you and me, just to insure that his security hasn't been breached." Sorren's hand curled around Shadow's knee, pushing her dress higher to touch softly against the underside of her thigh. "So shut up and play along."

Shadow did stop talking, but she could not adopt

the casual attitude that Sorren could affect, like an actor getting into character before stepping onto stage. She glanced to her left and saw Johnny looking at her, watching Sorren's hand playing lightly with her silky leg. Shadow wanted to pull her dress down to cover herself. She turned her face away from Johnny instead, hoping that out of sight would be, as Father Bradford had tried to explain so many times, out of mind.

"You're getting out of here tonight," Sorren said, turning his head slightly so he wouldn't have to raise his voice for Shadow. "LaRoux's becoming more tense all the time. And he's got something big planned for later this week. That's why the men haven't been as drunk lately. He sobers them up before an attack."

"But we're being watched all the time. You said yourself that LaRoux stations a guard outside the wagon every night."

Sorren leaned back in the saddle, and Shadow felt the heat of his body against her breasts. She did not move away. "I'll take care of the guards," Sorren said from the corner of his mouth. His hand trailed high along the underside of her thigh. "LaRoux's getting impatient. He wants to increase his hold on me. He's got to prove to me and himself that he's got power over me. The only way he's going to do that is to make me do something that he knows I don't want to do."

Sorren tried to ignore the pleasure he felt at touching Shadow's delicate, tanned flesh. In the time they had spent together in the wagon, he hadn't tried to make love. After seeing her contempt for him, he hadn't even tried to touch her. Also, after her confes

350

ion of love, when Sorren hadn't been able to speak the words of his heart, he felt her freeze up again. He was trying, misguidedly, but in the only way he knew how, not to hurt her more than he already had.

Fear chilled Shadow, and unconsciously she squeezed Sorren tighter, seeking the protection she believe he would give. "Like what?" she inquired in a voice that quivered slightly.

"I don't know yet. But he's got a sick mind. He's not the soldier he was ten years ago. He's different. He's crazy. He's not fighting a war because he has to; he's on the rampage because he likes it. The killing. The power. It excites him."

The entire notion of a man being consumed by his lust for power, by the desire to control other lives, made Shadow squeeze her eyes shut against the images that flashed across the surface of her mind. She tried not to think about the horrors that LaRoux was planning, but her imagination was running rampant. What would he make Sorren do? How would he prove to himself, to Sorren, and to every man and woman in his band of renegades and degenerates that he, General Jean-Jacques LaRoux, held their lives in his hands? And how far would Sorren go?"

"Just be ready for anything," Sorren continued. Shadow was thankful for his distraction. She didn't want to let her mind wander on it own for very long. "I don't know when this is going to happen so, for God's sake, be ready at all times." He patted her thigh reassuringly. "Don't worry too much. I don't want you to tip anyone off. Just keep thinking about being home again."

Home? thought Shadow. *Whose home? Yours, with all those empty rooms and a room filled with weapons? The MW Circle, where Carl practiced his duplicity and deception without restraint?* She had a sudden image of her small teepee on the shore with the cooking pot for one, lonely but secure.

Shadow squeezed Sorren a bit, placing her cheek against his back. He misread the reason for her touch, and said, "Don't worry, it'll work out. I'll get you out of here, Shadow . . . or I'll die trying."

Twilight came too slowly. Anxious seconds became anxious minutes, then finally turned into hours. Sorren resisted the unquenchable urge to check his watch, the heavy, accurate one that had been the gift of a wealthy and grateful lover. The time itself meant nothing. He needed the cover of darkness and the majority of LaRoux's soldiers to relax. This army did not operate on a time schedule.

After filling their bellies with food and sneaking a couple of quick swigs of whiskey from a stashed bottle, the men would be vulnerable. Only then, when the odds against Shadow's escape were reduced to a viable level, would Sorren make his move. His impatient nature, his desire for action, would not make him foolhardy. Not where Shadow's safety was concerned.

He hadn't talked to Shadow in several hours. Sorren had kept himself busy by talking with several soldiers, riding slowly along with them. He almost welcomed their conversation because it helped him keep his distance from Shadow. Sorren could never

352

be certain whether his true feelings for her would show on his face, in his eyes and the way he always seemed to have a little smile on his lips just because she was near him. LaRoux had been a leader of men for years. He would not miss signs like that. He couldn't be fooled into believing that Sorren was still trying to teach Shadow a lesson in subservience. He'd soon know that it was more than that with Sorren, and he'd have Shadow taken away — probably right after he took Sorren's gunbelt.

What would I do? Sorren asked himself. *If LaRoux made me give Shadow to one of the men, what would I do? Could I choose? If I didn't make any choice, he'd kill me. Or, more likely, he'd have Shadow raped and force me to watch it, then he'd kill me.*

Sorren closed his eyes against the thought. He wanted to ride to the wagon Shadow and the other women were in. Seeing her would make him feel good again. But it might also tip his hand, and he couldn't trust himself when he was with her.

A new kind of fear had crept into Sorren's soul, and what was strangest about it was that he fully understood what made him so frightened. Usually, his fears were imprecisely directed. He had, on many occasions, been afraid of dying. But if questioned directly, and if Sorren answered himself honestly, he could not say exactly *why* he wanted to live.

During the war, he had fought because he wanted to put an end to the bloody carnage that was happening all around him. But it was *people* that he didn't want to see die, not a *person*. His concern was generalized, not specific.

The fear that gnawed at Sorren's conscience was

now clear-cut with sharp edges, like a large and perfectly cut diamond. He was afraid that Shadow would die and he would have to live the rest of his life without her.

My God, Sorren thought, *I really am in love with her.*

If Shadow's life were not in such peril, that sudden moment of self-realization would have given him no end of consternation and pleasure.

The guards were posted, sentries in place, tents erected. Sorren stood looking at the fourteen triangular-shaped tents scattered around the small campfires. They were just barely big enough for two people to sleep in. Apparently the sleeping arrangements were not permanent, since Betty Sue, the bitter Pauline, and Janey never slept in the same tent two nights in a row. That meant one of the two men in the tent would have to move to another tent . . . unless, of course, the three of them didn't mind sharing each other.

Sorren leaned back against the wagon Smitty and Francine used. *Hookers*. That's what the women were called. He had known the man who had coined the phrase. He was just a foot soldier under General Hooker's command, and he called the stream of prostitutes who followed the officer and his men from battlefield to battlefield by the new nickname, *hookers*. Other soldiers, hearing of Hooker's liberal, if not enlightened, attitude toward his men's sexual appetites, soon picked up the expression. Before long, soldiers on both sides of the conflict were calling the prostitutes who followed them around *hookers*.

Sorren heard a noise inside the wagon. He decided it was time to move. He didn't want Francine coming out and talking to him. Her interest in him was getting stronger, he could tell, and he didn't need Smitty getting offended.

Walking slowly, Sorren put his hands behind his back, moving in what appeared to be aimless wandering. Natural enough, he told himself, for a man who had been sitting in a saddle all day. Sorren McKenna's casual meandering belied his mind's activity and the darting of his keen eyes. He was sizing up the camp and, in his mind, playing through the series of actions required on his part for Shadow's successful escape.

LaRoux had two soldiers watching the wagon Sorren and Shadow shared. One soldier was in close, about twenty-five feet away, with a view of the rear entrance of the Conestoga. The second guard was farther away and to the left, keeping the wagon between himself and the rest of the camp.

Sorren smiled. LaRoux's method made it possible to get past the first guard with a little luck, but doubly difficult to get to the second without being noticed. The second sentry was close enough to be within earshot, yet far enough away to make it a difficult dash from one post to the next.

Sorren felt grudging admiration for LaRoux. He was a madman. He was sick and thoroughly crazy . . . but he wasn't stupid. He was truly a worthy adversary for Sorren's skills, and the man dressed in black might even have taken conscious pleasure in this violent game if the stakes hadn't included a young woman of mixed-blood heritage who had no last name and just happened to have stolen his heart.

Four fires were burning. One fire for every five men. Most of the fires were vacated now. The hollow men with the shallow, melancholy eyes had stared morosely into the fire longer than usual tonight, probably in contemplation of the battle to come. With no home, no loved ones left, and no future, despair was their constant companion. Most of them knew their lives were over, but they still had to wait for Death to claim their bodies. Sorren had watched the three sentries leave shortly after they'd eaten. In four hours, they would be relieved by fresh men. The horses, including Sorren's mare, were kept in a rope corral on the opposite side of the camp from La-Roux's large, military-issue officer's tent. LaRoux's tent was separate from the others.

Rank has its privileges, Sorren understood.

Sorren made his way quietly over to the horses. Two men were at the edge of the corral, passing a bottle of rye whiskey back and forth. One would be the guard, the other his friend and half-owner of the liquor. Sorren hesitated a moment, quickly ad-libbing a plan of action, then moved forward.

"You men are going to make it easy for me," Sorren said, keeping his voice down enough so only the two soldiers could hear him. The men nearly jumped out of their skins at the sound of his voice. The soldier on the right, the older and much larger of the two, held the bottle behind his back. "Now we both knew what the general's standing orders are, don't we?" continued Sorren, affecting the sarcastically cruel tone of voice he'd heard so often in incompetent, power-hungry young officers who loved telling their men what to do. "What's behind your back, soldier?"

The big soldier swallowed, and Sorren could see his Adam's apple bob up and down. "N—nothing, sir."

Sorren moved closer, so close their bodies nearly touched. McKenna was shorter than the soldier by six inches. He looked unflinchingly into the man's eyes. "Are you calling me stupid, soldier?"

"No, sir! I wouldn't do that!"

"But you'd tell me a lie that only a very stupid man would believe. That tells me you think I'm stupid." Sorren watched beads of sweat pop out on the man's forehead. He began squirming, and Sorren could almost feel the guy's heart beating against his barrel chest. Sorren thought, *LaRoux's poisoned his men with fear. They're scared to death of officers.* "Should we try this one more time, boy? What's behind your back?"

The soldier closed his eyes for a moment. Finally, slowly and guiltily, he brought his hand around his body. The bottle was nearly full.

Perfect! thought Sorren. *Just perfect!*

"I'm going to make a deal with you men." Sorren took a step back and scratched his chin thoughtfully. He affected the posture and attitude of the young officers he hated with such passion. It wasn't easy to contain his happiness. "General LaRoux just sent me over to check on our backside. He's thinking somebody might have sent a posse looking for us after that incident with the stage." Both soldiers looked frightened, their sweaty faces gleaming in the moonlight. "Now I know how difficult it is to track at night, and so do you boys. But what the general wants, the

357

general gets. So instead of me riding back the last five miles or so, just to check on our backsides, what I'm going to do is have you two boys do it."

The little man to Sorren's right, who hadn't said anything so far, finally spoke up. "Why should we do that?"

"Because if you don't, I'll have to tell the general about your little drinking problem." Sorren cocked his head to the side, giving the small man a condescending look. "That would be a good way for me to make a few points with the general." Both men reacted to Sorren's words with pained expressions.

Sorren reached for the bottle and the big man put his hand protectively behind his back. *Alcoholic,* thought Sorren. He felt somewhat guilty for taking advantage of another man's weakness, but there was no other way around it.

"If you get tough with me," Sorren said slowly, drawling the words out in such a manner that made both soldiers tremble a little, "I'll beat the hell out of both of you. Is that what you really want?"

The big man looked into Sorren's eyes. He was not used to being threatened in such a manner. In a gunfight, he knew he didn't have a chance against Sorren McKenna. But in a fistfight? He was taller than Sorren and outweighed him by at least thirty pounds. The big man looked into Sorren's eyes . . . and then smiled weakly. There was something in McKenna's eyes that frightened him.

"No," he said. "No."

"No, *what?*"

"No, sir."

Sorren nodded his approval. "Okay, I know you

work hard for your money, so this is what I'm going to do. I'm giving you and your friend here five minutes to get mounted and on your way. Since it's my duty to take that bottle away from you, I'm going to do that. But if the bottle should happen to be empty by then?" Sorren spread his hands, turning his palms upward. He smiled broadly. "Is it *my* fault the bottle is empty?"

Sorren took a couple steps backward, then turned so that he was at a right angle to the men. From the corner of his eye, he could see them passing the bottle rapidly back and forth, pouring the cheap rye whiskey down their throats.

In twenty minutes, they would be two miles away and so drunk they could barely stay in the saddle.

This is going to be easier than I thought! Sorren told himself exuberantly.

When the men had gone on their imaginary exploration, Sorren stepped into the corral and quickly found his mare. She rubbed her head against his chest in greeting, just like she did every morning. The mare put her velvet-soft nose in Sorren's hand, but this time he had no apple to give her.

"What's wrong, girl? Did you miss me?" Sorren said with a smile. His affection for the mare was honest.

Sorren stroked the mare's neck. Sometimes he felt he could really speak to his horses. He knew they couldn't understand his words, but they knew what he was telling them. They responded to him with trust and love, and he responded in kind.

Sorren saddled his mare and bridled a well-mannered gelding he'd picked out earlier in the day. He didn't bother putting a saddle on for Shadow. He'd seen her ride, and she certainly didn't need the assistance of stirrups to stay astride a galloping horse.

Sorren took the reins of the gelding and tied them loosely to the saddle horn of his mare. Then, taking the reins of the mare, he ground-tied her. She could graze on the lush green grass but would not roam far with the reins touching the ground.

Step one was complete. Sorren's heart was pumping. He felt confident, despite the horrendous odds he faced. At any moment, he knew, the whole hastily concocted plan could blow up in his face. But at least for now, everything was working out as well as he had hoped for—or better.

Now the odds were only two against eighteen.

Chapter Twenty

Shadow sat in the Conestoga, waiting and wondering what Sorren was doing. She had been cursing him for the past hour or more. Cursing him because she had fallen in love with him, cursing him because he wasn't in love with her, and cursing him most of all because he was, at this very moment, probably doing some damn fool thing that would get him killed.

She couldn't bear the thought of Sorren not being in her life. In the span of a few short weeks, he had turned her life upside down, and she'd never once truly regretted it. The desolation of her life had been gently stripped away by his smile and his touch and the concern she saw in his eyes when he looked at her. He really did care for her. Nothing Sorren could say — or *not* say — would shake Shadow's belief in that. Someday he would come to love her as completely as she loved him. Someday . . . someday would come . . . if they lived.

Shadow felt her anger rising. She knew she had no right to be angry at Sorren. It wasn't his fault she was waiting in the broiling wagon. But she *was* angry. She was angry because that damn fool man of hers probably hadn't given her a single thought to whether or not he was driving her half out of her mind with worry.

"If we live through this," Shadow whispered to an absent Sorren in the closed-up Conestoga, "I'm going to hate you and love you for a long, long time, Sorren McKenna!"

Shadow rose to her feet once again and took the two steps necessary to reach the back of the wagon. Turning sharply, she took another two steps until she was at the edge of the mattress. Another sharp turn and two quick steps and she completed the circuit that she'd done a hundred times since Janey, Francine, Pauline, and Betty Sue had left her alone in the wagon to await Sorren's nightly arrival.

Gritting her teeth, Shadow gave her temper free rein. Being angry with Sorren was more preferable to worrying about whether or not Jean-Jacques LaRoux had figured out what he was up to. It was much more preferable to thinking about what would happen if Sorren ever got caught.

Squeezing her arms tightly around herself, Shadow sat on the edge of the mattress and waited. She rocked slowly forward and back, the motion caused by too much adrenaline and worry and not enough ways to get rid of her energy.

"I hate you," Shadow whispered to Sorren, wherever he was. "And when we get out of here, I'm going to tell you so. We'll escape tonight."

The last few hours had been slow torture for Shadow. After her confession of love to Sorren, a fissure had started between herself and him. With each passing hour, Shadow had felt that distance become greater and greater. Her confession of love was a mistake, she now concluded. It had frightened Sorren off. It seemed wildly absurd that a man who had proven his bravery countless times should be frightened by love. But he was, and there was no denying it. After she'd said she loved him, Sorren hadn't once tried to cross the invisible barrier that separated them. The only times he touched her was when they were outside where other people—those filthy-minded soldiers and the women who rode with them—could see him. Otherwise, Sorren had kept his distance.

She wanted to open the rear flaps of the wagon to let in some fresh air, but she did not. Sorren insisted. He didn't want any action to arouse suspicion, so she breathed in the stifling, stale air and wondered what the man she loved was doing just then.

"He doesn't care," Shadow said aloud. It was better to hear her own voice than to listen to the haunting silence. "He doesn't care about me or himself or anybody else."

Shadow was working herself into a frenzy, and she liked it. When Sorren showed up, she was going to give him a piece of her mind. She was going to tell him exactly what she thought of his foolhardy and dangerous stunts! And, furthermore, if Sorren thought he was going to sleep all by himself and withhold the pleasure that he had taught Shadow to hunger for, he had another guess coming! He wasn't going to distance himself from her. Not now. Not ever, damn it! Not in a thousand years!

Yes, Shadow told herself, *the moment he steps into this*

wagon I'm going to give that damned fool a piece of my mind!

When Sorren stepped through the rear flap of the Conestoga moments later, Shadow launched herself into his arms. She hugged him so tightly she could hardly breathe. She showered his face and neck with kisses because Sorren McKenna was a damn fool, but he was *her* damn fool and she loved him. Shadow was ridiculously, ecstatically, magnificently happy because the heady, masculine presence of one Sorren McKenna had been returned to her, to taunt her and tempt her and make her life worth living.

"Easy, precious," Sorren said, a broad smile curling his lips, causing the creases that started at the sides of his rather hawkish nose, arching down toward his mouth, to become more pronounced. "I'm okay. Everything is working out just fine."

Shadow took Sorren's face in her hands and kissed him on the mouth. The taste of his lips against her own was something that had been denied her too long, and now, the full length of her sensation-starved body pressed warmly against Sorren's, all she could think about was getting free of LaRoux and his men so that she could once again experience the exquisite, soul-searching satisfaction that came from the connoiseur's touch of Sorren McKenna, the man she quite foolishly and one-sidedly loved more than anything or anyone else in the world.

"Mmmm!" Sorren moaned, a hand sliding down from the small of Shadow's back. He cupped a taut buttock and playfully squeezed. "I really am not accustomed to saying things like this, but can we postpone pleasure until we're done with business?"

"Do you have time to hold me for just a minute?" Shadow asked, tucking her nose in under Sorren's chin. She loved the way he smelled. She wondered if all men were like Sorren or if there were just something so special about her man that made him universally attractive to women.

"A minute," Sorren murmured into Shadow's hair. "Only a minute."

He stroked her long jet hair, running his hand from the nape of her neck down her back. Sorren did not know the reason for Shadow's sudden change of heart, and he didn't care. Holding her in his arms again, feeling the warmth of her body against his own clarified all the chaotic thoughts that had been plaguing him. He knew he would risk everything to save her. He would not only risk everything to save her, he wanted to have her all to himself. He didn't want to share her with anyone. Not now . . . not ever.

"You're going to have to help me," Sorren said, still holding Shadow lightly against his chest. "There are two guards. It's impossible for me to get rid of both of them myself without alerting the whole camp."

With her eyes closed and the sinking feeling that this glorious moment was ending, Shadow asked, "What do you want me to do?"

"Distract one of the guards."

"How?"

She felt Sorren's chest move as he chuckled silently, and Shadow knew exactly how the man should be *distracted*.

"If you don't know that," Sorren said softly, "then you haven't looked in a mirror lately. You are a *very* distracting woman." Sorren curled his fingers into Shadow's hair and brought it to his face. He inhaled deeply. She was intoxicating to the senses. "What other clothes do you have with you?"

"Nothing. They stole my valise. Pauline and the others took my dresses."

"I'll buy you new ones. Dozens and dozens of gorgeous dresses that'll be the envy of every woman from God's Grace to San Francisco." Sorren took Shadow by the upper arms and pushed her gently away from his chest. "We've got to get started." He bent down and kissed Shadow's forehead, then the tip of her nose, and finally her mouth. They kissed softly for a moment, Sorren's palm resting lightly Shadow's smooth cheek. "There are two men watching us. One is directly behind the wagon; the other is that way" — he jerked a thumb toward the side of the wagon — "about thirty yards. He's the guy I want you to distract for me. I'll need about ten minutes, that's all. Just keep him looking at you and nothing else for ten minutes, and we're halfway home."

"Should I leave now?" Sorren nodded, and Shadow took a half step toward the rear flap of the Conestoga before she was stopped by a hand on her arm. "What? What's wrong?"

"First, you should give yourself some insurance," Sorren said in a silky purr. Shadow got the impression that he was acting cavalier so that she wouldn't be afraid. She loved him all the more for it. "Not that I have ever found this necessary, but this certainly isn't the time to take risks."

Shadow caught the direction of Sorren's gaze. Her hands came up and she unbuttoned the two top buttons of her dress, allowing the bodice to separate enough to show the alluring inner swell of her breasts.

"More?" she asked, her eyes on Sorren's face. He was looking at her bosom with the smouldering eyes that Shadow had seen before. She unbuttoned one more, then let her fingers toy with yet another button.

"I think that's enough," Sorren said, his voice a raspy whisper.

Shadow moistened her generous lips with the tip of her tongue. "You haven't — you haven't looked at me like that in a long time." She took Sorren's right wrist in her hand and raised it. Her dark eyes held Sorren's as she gently slipped his hand inside her dress. She felt his strong, smooth, slender fingers curling around the satiny swell of one lush breast. "There was a time when you liked to touch me."

Shadow put her hand over Sorren's, pressing his fingers deeper into her trembling breast.

"You'd better go now." Sorren eased his hand out of Shadow's dress. It hurt to see her once-immaculate dress now smudged with dirt, and the collar and bodice tainted with perspiration. "You'd better go *now* before I find that I can't let you go at all."

Shadow fastened one cloth button. "No matter what happens next, I want you to know that I love you."

She was out of the wagon so quickly that she never heard Sorren's response.

Her waist-length ebony hair fluffed in the small

367

breeze as she walked. Shadow glanced quickly to her right. The first sentry, sitting on a blanket, raised up to his knees.

"Hey," he said, "where do you think you're going?"

"Just over here," Shadow replied without stopping. "I'm bored."

"And I'm not?" He sounded disappointed in Shadow's choice of companionship.

Shadow saw the second sentry's eyes before anything else. With the small campfires at her back, he was bathed in a dim glow, and his watery eyes caught and reflected light. When Shadow was within ten feet of him, she saw that the man's face was covered with a scraggly, dark beard. He, too, sat on a blanket.

"Good evening," Shadow said as she approached. Her palms felt sweaty. She couldn't tell if her voice were trembling or not. "Mind if I sit down?"

The sentry nodded slowly, picking up his carbine and laying it across his lap. "Suit yourself," he said as Shadow was getting down in front of him.

"It was so hot in the wagon. I just had to get some fresh air."

"Open it up. You'll get all the fresh air you want."

Shadow tried to blush with embarrassment before she realized it made no difference. With her back to the campfires, she was just a silhouette to the sentry. He couldn't see anything but the outline of her body.

"But then people would be able to hear us—" Shadow left the sentence unfinished, and no matter how dim the light cast upon her face was, it couldn't mask the coy gleam of illicit pleasure in her eyes.

"That there wagon's got canvas walls," the sentry said matter-of-factly. "I been here every night and

I've never heard nothing but fighting twixt you two."

Shadow felt her throat constrict nervously. The man just wasn't responding to her as Sorren had said he would. Fear gripped her insides. *I'm no good at this,* she told herself. *He doesn't like me and there's nothing I can do to change that. He hates Indians, and no matter what I do or how I'm dressed, all he's going to see is a trampish Indian squaw sitting on the blanket beside him.*

"He likes me to be quiet," Shadow said on impulse. She forced words from her throat that her heart did not believe. "He's not really very imaginative." She looked to her right, at the wagon she'd just come from. The outline of it was clearly visible against the campfires. "He's not coming out, is he?"

"Ain't seen him," the sentry replied in a drawl.

"He must still be asleep."

The slow, creeping panic was insinuating itself into Shadow's pores, seeping into her flesh. Her hands began to tremble, so she sat on them to hide her fear from the bearded, uninterested sentry. In the back of her mind, an out-of-key chord was struck when she realized that the reaction she was trying to elicit from this unwashed and unshaven man was exactly what she had been trying to avoid for years. And now, for the first time in her life, when she wanted a lewd advance from a man, when she wanted a stranger to look at her with lust in his heart and soul, he was giving her little more than passing notice. *It's just not fair!* her angry mind screamed.

Together they heard the thump and the grunt that came a fraction of a second later. The sentry remained sitting, but he twisted on the blanket to look in the direction of the other guard. Shadow noticed

369

that his right hand had gone instinctively to the Winchester in his lap, the first finger curling around the trigger.

"Joey, you all right?" the sentry asked in a hushed voice, loud enough to carry the distance between himself and his friend but not so loud he would alarm the rest of the camp.

Sorren's on the move! Do something, Shadow! You're a woman and he's a man! You're not a shy little virgin! Do something!

"Hey, Joey!"

Shadow slipped sideways on the blanket, perhaps too fast, moving until she sat beside the sentry. She twisted so that the light of the campfires cast moving shadows across the front of her body. *Now,* she thought, *he can see what I'm offering.*

"Don't worry about him," Shadow purred, tugging on the bearded man's arm. "I want to talk with you."

The sentry glanced over at Shadow. Able to see her better now, his gaze travelled from her face down to her indecently exposed bosom. Shadow saw the way his eyes widened with interest.

"Yeah, yeah," the sentry said. He looked back in the direction of his comrade.

Sorren peered through the folds of the canvas curtain. He saw the two faces turn in Shadow's direction as she walked. When both guards were watching her, he slipped out of the Conestoga unnoticed, dropping to the ground soundlessly. Crouched over, he moved quickly, his boots silent against the grass, covering ground in a gait somewhere between a fast walk and a trot.

Sorren's eyes were trained on the guard's face. As he gazed at the man's profile, cold and deadly hatred exploded in his chest. Quite suddenly, the guard had become everything in Sorren's past that he'd tried so hard to run away from. If it hadn't been for LaRoux and his collection of misfits and murderers, Sorren wouldn't be here now, and neither would Shadow.

Ten feet separated Sorren from his prey. The guard heard the soft crunch of a boot pressing down dry grass and turned his attention away from Shadow toward the sound.

"Where'd she go? Have you see her?" Sorren asked in a rush of whispered words.

"Yeah. She went ov—"

Sorren's black boot came in an upswinging arc that connected solidly with the guard's chin. His head snapped back and his feet jerked from beneath him spastically. He lay on the blanket, arms and legs outstretched, unconscious. Sorren dropped to the blanket beside him. His heart was pounding.

Sorren heard the other sentry call.

"Sorren's not very imaginative," Shadow repeated, twisting her upper body to expose more of her ample bosom. When the sentry did not look at her, she placed a palm on his leg, midway between his crotch and knee. "But I bet you are. I bet you could make me scream, couldn't you? A woman could never stay quiet with you."

The guard had waited a lifetime for a woman who looked like Shadow to come on to him. What was most frustrating was that his fantasy was finally coming true, but something was going on with Joey that he just didn't understand. The heat of Shadow's palm against his thigh burned him through his trousers and long johns. He stared, bug-eyed, at her cleavage. Was there another woman in the whole world with breasts like those? he wondered.

The sentry, with great difficulty, pulled his gaze off Shadow. "Joey!" his hissed. Through the shadows he saw a seated figure raise a hand and wave it slowly over his head. The guard breathed a sigh of relief. "Dang fool probably tripped on his way back from taking a leak!"

"Forget about him," Shadow cooed, her tone warm and sultry. "Don't I interest you enough to keep your attention?" Shadow's fingers inched closer to the guard's crotch. The man was breathing deeply. His breath smelled foul.

The sentry continued to hold the Winchester with his right hand. But with his left he reached across his body, placing his palm over Shadow's breast, touching her through the dress.

"You sure enough do," he said through a lopsided grin. His dirty hand was rough against Shadow's breast. When he leaned toward her, trying to kiss her on the mouth, Shadow turned her face away.

"Slow down, honey," Shadow whispered. This ugly, dirty man's hand on her breast made her skin crawl. Somehow, though, his hand touching her body did not seem as disgusting as the notion of actually pressing her lips against his mouth. Kissing, in this instance, seemed much more personal. "We've got plenty of time."

Leaning away, Shadow tried to smile at the sentry. His clumsy hand went from one breast to the other. She looked into the man's eyes, hating him, wanting him to believe she loved his touch. It was impossible. Then, over his shoulder, Shadow saw the crouching approach of Sorren. He held a pistol in his right hand.

"What's the matter with you?" the guard asked accusingly. "You a teaser or something?"

"Of course not," Shadow replied. The man tried to shove his hands inside the neckline of her dress, but she stopped him by grabbing his wrist. "I just want to be courted a little bit first."

"Courted?" the man exclaimed, his voice rising. "Now?"

So intent was he on getting his hand inside Shadow's dress that the guard never heard Sorren's approach. Only at the very last second, when he saw the alarm in Shadow's eyes, did he realize something was terribly, terribly wrong. The butt of Sorren's Colt smashed against his skull, slamming his head down, jamming his chin into chest. He made a choking sound as he slumped to the side. Sorren struck him once more before the sentry was prone. Savagely, with all the strength he possessed, Sorren hit the man just above the ear.

"You son of a bitch!" Sorren hissed under his breath at the unconscious man. "If you touch her again, I'll kill you!"

Shadow looked at Sorren with mixed emotions. She had never seen such a vicious look on his face. Not even at Angie's Saloon, when he shot the four men, had he looked so angry. She knew the second blow to the guard's head was out of jealous rage. The guard was unconscious from the first strike. The second was to soothe Sorren's sense of possessiveness and honor.

"Are you okay?" Sorren touched Shadow's face lightly with his fingertips, as he so often did when he was searching her eyes honestly. "Did he hurt you?" The loving concern showed plainly on Sorren's handsome face.

"I'm fine," Shadow answered, new love blooming in her heart for Sorren's concern. "I'm okay. Now what do we do?"

"We find out how good I am at training horses." Sorren took Shadow's hand in his and stood. "Stay down and be quiet, but *hurry!*"

Shadow marveled that she wasn't frightened as long as Sorren was holding her hand. She had infinite faith in him. He could not love her—or at least couldn't *say* that he loved her—but he would protect her with his life, and of that Shadow had total confidence.

They moved quickly and silently along the outskirts of the encampment. The time between Sorren's attack on the first guard and their reaching the southernmost section of the camp was less than three minutes.

Sorren got down on one knee. The grass was higher here, covering him to the waist. Shadow knelt beside him, her small hand still secure inside his larger one.

"Now what?"

Sorren flashed Shadow a smile that made her confidence soar. "Now we find out if I'm as good as

374

I'd like to think I am."

Shadow's dark eyebrows pushed together in confusion. She looked at Sorren, loving the excitement she saw in his eyes, taking delight with him in the thrill of the escape. When she was with him, she felt invincible. She was fully aware of the potential for violence against her, but she wasn't afraid of it. Sorren would, as he had promised in the past, make everything all right.

Sorren gave a soft three-tone whistle. Low-high-low. He paused. He whistled low-high-low again. A neigh sounded in the distance, coming from the direction of the rope corral.

"You've got to be kidding me," Shadow whispered in awe, searching the darkness for an approaching horse.

She didn't have long to wait. In moments she heard a second answering neigh, then saw Sorren's white-faced mare making her way slowly along the edge of the camp. Shadow saw another horse at the side of the mare, following slightly behind. Glancing at Sorren, she saw a look of such exquisite, paternalistic pride and pleasure spreading across his face that she wanted to kiss him.

"Come to papa," Sorren murmured, though the mare was still too far away to hear. "Come on, sweetness. Come to papa."

Shadow realized that Sorren was using exactly the same tone of voice with his mare as he often used with her. *At least he's not calling her precious,* thought Shadow. Sorren's tone of voice irked Shadow unreasonably. She wanted something of Sorren's to be individually her own. She was painfully aware of the

375

many women he'd shared his body and passion with so she had at least stopped expecting that to truly be her own unique gift from him. She wanted something of his that he'd never given to anyone else.

When the horses were closer, Shadow saw that the second horse, a large roan male, had his reins tied to the saddle horn of Sorren's mare.

"Good girl," Sorren whispered, rubbing the mare's neck for a moment. He moved to the side and quickly untied the loosely knotted reins. He tossed them over his mare's back to Shadow. "Let's go while the going's good."

Shadow got on her horse. The long cloth dress was not like her doeskin dress. The voluminous folds and layers of cloth made it difficult for her to straddle the horses's back. She pulled the dress high on her legs and wished her sartorial finery was hanging neatly in her closet instead of clinging to her body.

"Nice and slow to begin with," Sorren whispered to Shadow. He tapped the mare on the ribs and she started walking. He was looking over his shoulder at the camp as he spoke. "If you hear anything, just follow me. My sweetheart can see in the dark."

Some horses can make their way through the night, and others cannot. There is a divergence of thought on whether this is a learned or an instinctive trait. One way or the other, Sorren's mare had chased and been chased through many black nights, and whether it was a matter of the mare trusting Sorren or the mare sensing Sorren's trust in her was unknown. So when Sorren heard the first warning sound behind him, he tapped his mare's ribs with his boot heels and whispered, "Now!" and she took off like the devil himself was after her.

At a hundred yards, Sorren realized the escape would not be without bloodshed. A guard — and Sorren hoped it was just one and not more — had been posted to watch over the valley. Sorren saw him step into the clearing, alerted by the pounding of hooves. He drew his Colt at the same time the guard hesitantly raised his rifle. Squeezing the pistol, Sorren felt his injured finger throb painfully.

"Stop!" the guard shouted, bringing the rifle up to his shoulder.

Sorren could picture the soldier's profound confusion. It was his job to keep people out of camp, not to prevent someone from leaving. He wanted to shoot, but he still could not recognize who was riding toward him at such a furious pace. Something was obviously wrong, but what? If he used his rifle, he could well kill a fellow soldier and would consequently face the wrath of General LaRoux; if he didn't, he might also find himself facing LaRoux. What to do?

"Stop!" the guard shouted again, apprehension and anger filling his voice.

At fifteen yards, at a full gallop, the guard recognized Sorren and made his decision. Sorren's right hand extended with the Colt, leaning over his mare's neck. He saw the red-yellow flash of flame spit from the muzzle of the guard's rifle. The sound of the rifle and pistol explosion came as one. The guard took two quick steps backward, and as Shadow passed him, she saw the deep round stain spreading across his shirtfront. He fell facedown and did not move. Sorren's finger stiffened as it began to swell.

Sorren and Shadow had put three hundred yards between themselves and the renegade army before anyone realized what exactly had happened. Before horses were saddled and riders mounted, the fleeing couple had put a mile between themselves and their hunter.

Shadow found the rhythm of the gelding's stride and rolled along with it smoothly. She leaned close to the horse, her face getting whipped by his long mane as his hooves pounded the green grass. The small valley south of the encampment swallowed Shadow and Sorren. Progress slowed drastically on the uphill side, but Shadow reasoned that if she was slowed by it, so would be the riders who followed her.

When they reached the far side of the valley, Sorren headed sharply to the right, heading east and away from the mountains. Shadow assumed, though she was not certain, that Sorren had picked this escape route in advance. Her appreciation of his cunning and forethought turned a fraction higher, and when he spun in his saddle to look over his shoulder at her, checking to see that she was still following, she made a solemn, silent vow that if they lived through this, she would break down the barriers that surrounded the black-clad's man hard heart and would reach the warm, tender, loving inner sanctum that she knew he was hiding and protecting.

If only they lived. If only the twenty—no, now nineteen—violent men who followed them wouldn't search forever. If only Sorren would give her a chance to truly show him how desperately, soulfully, completely in love she was with him.

The strenuous gallop slowed to a steady canter. After an hour, Sorren stopped his mare and Shadow moved beside him. She started to speak, but he silenced her by raising his palm. He listened to the wind, controlling his breathing and closing his eyes so that he shut out everything but sound. Shadow heard nothing.

"They're not—"

"Quiet!" Sorren hissed, and his eyes flashed dark in the night. He was like a wild animal, every nerve alive.

Thirty seconds ticked by. Then a minute. A grim smiled curled Sorren's lips. "They split up."

"Where?"

"At the rocks. Where we turned east." Sorren closed his eyes again, shutting out everything but his sense of hearing. "Damn," he whispered after a moment. "Damn."

It was then that Shadow, faintly in the evening breeze that carried the sound, heard the rumble of hooves. How, she asked herself, had Sorren heard that so much earlier than she had? What was it about him that made his senses so keen?

"Let's go," Sorren said. His tone carried an undercurrent of pleasure that Shadow did not understand. He headed his mare along a deer trail, pushing away from the open country and into the woods and forests. Shadow followed him into the dark forest, trusting Sorren's instincts, trusting him and fearing the angry, deadly soldiers who hunted them with the determination of a pack of hungry wolves.

Chapter Twenty-one

Jean-Jacques LaRoux bit harder on the unlighted cigar that was clamped between his even white teeth. The past hour had been holy hell for him and his men, and if there were any justice at all in this world, Sorren McKenna would soon be swinging from the end of a rope.

"Here's where we're not sure," Smitty said, pulling his horse to a halt next to LaRoux. "They coulda gone east or west. Ain't likely they continued straight, otherwise we coulda found their tracks." Smitty spit a long stream of tobacco juice to the ground. He had a look in his eyes that suggested he didn't need or want this kind of headache.

"What's your guess?" LaRoux asked.

Smitty scratched his chin. "I'd say they headed west. Moved up into the mountainland where the land's hard. Makes it a bitch to track somebody on. Especially at night. An' up there they gots the ambush advantage. Ain't no tellin' when they'll stop and take potshots down on us." Smitty nodded to the torch in his hand. "With these, he can see us before we sees him."

LaRoux let Smitty's guess dance around in his own mind. How would Sorren McKenna act when running? Would he do the logical thing, as Smitty had suggested? Or would he head east, into the woodlands? Tracking would be easier in the woodlands, even by torchlight, but visibility would be drastically reduced. There was absolutely no guessing when Sorren would set up a trap. Round a bend in the trail and there he'd be, shotgun at the ready, with the Colt at his hip waiting for the *coup de grace.*

LaRoux didn't like either option. Both were risky. But he wanted Sorren bad. Real bad. Sorren McKenna would not die quick, like Joey had. LaRoux was going to make McKenna beg for death. And that squaw he was with would see him die slowly, inch by inch, drop by drop.

Events of the past hour played through LaRoux's mind, the colors of death and blind rage blazing red and green in his mind's eye.

"Gen'ral, McKenna and the squaw got away," Smitty had said, slightly winded from running as he stood nervously at the entrance to LaRoux's tent. "They got horses. They're movin' fast."

LaRoux, with his shirttails flying as he leaped into his trousers, shouted, "Send out a preliminary expedition! Don't lose their trail, for Christ's sake!" He pushed his shoulder-length, wavy blond hair behind his ears and slapped his hand. "Get my horse! And I want to know who is responsible for this, Smitty! This camp's got two minutes!"

LaRoux's horse was saddled and brought to him.

The first expedition of three men—some of the better trackers among the army of misfits, in Smitty's opinion—had been sent ahead.

"Who's in charge of the wagons?" LaRoux asked, taking his horse and preparing to mount.

"Jackson."

"Tell him unless he keeps up, he's a dead man."

"Yes, sir," Smitty replied.

At the edge of the camp, LaRoux had Joey brought to him. Joey was bleeding from the mouth and missing several teeth from the kick to the jaw he'd received from Sorren.

"He sucker kicked me, General," Joey said, blood dribbling from the corner of his mouth. He was scared and in great pain, and it showed on his face as he looked up at his mounted leader. "I didn't have a chance. Honest to God, it ain't my fault!"

LaRoux never hesitated. He drew his revolver and, at point-blank range, put a bullet into Joey's mouth. He holstered his service revolver slowly, feeling the eyes of his own men on him.

"Let's move out," LaRoux said quietly. There was no need for him to raise his voice. Every ear was trained on him. Killing Joey had insured him that he would have every order followed instantly and without question.

LaRoux digested the information Smitty had given him. A cold, lethal rage was slowly bubbling to the boiling point inside him. McKenna! Out of the blue McKenna had showed up and, for reasons LaRoux could not fully understand at the time, had gone to great lengths to keep the Indian woman to himself and ingratiate himself to LaRoux. That would have een the tip-off, LaRoux surmised in retrospect. McKenna had never stayed with any woman long, and he had never done anything to ingratiate himself to Confederate officers. In fact, Sorren McKenna had usually done quite the opposite — openly ignoring orders, refusing to write reports, doing as he damn well pleased when he was back from an assignment across enemy lines. LaRoux had wanted to believe it was only the years that had made Sorren change.

LaRoux had bought the whole crazy story because he wanted to believe in McKenna. He had wanted a soldier of McKenna's caliber riding with him. In the back of LaRoux's mind, he knew why it was important to him that he have Sorren McKenna in his private army, too. To have McKenna riding with him and taking orders from him would, vicariously, prove LaRoux's leadership, would prove beyond any doubt that he was a great soldier and a leader of men. If he weren't so masterful, then why would Sorren McKenna be riding with him?

McKenna had outsmarted LaRoux, and any way the general looked at it, he would come up with no other conclusion. Sorren had played with him, moving him about like a piece on a chess board, manipulating him, directing him however he chose until he finally made his break.

"We'll split up, you taking half the men and me taking the other half," LaRoux said, his pale eyes glittering with feral blood lust. He had no need to raise his voice. Every rider there knew who to take orders from. As he studied the faces of his soldiers in the torchlight, he saw the fear they had for him in their eyes. LaRoux knew then that it had been a

smart leadership decision to kill Joey in front o
them. Now they all knew the price to be paid fo
failure. "No matter what happens, McKenna is to be
taken alive."

LaRoux would not be denied his revenge. Th
South had lost the war because of men like
McKenna. Revenge, when it came, would be swee
on LaRoux's tongue. It would taste of the blood and
flesh of Sorren McKenna, and would be heard in hi
screams as he begged for death to take him.

The deer trail eventually emptied out into one o
the many long, grassy valleys so characteristic of th
Colorado territories. Sorren pulled his mare to a sto
at the edge of the valley and waited until Shadow wa
beside him.

"We'll cross here," Sorren said. Shadow saw that h
was breathing deeply. *So, he is not inexhaustable, either*
The strain was showing on him, though the effect
were far less noticeable on Sorren than on herself
"From the other side we can watch the valley. We ca
rest there. If they want to follow us, they'll have t
come into the open." He gave Shadow a half smile a
he patted the Remington Rolling Block with th
telescopic sight in the scabbard running parallel t
the left side of his mare. "That's what this baby's for.

"Okay," Shadow replied. She did not like the eu
phoria she saw on Sorren's face. Shadow couldn't tel
whether he was happy that they were making such
good progress, or if he was thrilling at the action. I
was impossible for her to tell whether Sorren wa
looking forward with anticipation to using his long

range rifle, or if he simply understood that if the need arose, he was prepared.

They crossed the valley at an easy trot. It didn't take long for Sorren to find another animal trail that led into the forest on the far side. The clear blue stream that split the valley continued into the woods, and he stopped at an area where the stream widened and took a ninety-degree turn. The water, only inches deep in most places, was deeper here, nearly a foot deep at the elbow of the turn where the spring rains, flooding the stream, had eroded the soil the most.

Sorren looped a long, lean leg over the rump of his mare and went to Shadow. "Let me help you down," he said, taking the reins of her gelding. He dropped the reins, and when Shadow twisted on the back of her mount, she felt his strong hands encircle her waist. He eased her to the ground and she sighed softly, happy both for the feel of his hands on her and relief for finally having gotten off the hard-backed but well-trained animal.

The horses were as thirsty as their riders. Sorren let them drink downstream from himself. He lay on his belly, his hat on the ground beside him as he dipped his face into the clear, cool stream and gulped water in greedily. Though Shadow was as thirsty as Sorren, she waited a moment, watching him as he drank. It was always easier to look at Sorren when he didn't know she was watching him. When he was unguarded, Shadow believed she had a better understanding of the man behind the cold, deadly persona of whoever it was who always wore black and carried rifles designed for killing people at great range.

"If you want to wash up," Sorren said when he'd finally finished drinking, "now's the time to do it. I'll keep a watch on the valley." His face was wet. He removed his neckerchief and used it to dry his face.

"I'd like that," Shadow replied softly. Sometimes Sorren talked to her in a tone and manner that suggested she meant nothing more to him than a riding companion, a friend who had been through arduous times with him. She wished his tone always carried that special timbre that suggested, without words, the intimacy they had once shared.

"Just give me a holler when you're finished." Sorren went to his mare as she drank. He removed the scoped rifle from its scabbard. "I'll be at the edge. Take your time, but not too much."

Shadow watched him walk away. Her eyes lingered on the taut movement of his buttocks inside the snug denim slacks and the gentle swaying motion of his broad shoulders. She whispered "Damn you" under her breath, into the moonlit night air, soft enough so that Sorren couldn't hear her, then went to the stream where he had drank.

Sorren sat at the edge of the valley with his back against a tree and the Remington across his lap. He closed his eyes for a moment, breathing deeply, wishing upon whatever powers there were in the universe that Things would be All Right.

The feelings he had for Shadow changed constantly, not by the hour or day, but by the minute. There were things about him that Sorren knew she could never understand or accept. They were as foreign and arcane to Shadow as her Kiowan language and customs were to him. She could never understand the intense loneliness of a man who is adored too much by too many people; the fear of intimacy that a man who has loved too many women too shallowly develops; and, most of all, Shadow could never understand Sorren's belief that on an intrinsic level, he was not truly *good* for women, that he would eventually hurt Shadow, and that since he believed this and since he truly did love her, he did not want her to love him because he knew that eventually he would hurt her.

In time, Sorren would feel the need to stray, and he'd find himself in the arms and bed of a woman who could not match up to Shadow. But he would go to bed with her nevertheless, just to prove that he wasn't captivated by Shadow, wasn't imprisoned by her charms. He would prove his independence by sharing his body with another woman, and when it was over, he would feel hollow inside for what he'd done. And, when Shadow finally discovered his infidelity, he would not lie to her about it; he'd confess without blinking and say that she had no claims to him. He was a man—he was Sorren McKenna, after all—and he'd be damned if he'd let a woman dictate the terms of his life to him.

Of course, a woman like Shadow could never accept him after that. She would leave him. Sorren would pretend he wasn't lonely by surrounding himself with women who adored him but couldn't possibly love him since all they'd ever gotten from him was some of his charm and love words and the skill of his hands and body to make them feel wanted.

Sorren took his hat off. He tilted his head back against the tree trunk and sighed. The knowledge of what the future held in store carried no comfort. He sometimes wondered whether it was good that he could look at himself, at his strengths and weaknesses so clearly, without any deception. If he could make himself believe he wouldn't hurt Shadow, he would willingly accept the love she so freely offered. Until that time, his conscience would be clear of the guilt of intentionally hurting Shadow.

Now is not the time to let your mind wander! he chided himself, his heart's self-defense mechanism still intact. Worrying about the men following him was less disquieting than thinking about a voluptuous young woman with doe eyes and long legs and full lips and firm breasts splashing in the stream a scant twenty yards away. *Stop it right now! Don't think about her!*

Sorren scanned the far edge of the valley where the woods met the long, grassy plain. He studied the valley, sadly realizing that at one time — a time not that many years ago — Indians and buffalo controlled this land. Now the Indians were mostly on reservations and the buffalo had been slaughtered nearly to extinction.

Sorren wondered how large the group of soldiers was that followed him and Shadow. Was LaRoux with them? A grim, determined smile curled his mouth, and his left hand slid along the walnut forearm stock of the Remington. When the soldiers crossed the valley, they would be in the open. For a period of no less than a hundred yards, the soldiers would be well within his range but he would be out of theirs. If Jean-Jacques LaRoux was in the hunting party, Sorren would hold off on his first shot until he was absolutely certain his mark was within killing range.

Then he'd take LaRoux out with a single shot. What happened after that was in doubt. Perhaps some of LaRoux's men would attempt to fight back, but more likely, they would turn tail and run. It wouldn't take long for the men to split up. Then, on an individual basis, they would not be strong and brave and vicious; they would be scared, hungry, displaced soldiers. Some would drift, looking for a new army to join. Others would become alcoholics and die in a muddy gutter someplace, perhaps even in God's Grace. But the majority of the men would end up working as cowpunchers and ranch hands, driving cattle to the Kansas City and St. Louis stockyards and railroad terminals, making just enough money to have an occasional wild night or two in those thriving cities, spending everything they'd made on a rush of alcohol and women and card games for stakes they couldn't afford. Sorren remembered what he'd read in Benjamin Franklin's *Poor Richard's Almanac*: "Nine men in ten are suicides." In his own way, was he among them?

All this was possible, even likely . . . but not until Jean-Jacques LaRoux tasted death on his tongue, felt the last vile beat of his ignoble heart. Not until LaRoux died in the same violet manner that he had lived and ruled would the men who followed him become harmless derelicts.

Sorren glanced over to the stream and his heart skipped a beat. Shadow was kneeling naked in the shallow, cool stream, cupping water in her hands to wash her face. She was, in that heart-stopping instant, more astonishingly beautiful, more guileless and alluring, than Sorren could ever believe possible.

He saw her in the glow of partial moonlight, her glorious profile electrifying. His eyes lingered on her tawny flesh, her flawless form. Sorren saw her in a way that he never had before. She was an illusion, a dream come to life. There was nothing in the world, he decided then and there, more erotic than an innocently beguiling woman. As Shadow washed the perspiration from her face, Sorren saw the taut, gentle sway of her heavy breasts. Her hair, black as midnight, was spread over her rounded shoulders, fanning out luxuriously over her back, tucked behind her ears.

When Shadow raised her head, the ends of her hair touched the water. Still kneeling, she splashed cool water with cupped hands onto her bosom and stomach.

"Sweet Jesus," Sorren murmured, his eyes glazed as he watched Shadow's hands run softly, blamelessly over her breasts and stomach.

Everything in Sorren's emotional makeup screamed in silent protest of this torture. And for Sorren, what had at first been an event of erotic voyeurism was now stark, agonizing torture. The devilish naughtiness of watching Shadow bathe herself only served to reinforce his bone-marrow-deep belief that he had become too jaundiced to the simple and honest pleasures in life and love for him to, with a clear conscience, involve himself deeply and permanently in Shadow's life. She deserved a steady and constant man, a man who was not trying to outrun his past. Shadow, despite the tough exterior she struggled so vainly at times to show the world, was a fragile-hearted, loving young woman.

Woman? thought Sorren. *She's still a teenager!*

She stood and, still bent over, washed the pebbles of sand from her knees. Sorren, afraid that she would face him, presenting him with the full, spine-tingling force of her beauty, jerked his gaze violently from her. He squeezed his eyes shut as a shudder of frustration passed through him.

"Damn me," he whispered aloud, hating the fact that he was talking to himself, yet taking a certain comfort in the sound of his own voice. "Damn, damn, goddamn me."

It wasn't until Sorren was absolutely certain he had regained his self-control that he opened his eyes. He turned his attention to the far side of the moonlit valley and smiled wanly as he saw the pinpricks of light from torches carried by the men who lived with the desire to see him die.

At first it appeared to be just one torch, but then the riders separated and Sorren saw that it was three riders. One rider headed into the valley, moving slowly while the other two remained at the treeline.

"Come on," Sorren purred, resisting the urge to pick up the Rolling Block that lay across his lap. "Don't stop now."

But the single lead rider did not continue. In the bowl of the valley, he stopped and turned, returning to the other two. Sorren sighed, understanding why the tracker had stopped. He had no real knowledge of how far ahead Sorren and Shadow were, so he had decided to call it quits, at least for the evening. In the morning, it would be easy enough to track Sorren through the valley. Starting fresh in the morning would also give the riders the advantage of daylight. If they headed across the long valley with their torches, Sorren could stay hidden in the night, shooting them without any danger whatsoever of them returning fire.

LaRoux got off his horse and looked over the valley. It was, he knew, the smart thing to do to stop tracking McKenna and his woman. He wanted McKenna's blood, but not at the cost of his. He wasn't overly concerned about the lives of his men — they were soldiers, weren't they? — but if too many of them should die in what amounted to nothing more than a mission of vengeance, he could find the control he had over his soldiers slip. He knew they followed his command only because they felt it was in their best interests to do so. There wasn't a one of them who would not, for the right price, put a bullet in his back. And that included Smitty.

Besides, a good general doesn't waste men, La-Roux assured himself. The valley would be the ideal spot for an ambush. Hidden in the trees on the opposite side of the valley, McKenna could pick LaRoux's men off at will with almost no danger to himself. He could pick his shot, kill one of the trackers, then ride on. That action alone would slow down LaRoux enormously.

"We'll stop here until sunup," LaRoux said quietly to Johnny, who hovered near his elbow, waiting for orders. "We'll start again in the morning. He can't be that far ahead of us."

"No, sir, he can't be too far," Johnny readily agreed. "An' he's got that squaw with him. That'll slow him down."

LaRoux wasn't sure of that, but he said nothing to Johnny. The woman McKenna had kept at his side had a look in her eyes, a defiance that never left her, which indicated to LaRoux that she wouldn't slow down a man on the run.

A campfire was started and LaRoux waited impatiently for someone to bring him his coffee. He did not mingle with the six men who rode in his group. They were underlings, inferiors, and no matter how much LaRoux needed their services, he couldn't possibly see himself as being one of them.

In the pit of his stomach, LaRoux could feel small tremors of fear working their way slowly through his system. The fear had a name, and that name was Sorren McKenna. He looked out over the valley, wondering where the man he hunted was. *Are you still running? Are you laying in wait, hiding in the trees for me? Damn you, McKenna, you'll pay dearly for this.*

To realize that he was afraid of McKenna left a foul taste in LaRoux's mouth. Sorren McKenna was a man accustomed to hunting alone, to fighting alone. His power rested in his ability to act quickly, independently, and decisively. LaRoux's power rested in his ability to direct other men to act and react that way.

In a one-on-one battle, LaRoux sensed that he really was no match for Sorren. Still, he also knew that whatever he lacked in physical skill against McKenna, he more than made up for in manpower. Sorren McKenna was a great fighter, a fearsome soldier . . . But he was just one soldier against many, and LaRoux would use that to his best advantage.

Francine wasn't certain what it meant, but she di
know it was important. It was her ticket back int
Jean-Jacques LaRoux's big, comfortable tent and ou
of Smitty's bed.

Though sweat stung her eyes and a thin trickle o
blood came from the scratch of her cheek, sh
pushed on, moving farther and farther ahead o
Jackson and the wagons, getting closer — she hoped —
to LaRoux.

She hadn't anticipated Sorren McKenna and th
squaw taking off like they had, but that wasn't goin
to change her plans. Not one little bit. Her plan
weren't going to change because she knew that La
Roux hadn't made love in several days, and when h
saw her he would want her just like he used to. Jean
Jacques LaRoux would want Francine all to himsel
He wouldn't want to share her glorious body an
sexual skills with anyone — certainly not with a to
bacco-chewing cretin like Smitty!

Should I get spruced up a little before I see him
she wondered.

Francine squeezed the fat leather envelope she hel
and a surge of confidence went through her. Whe
the man had gone through Shadow's possessions
looking through her valise, they had found the thic
pile of papers tucked in a leather envelope. Seein
that it wasn't money and therefore was, at least t
them, without value, they had discarded it. Bu
Francine could read. She could see that there wer
four names on the contract. There had been space
for only two names, but four had been written in

She recognized two of the names: Sorren McKenna, esquire, and Shadow.

Francine was certain LaRoux would be pleased with her when she showed him the contract. Once he saw what she had done for him, riding ahead of the wagons and risking her life — at least that's the way she would make it sound to him — she would be taken back into his arms and into his warm, dry tent, and she wouldn't have to spread her legs for Smitty or anyone else ever again.

Even though the stream was very shallow, the water was quite cool. Shadow shivered a little as she splashed water onto the lower part of her legs. It felt amazingly refreshing to wash away the dirt and sweat of the hard ride, to rid herself symbolically as well as physically of General Jean-Jacques LaRoux and his band of cutthroats.

Unembarrassed by her own nudity, Shadow wondered if Sorren was watching her. She'd done nothing to hide herself as she bathed. What possible difference could it make, she reasoned, if he did look at her? He'd made it clear that he wasn't going to make love to her again. If he had such thoughts, he hadn't acted upon them, even though he had more than ample opportunity when they were locked in the Conestoga together.

When she glanced over to where Sorren stood at look out, she saw the last turn of his head away from her. *So he is watching!* she thought.

It struck her as particularly absurd that, on the run from a band of lunatics who wanted to see them dead, she should be concerning herself with the less-than-subtle art of breaking down a man's emotional barriers. Even Shadow realized that now was hardly the time for such frivolous pursuits. The logical side of her brain told her to set aside Sorren and the feelings he had toward her and their future together until later, when they were safe and snug in a hotel together or perhaps comfortably seated in Sorren's gun room. But this wasn't a matter for logic. This was a matter of the heart, an *affair* of the heart, and whatever dangers life presented them weren't at hand this very moment.

Shadow thought, *I have become impatient. Nothing used to bother me very much. Now I can't stand being without what I want.*

A coy smile spread gently across her wide, lovely face as she dismissed this bout of childlike impatience to the Weatherly side of her bloodline. Shadow saw herself, with amusement, becoming more and more like Catherine Weatherly all the time.

"Uh-oh," Sorren said.

Shadow, washing the last pebbles of dirt from her knees, looked over again to where he was. The field glasses were at his eyes. She stepped out of the stream and pressed her dress to her body with one hand, letting her moccasins dangle from two fingers of the left hand.

"What do you see?" Shadow asked softly, walking barefooted to where Sorren was.

"A minute ago they were setting up camp." Sorren did not take the field glasses from his eyes as he spoke. "Now it looks like they're leaving. Damn!"

"Let me see." Shadow waited for the field glasses

She was on her knees beside Sorren, slightly behind him at the treeline. When he finally put the glasses down and handed them to her, she saw his eyes widen in shock as he saw that she had not put the dress on but was only pressing it to her body. "Thank you," Shadow replied, taking the proffered field glasses from Sorren. For only an instant her fingers touched his as she took the glasses from him. She held them in her left hand, looking through the twin optics, her right hand only casually attempting to keep her garment in place.

"We may not be able to stay here tonight."

"Okay," Shadow replied. At first she saw nothing but midnight darkness. Then, finally, she picked up the campfire across the valley at the edge of the trees. Shadow was surprised at how much light the field glasses collected. Not only did everything look closer, but it seemed they saw more moonlight.

"It all depends on what LaRoux's going to do."

"Of course." Shadow continued looking through the field glasses, but she really wasn't paying attention to what she saw. What was more important was the tone of Sorren's voice. She wondered what was going through his mind, and though she felt a little shameful for her wanton behavior, she did not in any way regret what she was doing. Her words came out in a slow, precise, matter-of-fact fashion. "Whatever you think is best. You know more about these things than I do."

"Yes," Sorren said, and in that single word was a tautness that showed his casual manner was a facade for rioting emotions. "Are you tired?" Sorren cleared his throat. "Can you keep riding?"

"As long as necessary." Shadow finally took the field glasses from her eyes. She handed them back to Sorren. "Well, I'd better get ready to ride, I suppose."

"I suppose."

The artificially nonchalant conversation gnawed at Shadow's patience. Unreasonably, she suddenly wanted to scream at Sorren. She wanted him to either set her free or tell her he loved her. Anything was preferable to leaving her in the emotional limbo she now hung suspended in. If she were hurt by his words, whatever they might be, Shadow could live with that hurt. But to be told that she simply would not and could not understand explained absolutely nothing. It also—and this notion had just crept into her mind poisonously—implied that she was incapable of the same powers of intellect as Sorren McKenna.

Shadow looked directly into Sorren's eyes. She found it irritating that the strain which showed so plainly on his face did nothing to take away his handsomeness. In the moonlight, the lines of fatigue and the years that Shadow had not yet seen only made Sorren look more masculine to her.

"I could always make enough noise to draw their attention," Shadow said acidly. Her anger was rising, and though she realized this was not the time for it, she would not be denied an opportunity to prick his conscience.

"What are you talking about?"

"I'm saying that I could get them to chase us again. Then you wouldn't have to look at me or talk to me or do anything. That's what you want, isn't it?"

"You're losing your mind." Sorren took the glasses

and raised them to his eyes as Shadow's dark, angry gaze sliced into him.

"I'm losing my mind? I'm not the one who—"

"They're moving," Sorren cut in. "What the hell is LaRoux up to now?"

"I'm not interested in what—"

"Be quiet, will you?" Sorren cut in again, still peering carefully through the field glasses. His concentration on the far side of the valley did absolutely nothing to assuage Shadow's escalating temper. "What's he got planned?"

"Don't tell me to shut up."

"I didn't. I told you to be quiet."

"It's the same thing." Shadow looked at where the camp was, and to her surprise, she saw the pinholes of light that were the torches of the lead riders. They were moving horizontally. "What are they doing?"

"I haven't the slightest idea. But he's moving fast. Damn fast. Hmmm? . . . He's up to something, but he's not after us."

"Are they giving up? You're sure?" Shadow could not keep her anger focused on Sorren when it appeared as though the ordeal of the past days was finally over. "Are they going to leave us alone?"

Sorren still had the field glasses to his eyes as the torches advanced into the bowl of the valley, moving steadily away. "Maybe. But it could be a trick." He paused a long moment. "Damn it, yes! I don't know why, but they are definitely giving up the chase." Not until the torches had disappeared over a ridge and out of sight did Sorren put the glasses down. His face was bright with relief, his eyes glittering triumphantly as he looked at Shadow. "We did it, precious." Sorren smiled and sighed wearily, tension oozing form him. "We've won."

"We're safe?" Shadow asked the question in a tone that suggested she couldn't quite believe they were no longer in danger. She needed to hear it from Sorren's lips before she could allow herself to believe it.

"Yes, precious, We're safe." A soft chuckle came from Sorren's chest, rumbling through him with warm satisfaction. He tilted his head back until it touched the tree he was leaning against. He closed his eyes and sighed again. "We're safe, precious. For now, we're safe."

Chapter Twenty-two

Shadow smiled weakly at Sorren. Her lips quivered. "We're safe? We're really safe?" Sorren nodded his head and Shadow felt hot tears or relief misting her eyes. It was only then that she realized how truly frightened she had been. "Thank you," she whispered. "Thank you, Sorren."

Sorren reached out to touch Shadow's face. She took his hand in hers and squeezed it. "Ouch!" he hollered, his eyes alive with pleasure. "My finger is still sore."

Shadow laughed then, too. She took Sorren's hand and studied the marks where her teeth had sank through the skin. The finger was swollen still, but it was showing the signs of healing. As Sorren had so often done to her, Shadow closed her eyes and kissed the inside of his hand.

"I'm sorry," she whispered into Sorren's palm. "I didn't mean to hurt you. Not really. I was angry and frightened. That's why I bit your finger."

"It's okay. Don't think about it."

Shadow softly pressed her lips to Sorren's wounded finger. "Such gentle hands," she purred softly. "They shouldn't be hurt by me or anyone else. Never." Shadow took her left hand away from her bosom, no longer clutching her dress to herself. "You saved my life, Sorren."

"Don't think about that. It's all over now," Sorren said. Shadow's dress fell away from her breasts. The soft brown areolas drew his eyes. The nipples were hard. Was it because of the cool night air? He watched Shadow kiss the inside of his wrist. "Shadow . . . precious . . . you don't know what it is you do to me."

Shadow inched closer to Sorren, keeping her knees beneath her. She sat on the backs of her heels, softly kissing Sorren's forearm, her eyes holding his. "Make love to me, Sorren," she whispered. "Please. I'm in love with you. I know you don't—"

"Shadow, I'm in—"

"No!" Shadow said quickly. "Don't tell me that. Please don't. Not now. You're saying it because I want to make love to you and I tell you that I love you. You think that it's the gentlemanly thing to say. But it's not really what I want to hear. Not if it's not true." She released Sorren's hand. Her hands roamed slowly up his arms until she cupped his face between her palms. "Make love to me like you love me. Please, Sorren. I won't ask you for anything else ever again." She leaned closer until her soft, shimmering lips were an inch from his mouth. "Kiss me softly and make love to me." Shadow kissed Sorren. The tip of her tongue flicked against his lips, then followed them, tracing a moist line around his mouth. "I love the way you kiss," she purred, her lips touching his, her fingertips trailing light as a feather down Sorren's neck until she reached the top button of his black silk shirt. She unfastened it and leaned back, sitting once again on her heels, her eyes smoky with love and passion. "I've never really told you how the sight of you affects me, have I?"

Sorren tried to calm his uneven breathing. He felt another button come unfastened. His eyes danced from Shadow's face down to her breasts. He watched them move, swaying slightly from side to side as her fingers worked free yet another button of his shirt. He brought a hand to one breast, raising it, catching the nipple between his first finger and thumb.

"Ohhh!" Shadow sighed. "I love how you touch me. You know now to be just strong enough and just gentle enough." Shadow pulled the shirttails out of Sorren's slacks. She spread her hands across his chest, feeling the sinewy muscles just beneath the surface of his skin. "You're like a puma. I've thought that sometimes. Just like a cougar." The heat of Sorren's flesh burned through Shadow's palms. His fingers stroked and rolled her nipples until they were fiercely erect and intensely aroused. "With the Kiowas, we revere and fear the puma. We're frightened of the puma's power and cunning, but we respect him for the same things we fear."

Sorren's hands left Shadow's breasts to slide around her trim waist. He pulled her close. She shivered. Shadow came off her knees, falling a little to one side. Sorren pulled her tighter still until her breasts pressed against his naked chest and her weight was on his thighs. He dipped his head down, his hand pushing into the heavy fall of her ebony hair, bringing his mouth to hers. The kiss was soft and deep,

Shadow opening her lips for Sorren and tasting his tongue.

A tremor worked its way through Shadow. She gave herself over freely to the pleasure that shivered through her body like a vital force. Sorren would make love to her. At least one more time she would know the passion that only he could draw from her senses. She kissed his mouth and neck, loving the feel of his chest against her sensitive breasts. His hand slipped from her back, curling around her hip to squeeze one buttock, and Shadow snuggled in closer to him.

Tomorrow they might die, but tonight she could live one more time.

"I won't expect anything of you," Shadow whispered. She kissed Sorren's cheek. The tip of her tongue flicked against his earlobe. "No demands. Just don't shut me out."

"Shadow, I—"

"No." Shadow put her fingers to Sorren's lips to stop his words. "Don't say that. When you touch me, I can feel the desire you have for me in everything you do. In the way you touch me, in the way you make love to me. That's—that's enough for me. That's all I need to know. If you say that—" Shadow couldn't force the words she really wanted to speak from her throat. "I just don't want you to say something to me that isn't true. When you touch me, it's not a lie."

Sorren kissed Shadow again, their lips pressed together for long, breathtaking moments. When they parted, he was shaking his head. "Shadow, you fool," he whispered. "You beautiful little fool. You don't understand, do you?"

It was Shadow who shook her head in negation this time. "Please. don't. I don't want to hear that I don't understand."

"I love you." Sorren's eyes were shiny as he looked down into the lovely face so intimately close to his own. "Don't you understand that? I am in love with you. I think I always have been. Right from the very beginning." Sorren tilted his head back on his shoulders, leaning against the trunk of the tree. He stared out into the night as though it were too much for him to look at Shadow and say the words he knew were the truth. "I am so afraid of hurting you. That's why—"

Shadow pulled Sorren's head down, kissing him, their lips barely touching yet the contact searingly intimate. "Your love won't hurt me," she whispered, twisting in his arms to press more of herself against him. "Your love could never hurt me. Love me, Sorren. Love me."

They made love beneath the stars, loving each other tenderly, always looking into each others eyes, making love as though it were the first time for them. Later, in Sorren's bedroll, Shadow held his head to her breast while he slept, holding him gently, whispering that everything would be all right, assuring Sorren that his love for her was beautiful and shouldn't frighten him.

It was on that night, when Shadow first realized Sorren, too, could be vulnerable and frightened, that she loved him more deeply than life itself.

Chapter Twenty-three

Shadow awoke first. She had Sorren's head cradled in her arm. A sleepy smile spread gently across her mouth and up into the corners of her eyes. Last night had been the most beautiful night of her life, and now, waking up with the man she loved—the man who loved her and said so—was magnificent. She hugged Sorren a little closer. He moaned groggily, snuggling in tighter to the warmth of her body.

Shadow kissed Sorren's forehead. With one finger she smoothed his mussed hair away from a closed eye.

He's so handsome, Shadow thought. *Especially now, when his hair isn't neatly combed and he's not dressed in menacing black. He looks even more exciting when he's not so composed.*

Content to drift in and out of sleep, holding Sorren softly to her side, Shadow welcomed the soft golden rays of dawn filtering through the trees, but not the harsh sunlight of morning she knew would soon follow. She didn't want anything—not even something as wonderful as a new morning—to disturb the way she felt right now.

With eyes closed, Shadow listened to the peaceful world around her. She heard the chirping of grackles as they, too, awoke. She listened to the high-pitched squeak of a chipmunk nearby. Shadow thought, *Don't worry, little chipmunk. We are intruders into your land, but we will not hurt you. There will be no violence today.*

Had there ever, in the history of the world, been a morning so beautiful as this one? It didn't matter that Shadow and Sorren were sleeping on the ground, with only a rough-textured wool blanket to protect them from the cold. Sorren's body was warm and naked beside her. She could feel his breath against her cheek, could feel the strong, even beating of his pulse from his arm that lay across her stomach.

Shadow's life was different now. It was absurd, she realized, to believe the air smelled fresher on this morning than any other morning—though it did. It was ridiculous to think the songbirds sang their lovesong on this one morning in greeting to her and Sorren—but they did. It was utter nonsense to believe that the sun had risen just to wake Shadow, so that she would know her dreams had become reality—though that is exactly why the sun had risen.

In the half-consciousness of early morning, Shadow was vaguely aware that she really was quite delirious with love and that she had lost all her powers of reasoning.

It seemed an insignificant price to pay for love.

Sorren shifted again. Shadow sighed, realizing he was waking up. She did not want Sorren awake. She wanted him to stay just the way he was now. She wanted this moment to last a moment longer.

"Ohhh!" Sorren sighed. He blinked his eyes. "Good

morning." Sorren pushed himself away from Shadow, taking his head from her bosom. He moved as though the position weren't proper for him. *He* should be the one cradling Shadow's head to his chest, not the other way around. "How long have you been awake?"

"A while." Shadow, with her arm around Sorren, tried to pull him down to where he had been. He resisted her. "Don't go yet. I'm not ready for the world."

Sorren smiled sleepily, but instead of putting his head on her bosom, he rolled so that he was half atop Shadow, the long, masculine length of his sinewy body pressed upon her. He kissed her lightly on the mouth, then put a soft kiss on each eyelid.

Putting his cheek against Shadow's, Sorren relaxed, content to let the morning and consciousness come to him slowly, gradually. On this one day, he would not attack the morning in an explosion of energy. The rest of his life could wait for a while. *Just a little while longer*, he thought. All he wanted was this one morning with Shadow. This one, and the next . . . and the next . . . and the one after that . . . and . . .

A final stretch put an end to the peaceful morning. Sorren rolled off Shadow, but she moved so that she was nestled under his arm. His fingertips trailed lightly over her smooth shoulder.

"Are you thinking about LaRoux?"

He nodded. "I just can't figure out why he gave up the chase. He had to have known we were close. That's why he stopped at the edge of the valley. He knew it was a great place for an ambush. He had to know that's where I could pick off a couple of his men. I can understand that he would wait, but I've never known him to quit. Lord knows, he doesn't care about his men that much."

It disturbed Shadow that Sorren could talk about killing men so casually. It would not be easy loving a man who often found himself in dangerous and violent situations, and knew how to react to those situations. Sorren McKenna was a warrior. He had been one before Shadow had fallen so deeply in love with him, and no amount of love she could give him would change him.

Shadow kissed Sorren's muscled upper arm and tried not to think about it.

"Something made him turn around," Sorren continued. He was staring at the canopy of trees overhead, but his mind was miles away. "Something . . . but what?"

"Maybe he got scared," Shadow offered in explanation. "Maybe he was frightened of you." Sorren shook his head. "Why not? He's a man. He gets frightened just the same as anyone else."

"No. Not LaRoux. He's insane. He doesn't think the same as a sane man. *Something* made him turn tail and run. I don't know what it was, but it wasn't because he's afraid of me." Sorren nibbled on his bottom lip, thinking. Shadow had the almost irresistible urge to kiss him. "Think it through," Sorren continued, talking to himself. Though his fingers moved gently along Shadow's shoulder, he did not feel the silkiness of her skin or the warmth of her voluptuous body pressed intimately against him. "What would make Jake-Jacques LaRoux run away from me?"

Shadow giggled softly. "Maybe he was running away from *me*. You didn't think of that, did you?"

"Unless, of course, he wasn't running away," Sorren continued, and Shadow realized he hadn't heard a word she'd said. "What if he wasn't running *away?* What if he was running *to* something or someone? What if something else had become more important than killing me?"

"Like making love?"

Sorren's mind twisted over what he knew about LaRoux, oblivious to the satiny contact of a thigh brushing across his legs. "They were riding fast last night when they left. That means they had a time schedule. A special purpose."

"Yes, of course," Shadow murmured, sliding further over, twisting as she raised her hips so that she straddled Sorren's lean waist with her thighs. "We must all have a special purpose, mustn't we?"

Sorren was still distracted. It wasn't until warm, soft breasts were brushing from side to side across his naked chest and feminine hips were moving in a gentle, erotic circular motion that he was fully aware of what Shadow was doing to him, and how his body had reacted independently of his mind.

"Like I said," Shadow whispered, holding Sorren's arousal to guide him into her, "we all must have a special purpose in life."

Sorren sighed as he felt himself driving deep into Shadow. He slipped his fingers into her hair, pulling her face down. He kissed her passionately, his tongue playing with hers. His fingertips followed her spine, touching lightly, gliding across the smooth curves of er buttocks. Together, they rolled over, Sorren positioning himself above Shadow. He watched the warmth of passion color her face as he pushed deeper and deeper.

"Precious, you are so beautiful," he said, his tone warm and silky with love.

An hour later, Shadow again lay with her head on Sorren's arm, her body tingling from head to toe in the glorious, golden afterglow of lovemaking. Sorren, to Shadow's intense disapproval, was chewing on a blade of grass, staring up at the trees with the same distant look in his dark eyes as before they made love.

"I'm not sure what the etiquette is for this sort of thing," Shadow began, her voice warm and indolent with thoughts and feelings still fresh, "but aren't you supposed to be thinking about me and what we've just done, instead of thinking about a man?"

If Shadow hadn't been watching Sorren at that precise moment, she would not believe such a rapid change was possible. The blood simply drained from his face, leaving him pale. And what she saw in his eyes was a mixture of sudden realization and terror.

"Damn. Sweet Jesus. Shadow, what happened to the contracts? What happened to them?" Sorren twisted on the bedroll so he could look directly into her eyes.

"I—I don't know. The contracts were in my valise. When the stage was held up, the valise was taken from me." A coldness was spreading through Shadow's slender limbs. It chilled her soul. It was horrifying to see this fear on Sorren's face and in his dark eyes that so often flashed with bravery. "The

411

women stole my dresses after that. I didn't have time to worry about the contracts." Sorren rolled away from Shadow, putting his forearm across his eyes as though the world had suddenly become too ugly a place for him to look at. "What's wrong? I don't understand what the contracts have to do with La Roux. He wasn't a part of the deal, was he?"

"He wasn't part of the deal," Sorren said, realizing he was giving Shadow a half-truth. If it hadn't been for Sorren agreeing to put an end to LaRoux, there would have been no contract. Now wasn't the time to explain that to Shadow. "But if he sees the contracts he'll know how you and I are tied together." Sorren's eyes glittered darkly. "He's going to wait for us at the MW Circle. He knows we've got to go back there eventually."

Shadow shook her head. "How would he know about the MW Circle?"

"The contract had Matthew's name on it. You, Carl, and Catherine signed on behalf of the MW Circle." Sorren paused, hoping he was wrong, knowing he was right. "There isn't a person in the territory who hasn't heard of the Weatherlys and the MW Circle."

Shadow was beginning to shake. "You're sure?"

"No. But I'm sure enough." Sorren pulled away from Shadow, reaching for his clothes. "If we can beat them back to the ranch, we've got a chance."

Shadow didn't believe the situation was as grave as Sorren was making it appear. "But what about all of Carl's hired men?"

Sorren stood and pulled on his shirt. *Akana, he's handsome,* she thought. "They're cowboys, not killers.

And how many will be at the ranch when LaRoux arrives? How many with the stock?" Shadow watched Sorren's hands moving rapidly as he strapped on the hand-tooled gunbelt. "Carl doesn't pay his men to sit around the bunkhouse playing cards. He also doesn't pay them to get in gunfights with lunatic armies. He sure as hell doesn't have the loyalty of his men like Matthew had."

Vague, horrific images began forming in Shadow's mind. She saw evil things happening to Carl and Catherine. Carl treated her cruelly, but he was her half brother, and Shadow's forgiving heart could not forget that. And there was Emma, who had accepted Shadow with an open mind and heart. Emma had been on her side from the very beginning. Shadow had heard LaRoux talk of the "darkies," and she knew that he hated blacks even more than he hated Indians, carpetbaggers, and Yankees.

As Shadow hurriedly pulled on her dress with trembling hands, she wondered if, somehow, she would be responsible for whatever harm should befall Emma and her family. Shadow did not want to believe that she would have to pay a still higher price for the love she had found with Sorren.

Chapter Twenty-four

Sorren knew he should slow down. His mare, born, bred, and raised to run, had held the pace he'd set. But now, with miles and miles of grassland between where they were and where he'd made camp with Shadow, she was showing the strain. The mare's nostrils were wider than gold dollars, and she was foaming at the mouth and at the saddle straps that held tight to her ribs. She'd keep running until her heart exploded. Sorren had seen such things happen before when a rider pushed a well-trained, noble-hearted mount beyond the limits of physical endurance.

But he also knew that LaRoux had a five-hour head start. Riding this hard, Sorren might catch up to him in three or four hours. If LaRoux got side-tracked or lost, Sorren had a good chance of beating him to the MW Circle.

Sorren was too logical a soldier to put too much hope in LaRoux getting lost. He steeled himself; the wise move was to prepare for the worst and hope for the best.

Sorren listened to his mare panting. He had to remind himself that she was, after all, just a horse. A beast with no name. A stupid beast with more loyalty than most men had for their wives; a stupid beast who greeted him every morning with a friendly nuzzle and a neigh.

"Come on, girl, ease up just a little," Sorren said, not sure if he'd actually spoken the words or just thought them. The mare slowed. Sorren rationalized his actions by thinking that if the mare collapsed beneath him, he wouldn't get to the MW Circle at all. Behind him, he sensed Shadow. Sometimes she was so close he could hear the labored breathing of her horse. When he glanced back, his heart thrilled to see her flowing smoothly with the action of her mount. She occasionally caught his eye and smiled. She knew he recognized and appreciated her superior horsemanship. He marveled at her skill. It felt good to have a strong partner.

Hours later, with the sun just past its zenith in the midday sky, Sorren and Shadow gulped in icy artesian water from a deep natural pool.

"The horses can't keep this up much longer," Shadow said between pants of air and gulps of water. She was on her stomach beside Sorren. "We'll kill them."

Sorren just nodded his head. Crystalized in his mind was the promise he'd made to Matthew Weatherly. If Sorren didn't feel just right about having Catherine as his Mrs. McKenna, Matthew had said with slurred words in a sad tone, could he keep an eye out for her just the same? Sorren had promised Matthew he'd look after Catherine. He'd made the promise, and though the only person who knew of the promise was dead, its binding force was just as strong as the day Sorren had said it.

"They — they won't be riding as hard as we are," Sorren said, splashing cool water onto the back of his neck. "If LaRoux really is headed to the MW Circle, we're making up ground on him. A lot of it."

"Can we beat him there?"

Sorren rolled away from the well onto his back. He shielded his eyes from the sun with a forearm. Why did she have to ask such straightforward questions? There were times when Sorren wished Shadow were more like other women. He stopped himself. No, that wasn't true.

"I honestly don't know," Sorren answered. "We'll take it slow for a while. The horses have bloated themselves with water. They'll cramp up if we push them."

Sorren turned his head to look at Shadow from beneath his forearm. He thought, *She's tired, too, but hasn't complained once. Thank God for her Indian blood. Someday I'll make this all up to you,* he promised silently. *Soon. I'm going to pamper you like you've never been pampered before.*

A mirthless smile turned the corners of Sorren's mouth when he remembered that Shadow *never* had been pampered. He was going to make up for that.

Jean-Jacques LaRoux stretched out on the ground and looked down at the MW Circle. Everything was working out so much better than he had ever thought possible. He felt like shouting. Too bad Smitty wasn't with him. Now would be a good time to talk with him. It would be like the old days during the war. How many Union camps had they stalked in the early dawn hours like this? After the raid, when the Yanks had been slaughtered and the wounded Confederate soldiers had been tended to, LaRoux would smoke his cigar and Smitty would chew his tobacco and they would sip some of LaRoux's private stock of liquor.

Johnny crawled beside LaRoux. There was a smile on his boyish face. "Ain't that many down there, General. Right now my guess is somewheres around ten or twelve men. Ain't no tellin' how many will show up later for breakfast grub."

Quietly, menacingly, LaRoux replied, "We'll have control of the house by then. That's all that matters. Once we control the house, we control everything."

"Yes, sir," Johnny agreed quickly.

"The sun'll be up soon," LaRoux said in a hushed voice. He knew that in the still morning hours, a man's voice carries far. "That'll be all," he added in dismissal.

The plan wasn't yet fully formed in LaRoux's mind. He did not, by nature, like raids of this sort. It was always a chancy proposition going outnumbered into an enemy camp. The best hope for success lay in surprise. LaRoux didn't have the time to wait a single day, let alone the necessary two or three days, to watch the MW Circle. With intelligence reports on the comings and goings at the MW Circle in his hands, LaRoux would feel confident. Since he'd be in the initial invasion, this was one raid he simply could not afford to have go wrong.

LaRoux looked to the east. The horizon held a slight pink hue. He had an hour to get cleaned up, to wash away the sweat and dirt and fatigue of being on the run. A conquering commander riding into a defeated city had to be clean, calm, and poised.

He crawled backward until he was well behind the knoll before getting to his feet. There was no stream nearby, but LaRoux knew his men carried enough water in their canteens for him to wash his hands and face. Touching his face as he walked to where Francine, Johnny, and six men stood waiting for new orders, LaRoux decided he would also shave. He wanted to look his best for Catherine.

Catherine Weatherly would be his next bauble. There would be a moment, one glorious moment, when her interest in him would change, when coquetry would turn to terror. He relished the thought of the look in her eyes when Catherine would realize she had no choice as to whether or not she wanted to have sex with him; in a moment, Miss Catherine Weatherly would realize all power rested with La-Roux, and that whatever happened would be dictated by him. That was the moment LaRoux mentally savored. It was so real to him he could almost taste her frightened kisses.

He would show them all. Everyone would soon know that General Jean-Jacques LaRoux was a man to be reckoned with. Sorren McKenna and his squaw, Carl Weatherly, and Catherine . . . very soon they would all know that he, General Jean-Jacques LaRoux, was a man who could not be crossed without paying a heavy price.

* * *

Catherine wasn't usually awake at this time of the morning. The news that Shadow's stage had been ambushed had kept her awake, tossing fitfully most of the night. Also playing on her mind was Carl's heartless, even cruel reaction to what had happened to Shadow. Since their father's death, he had never once shown any true sadness. He had put up a good front, but his acting job was incomplete, and eventually even Catherine was able to see the charade for what it was.

Catherine was disturbed by other news about Carl, too. Was this a new side of him, or was she just taking notice now? Had she willingly just closed her eyes all these years? While on a recent expedition to God's Grace, Catherine was accepting condolences from several friends who commiserated with her for both her father's recent death and the revelation that she had a half sister who was half-Kiowan Indian. Catherine was told at the same time, in the tones of someone who enjoys relaying a painful story but pretends not to, of Carl's most recent violent escapade at Beth Ann's bordello.

Rumor had it that Carl had been unable to perform sexually, and he had blamed this inadequacy on the prostitute he had selected. Though there were conflicting stories of whether or not Carl was so drunk that he was impotent, or whether he had gotten drunk later, one thing was clear — he had beaten the prostitute severely.

Catherine had known for years that her brother

frequented Beth Ann's, procuring her working girls to satisfy his sexual needs. She did not approve of this, but she did not openly frown upon it, either. It was a weakness, she believed, but a fairly harmless weakness. Hadn't her father, whom she adored more than any man, shown a similar weakness of the flesh, though he hadn't purchased the woman he slept with?

After hearing the story, Catherine visited the woman, offering her money to leave town. She was pretty, and too young and confused to refuse. It was difficult to judge which of the women was more humiliated. Afterwards, Catherine was pale and shaken. The vision of Carl, wild with rage, striking the defenseless woman, hounded her into her sleep. In the nightmares of Carl beating the prostitute, Catherine saw him beating Shadow to the ground and kicking her.

Catherine was still sleepy and disoriented when she heard the knock again on the front door of the mansion. It was too early for Emma to be in the mansion, so she resigned herself to shooing away the intruder.

She pulled the shimmering ivory nightgown tighter around her body. Her slippered feet swished against the wooden floor, then turned soundless when she padded across the carpet in the front room. She stroked her golden hair, not sure of how it looked. She thought, *What difference does it make? It's only one of the hired hands*.

Catherine opened the door several inches, a petulant look of indignation already on her lovely face. She peered through the opening, keeping her body hidden by the door.

"Good morning, Miss Weatherly," Jean-Jacques La-Roux said. He touched the brim of his hat and gave a curt nod. "Please forgive my early morning arrival. I realize this is inconvenient for you, but there are vital business matters that I must discuss with your brother immediately."

Catherine, no longer sleepy-eyed but wildly embarrassed by her unimpressive dishabille in front of the distinguished Southern gentleman, gave him a sheepish smile. "My brother is still asleep, and Emma isn't on duty yet."

"Yes, of course. I understand perfectly," LaRoux said. "But would you mind terribly if we waited inside?" He looked at the two men flanking him. "My colleagues, Johnny and Jeremiah, have ridden through the night to bring news that your brother needs to hear. They're quite exhausted. Perhaps if you would allow us to just sit and rest a moment?" LaRoux smiled again, and Catherine, seeing the fatigue showing on the faces of the two young men, felt herself weakening inside. She couldn't turn the men away, especially not after they had gone through such exhausting lengths to help Carl. "I am truly sorry," LaRoux continued. He put a boot inside the doorway, making it impossible for Catherine to close the door. "Truly, I am terribly sorry for the inconvenience, Miss Weatherly. Please try to understand."

Catherine was shocked when LaRoux put a hand on the door and gave it a slow but determined push. She was forced backward a step. LaRoux and his two men moved into the house as she clutched her nightdress and gown at her throat. "If you would wait in the library until my brother can see you . . ."

"Of course, Miss Weatherly. We do appreciate your kindness."

Catherine hurried up the stairs to her brother's bedroom. Carl, she was certain, had gotten himself into some kind of trouble. Legitimate business was not conducted at dawn.

LaRoux went past the library into the study. Jeremiah and Johnny followed close at his heels.

He crossed the room and sat in Carl's chair, behind the brightly polished desk. On one corner of the desktop, LaRoux saw scratches where Carl's boots had scarred the wood.

"He has no appreciation for what is good in life," LaRoux said aloud, speaking to himself.

Johnny and Jeremiah positioned themselves near the door, standing on either side. Johnny had the heel of his right hand resting on the handle of his revolver. LaRoux matched Johnny's gaze and, without words, warned the young man to wait for his signal.

It took Catherine several minutes to roust Carl out of bed. LaRoux heard the library door open and close and the muffled sounds of the siblings talking. A cruel smile curled up the corners of his mouth, and he twisted the end of his blond moustache, smoothing it in a downward arch.

"Wait for me to give the word," LaRoux instructed his men.

A moment later the door opened and Carl took one step into the study. He saw LaRoux sitting behind the desk. Carl's eyes, bloodshot from drinking and lack of sleep, blazed with hellish rage.

"What in God's name do you think you're doing?" Carl spat. He started toward LaRoux, moving to within a couple of feet of the desk before he realized he had men standing behind him. Carl stopped and looked over his shoulder. He was too angry to be afraid. With a wicked sneer, he spat, "Perhaps you don't understand, LaRoux. I own this goddamn town. I own this valley. And unless you get your Johnny Reb ass out of my chair in two seconds, I'll own *you!*"

Unflustered by Carl's outburst, LaRoux drawled, "Do you know what power is, Carl? True power?" He grinned. "This is power."

LaRoux snapped his fingers. There was a second in time when Carl just looked at LaRoux, wondering if the Southern businessman had actually lost his mind. Didn't LaRoux realize that he could crush him? Carl believed he held the power of the moment right up to the time that the toe of Johnny's boot connected solidly with his testicles. Carl doubled over, clutching his groin. Before he could fall to his knees, Johnny and Jeremiah grabbed him by the arms and hauled him upright. Carl's face was a mask of agony. Simultaneously, Johnny and Jeremiah punched him in the kidneys, low and hard, just beneath his rib cage. They released Carl and he dropped to the floor, writhing in pain.

"That," LaRoux said impassively, "is what power is. Now please, Carl, compose yourself quickly. Then go to your safe and withdraw the money that you owe me." LaRoux watched Carl squirming on the floor. He was a little disappointed that Weatherly hadn't lost bladder control. The last time LaRoux had

Johnny and Jeremiah kidney punch someone, the man wet his pants. Perhaps they'll get a second chance, he thought. "Where's Catherine?"

LaRoux waited for Carl to raise his head. Once again, he was a little disappointed in what he saw. LaRoux had hoped to see a sibling protectiveness in Carl's expression, wanted to see some kind of fear for his sister's well-being. He saw nothing of that whatsoever.

"She's — she's upstairs . . . in —" The words were coming slowly to Carl, forced through a throat constricted with pain. Carl, on his knees, was still holding his groin. "Bedroom . . . she's getting dolled up for you."

"Good. That's very, very good." From his pocket LaRoux extracted a long, slender cigar. He scratched a match against the sole of his boot and puffed lazily on the cigar. "Up now, onto your feet." LaRoux jabbed Carl with the toe of his boot. The contact was meant to threaten, not punish. "The safe is in here, correct?" Carl nodded. "Get him to his feet," LaRoux told Johnny and Jeremiah.

His legs didn't want to support his weight, so Johnny and Jeremiah had to drag Carl to the portrait of George Washington on the wall. Shards of agony laced up from Carl's abused groin, exploding in his brain. He kept his left hand cupped over his groin while with his right he pulled back the painting and spun the dial on the safe. Sweat dribbled down his forehead and stung his eyes, but he managed to find all the right numbers to open the safe.

"Take it," Carl said, doubling over as fresh pain ripped through him. "Take it all. I don't care."

LaRoux reached into the safe. There were several legal documents and one small stack of cash. He thumbed through the money, not counting it accurately but guessing around three hundred was there. "What's this? A joke, Carl? Is this your idea of a joke?"

"When—when you didn't come to collect . . . I thought you left the territory," Carl said weakly.

"I always collect on my debts," LaRoux hissed. "You must be punished! Johnny and Jeremiah will show you what it means to disobey me." He looked at his men. "Do it quietly."

Carl staggered away from the men, moving to the center of the room. The pain in his groin was nearly matched by the pain in his kidneys. Johnny stepped up behind Carl and put a foot against the back of his knee. Carl struggled as best he could. His breath came in labored gasps. He had little strength to fight with when Johnny and Jeremiah twisted his hands behind his back and tied them tightly with a piece of rough hemp rope. A bandanna was tied around his mouth to gag him.

Carl's red-rimmed eyes were filled with horror. LaRoux crossed the room slowly, his strides measured and confident.

"Make sure he doesn't make too much noise." LaRoux looked down at Carl. He shook his head in weary disgust. "You are such a pathetic little man."

LaRoux waited until Johnny kicked Carl in the back, knocking him onto his belly. Carl bit the bandanna with all the strength in his jaws as fresh waves of agony lanced through his body. Johnny delivered another heart-stopping kick to the groin.

"He squirms like a lizard," LaRoux said as h[e]
walked out of the study. "Be sure he stays quiet.
don't want to be disturbed."

LaRoux closed the study door and waited a mo[-]
ment outside it. Johnny and Jeremiah began th[e]
beating in earnest, but all LaRoux could hear wa[s]
the muffled sound of Carl squealing with each ne[w]
assault. LaRoux wondered if Johnny would kill Ca[rl]
before he was through with Catherine. LaRou[x]
wanted Catherine to see her own brother's death[.]

Upstairs, Catherine Weatherly frowned pretti[ly]
into the mirror attached to her dressing table. Wh[at]
was General LaRoux doing here so early, anyway[?]
He had been commanding, almost forcing his wa[y]
past her. Though this had bothered her, Catherin[e]
also realized that many of her father's, and no[w]
brother's, business associates were men accustomed [to]
having their own way. They were forceful, perha[ps]
even domineering men who cut a wide swath whe[n]
they walked. As Catherine thought this, she chastise[d]
herself mildly. How would she expect a man lik[e]
LaRoux to act? Like a weak-willed, simpering foo[l?]
Like the sycophant boys who courted her, begging f[or]
a kiss or just to hold her hand? Is that really the wa[y]
Catherine expected Jean-Jacques LaRoux to act, [or]
even wanted him to?

Catherine pinched her cheeks, making them a litt[le]
more rosy, highlighting her cheekbones, defining h[er]
fair skin. The single ribbon she used to tie her ha[ir]
back looked fine, but she wished she had the time [to]
have Emma do her coiffure. Emma was a real arti[st]
at that, and she took such joy in helping Catheri[ne]
get ready.

Catherine was still studying herself in the mirror when she heard the bedroom door open. "Emma, thank goodness you're early! Remember Mr. LaRoux? He's come so frightfully early to see Carl. But now that you're here, you can help me do something special with my hair." Catherine smiled at herself in the mirror. "I want him to notice me."

"Rest assured," LaRoux said in his perfectly modulated tone, "I have indeed taken notice of you."

Catherine's gasp was muffled in the rustle of hand-sewn petticoats and a beautiful pink dress tailored for her by Mrs. Anderson. Sapphire-blue eyes were wide with shock as Catherine stared in surprise at the tall, grim man leaning against the frame of her bedroom door.

"Mr. LaRoux, you really shouldn't be here!" Catherine rose quickly, heading for the door. She knew then that LaRoux had never done business with her father. Matthew Weatherly would never have associated with, let alone done business with, anyone so forward as to enter unannounced into a woman's bedroom. "If Emma sees you here, she'll skin you alive!"

"Emma?" LaRoux softly inquired. He made no move to step out of the doorway. Catherine stopped.

"Yes. Emma is my maid." Catherine saw the condescending twist to LaRoux's mouth and didn't appreciate it. "Emma is very protective of me."

LaRoux gave his most charming smile to Catherine. He reached out and touched his fingertips lightly to the side of her face. Catherine was nervous, but she did not back away.

"You don't need anyone to protect you from me,"

LaRoux said, his voice soft and yet commanding. "
always get whatever and whomever I want. And m
women are always satisfied."

Catherine was too confused to say anything. Sh
didn't know whether to be fascinated by this arrogan
Southern man or repulsed by his egotism. Was he th
man she had been waiting for, saving herself for
Tall, handsome, rich, educated—he had all the trait
that she wanted in a man. But there was somethin
else there, too. Some frightening thing that lurke
just behind the surface of his eyes when he looked a
her.

She took a small step backward, moving out of hi
reach. Though she tried, Catherine could not muste
a smile for LaRoux.

"Would you . . . um . . . mind if we went down
stairs?" Her composure was slowly returning. No
she managed a weak smile. "Can I make you som
tea? Emma usually handles things like that, but
would be honored if you'd allow me."

LaRoux nodded his head slowly several time:
"That's very nice. I do believe you are beginning t
understand what is expected of you." LaRoux steppe
forward and took Catherine's hand in his. He tugge
her closer to him, his heated gaze boring into he
soft blue eyes. "There's another favor I must ask (
you, Miss Catherine. It's very, very important."

"Of course," Catherine replied. She was pleased th
conversation had turned away from its intimate be
ginning and that they were now headed out of he
bedroom. Catherine would be glad to see her brotl
er's face.

"I want you to send the hired hands away," LaRou

428

said as they left Catherine's bedroom.

"What can you see?" Shadow asked quietly, her heart pounding in her chest from exertion and fear.

Sorren squinted into the field glasses. "Nothing. Not a damn thing."

Shadow looked at the MW Circle. It took her a moment to realize what was wrong. There wasn't a ranch hand in sight. The MW Circle, which Shadow had come to know as a busy, noisy enterprise, looked deserted.

"Where do you think everybody is?" Shadow asked. She moved closer to Sorren, her shoulder now touching his as they lay on the ground.

"The men were sent away." Sorren delivered the words as a statement, not a question. He wasn't sure how LaRoux had managed to get the hired hands to leave, but he knew it was the only explanation. "Carl or Catherine said the words, but LaRoux gave the orders." Sorren handed the field glasses over to Shadow. "Maybe you can see something I can't."

Shadow took the glasses. Sorren went to his mare and withdrew the Remington. He went back to Shadow and lay down on the ground beside her. He put the stock against his shoulder, peering through the telescopic sight. The cross hairs centered on the large double front doors of the mansion.

"Check all the windows. Maybe you'll see something." A movement caught Sorren's attention. The cross hairs slashed across thirty yards of ground and focused on a short, stout black woman. "Oh, no. Damn you, Emma! Don't go in the house. Please

429

don't go in the house."

His finger twitched on the trigger as if to fire a warning shot, but he knew that would force him to squander the one advantage he had over LaRoux— surprise.

He watched helplessly as Emma calmly walked through the front doors of the MW Circle, just the same as she had done every morning for years.

Shadow read the scene exactly as Sorren had. She set the field glasses on the ground in front of her. Closing her eyes, she hung her head in despair. "We could have stopped her," Shadow whispered. "We could have and we didn't."

"We would have killed Carl and Catherine."

Shadow looked at Sorren. She knew that he was right. It wasn't a time to let emotions interfere with what must be done, but damn him! Was he devoid of all emotions?

"Now what?" Shadow asked, afraid of the answer.

"Wait. Watch. I don't know." Sorren rubbed his eyebrows together with a finger and thumb, against the natural growth of the hair. Shadow had seen him to this before. He did it whenever he had a very painful decision to make.

"No matter what happens, I'll back you up," Shadow whispered, not sure why she felt the need to tell Sorren what she was certain he already knew. "Just tell me what you want."

Sorren took Shadow's eyes in with his own. Though no more words were exchanged, with that one look, Sorren drew strength from the woman who had captured his heart and captivated his soul.

"I never knew I could love this much," he said

softly, unable to look at Shadow as he spoke. He couldn't speak from the heart and look into her eyes at the same time.

Catherine was too scared to even cry. As soon as the ranch hands rode off, Johnny and Jeremiah had begun to beat Carl in the face.

"I heard you were something of a ladies' man," LaRoux said, sitting behind the desk. Carl, on his knees with his hands still tied behind his back, raised his head. His left eye was swollen shut. Soon the right eye would be shut, too. His lips were puffy, and he was bleeding from his ear. "I wonder what your lady would think if she saw you now?" LaRoux smiled wickedly. "You have got a lady, haven't you, Carl? Tell me her name. I may want her for myself when we're finished here."

"I haven't got . . . a woman." Carl coughed and blood spilled from the corner of his mouth, dribbling down his chin.

"Stop it! Stop it right now!" Emma shrieked. She started to rise from the sofa, where she sat beside Catherine, but was stopped when Jeremiah withdrew his pistol and touched it to the back of Carl's head. Jeremiah thumbed back the hammer and Emma sat down.

"Listen," LaRoux hissed, his eyes alive with feral anger, "I don't like my darkies talking to me in that tone of voice. Now, if you take your black ass off that sofa again, Jeremiah is going to put a bullet through your master's skull. Do you hear me?" Emma glared angrily at LaRoux, saying nothing. "I asked you a question, nigger. Do you hear me?"

"Yes, sir," Emma whispered. She put her arm around Catherine's shoulders.

Emma watched in horror as the vicious young man named Johnny stepped up to Carl and delivered a brutal kick to the ribs. Carl screamed in pain, writhing on the floor. Everyone in the room heard the unmistakable sound of ribs breaking. Johnny drank from the crystal decanter, laughed gleefully, then delivered another punishing kick to Carl's ribs.

LaRoux rose slowly from his chair. He walked past Carl, looking down at the slumped and panting figure on the floor in disgust. He stepped up to Catherine and extended a hand politely.

"Miss Catherine, I would be honored if you would give me a tour of your fine home," LaRoux said in the cultured tone of an educated man.

"You ain't goin' nowheres with him," Emma hissed, speaking to Catherine but glowering at LaRoux.

"Jeremiah, once again, please."

Jeremiah stepped up to Emma. In a lightning move, he brought the back of his hand across her face. His knuckles smacked loudly against her fleshy cheek.

"You will learn to keep your tongue still," LaRoux said, shaking his head in amazement, as though Emma's behavior completely baffled him. To Jeremiah, LaRoux said, "I'll be busy for some time. If the nigger tries anything, put a bullet in Carl's ear. If she talks, teach her some manners."

"Yes, sir," Jeremiah said. He massaged the knuckles of his right hand. They were sore from hitting Carl's face.

LaRoux pulled Catherine to her feet. She did not resist. Her blue eyes were glassy with tears that she refused to allow to spill from them. "Don't worry," she whispered tremulously to Emma. "I'll be all right. Don't do anything that will get you hurt. Please don't, Emma. Not on account of me." Catherine looked up at LaRoux and said, "All right, I'll show you the house. I know what room you want to see. Just leave Emma alone."

LaRoux smiled and it sickened Catherine. She silently promised herself that she wouldn't break down in front of him. No matter what he did to her, she wouldn't let him see her tears.

Just then, Catherine would have made her father proud.

Shadow wished she had her bow and arrows instead of the Winchester. Though she was aware of the awesome killing power of the repeater rifle, she had never fired one in her life. Her arrows required more skill, but she was more confident with her simple, quiet weapons.

Through the cotton mesh of the window curtain, Shadow studied the kitchen. It was empty. She had hoped Emma would be in there, but she wasn't. Forcing her courage to push her into doing what her instincts said she should not do, Shadow leaned through the window and set the carbine down lightly on the counter. Then she slithered through the opening. She remained perched on the counter briefly, holding the Winchester tightly in steady hands, waiting for one of LaRoux's men to step into the kitchen.

When nobody came, Shadow slipped off the counter, her moccasin-shod feet soundless against the hard wooden floor.

Taking each step with careful deliberation, Shadow headed for the hallway. If LaRoux's men weren't in the kitchen, they were in another room. All she had to do was find out which one. Then she had to signal Sorren, who was entering from the rear. She and Sorren had to free Emma, Catherine, and Carl, then make sure they got out of the mansion alive.

Shadow had never been so terrified in her life.

Catherine's fear was heightened when LaRoux finished the meal Emma had prepared. He had a look of quiet contentment in his eyes, and that was what worried Catherine the most.

"Delicious," LaRoux said, dabbing at the corner of his mouth with a napkin. He leaned back in the settee in Catherine's bedroom, his cool eyes sweeping over her approvingly. "She should be whipped more often, but she is a wonderful cook." LaRoux smiled again with mocking indulgence. "If I hadn't told her you would be eating with me, she would have poisoned the food."

"Whipped?" Catherine asked, immediately wishing she'd kept quiet.

"Yes. It's the only way you can keep the slaves in line." LaRoux withdrew a cigar from his pocket. He bit off the tip. Also from an inside pocket he produced a wooden match. He extended the unlit match to Catherine, his eyes steady on hers. "The darkies forget who owns them unless you whip them. They forget their proper place otherwise."

Catherine took the match from LaRoux. Her hand was trembling, but not as much as it had before, when she had first led LaRoux upstairs to her bedroom. She looked around for a suitable place to strike the match. Finding nothing appropriate, she scratched the match on the tea set's silver tray. The match flared to life, leaving a black mark on the silver. Catherine brought the match to the end of LaRoux's cigar. He touched her hand with his, steadying the small hand. As he took several puffs, his eyes never left Catherine's.

"Thank you." LaRoux leaned away from Catherine, his long legs crossed casually at the ankle in front of him. He was at ease with his world. "A good meal. A good cigar. The company of a beautiful woman. What else could a man ask for?"

Catherine thought, *Why doesn't he just get on with it?* It was a subtle act of torture the way he was making her behave, acting as though he were courting her, all the polite banter, the sly touching of hands and the way he always managed to brush against her knee or shoulder, briefly, when they talked. It was eating away at Catherine's strength, wearing down her willpower. It had all the outward appearances of civilized conduct. What made it molestation was that Catherine knew when LaRoux tired of the game, he would defile her. She was resigned to this. She knew that people she loved would face his rage if he was not pleased.

Catherine Weatherly really had no choice at all. All her money and grace and charm wouldn't help her now.

"Can I get you anything else?" Catherine asked. Her voice was steady now. "Perhaps some dessert? Emma makes wonderful desserts."

LaRoux smiled lazily. "I'm looking at my dessert." LaRoux sent a plume of smoke spiraling toward the ceiling. He smoothed his moustache with a fingertip. "Stand up, please. I would like to look at you."

"But Mr. La—"

Catherine gave LaRoux a stunned look, at first not even realizing that he'd slapped her. When anger flashed in her eyes, LaRoux slapped her a second time. He didn't slap her hard. It was a gesture of his power, of his complete domination. If Catherine continued to show any signs of resistance, he would become more violent. Catherine understood all this without having to be told.

She got to her feet and took several steps away. She stood with her hands at her sides. Catherine Weatherly, with a dazed, defeated glaze to her eyes, waited for her orders.

"Much better," LaRoux said through a broad smile. "I find obedient women very . . . satisfying. Now please, Miss Catherine, remove your clothes."

Catherine's eyes grew wider. She slowly turned away, her hand moving to the top button. "No, Miss Catherine," LaRoux said, a thinly disguised hard, lethal edge to his tone, "let me see you. And please, do it slowly. Very slowly. We're in no hurry at all. I've got everything under control."

Sorren flattened himself against the side of the house. He held the Colt in both hands, high near his right ear, the left hand curled over the right. He breathed in slowly, deeply, forcing himself to remain calm.

Seeing Carl being beaten in Matthew's study had shocked him. What worried Sorren was the look on Emma's face. He saw in her eyes the rapid workings of her mind. She was thinking of a plan of attack. She would eventually try to play the heroine, and when she did, she would die. Sorren just couldn't allow that to happen.

He moved to the next window. Slowly, with just one eye, he checked the room through the white cotton curtain. It was the library. Three men were drinking with Francine. He could see the men were interested in having something more than conversation with Francine. The men didn't appear too drunk, and they also didn't look wary. It made Sorren wonder why.

Judging by the number of horses tied to the hitching rail in front, there was one more rider from LaRoux's army in the house.

Sorren felt the blood turn cold in his veins. Only two people weren't accounted for: Catherine Weatherly and Jean-Jacques LaRoux.

Before Sorren could make his move, he needed to know where Catherine was. Where was she? And where was Shadow? He should have kept Shadow with him. No. He shouldn't have let her get involved in this at all.

Catherine had to be upstairs. That's where the bedrooms were. It was impossible to get to a second-floor window. Sorren would have to enter on the ground floor and make his way up without being noticed by the soldiers.

The window to the room that Emma did her sewing in was open. Sorren slipped into the house without a sound. He crossed the small room and placed his ear against the door. He stopped breathing. Concentrating, he heard nothing. He opened the door and peered into the hallway. It was empty.

Where was Shadow? She had looked so unsure of herself when he handed her the rifle. Sorren had given her quick instructions on its use, and now he knew he should have made her stay behind. Sorren thought, *She wouldn't have stayed behind. I couldn't have stopped her. Not as long as Emma is in danger. Nothing could have stopped her.*

It didn't help to know this.

Sorren moved out of the sewing room and into the hallway. He had taken just a few steps toward the stairway leading to the upstairs bedroom when he heard the scrape of a boot heel against the wooden floor. He spun, extending the Colt in both hands, thumbing back the hammer.

Shadow was at the other end of the hallway when she heard the sound. A single shot roared through the house, and a volley of gunfire immediately followed. "Sorren!" she shouted, stepping into the hallway, staying low. Sorren was to her right. To her left were three men, one on the floor, two standing.

Sorren glanced at Shadow. "Get back!" he shouted. He was suddenly catapulted backward. Shadow saw blood splash the wall behind him. He continued firing, shooting twice more.

Shadow pivoted, thrusting the Winchester in front of her awkwardly. The last of the three men went facedown in the hallway. Just behind them, the study door opened and Jeremiah leaped out. Shadow squeezed the trigger of the Winchester. She had never fired a rifle before and was not ready for the recoil. It knocked her backward against the wall. Wood splintered above Jeremiah's head.

"Get back!" she heard Sorren shout again.

Shadow worked the lever of the Winchester, ejecting the spent cartridge. She heard the explosion of Jeremiah's pistol and felt his slug push her body backward. There was no pain. Just an instant numbness that started in her left shoulder and spread throughout her body. She fell to her knees, reflexively squeezing the trigger. Shadow did not see her bullet hitting Jeremiah's chest. He was knocked backward into Johnny.

This is happening too fast, Shadow thought in a daze. *I'm losing blood. Sorren never said it would happen like this.*

Shadow's head lagged to the side, the muscles in her neck suddenly so weak she couldn't hold her head upright even when leaning against the door frame. Deafening explosions of gunfire came from her right and left. With what remained of her strength, she looked at Johnny. She saw his gun pointing at her and thought, *I want to kiss Sorren good-bye.*

Suddenly, one more shot filled the hallway with noise. Johnny grabbed his stomach and fell face first. He died with his eyes wide open, fixed on Shadow.

Forcing strength from where she thought there was none, Shadow turned her head and looked at Sorren. *Sorren's hurt. He's bleeding.*

He was sitting, leaning against the hallway wall, holding his chest. Shadow watched blood ooze through his fingers. His gun hand was bloody, limp at his side. She remembered how much pleasure his hands had brought to her. Sorren's eyes were closed, and for an agonizing moment Shadow thought he was dead. Then he raised his knee, pushing himself against the wall.

"Sorren," she said, her voice barely above a whisper.

Shadow tried to crawl to him, but she had no strength left. She fell to her side, unable to move. She looked into Sorren's half-opened eyes and thought, *He's dying. Please, Akana, don't let him die.*

Shadow's cheek was against the floor when she saw the stocking feet. She heard the deep chuckle and recognized it was LaRoux.

"McKenna, are you dead?" LaRoux asked in a conversational tone. He kicked the Winchester Shadow had used beyond her reach. "By God, you're not dead yet. Good. That's very good." LaRoux touched Shadow's face with his toe and she blinked. "Hmmm. You're still alive, too. This is getting better all the time. I wanted to be the one to kill both of you." LaRoux put his toe under Shadow's chin, tilting his foot up so that she was forced to look into his face. "I'm going to cut Sorren's throat. You're going to watch me do it. And when I'm done, I'm going to cut your throat."

Shadow tried to speak but couldn't. She had no strength left. All she could do was watch. Catherine stepped up next to LaRoux. She wore only a corset and stockings.

"Oh, my God!" Catherine cried through her hands, her face pale. She turned to LaRoux, clutching his arm. "Leave them alone!" she screamed.

LaRoux struck her viciously, knocking Catherine to the floor. When he moved his foot, Shadow's head again rolled to the side, her cheek against the floor.

She watched LaRoux's feet move out of view. Shadow looked at Sorren. He blinked, and when he opened his eyes, he did it with difficulty, as though his eyelids were very, very heavy.

LaRoux returned with Johnny's huge bowie knife. He squatted beside Sorren, touching the long, sharp blade to his throat.

"Can you see?" LaRoux asked Shadow, looking over his shoulder at her. He moved so that she had an unobstructed view of Sorren. "Watch how lover boy bleeds." LaRoux turned to Sorren. He put an ounce of pressure behind the knife and a drop of blood formed on the blade. "What's wrong, McKenna? Are you scared? Yes, that's it. That's what I see in your eyes, isn't it? Fear. You're scared, McKenna."

Shadow looked at Sorren and thought, *He doesn't look scared.* Sorren was looking unflinchingly into LaRoux's eyes. He made no move to push the knife from his throat.

"Come on, McKenna," LaRoux said in a voice that was too loud. "Let me hear you beg for your life." LaRoux's tone turned maniacal when he hissed, "Beg me, you bastard! Beg me or I'll castrate you!"

LaRoux was looking straight into Sorren's eyes, waiting to see the fear that would come from Sorren's soul. He never saw that fear. And he never saw

Sorren's bloody hand slide into the top of his boot remove the hideaway derringer. LaRoux grunte when the bullet popped and hit him low in th stomach, knocking him backward. He dropped th knife, looking at his stomach, then at Sorren.

"You bastard," LaRoux said in disbelief. "You ha no right to do that."

Sorren thumbed back the hammer and fired int LaRoux's chest.

The derringer dropped from Sorren's hand. H looked at Shadow.

LaRoux is dead, Shadow thought. *Now Sorren is goin to make everything all right, just like he promised.*

Sorren pulled himself across the floor, each move torturous struggle against a weak and unwilling body He dragged himself inch by inch across the floo until he was beside Shadow. His strength could tak him no further.

Sorren put his hand over Shadow's. "I will lov you," he whispered hoarsely, "for all eternity."

Chapter Twenty-five

Phillip Sanders was proud of his clientele. His was the finest restaurant in Philadelphia, and if you had money, it was the place to be. Business leaders, politicians, industrial giants, railroad tycoons, bankers. Even the rich and mysterious, like Stephen and Sasha Kennedy.

Mr. Kennedy was an enigmatic businessman who was reputed to own several companies of vague description. Rumor had it that his wife had an equal hand in running the enterprise. But they just didn't seem like entrepreneurs. He didn't know what Mr. Kennedy did, but he was more than just a business owner. And Mrs. Kennedy? She was another enigma. Definitely foreign, perhaps Egyptian. Very dignified. Sanders wondered if Sasha were an Egyptian name, and if she were a princess or something. Maybe that's where their money came from. Mr. Kennedy could be her bodyguard. He had that look to him.

"Good evening, Mr. and Mrs. Kennedy," Sanders

said, moving quickly to greet the couple at th
entrance. Sanders always seated customers of th
Kennedy's stature himself. "I have your table waitin
for you."

"Thank you," Stephen said. He took Sasha by th
arm, leading her slowly past several couples waitin
to be seated. "You look lovely tonight, precious. Th
new fashion becomes you."

"Don't tease," she smiled.

In a whisper, Stephen asked, "How are you fee
ing?"

"I'm okay," Sasha replied. She patted her rounde
stomach. "Baby is getting restless though."

"Just one more month."

Sanders pulled the chair for Mrs. Kennedy. On
month until the baby was due? When the chil
arrived, he'd send an appropriate gift.

After Sanders withdrew, Sasha gave her husband
gentle smile. "You're anxious about becoming a fa
ther, aren't you?"

"Petrified," he said, stony-faced. He reached acros
the table to place his hand over his wife's, and th
false solemnity broke into a happy grin. "Petrifie
and proud."

"Try to be brave," Sasha teased. Moments later, sh
blinked and a tear formed in the corner of her eye
"We can't go back?"

"No," Stephen replied softly, sadly. "It's too danger
ous. I want the baby to be born there, too, but it jus
isn't worth the risk." He squeezed her hand. "Yo
know there are too many people who know about m
now, too many of LaRoux's followers who would lik
to see me —" His words trailed off when he saw th

444

pain in Sasha's eyes.

"But it's been three years." Sasha blinked and a tear trickled down a high cheekbone. She looked down, wanting to hide her tears. When she looked up again, Stephen was smiling. "What's so funny?"

"We can't go west for our baby's birth, so I've brought the best of the west to us."

Sasha's eyebrows pushed together.

Stephen's face exploded into an even broader, beaming smile. "Right now, even as we speak—"

"Stephen—"

"—Emma is home waiting for us."

"What?" Sasha's eyes were big and round. "Are you serious?"

He nodded in triumph. "And John, too. Emma wanted to get cleaned up before she saw you. She'll be here to help you until after the baby arrives."

Sasha grabbed the arms of the chair, pushing herself to her feet. It wasn't an easy thing to do being eight months pregnant. "Sorren McKenna, you take me home this instant!"

He chuckled and hissed behind a cupped hand, "The name is Stephen. Stephen Kennedy."

Phillip Sanders hurried over to the Kennedys, his face showing the concern of a man who did not want a baby—however highborn—to come into this world in his restaurant.

"Is anything wrong, sir?"

"No, everything is fine," Sorren said. He patted Sanders's shoulder to confirm his words. "Send for our carriage, will you?"

"Yes, Mr. Kennedy. Of course."

When they were outside, waiting for their carriage

to be brought around, Shadow grabbed Sorren's tie
pulling him down so their noses were nearly touch
ing. "I'm going to get even with you for keeping thi
a secret from me."

Sorren smiled and placed his hand lightly on hi
wife's stomach. "Maybe you'd better wait a while fo
that kind of challenge."

The carriage, drawn by two shining black stallions
was one of the most lavish in all of Philadelphia
Sorren helped Shadow in. Just before he was abou
to step up himself, Sanders called his name and ra
up to him, puffing from exertion and self-impor
tance.

"Sir, this was just delivered by a man in uniform.

Sorren took the envelope from Sanders and turne
it around in his hands. There was no name on it. I
was sealed with wax. Pressed into the wax was th
seal of the President of the United States.

Sorren McKenna stuffed the envelope into his coa
pocket and mounted the carriage.

<u>FREE</u> Preview Each Month and $ave

Zebra has made arrangements for you to preview 4 brand new HEARTFIRE novels each month...FREE for 10 days. You'll get them as soon as they are published. If you are not delighted with any of them, just return them with no questions asked. But if you decide these are everything we said they are, you'll pay just $3.25 each— a total of $13.00 (a $15.00 value). **That's a $2.00 saving each month off the regular price.** Plus there is NO shipping or handling charge. These are delivered right to your door absolutely free! There is no obligation and there is no minimum number of books to buy.

TO GET YOUR FIRST MONTH'S PREVIEW... Mail the Coupon Below!